VICTORIAN GHOST STORIES

VICTORIAN GHOST STORIES

This edition published in 2024 by Arcturus Publishing Limited
26/27 Bickels Yard, 151–153 Bermondsey Street,
London SE1 3HA

AD011557UK

Printed in the UK

CONTENTS

INTRODUCTION..7

THE DREAM – *Joseph Sheridan Le Fanu*.......................9

A CHAPTER IN THE HISTORY OF A TYRONE FAMILY – *Joseph Sheridan Le Fanu*... 23

THE DEAD SEXTON – *Joseph Sheridan Le Fanu* 65

THE ITALIAN'S STORY – *Catherine Crowe* 87

ROUND THE FIRE – *Catherine Crowe* 107

THE MYSTERIOUS STRANGER..121

THE GHOST DETECTIVE – *Mark Lemon* 165

THE SHADOW OF A SHADE – *Tom Hood*............................ 179

THE DEAD MAN OF VARLEY GRANGE – *Anonymous*..... 197

THE STORY OF MEDHANS LEA – *E. and H. Heron* 213

THE TOMB OF SARAH – *Frederick George Loring*................229

EVELINE'S VISITANT – *Mary Elizabeth Braddon* 245

HUGUES, THE WER-WOLF – *Sutherland Menzies* 257

THE BODY SNATCHER – *Robert Louis Stevenson*................ 281

INTRODUCTION

Known for its overtly gothic tropes, dark settings and supernatural entities, Victorian literature has been evoking intrigue and fear in readers for almost two centuries. Filled with urban cities where poverty and prosperity sit side by side and opulent architecture is haunted by sinister spirits, the tales from this bygone era are still popular today. The Victorian era spanned most of the nineteenth century and continued until the death of Queen Victoria in 1901. During this time, Great Britain underwent huge social change and literature evolved from primarily larger volumes to shorter serial forms of publishing that were printed more frequently and easily available in magazines.

Writers such as Charles Dickens, Robert Louis Stevenson and Elizabeth Gaskell all published at least some of their work in serial form. Most writers who published works during the Victorian era would have also tried their hand at writing ghost stories. Ghost stories have long fascinated humans, and in the nineteenth century readers found themselves drawn towards ghoulish tales that featured the candlelit houses in which they lived and the cobbled streets on which they walked. Also included were vampires, mummies, werewolves, apparitions and many other terrors. Filled with ambiguity and mystery, the tales in this collection take you over

Victorian thresholds and into dimly lit parlours, darkened corridors and abandoned libraries where supernatural beings linger.

This collection showcases the finest ghost stories penned by a variety of masterful storytellers such as Joseph Sheridan Le Fanu, Mark Lemon, Mary Elizabeth Braddon and many more. Mark Lemon's 'The Ghost Detective' is a curious tale of a mysterious apparition that helps to uncover the truth when a respectable Mr Loxley is arrested unjustly for embezzlement. In 'The Dream', Le Fanu tells a chilling story about the 'drunkard' who returns to the living world from death's door after making an ominous deal in order to survive.

The short stories in this collection will fascinate and terrify you as you grapple with the unexplained sounds and feelings that haunt our characters. So, pull the curtains tight, dim the lights (if you dare!) and settle down with this thrilling book of Victorian ghost stories.

THE DREAM
by Joseph Sheridan Le Fanu

Dreams! What age, or what country of the world, has not felt and acknowledged the mystery of their origin and end? I have thought not a little upon the subject, seeing it is one which has been often forced upon my attention, and sometimes strangely enough; and yet I have never arrived at anything which at all appeared a satisfactory conclusion. It does appear that a mental phenomenon so extraordinary cannot be wholly without its use. We know, indeed, that in the olden times it has been made the organ of communication between the Deity and His creatures; and when, as I have seen, a dream produces upon a mind, to all appearance hopelessly reprobate and depraved, an effect so powerful and so lasting as to break down the inveterate habits, and to reform the life of an abandoned sinner, we see in the result, in the reformation of morals which appeared incorrigible, in the reclamation of a human soul which seemed to be irretrievably lost, something more than could be produced by a mere chimera of the slumbering fancy, something more than could arise from the capricious images of a terrified imagination; And while Reason rejects as absurd the superstition which will read a prophecy in every dream, she may, without violence to herself, recognise, even in the wildest and most incongruous of the wanderings of a slumbering intellect, the evidences and the fragments of a language

which may be spoken, which *has* been spoken, to terrify, to warn and to command. We have reason to believe too, by the promptness of action which in the age of the prophets followed all intimations of this kind, and by the strength of conviction and strange permanence of the effects resulting from certain dreams in latter times – which effects we ourselves may have witnessed – that when this medium of communication has been employed by the Deity, the evidences of His presence have been unequivocal. My thoughts were directed to this subject, in a manner to leave a lasting impression upon my mind, by the events which I shall now relate, the statement of which, however extraordinary, is nevertheless accurate.

About the year 17———, having been appointed to the living of C———h, I rented a small house in the town, which bears the same name: one morning in the month of November, I was awakened before my usual time by my servant, who bustled into my bedroom for the purpose of announcing a sick call. As the Catholic Church holds her last rites to be totally indispensable to the safety of the departing sinner, no conscientious clergyman can afford a moment's unnecessary delay, and in little more than five minutes I stood ready cloaked and booted for the road, in the small front parlour, in which the messenger, who was to act as my guide, awaited my coming. I found a poor little girl crying piteously near the door, and after some slight difficulty I ascertained that her father was either dead or just dying.

'And what may be your father's name, my poor child?' said I. She held down her head, as if ashamed. I repeated the question, and the wretched little creature burst into floods of tears still more bitter than she had shed before. At length, almost provoked by conduct which appeared to me so unreasonable, I began to lose patience, and I said rather harshly:

'If you will not tell me the name of the person to whom you would lead me, your silence can arise from no good motive, and I might be justified in refusing to go with you at all.'

'Oh, don't say that – don't say that!' cried she. 'Oh, sir, it was that I was afeard of when I would not tell you – I was afeard, when you heard his name, you would not come with me; but it is no use hidin' it now – it's Pat Connell, the carpenter, your honour.'

She looked in my face with the most earnest anxiety, as if her very existence depended upon what she should read there; but I relieved her at once. The name, indeed, was most unpleasantly familiar to me; but, however fruitless my visits and advice might have been at another time, the present was too fearful an occasion to suffer my doubts of their utility or my reluctance to re-attempting what appeared a hopeless task to weigh even against the lightest chance that a consciousness of his imminent danger might produce in him a more docile and tractable disposition. Accordingly I told the child to lead the way, and followed her in silence. She hurried rapidly through the long narrow street which forms the great thoroughfare of the town. The darkness of the hour, rendered still deeper by the close approach of the old-fashioned houses, which lowered in tall obscurity on either side of the way; the damp, dreary chill which renders the advance of morning peculiarly cheerless, combined with the object of my walk – to visit the death-bed of a presumptuous sinner, to endeavour, almost against my own conviction, to infuse a hope into the heart of a dying reprobate – a drunkard but too probably perishing under the consequences of some mad fit of intoxication; all these circumstances served to enhance the gloom and solemnity of my feelings, as I silently followed my little guide, who with quick steps traversed the uneven pavement of the main street. After a walk of about five minutes she turned off into a narrow lane, of that obscure and comfortless class which is to be found in almost all small old-fashioned towns, chill, without ventilation, reeking with all manner of offensive effluvia, and lined by dingy, smoky, sickly and pent-up buildings, frequently not only in a wretched but in a dangerous condition.

'Your father has changed his abode since I last visited him and, I am afraid, much for the worse,' said I.

'Indeed he has, sir; but we must not complain,' replied she. 'We have to thank God that we have lodging and food, though it's poor enough, it is, your honour.'

Poor child! thought I. How many an older head might learn wisdom from thee – how many a luxurious philosopher, who is skilled to preach but not to suffer, might not thy patient words put to the blush! The manner and language of my companion were alike above her years and station; and, indeed, in all cases in which the cares and sorrows of life have anticipated their usual date, and have fallen, as they sometimes do, with melancholy prematurity to the lot of childhood, I have observed the result to have proved uniformly the same. A young mind, to which joy and indulgence have been strangers, and to which suffering and self-denial have been familiarised from the first, acquires a solidity and an elevation which no other discipline could have bestowed, and which, in the present case, communicated a striking but mournful peculiarity to the manners, even to the voice, of the child. We paused before a narrow, crazy door, which she opened by means of a latch, and we forthwith began to ascend the steep and broken stairs which led to the sick man's room.

As we mounted flight after flight towards the garret-floor, I heard more and more distinctly the hurried talking of many voices. I could also distinguish the low sobbing of a female. On arriving upon the uppermost lobby these sounds became fully audible.

'This way, your honour,' said my little conductress; at the same time, pushing open a door of patched and half-rotten plank, she admitted me into the squalid chamber of death and misery. But one candle, held in the fingers of a scared and haggard-looking child, was burning in the room, and that so dim that all was twilight or darkness except within its immediate influence. The general obscurity, however, served to throw into prominent and startling

relief the death-bed and its occupant. The light fell with horrible clearness upon the blue and swollen features of the drunkard. I did not think it possible that a human countenance could look so terrific. The lips were black and drawn apart; the teeth were firmly set; the eyes a little unclosed, and nothing but the whites appearing. Every feature was fixed and livid, and the whole face wore a ghastly and rigid expression of despairing terror such as I never saw equalled. His hands were crossed upon his breast, and firmly clenched; while, as if to add to the corpse-like effect of the whole, some white cloths, dipped in water, were wound about the forehead and temples.

As soon as I could remove my eyes from this horrible spectacle, I observed my friend Dr D——— , one of the most humane of a humane profession, standing by the bedside. He had been attempting, but unsuccessfully, to bleed the patient, and had now applied his finger to the pulse.

'Is there any hope?' I inquired in a whisper.

A shake of the head was the reply. There was a pause while he continued to hold the wrist; but he waited in vain for the throb of life – it was not there: and when he let go the hand, it fell stiffly back into its former position upon the other.

'The man is dead,' said the physician, as he turned from the bed where the terrible figure lay.

Dead! thought I, scarcely venturing to look upon the tremendous and revolting spectacle. Dead! without an hour for repentance, even a moment for reflection. Dead without the rites which even the best should have. Is there a hope for him? The glaring eyeball, the grinning mouth, the distorted brow – that unutterable look in which a painter would have sought to embody the fixed despair of the nethermost hell. These were my answer.

The poor wife sat at a little distance, crying as if her heart would break – the younger children clustered round the bed, looking with wondering curiosity upon the form of death never seen before.

When the first tumult of uncontrollable sorrow had passed away, availing myself of the solemnity and impressiveness of the scene, I desired the heart-stricken family to accompany me in prayer, and all knelt down while I solemnly and fervently repeated some of those prayers which appeared most applicable to the occasion. I employed myself thus in a manner which, I trusted, was not unprofitable, at least to the living, for about ten minutes; and having accomplished my task, I was the first to arise.

I looked upon the poor, sobbing, helpless creatures who knelt so humbly around me, and my heart bled for them. With a natural transition I turned my eyes from them to the bed in which the body lay; and, great God! what was the revulsion, the horror which I experienced on seeing the corpse-like terrific thing seated half upright before me; the white cloths which had been wound about the head had now partly slipped from their position, and were hanging in grotesque festoons about the face and shoulders, while the distorted eyes leered from amid them –

'A sight to dream of, not to tell.'

I stood actually riveted to the spot. The figure nodded its head and lifted its arm, I thought, with a menacing gesture. A thousand confused and horrible thoughts at once rushed upon my mind. I had often read that the body of a presumptuous sinner who, during life, had been the willing creature of every satanic impulse, after the human tenant had deserted it, had been known to become the horrible sport of demoniac possession.

I was roused from the stupefaction of terror in which I stood, by the piercing scream of the mother, who now, for the first time, perceived the change which had taken place. She rushed towards the bed, but stunned by the shock, and overcome by the conflict of violent emotions, before she reached it she fell prostrate upon the floor.

I am perfectly convinced that had I not been startled from the torpidity of horror in which I was bound by some powerful and arousing stimulant, I should have gazed upon this unearthly apparition until I had fairly lost my senses. As it was, however, the spell was broken – superstition gave way to reason: the man whom all believed to have been actually dead was living!

Dr D—— was instantly standing by the bedside, and upon examination he found that a sudden and copious flow of blood had taken place from the wound which the lancet had left; and this, no doubt, had effected his sudden and almost preternatural restoration to an existence from which all thought he had been for ever removed. The man was still speechless, but he seemed to understand the physician when he forbade his repeating the painful and fruitless attempts which he made to articulate, and he at once resigned himself quietly into his hands.

I left the patient with leeches upon his temples, and bleeding freely, apparently with little of the drowsiness which accompanies apoplexy. Indeed, Dr D—— told me that he had never before witnessed a seizure which seemed to combine the symptoms of so many kinds, and yet which belonged to none of the recognised classes; it certainly was not apoplexy, catalepsy, nor *delirium tremens*, and yet it seemed, in some degree, to partake of the properties of all. It was strange, but stranger things are coming.

During two or three days Dr D—— would not allow his patient to converse in a manner which could excite or exhaust him, with anyone; he suffered him merely as briefly as possible to express his immediate wants. And it was not until the fourth day after my early visit, the particulars of which I have just detailed, that it was thought expedient that I should see him, and then only because it appeared that his extreme importunity and impatience to meet me were likely to retard his recovery more than the mere exhaustion attendant upon a short conversation could possibly do. Perhaps, too, my friend entertained some hope that if by holy confession his patient's bosom

were eased of the perilous stuff which no doubt oppressed it, his recovery would be more assured and rapid. It was then, as I have said, upon the fourth day after my first professional call that I found myself once more in the dreary chamber of want and sickness.

The man was in bed, and appeared low and restless. On my entering the room he raised himself in the bed, and muttered, twice or thrice:

'Thank God! Thank God!'

I signed to those of his family who stood by to leave the room, and took a chair beside the bed. So soon as we were alone, he said, rather doggedly:

'There's no use in telling me of the sinfulness of bad ways – I know it all. I know where they lead to – I seen everything about it with my own eyesight, as plain as I see you.' He rolled himself in the bed, as if to hide his face in the clothes; and then suddenly raising himself, he exclaimed with startling vehemence: 'Look, sir! there is no use in mincing the matter: I'm blasted with the fires of hell; I have been in hell. What do you think of that? In hell – I'm lost for ever – I have not a chance. I am damned already – damned – damned!'

The end of this sentence he actually shouted. His vehemence was perfectly terrific; he threw himself back, and laughed, and sobbed hysterically. I poured some water into a tea-cup, and gave it to him. After he had swallowed it, I told him if he had anything to communicate to do so as briefly as he could, and in a manner as little agitating to himself as possible; threatening at the same time, though I had no intention of doing so, to leave him at once, in case he again gave way to such passionate excitement.

'It's only foolishness,' he continued, 'for me to try to thank you for coming to such a villain as myself at all. It's no use for me to wish good to you, or to bless you; for such as me has no blessings to give.'

I told him that I had but done my duty, and urged him to proceed to the matter which weighed upon his mind. He then spoke nearly as follows:

'I came in drunk on Friday night last, and got to my bed here; I don't remember how. Sometime in the night it seemed to me I wakened, and feeling uneasy in myself, I got up out of the bed. I wanted the fresh air; but I would not make a noise to open the window, for fear I'd waken the crathurs. It was very dark and troublesome to find the door; but at last I did get it, and I groped my way out, and went down as easy as I could. I felt quite sober, and I counted the steps one after another, as I was going down, that I might not stumble at the bottom.

'When I came to the first landing-place – God be about us always! – the floor of it sunk under me, and I went down – down – down, till the senses almost left me. I do not know how long I was falling, but it seemed to me a great while. When I came rightly to myself at last, I was sitting near the top of a great table; and I could not see the end of it, if it had any, it was so far off. And there was men beyond reckoning, sitting down all along by it, at each side, as far as I could see at all. I did not know at first was it in the open air; but there was a close smothering feel in it that was not natural. And there was a kind of light that my eyesight never saw before, red and unsteady; and I did not see for a long time where it was coming from, until I looked straight up, and then I seen that it came from great balls of blood-coloured fire that were rolling high overhead with a sort of rushing, trembling sound, and I perceived that they shone on the ribs of a great roof of rock that was arched overhead instead of the sky. When I seen this, scarce knowing what I did, I got up, and I said, "I have no right to be here; I must go." And the man that was sitting at my left hand only smiled, and said, "Sit down again; you can *never* leave this place." And his voice was weaker than any child's voice I ever heard; and when he was done speaking he smiled again.

'Then I spoke out very loud and bold, and I said, "In the name of God, let me out of this bad place." And there was a great man that I did not see before, sitting at the end of the table that I was near; and he was taller than twelve men, and his face was very proud and terrible to look at. And he stood up and stretched out his hand before him; and when he stood up, all that was there, great and small, bowed down with a sighing sound, and a dread came on my heart, and he looked at me, and I could not speak. I felt I was his own, to do what he liked with, for I knew at once who he was; and he said, "If you promise to return, you may depart for a season;" and the voice he spoke with was terrible and mournful, and the echoes of it went rolling and swelling down the endless cave, and mixing with the trembling of the fire overhead; so that when he sat down there was a sound after him, all through the place, like the roaring of a furnace. And I said, with all the strength I had, "I promise to come back – in God's name let me go!"

'And with that I lost the sight and the hearing of all that was there, and when my senses came to me again, I was sitting in the bed with the blood all over me, and you and the rest praying around the room.'

Here he paused and wiped away the chill drops of horror which hung upon his forehead.

I remained silent for some moments. The vision which he had just described struck my imagination not a little, for this was long before *Vathek* and the *Hall of Eblis* had delighted the world; and the description which he gave had, as I received it, all the attractions of novelty beside the impressiveness which always belongs to the narration of an *eye-witness*, whether in the body or in the spirit, of the scenes which he describes. There was something, too, in the stern horror with which the man related these things, and in the incongruity of his description, with the vulgarly received notions of the great place of punishment, and of its presiding spirit, which struck my mind with awe, almost with fear. At length he said, with an expression of horrible, imploring earnestness, which I shall never forget:

'Well, sir, is there any hope; is there any chance at all? or, is my soul pledged and promised away for ever? is it gone out of my power? must I go back to the place?'

In answering him, I had no easy task to perform; for however clear might be my internal conviction of the groundlessness of his tears, and however strong my scepticism respecting the reality of what he had described, I nevertheless felt that his impression to the contrary, and his humility and terror resulting from it, might be made available as no mean engines in the work of his conversion from profligacy, and of his restoration to decent habits, and to religious feeling.

I therefore told him that he was to regard his dream rather in the light of a warning than in that of a prophecy; that our salvation depended not upon the word or deed of a moment, but upon the habits of a life; that, in fine, if he at once discarded his idle companions and evil habits, and firmly adhered to a sober, industrious and religious course of life, the powers of darkness might claim his soul in vain, for that there were higher and firmer pledges than human tongue could utter, which promised salvation to him who should repent and lead a new life.

I left him much comforted, and with a promise to return upon the next day. I did so, and found him much more cheerful and without any remains of the dogged sullenness which I suppose had arisen from his despair. His promises of amendment were given in that tone of deliberate earnestness, which belongs to deep and solemn determination; and it was with no small delight that I observed, after repeated visits, that his good resolutions, so far from failing, did but gather strength by time; and when I saw that man shake off the idle and debauched companions, whose society had for years formed alike his amusement and his ruin, and revive his long discarded habits of industry and sobriety, I said within myself, there is something more in all this than the operation of an idle dream.

One day, sometime after his perfect restoration to health, I was surprised on ascending the stairs, for the purpose of visiting this man, to find him busily employed in nailing down some planks upon the landing-place, through which, at the commencement of

his mysterious vision, it seemed to him that he had sunk. I perceived at once that he was strengthening the floor with a view to securing himself against such a catastrophe, and could scarcely forbear a smile as I bid 'God bless his work.'

He perceived my thoughts, I suppose, for he immediately said:

'I can never pass over that floor without trembling. I'd leave this house if I could, but I can't find another lodging in the town so cheap, and I'll not take a better till I've paid off all my debts, please God; but I could not be easy in my mind till I made it as safe as I could. You'll hardly believe me, your honour, that while I'm working, maybe a mile away, my heart is in a flutter the whole way back, with the bare thoughts of the two little steps I have to walk upon this bit of a floor. So it's no wonder, sir, I'd try to make it sound and firm with any idle timber I have.'

I applauded his resolution to pay off his debts, and the steadiness with which he perused his plans of conscientious economy, and passed on.

Many months elapsed, and still there appeared no alteration in his resolutions of amendment. He was a good workman, and with his better habits he recovered his former extensive and profitable employment. Everything seemed to promise comfort and respectability. I have little more to add, and that shall be told quickly. I had one evening met Pat Connell, as he returned from his work, and as usual, after a mutual, and on his side respectful salutation, I spoke a few words of encouragement and approval. I left him industrious, active, healthy – when next I saw him, not three days after, he was a corpse.

The circumstances which marked the event of his death were somewhat strange – I might say fearful. The unfortunate man had accidentally met an old friend just returned, after a long absence, and in a moment of excitement, forgetting everything in the warmth of his joy, he yielded to his urgent invitation to accompany him into a public-house, which lay close by the spot where the encounter had

taken place. Connell, however, previously to entering the room, had announced his determination to take nothing more than the strictest temperance would warrant.

But oh! who can describe the inveterate tenacity with which a drunkard's habits cling to him through life? He may repent, he may reform, he may look with actual abhorrence upon his past profligacy; but amid all this reformation and compunction, who can tell the moment in which the base and ruinous propensity may not recur, triumphing over resolution, remorse, shame, everything, and prostrating its victim once more in all that is destructive and revolting in that fatal vice?

The wretched man left the place in a state of utter intoxication. He was brought home nearly insensible, and placed in his bed, where he lay in the deep calm lethargy of drunkenness. The younger part of the family retired to rest much after their usual hour; but the poor wife remained up sitting by the fire, too much grieved and shocked at the occurrence of what she had so little expected, to settle to rest. Fatigue, however, at length overcame her, and she sank gradually into an uneasy slumber. She could not tell how long she had remained in this state; but she awakened, and immediately on opening her eyes, she perceived by the faint red light of the smouldering turf embers, two persons, one of whom she recognised as her husband, noiselessly gliding out of the room.

'Pat, darling, where are you going?' said she.

There was no answer – the door closed after them; but in a moment she was startled and terrified by a loud and heavy crash, as if some ponderous body had been hurled down the stair.

Much alarmed, she started up, and going to the head of the staircase, she called repeatedly upon her husband, but in vain.

She returned to the room, and with the assistance of her daughter, whom I had occasion to mention before, she succeeded in finding and lighting a candle, with which she hurried again to the head of the staircase.

At the bottom lay what seemed to be a bundle of clothes, heaped together, motionless, lifeless – it was her husband. In going down the stair, for what purpose can never now be known, he had fallen helplessly and violently to the bottom, and coming head foremost, the spine at the neck had been dislocated by the shock, and instant death must have ensued.

The body lay upon that landing-place to which his dream had referred.

It is scarcely worth endeavouring to clear up a single point in a narrative where all is mystery; yet I could not help suspecting that the second figure which had been seen in the room by Connell's wife on the night of his death, might have been no other than his own shadow.

I suggested this solution of the difficulty; but she told me that the unknown person had been considerably in advance of the other, and on reaching the door, had turned back as if to communicate something to his companion.

It was then a mystery.

Was the dream verified? – whither had the disembodied spirit sped? – Who can say? We know not. But I left the house of death that day in a state of horror which I could not describe. It seemed to me that I was scarce awake. I heard and saw everything as if under the spell of a nightmare. The coincidence was terrible.

A CHAPTER IN THE HISTORY OF A TYRONE FAMILY
by Joseph Sheridan Le Fanu

In the following narrative, I have endeavoured to give as nearly as possible the *ipsissima verba* of the valued friend from whom I received it, conscious that any aberration from *her* mode of telling the tale of her own life, would at once impair its accuracy and its effect.

Would that, with her words, I could also bring before you her animated gesture, her expressive countenance, the solemn and thrilling air and accent with which she related the dark passages in her strange story; and, above all, that I could communicate the impressive consciousness that the narrator had seen with her own eyes, and personally acted in the scenes which she described. These accompaniments, taken with the additional circumstance, that she who told the tale was one far too deeply and sadly impressed with religious principle, to misrepresent or fabricate what she repeated as fact, gave to the tale a depth of interest which the events recorded could hardly have produced.

I became acquainted with the lady from whose lips I heard this narrative nearly twenty years since, and the story struck my fancy so much, that I committed it to paper while it was still fresh in my mind, and should its perusal afford you entertainment for a

listless half-hour, my labour shall not have been bestowed in vain.

I find that I have taken the story down as she told it, in the first person and perhaps, this is as it should be.

She began as follows.

My maiden name was Richardson, the designation of a family of some distinction in the county of Tyrone. I was the younger of two daughters, and we were the only children. There was a difference in our ages of nearly six years, so that I did not, in my childhood, enjoy that close companionship which sisterhood, in other circumstances, necessarily involves; and while I was still a child, my sister was married.

The person upon whom she bestowed her hand, was a Mr Carew, a gentleman of property and consideration in the north of England.

I remember well the eventful day of the wedding; the thronging carriages, the noisy menials, the loud laughter, the merry faces and the gay dresses. Such sights were then new to me, and harmonised ill with the sorrowful feelings with which I regarded the event which was to separate me, from a sister whose tenderness alone had hitherto more than supplied all that I wanted in my mother's affection.

The day soon arrived which was to remove the happy couple from Ashtown House. The carriage stood at the hall-door, and my poor sister kissed me again and again, telling me that I should see her soon.

The carriage drove away, and I gazed after it until my eyes filled with tears and, returning slowly to my chamber, I wept more bitterly, and so, to speak more desolately than ever I had done before.

My father had never seemed to love, or to take an interest in me. He had desired a son, and I think he never thoroughly forgave me my unfortunate sex.

My having come into the world at all as his child, he regarded as a kind of fraudulent intrusion and, as his antipathy to me had its origin in an imperfection of mine, too radical for removal, I never even hoped to stand high in his good graces.

My mother was, I dare say, as fond of me as she was of anyone; but she was a woman of a masculine and a worldly cast of mind. She had no tenderness or sympathy for the weaknesses, or even for the affections of woman's nature, and her demeanour towards me was peremptory, and often even harsh.

It is not to be supposed, then, that I found in the society of my parents much to supply the loss of my sister. About a year after her marriage, we received letters from Mr Carew, containing accounts of my sister's health which, though not actually alarming, were calculated to make us seriously uneasy. The symptoms most dwelt upon, were loss of appetite and a cough.

The letters concluded by intimating that he would avail himself of my father and mother's repeated invitation to spend some time at Ashtown, particularly as the physician who had been consulted as to my sister's health had strongly advised a removal to her native air.

There were added repeated assurances that nothing serious was apprehended, as it was supposed that a deranged state of the liver was the only source of the symptoms which seemed to intimate consumption.

In accordance with this announcement, my sister and Mr Carew arrived in Dublin, where one of my father's carriages awaited them, in readiness to start upon whatever day or hour they might choose for their departure.

It was arranged that Mr Carew was, as soon as the day upon which they were to leave Dublin was definitely fixed, to write to my father, who intended that the two last stages should be performed by his own horses, upon whose speed and safety far more reliance might be placed than upon those of the ordinary post-horses, which were, at that time, almost without exception, of the very worst order. The journey, one of about ninety miles, was to be divided; the larger portion to be reserved for the second day.

On Sunday, a letter reached us, stating that the party would leave Dublin on Monday and, in due course reach Ashtown upon Tuesday evening.

Tuesday came: the evening closed in, and yet no carriage; darkness came on, and still no sign of our expected visitors.

Hour after hour passed away, and it was now past twelve; the night was remarkably calm, scarce a breath stirring, so that any sound, such as that produced by the rapid movement of a vehicle, would have been audible at a considerable distance. For some such sound I was feverishly listening.

It was, however, my father's rule to close the house at nightfall, and the window-shutters being fastened, I was unable to reconnoitre the avenue as I would have wished. It was nearly one o'clock, and we began almost to despair of seeing them upon that night, when I thought I distinguished the sound of wheels, but so remote and faint as to make me at first very uncertain. The noise approached; it become louder and clearer; it stopped for a moment.

I now heard the shrill screaming of the rusty iron, as the avenue gate revolved on its hinges; again came the sound of wheels in rapid motion.

'It is they,' said I, starting up, 'the carriage is in the avenue.'

We all stood for a few moments, breathlessly listening. On thundered the vehicle with the speed of a whirlwind; crack went the whip, and clatter went the wheels, as it rattled over the uneven pavement of the court. A general and furious barking from all the dogs about the house hailed its arrival.

We hurried to the hall in time to hear the steps let down with the sharp clanging noise peculiar to the operation, and the hum of voices exerted in the bustle of arrival. The hall door was now thrown open, and we all stepped forth to greet our visitors.

The court was perfectly empty; the moon was shining broadly and brightly upon all around; nothing was to be seen but the tall trees with their long spectral shadows, now wet with the dews of midnight.

We stood gazing from right to left, as if suddenly awakened from a dream; the dogs walked suspiciously, growling and snuffling about

the court, and by totally and suddenly ceasing their former loud barking expressed the predominance of fear.

We stared one upon the other in perplexity and dismay, and I think I never beheld more pale faces assembled. By my father's directions, we looked about to find anything which might indicate or account for the noise which we had heard; but no such thing was to be seen – even the mire which lay upon the avenue was undisturbed. We returned to the house, more panic stricken than I can describe.

On the next day, we learned by a messenger, who had ridden hard the greater part of the night, that my sister was dead. On Sunday evening, she had retired to bed rather unwell and, on Monday, her indisposition declared itself unequivocally to be malignant fever. She became hourly worse and, on Tuesday night, a little after midnight, she expired.

I mention this circumstance, because it was one upon which a thousand wild and fantastical reports were founded, though one would have thought that the truth scarcely required to be improved upon; and again, because it produced a strong and lasting effect upon my spirits, and indeed, I am inclined to think, upon my character.

I was, for several years after this occurrence, long after the violence of my grief subsided, so wretchedly low-spirited and nervous, that I could scarcely be said to live; and during this time, habits of indecision, arising out of a listless acquiescence to the will of others, a fear of encountering even the slightest opposition, and a disposition to shrink from what are commonly called amusements, grew upon me so strongly, that I have scarcely even yet, altogether overcome them.

We saw nothing more of Mr Carew. He returned to England as soon as the melancholy rites attendant upon the events which I have just mentioned were performed; and not being altogether inconsolable, he married again within two years; after which, owing to the remoteness of our relative situations, and other circumstances, we gradually lost sight of him.

I was now an only child; and as my elder sister had died without issue, it was evident that, in the ordinary course of things, my father's property, which was altogether in his power, would go to me; and the consequence was, that before I was fourteen, Ashtown House was besieged by a host of suitors. However, whether it was that I was too young, or that none of the aspirants to my hand stood sufficiently high in rank or wealth, I was suffered by both parents to do exactly as I pleased; and well was it for me, as I afterwards found, that fortune, or, rather Providence, had so ordained it, that I had not suffered my affections to become in any degree engaged, for my mother would never have suffered any silly fancy of mine, as she was in the habit of styling an attachment, to stand in the way of her ambitious views – views which she was determined to carry into effect, in defiance of every obstacle, and in order to accomplish which she would not have hesitated to sacrifice anything so unreasonable and contemptible as a girlish passion.

When I reached the age of sixteen, my mother's plans began to develop themselves and, at her suggestion, we moved to Dublin to sojourn for the winter, in order that no time might be lost in disposing of me to the best advantage.

I had been too long accustomed to consider myself as of no importance whatever, to believe for a moment that I was in reality the cause of all the bustle and preparation which surrounded me, and being thus relieved from the pain which a consciousness of my real situation would have inflicted, I journeyed towards the capital with a feeling of total indifference.

My father's wealth and connection had established him in the best society, and consequently, upon our arrival in the metropolis, we commanded whatever enjoyment or advantages its gaieties afforded.

The tumult and novelty of the scenes in which I was involved did not fail considerably to amuse me, and my mind gradually recovered its tone, which was naturally cheerful.

It was almost immediately known and reported that I was

an heiress, and of course my attractions were pretty generally acknowledged.

Among the many gentlemen whom it was my fortune to please, one, ere long, established himself in my mother's good graces, to the exclusion of all less important aspirants. However, I had not understood or even remarked his attentions, nor, in the slightest degree, suspected his or my mother's plans respecting me, when I was made aware of them rather abruptly by my mother herself.

We had attended a splendid ball, given by Lord M———, at his residence in Stephen's Green, and I was, with the assistance of my waiting-maid, employed in rapidly divesting myself of the rich ornaments which, in profuseness and value, could scarcely have found their equals in any private family in Ireland.

I had thrown myself into a lounging chair beside the fire, listless and exhausted after the fatigues of the evening, when I was aroused from the reverie into which I had fallen, by the sound of footsteps approaching my chamber, and my mother entered.

'Fanny, my dear,' said she, in her softest tone. 'I wish to say a word or two with you before I go to rest. You are not fatigued, love, I hope?'

'No, no, madam, I thank you,' said I, rising at the same time from my seat with the formal respect so little practised now.

'Sit down, my dear,' said she, placing herself upon a chair beside me; 'I must chat with you for a quarter of an hour or so. Saunders (to the maid), you may leave the room; do not close the room door, but shut that of the lobby.'

This precaution against curious ears having been taken as directed, my mother proceeded.

'You have observed, I should suppose, my dearest Fanny; indeed, you *must* have observed, Lord Glenfallen's marked attentions to you?'

'I assure you, madam –' I began.

'Well, well, that is all right,' interrupted my mother; 'of course you must be modest upon the matter; but listen to me for a few

moments, my love, and I will prove to your satisfaction that your modesty is quite unnecessary in this case. You have done better than we could have hoped, at least, so very soon. Lord Glenfallen is in love with you. I give you joy of your conquest,' and saying this, my mother kissed my forehead.

'In love with me!' I exclaimed, in unfeigned astonishment.

'Yes, in love with you,' repeated my mother; 'devotedly, distractedly in love with you. Why, my dear, what is there wonderful in it; look in the glass, and look at these,' she continued, pointing with a smile to the jewels which I had just removed from my person, and which now lay a in glittering heap upon the table.

'May there not –' said I, hesitating between confusion and real alarm; 'is it not possible that some mistake may be at the bottom of all this?'

'Mistake, dearest! None,' said my mother. 'None, none in the world; judge for yourself; read this, my love.' And she placed in my hand a letter, addressed to herself, the seal of which was broken. I read it through with no small surprise. After some very fine complimentary flourishes upon my beauty and perfections, as also upon the antiquity and high reputation of our family, it went on to make a formal proposal of marriage, to be communicated or not to me at present, as my mother should deem expedient; and the letter wound up by a request that the writer might be permitted, upon our return to Ashtown House, which was soon to take place, as the spring was now tolerably advanced, to visit us for a few days, in case his suit was approved.

'Well, well, my dear,' said my mother, impatiently; 'do you know who Lord Glenfallen is?'

'I do, madam,' said I rather timidly, for I dreaded an altercation with my mother.

'Well, dear, and what frightens you?' continued she. 'Are you afraid of a title? What has he done to alarm you? He is neither old nor ugly.'

I was silent, though I might have said, 'He is neither young nor handsome.'

'My dear Fanny,' continued my mother, 'in sober seriousness you have been most fortunate in engaging the affections of a nobleman such as Lord Glenfallen, young and wealthy, with first-rate – yes, acknowledged *first-rate* abilities, and of a family whose influence is not exceeded by that of any in Ireland. Of course you see the offer in the same light that I do – indeed I think you *must.*'

This was uttered in no very dubious tone. I was so much astonished by the suddenness of the whole communication that I literally did not know what to say.

'You are not in love?' said my mother, turning sharply, and fixing her dark eyes upon me with severe scrutiny.

'No, madam,' said I, promptly; horrified, as what young lady would not have been, at such a query.

'I am glad to hear it,' said my mother, dryly. 'Once, nearly twenty years ago, a friend of mine consulted me as to how he should deal with a daughter who had made what they call a love match – beggared herself, and disgraced her family; and I said, without hesitation, take no care for her, but cast her off. Such punishment I awarded for an offence committed against the reputation of a family not my own; and what I advised respecting the child of another, with full as small compunction I would *do* with mine. I cannot conceive anything more unreasonable or intolerable than that the fortune and the character of a family should be marred by the idle caprices of a girl.'

She spoke this with great severity, and paused as if she expected some observation from me.

I, however, said nothing.

'But I need not explain to you, my dear Fanny,' she continued, 'my views upon this subject; you have always known them well, and I have never yet had reason to believe you are likely to offend me voluntarily, or to abuse or neglect any of those advantages which reason and duty tell you should be improved. Come hither, my dear, kiss me, and do not look so frightened. Well, now, about this letter – you need not answer it yet; of course, you must be allowed time to make up your mind. In the meantime, I will write to his lordship to give him my permission to visit us at Ashtown. Good night, my love.'

And thus ended one of the most disagreeable, not to say astounding, conversations I had ever had. It would not be easy to describe exactly what were my feelings towards Lord Glenfallen; whatever might have been my mother's suspicions, my heart was perfectly disengaged – and hitherto, although I had not been made in the slightest degree acquainted with his real views, I had liked him very much as an agreeable, well informed man, whom I was always glad to meet in society. He had served in the navy in early life, and the polish which his manners received in his after intercourse with courts and cities had not served to obliterate that frankness of manner which belongs proverbially to the sailor.

Whether this apparent candour went deeper than the outward bearing, I was yet to learn. However, there was no doubt that as far as I had seen of Lord Glenfallen, he was, though perhaps not so young as might have been desired in a lover, a singularly pleasing man, and whatever feeling unfavourable to him had found its way into my mind, arose altogether from the dread, not an unreasonable one, that constraint might be practised upon my inclinations. I reflected, however, that Lord Glenfallen was a wealthy man, and one highly thought of; and although I could never expect to love him in the romantic sense of the term, yet I had no doubt but that, all things considered, I might be more happy with him than I could hope to be at home.

When next I met him it was with no small embarrassment, his tact and good breeding, however, soon reassured me, and effectually prevented my awkwardness being remarked upon; and I had the satisfaction of leaving Dublin for the country with the full conviction

that nobody, not even those most intimate with me, even suspected the fact of Lord Glenfallen's having made me a formal proposal.

This was to me a very serious subject of self-gratulation, for, besides my instinctive dread of becoming the topic of the speculations of gossip, I felt that if the situation which I occupied in relation to him were made publicly known, I should stand committed in a manner which would scarcely leave me the power of retraction.

The period at which Lord Glenfallen had arranged to visit Ashtown House was now fast approaching, and it became my mother's wish to form me thoroughly to her will, and to obtain my consent to the proposed marriage before his arrival, so that all things might proceed smoothly without apparent opposition or objection upon my part. Whatever objections, therefore, I had entertained were to be subdued; whatever disposition to resistance I had exhibited or had been supposed to feel, were to be completely eradicated before he made his appearance, and my mother addressed herself to the task with a decision and energy against which even the barriers her imagination had created, could hardly have stood.

If she had, however, expected any determined opposition from me, she was agreeably disappointed. My heart was perfectly free, and all my feelings of liking and preference were in favour of Lord Glenfallen, and I well knew that in case I refused to dispose of myself as I was desired, my mother had alike the power and the will to render my existence as utterly miserable as even the most ill-assorted marriage could possibly have made it.

You will remember, my good friend, that I was very young and very completely under the control of my parents, both of whom, my mother particularly, were unscrupulously determined in matters of this kind, and willing, when voluntary obedience on the part of those within their power was withheld, to compel a forced acquiescence by an unsparing use of all the engines of the most stern and rigorous domestic discipline.

All these combined, not unnaturally, induced me to resolve upon yielding at once, and without useless opposition, to what appeared almost to be my fate. The appointed time was come, and my now accepted suitor arrived; he was in high spirits, and, if possible, more entertaining than ever.

I was not, however, quite in the mood to enjoy his sprightliness; but whatever I wanted in gaiety was amply made up in the triumphant and gracious good humour of my mother, whose smiles of benevolence and exultation were showered around as bountifully as the summer sunshine.

I will not weary you with unnecessary details. Let it suffice to say, that I was married to Lord Glenfallen with all the attendant pomp and circumstance of wealth, rank and grandeur. According to the usage of the times, now humanely reformed, the ceremony was made until long past midnight, the season of wild, uproarious and promiscuous feasting and revelry.

Of all this I have a painfully vivid recollection, and particularly of the little annoyances inflicted upon me by the dull and coarse jokes of the wits and wags who abound in all such places, and upon all such occasions.

I was not sorry, when, after a few days, Lord Glenfallen's carriage appeared at the door to convey us both from Ashtown; for any change would have been a relief from the irksomeness of ceremonial and formality which the visits received in honour of my newly-acquired titles hourly entailed upon me.

It was arranged that we were to proceed to Cahergillagh, one of the Glenfallen estates, lying, however, in a southern county; so that, owing to the difficulty of the roads, a tedious journey of three days intervened.

I set forth with my noble companion, followed by the regrets of some, and by the envy of many, though God knows I little deserved the latter; the three days of travel were now almost spent, when passing the brow of a wild heathy hill, the domain of Cahergillagh opened suddenly upon our view.

It formed a striking and a beautiful scene. A lake of considerable extent stretching away towards the west, and reflecting from its broad, smooth waters, the rich glow of the setting sun, was overhung by steep hills, covered by a rich mantle of velvet sward, broken here and there by the grey front of some old rock, and exhibiting on their shelving sides, and on their slopes and hollows every variety of light and shade. A thick wood of dwarf oak, birch and hazel skirted these hills, and clothed the shores of the lake, running out in rich luxuriance upon every promontory, and spreading upward considerably upon the side of the hills.

'There lies the enchanted castle,' said Lord Glenfallen, pointing towards a considerable level space intervening between two of the picturesque hills, which rose dimly around the lake.

This little plain was chiefly occupied by the same low, wild wood which covered the other parts of the domain; but towards the centre a mass of taller and statelier forest trees stood darkly grouped together, and among them stood an ancient square tower, with many buildings of a humbler character, forming together the manor-house, or, as it was more usually called, the Court of Cahergillagh.

As we approached the level upon which the mansion stood, the winding road gave us many glimpses of the time-worn castle and its surrounding buildings; and seen as it was through the long vistas of the fine old trees, and with the rich glow of evening upon it, I have seldom beheld an object more picturesquely striking.

I was glad to perceive, too, that here and there the blue curling smoke ascended from stacks of chimneys now hidden by the rich, dark ivy which, in a great measure, covered the building; other indications of comfort made themselves manifest as we approached; and indeed, though the place was evidently one of considerable antiquity, it had nothing whatever of the gloom of decay about it.

'You must not, my love,' said Lord Glenfallen, 'imagine this place worse than it is. I have no taste for antiquity, at least I should not choose a house to reside in because it is old. Indeed I do not recollect that I was even so romantic as to overcome my aversion to rats and rheumatism, those faithful attendants upon your noble relics of feudalism; and I much prefer a snug, modern, unmysterious bedroom, with well-aired sheets, to the waving tapestry, mildewed cushions, and all the other interesting appliances of romance. However, though I cannot promise you all the discomfort generally pertaining to an old castle, you will find legends and ghostly lore enough to claim your respect; and if old Martha be still to the fore, as I trust she is, you will soon have a supernatural and appropriate anecdote for every closet and corner of the mansion. But here we are – so, without more ado, welcome to Cahergillagh.'

We now entered the hall of the castle, and while the domestics were employed in conveying our trunks and other luggage which we had brought with us for immediate use to the apartments which Lord Glenfallen had selected for himself and me, I went with him into a spacious sitting room, wainscoted with finely polished black oak, and hung round with the portraits of various worthies of the Glenfallen family.

This room looked out upon an extensive level covered with the softest green sward, and irregularly bounded by the wild wood I have before mentioned, through the leafy arcade formed by whose boughs and trunks the level beams of the setting sun were pouring. In the distance, a group of dairy maids were plying their task, which they accompanied throughout with snatches of Irish songs which, mellowed by the distance, floated not unpleasingly to the ear; and beside them sat or lay, with all the grave importance of conscious protection, six or seven large dogs of various kinds. Farther in the distance, and through the cloisters of the arching wood, two or three ragged urchins were employed in driving such stray kine as had wandered farther than the rest to join their fellows.

As I looked upon this scene which I have described, a feeling of tranquillity and happiness came upon me, which I have never

experienced in so strong a degree; and so strange to me was the sensation that my eyes filled with tears.

Lord Glenfallen mistook the cause of my emotion, and taking me kindly and tenderly by the hand he said:

'Do not suppose, my love, that it is my intention to settle here, whenever you desire to leave this, you have only to let me know your wish and it shall be complied with, so I must entreat of you not to suffer any circumstances which I can control to give you one moment's uneasiness. But here is old Martha, you must be introduced to her, one of the heirlooms of our family.'

A hale, good-humoured, erect, old woman was Martha, and an agreeable contrast to the grim, decrepit hag, which my fancy had conjured up, as the depository of all the horrible tales in which I doubted not this old place was most fruitful.

She welcomed me and her master with a profusion of gratulations, alternately kissing our hands and apologising for the liberty, until at length Lord Glenfallen put an end to this somewhat fatiguing ceremonial, by requesting her to conduct me to my chamber if it were prepared for my reception.

I followed Martha up an old-fashioned oak staircase into a long, dim passage at the end of which lay the door which communicated with the apartments which had been selected for our use; here the old woman stopped, and respectfully requested me to proceed.

I accordingly opened the door and was about to enter, when something like a mass of black tapestry, as it appeared, disturbed by my sudden approach, fell from above the door, so as completely to screen the aperture; the startling unexpectedness of the occurrence, and the rustling noise which the drapery made in its descent, caused me involuntarily to step two or three paces backwards, I turned, smiling and half ashamed to the old servant, and said,

'You see what a coward I am.'

The woman looked puzzled and, without saying any more, I was about to draw aside the curtain and enter the room, when, upon

turning to do so, I was surprised to find that nothing whatever interposed to obstruct the passage.

I went into the room, followed by the servant woman, and was amazed to find that it, like the one below, was wainscoted, and that nothing like drapery was to be found near the door.

'Where is it,' said I; 'what has become of it?'

'What does your ladyship wish to know?' said the old woman.

'Where is the black curtain that fell across the door, when I attempted first to come to my chamber,' answered I.

'The Cross of Christ about us!' said the old woman, turning suddenly pale.

'What is the matter, my good friend?' said I; 'you seem frightened.'

'Oh, no, no, your ladyship,' said the old woman, endeavouring to conceal her agitation; but in vain, for tottering towards a chair, she sunk into it, looking so deadly pale and horror-struck that I thought every moment she would faint.

'Merciful God, keep us from harm and danger!' muttered she at length.

'What can have terrified you so?' said I, beginning to fear that she had seen something more than had met my eye. 'You appear ill, my poor woman!'

'Nothing, nothing, my lady,' said she, rising. 'I beg your ladyship's pardon for making so bold; may the great God defend us from misfortune!'

'Martha,' said I, 'something *has* frightened you very much, and I insist on knowing what it is; your keeping me in the dark upon the subject will make me much more uneasy than anything you could tell me. I desire you, therefore, to let me know what agitates you; I command you to tell me.'

'Your ladyship said you saw a black curtain falling across the door when you were coming into the room,' said the old woman.

'I did,' said I; 'but though the whole thing appears somewhat strange I cannot see anything in the matter to agitate you so excessively.'

'It's for no good you saw that, my lady,' said the crone; 'something terrible is coming. It's a sign, my lady – a sign that never fails.'

'Explain, explain what you mean, my good woman,' said I, in spite of myself, catching more than I could account for, of her superstitious terror.

'Whenever something – something *bad* is going to happen to the Glenfallen family, some one that belongs to them sees a black handkerchief or curtain just waved or falling before their faces. I saw it myself,' continued she, lowering her voice, 'when I was only a little girl, and I'll never forget it. I often heard of it before, though I never saw it till then, nor since, praised be God. But I was going into Lady Jane's room to waken her in the morning; and sure enough when I got first to the bed and began to draw the curtain, something dark was waved across the division, but only for a moment; and when I saw rightly into the bed, there was she lying cold and dead, God be merciful to me! So, my lady, there is small blame to me to be daunted when any one of the family sees it, for it's many the story I heard of it, though I saw it but once.'

I was not of a superstitious turn of mind; yet I could not resist a feeling of awe very nearly allied to the fear which my companion had so unreservedly expressed; and when you consider my situation, the loneliness, antiquity and gloom of the place, you will allow that the weakness was not without excuse.

In spite of old Martha's boding predictions, however, time flowed on in an unruffled course. One little incident, however, though trifling in itself, I must relate as it serves to make what follows more intelligible.

Upon the day after my arrival, Lord Glenfallen of course desired to make me acquainted with the house and domain; and accordingly we set forth upon our ramble. When returning, he became for some time silent and moody, a state so unusual with him as considerably to excite my surprise.

I endeavoured by observations and questions to arouse him –

but in vain. At length as we approached the house, he said, as if speaking to himself:

"Twere madness – madness – madness,' repeating the word bitterly – 'sure and speedy ruin.'

There was here a long pause; and at length, turning sharply towards me, in a tone very unlike that in which he had hitherto addressed me, he said:

'Do you think it possible that a woman can keep a secret?'

'I am sure,' said I, 'that women are very much belied upon the score of talkativeness, and that I may answer your question with the same directness with which you put it – I reply that I *do* think a woman can keep a secret.'

'But I do not,' said he, dryly.

We walked on in silence for a time. I was much astonished at his unwonted abruptness – I had almost said rudeness.

After a considerable pause he seemed to recollect himself, and with an effort resuming his sprightly manner, he said:

'Well, well, the next thing to keeping a secret well is not to desire to possess one – talkativeness and curiosity generally go together. Now I shall make test of you in the first place, respecting the latter of these qualities. I shall be your *Bluebeard* – tush, why do I trifle thus? Listen to me, my dear Fanny, I speak now in solemn earnest. What I desire is intimately, inseparably, connected with your happiness and honour as well as my own; and your compliance with my request will not be difficult. It will impose upon you a very trifling restraint during your sojourn here, which certain events which have occurred since our arrival have determined me shall not be a long one. You must promise me, upon your sacred honour, that you will visit *only* that part of the castle which can be reached from the front entrance, leaving the back entrance and the part of the building commanded immediately by it to the menials, as also the small garden whose high wall you see yonder; and never at any time seek to pry or peep into them, nor to open the door which communicates from the front part of the house through the corridor with the back. I do not urge this in jest or in caprice, but from a solemn conviction that danger and misery will be the certain consequences of your not observing what I prescribe. I cannot explain myself further at present. Promise me, then, these things as you hope for peace here and for mercy hereafter.'

I did make the promise as desired, and he appeared relieved; his manner recovered all its gaiety and elasticity, but the recollection of the strange scene which I have just described dwelt painfully upon my mind.

More than a month passed away without any occurrence worth recording; but I was not destined to leave Cahergillagh without further adventure. One day, intending to enjoy the pleasant sunshine in a ramble through the woods, I ran up to my room to procure my hat and cloak. Upon entering the chamber, I was surprised and somewhat startled to find it occupied. Beside the fireplace, and nearly opposite the door, seated in a large, old-fashioned elbow-chair, was placed the figure of a lady. She appeared to be nearer fifty than forty, and was dressed suitably to her age, in a handsome suit of flowered silk; she had a profusion of trinkets and jewellery about her person, and many rings upon her fingers. But although very rich, her dress was not gaudy or in ill taste. But what was remarkable in the lady was, that although her features were handsome, and upon the whole pleasing, the pupil of each eye was dimmed with the whiteness of cataract, and she was evidently stone-blind. I was for some seconds so surprised at this unaccountable apparition, that I could not find words to address her.

'Madam,' said I, 'there must be some mistake here – this is my bedchamber.'

'Marry come up,' said the lady, sharply; '*your* chamber! Where is Lord Glenfallen?'

'He is below, madam,' replied I; 'and I am convinced he will be not a little surprised to find you here.'

'I do not think he will,' said she; 'with your good leave, talk of

what you know something about. Tell him I want him; why does the minx dilly-dally so?'

In spite of the awe which this grim lady inspired, there was something in her air of confident superiority which, when I considered our relative situations, was not a little irritating.

'Do you know, madam, to whom you speak?' said I.

'I neither know nor care,' said she; 'but I presume that you are someone about the house, so again, I desire you, if you wish to continue here, to bring your master hither forthwith.'

'I must tell you, madam,' said I, 'that I am Lady Glenfallen.'

'What's that?' said the stranger, rapidly.

'I say, madam,' I repeated, approaching her, that I might be more distinctly heard, 'that I am Lady Glenfallen.'

'It's a lie, you trull!' cried she, in an accent which made me start, and, at the same time, springing forward, she seized me in her grasp and shook me violently, repeating, 'It's a lie, it's a lie!' with a rapidity and vehemence which swelled every inch of her face. The violence of her action, and the fury which convulsed her face, effectually terrified me, and disengaging myself from her grasp, I screamed as loud as I could for help. The blind woman continued to pour out a torrent of abuse upon me, foaming at the mouth with rage, and impotently shaking her clenched fists towards me.

I heard Lord Glenfallen's step upon the stairs, and I instantly ran out; as I passed him I perceived that he was deadly pale, and just caught the words, 'I hope that demon has not hurt you?'

I made some answer, I forget what, and he entered the chamber, the door of which he locked upon the inside. What passed within I know not; but I heard the voices of the two speakers raised in loud and angry altercation.

I thought I heard the shrill accents of the woman repeat the words, 'Let her look to herself'; but I could not be quite sure. This short sentence, however, was, to my alarmed imagination, pregnant with fearful meaning.

The storm at length subsided, though not until after a conference of more than two long hours. Lord Glenfallen then returned, pale and agitated.

'That unfortunate woman,' said he, 'is out of her mind. I dare say she treated you to some of her ravings, but you need not dread any further interruption from her, I have brought her so far to reason. She did not hurt you, I trust.'

'No, no,' said I; 'but she terrified me beyond measure.'

'Well,' said he, 'she is likely to behave better for the future, and I dare swear that neither you nor she would desire after what has passed, to meet again.'

This occurrence, so startling and unpleasant, so involved in mystery, and giving rise to so many painful surmises, afforded me no very agreeable food for rumination.

All attempts on my part to arrive at the truth were baffled; Lord Glenfallen evaded all my enquiries, and at length peremptorily forbade any further allusion to the matter. I was thus obliged to rest satisfied with what I had actually seen, and to trust to time to resolve the perplexities in which the whole transaction had involved me.

Lord Glenfallen's temper and spirits gradually underwent a complete and most painful change; he became silent and abstracted, his manner to me was abrupt and often harsh, some grievous anxiety seemed ever present to his mind; and under its influence his spirits sank and his temper became soured.

I soon perceived that his gaiety was rather that which the stir and excitement of society produce, than the result of a healthy habit of mind; and every day confirmed me in the opinion, that the considerate good nature which I had so much admired in him was little more than a mere manner; and to my infinite grief and surprise, the gay, kind, open-hearted nobleman who had for months followed and flattered me, was rapidly assuming the form of a gloomy, morose and singularly selfish man. This was a bitter discovery, and I strove to conceal it from myself as long as I could, but the truth was not to be denied, and I was forced to believe that my husband no longer loved me, and that he was at little pains to conceal the alteration in his sentiments.

One morning after breakfast, Lord Glenfallen had been for some time walking silently up and down the room, buried in his moody reflections, when, pausing suddenly, and turning towards me, he exclaimed:

'I have it! – I have it! We must go abroad, and stay there, too, and if that does not answer, why – why we must try some more effectual expedient. Lady Glenfallen, I have become involved in heavy embarrassments. A wife you know must share the fortunes of her husband, for better for worse, but I will waive my right if you prefer remaining here – here at Cahergillagh. For I would not have you seen elsewhere without the state to which your rank entitles you; besides it would break your poor mother's heart,' he added, with sneering gravity. 'So make up your mind – Cahergillagh or France. I will start if possible in a week, so determine between this and then.'

He left the room and in a few moments I saw him ride past the window, followed by a mounted servant. He had directed a domestic to inform me that he should not be back until the next day.

I was in very great doubt as to what course of conduct I should pursue, as to accompanying him on the continental tour so suddenly determined upon, I felt that it would be a hazard too great to encounter; for at Cahergillagh I had always the consciousness to sustain me, that if his temper at any time led him into violent or unwarrantable treatment of me, I had a remedy within reach, in the protection and support of my own family, from all useful and effective communication with whom, if once in France, I should be entirely debarred.

As to remaining at Cahergillagh in solitude, and, for aught I knew, exposed to hidden dangers, it appeared to me scarcely less objectionable than the former proposition; and yet I feared that with one or other I must comply, unless I was prepared to come

to an actual breach with Lord Glenfallen. Full of these unpleasing doubts and perplexities, I retired to rest.

I was wakened, after having slept uneasily for some hours, by some person shaking me rudely by the shoulder; a small lamp burned in my room, and by its light, to my horror and amazement, I discovered that my visitant was the self-same blind old lady who had so terrified me a few weeks before.

I started up in the bed, with a view to ring the bell, and alarm the domestics, but she instantly anticipated me by saying:

'Do not be frightened, silly girl! If I had wished to harm you I could have done it while you were sleeping, I need not have wakened you. Listen to me, now, attentively and fearlessly; for what I have to say interests you to the full as much as it does me. Tell me, here, in the presence of God, did Lord Glenfallen marry you – *actually marry* you? Speak the truth, woman.'

'As surely as I live and speak,' I replied, 'did Lord Glenfallen marry me in presence of more than a hundred witnesses.'

'Well,' continued she, 'he should have told you *then*, before you married him, that he had a wife living – that I am his wife. I feel you tremble – tush! do not be frightened. I do not mean to harm you. Mark me now – you are *not* his wife. When I make my story known you will be so, neither in the eye of God nor of man. You must leave this house upon tomorrow. Let the world know that your husband has another wife living; go, you, into retirement, and leave him to justice, which will surely overtake him. If you remain in this house after tomorrow, you will reap the bitter fruits of your sin.'

So saying, she quitted the room, leaving me very little disposed to sleep.

Here was food for my very worst and most terrible suspicions; still there was not enough to remove all doubt. I had no proof of the truth of this woman's statement.

Taken by itself there was nothing to induce me to attach weight to it; but when I viewed it in connection with the extraordinary mystery of some of Lord Glenfallen's proceedings, his strange anxiety to exclude me from certain portions of the mansion, doubtless, lest I should encounter this person – the strong influence, nay, command, which she possessed over him, a circumstance clearly established by the very fact of her residing in the very place, where, of all others, he should least have desired to find her – her thus acting, and continuing to act in direct contradiction to his wishes; when, I say, I viewed her disclosure in connection with all these circumstances, I could not help feeling that there was at least a fearful verisimilitude in the allegations which she had made.

Still I was not satisfied, nor nearly so. Young minds have a reluctance almost insurmountable to believing upon anything short of unquestionable proof, the existence of premeditated guilt in anyone whom they have ever trusted; and in support of this feeling I was assured that if the assertion of Lord Glenfallen, which nothing in this woman's manner had led me to disbelieve, were true, namely that her mind was unsound, the whole fabric of my doubts and fears must fall to the ground.

I determined to state to Lord Glenfallen freely and accurately the substance of the communication which I had just heard, and in his words and looks to seek for its proof or refutation; full of these thoughts I remained wakeful and excited all night, every moment fancying that I heard the step, or saw the figure of my recent visitor towards whom I felt a species of horror and dread which I can hardly describe.

There was something in her face, though her features had evidently been handsome, and were not, at first sight, unpleasing, which, upon a nearer inspection, seemed to indicate the habitual prevalence and indulgence of evil passions, and a power of expressing mere animal anger, with an intenseness that I have seldom seen equalled, and to which an almost unearthly effect was given by the convulsive quivering of the sightless eyes.

You may easily suppose that it was no very pleasing reflection to

me to consider that, whenever caprice might induce her to return, I was within the reach of this violent and, for aught I knew, insane woman, who had, upon that very night, spoken to me in a tone of menace, of which her mere words, divested of the manner and look with which she uttered them, can convey but a faint idea.

Will you believe me when I tell you that I was actually afraid to leave my bed in order to secure the door, lest I should again encounter the dreadful object lurking in some corner or peeping from behind the window curtains, so very a child was I in my fears.

The morning came, and with it Lord Glenfallen. I knew not, and indeed I cared not, where he might have been; my thoughts were wholly engrossed by the terrible fears and suspicions which my last night's conference had suggested to me; he was, as usual, gloomy and abstracted, and I feared in no very fitting mood to hear what I had to say with patience, whether the charges were true or false.

I was, however, determined not to suffer the opportunity to pass, or Lord Glenfallen to leave the room, until, at all hazards, I had unburdened my mind.

'My Lord,' said I, after a long silence, summoning up all my firmness, 'my lord, I wish to say a few words to you upon a matter of very great importance, of very deep concernment to you and to me.'

I fixed my eyes upon him to discern, if possible, whether the announcement caused him any uneasiness, but no symptom of any such feeling was perceptible.

'Well, my dear,' said he, 'this is, no doubt, a very grave preface, and portends, I have no doubt, something extraordinary. Pray let us have it without more ado.'

He took a chair, and seated himself nearly opposite to me.

'My lord,' said I, 'I have seen the person who alarmed me so much a short time since, the blind lady, again, upon last night.' His face, upon which my eyes were fixed, turned pale, he hesitated for a moment, and then said:

'And did you, pray madam, so totally forget or spurn my express

command, as to enter that portion of the house from which your promise, I might say, your oath, excluded you? Answer me that!' he added, fiercely.

'My lord,' said I, 'I have neither forgotten your *commands*, since such they were, nor disobeyed them. I was, last night, wakened from my sleep, as I lay in my own chamber, and accosted by the person whom I have mentioned. How she found access to the room I cannot pretend to say.'

'Ha! this must be looked to,' said he, half reflectively. 'And pray,' added he, quickly, while in turn he fixed his eyes upon me, 'what did this person say, since some comment upon her communication forms, no doubt, the sequel to your preface.'

'Your lordship is not mistaken,' said I, 'her statement was so extraordinary that I could not think of withholding it from you; she told me, my lord, that you had a wife living at the time you married me, and that she was that wife.'

Lord Glenfallen became ashy pale, almost livid; he made two or three efforts to clear his voice to speak, but in vain, and turning suddenly from me, he walked to the window. The horror and dismay, which, in the olden time, overwhelmed the woman of Endor, when her spells unexpectedly conjured the dead into her presence, were but types of what I felt, when thus presented with what appeared to be almost unequivocal evidence of the guilt, whose existence I had before so strongly doubted.

There was a silence of some moments, during which it were hard to conjecture whether I or my companion suffered most.

Lord Glenfallen soon recovered his self command; he returned to the table, again sat down and said:

'What you have told me has so astonished me, has unfolded such a tissue of motiveless guilt, and in a quarter from which I had so little reason to look for ingratitude or treachery, that your announcement almost deprived me of speech; the person in question, however, has one excuse, her mind is, as I told you

before, unsettled. You should have remembered that, and hesitated to receive as unexceptionable evidence against the honour of your husband, the ravings of a lunatic. I now tell you that this is the last time I shall speak to you upon this subject and, in the presence of the God who is to judge me, and as I hope for mercy in the day of judgment, I swear that the charge thus brought against me, is utterly false, unfounded and ridiculous; I defy the world in any point to taint my honour; and, as I have never taken the opinion of madmen touching your character or morals, I think it but fair to require that you will evince a like tenderness for me; and now, once for all, never again dare to repeat to me your insulting suspicions, or the clumsy and infamous calumnies of fools. I shall instantly let the worthy lady who contrived this somewhat original device understand fully my opinion upon the matter. Good morning.'

And with these words he left me again in doubt, and involved in all horrors of the most agonising suspense.

I had reason to think that Lord Glenfallen wreaked his vengeance upon the author of the strange story which I had heard, with a violence which was not satisfied with mere words, for old Martha, with whom I was a great favourite, while attending me in my room, told me that she feared her master had ill – used the poor, blind, Dutchwoman, for that she had heard her scream as if the very life were leaving her, but added a request that I should not speak of what she had told me to any one, particularly to the master.

'How do you know that she is a Dutchwoman?' inquired I, anxious to learn anything whatever that might throw a light upon the history of this person, who seemed to have resolved to mix herself up in my fortunes.

'Why, my lady,' answered Martha, 'the master often calls her the Dutch hag, and other names you would not like to hear, and I am sure she is neither English nor Irish; for, whenever they talk together, they speak some queer foreign lingo, and fast enough, I'll be bound. But I ought not to talk about her at all; it might be as much as my place is worth to mention her, only you saw her first yourself, so there can be no great harm in speaking of her now.'

'How long has this lady been here?' continued I.

'She came early on the morning after your ladyship's arrival,' answered she; 'but do not ask me any more, for the master would think nothing of turning me out of doors for daring to speak of her at all, much less to *you*, my lady.'

I did not like to press the poor woman further; for her reluctance to speak on this topic was evident and strong.

You will readily believe that upon the very slight grounds which my information afforded, contradicted as it was by the solemn oath of my husband, and derived from what was, at best, a very questionable source, I could not take any very decisive measures whatever; and as to the menace of the strange woman who had thus unaccountably twice intruded herself into my chamber, although, at the moment, it occasioned me some uneasiness, it was not, even in my eyes, sufficiently formidable to induce my departure from Cahergillagh.

A few nights after the scene which I have just mentioned, Lord Glenfallen having, as usual, early retired to his study, I was left alone in the parlour to amuse myself as best I might.

It was not strange that my thoughts should often recur to the agitating scenes in which I had recently taken a part.

The subject of my reflections, the solitude, the silence, and the lateness of the hour, as also the depression of spirits to which I had of late been a constant prey, tended to produce that nervous excitement which places us wholly at the mercy of the imagination.

In order to calm my spirits, I was endeavouring to direct my thoughts into some more pleasing channel, when I heard, or thought I heard, uttered, within a few yards of me, in an odd half-sneering tone, the words:

'There is blood upon your ladyship's throat.'

So vivid was the impression, that I started to my feet, and involuntarily placed my hand upon my neck.

I looked around the room for the speaker, but in vain.

I went then to the room door, which I opened, and peered into the passage, nearly faint with horror, lest some leering, shapeless thing should greet me upon the threshold.

When I had gazed long enough to assure myself that no strange object was within sight,

'I have been too much of a rake, lately; I am racking out my nerves,' said I, speaking aloud, with a view to reassure myself.

I rang the bell and, attended by old Martha, I retired to settle for the night.

While the servant was, as was her custom, arranging the lamp which I have already stated always burned during the night in my chamber, I was employed in undressing and, in doing so, I had recourse to a large looking-glass which occupied a considerable portion of the wall in which it was fixed, rising from the ground to a height of about six feet; this mirror filled the space of a large panel in the wainscoting opposite the foot of the bed.

I had hardly been before it for the lapse of a minute, when something like a black pall was slowly waved between me and it.

'Oh, God! there it is,' I exclaimed wildly. 'I have seen it again, Martha – the black cloth.'

'God be merciful to us, then!' answered she, tremulously crossing herself. 'Some misfortune is over us.'

'No, no, Martha,' said I, almost instantly recovering my collectedness; for, although of a nervous temperament, I had never been superstitious. 'I do not believe in omens. You know I saw, or fancied I saw, this thing before, and nothing followed.'

'The Dutch lady came the next morning,' replied she.

'But surely her coming scarcely deserved such a dreadful warning,' I replied.

'She is a strange woman, my lady,' said Martha, 'and she is not *gone* yet – mark my words.'

'Well, well, Martha,' said I, 'I have not wit enough to change your opinions, nor inclination to alter mine; so I will talk no more of the matter. Good night,' and so I was left to my reflections.

After lying for about an hour awake, I at length fell into a kind of doze; but my imagination was very busy, for I was startled from this unrefreshing sleep by fancying that I heard a voice close to my face exclaim as before:

'There is blood upon your ladyship's throat.'

The words were instantly followed by a loud burst of laughter.

Quaking with horror, I awakened, and heard my husband enter the room. Even this was a relief.

Scared as I was, however, by the tricks which my imagination had played me, I preferred remaining silent, and pretending to sleep, to attempting to engage my husband in conversation, for I well knew that his mood was such, that his words would not, in all probability, convey anything that had not better be unsaid and unheard.

Lord Glenfallen went into his dressing-room, which lay upon the right-hand side of the bed. The door lying open, I could see him by himself, at full length upon a sofa, and, in about half an hour, I became aware, by his deep and regularly drawn respiration, that he was fast asleep.

When slumber refuses to visit one, there is something peculiarly irritating, not to the temper, but to the nerves, in the consciousness that some one is in your immediate presence, actually enjoying the boon which you are seeking in vain; at least, I have always found it so, and never more than upon the present occasion.

A thousand annoying imaginations harassed and excited me, every object which I looked upon, though ever so familiar, seemed to have acquired a strange phantom-like character, the varying shadows thrown by the flickering of the lamplight, seemed shaping themselves into grotesque and unearthly forms, and whenever my eyes wandered to the sleeping figure of my husband, his features appeared to undergo the strangest and most demoniacal contortions.

Hour after hour was told by the old clock, and each succeeding one found me, if possible, less inclined to sleep than its predecessor.

It was now considerably past three; my eyes, in their involuntary wanderings, happened to alight upon the large mirror which was, as I have said, fixed in the wall opposite the foot of the bed. A view of it was commanded from where I lay, through the curtains. As I gazed fixedly upon it, I thought I perceived the broad sheet of glass shifting its position in relation to the bed; I rivetted my eyes upon it with intense scrutiny; it was no deception, the mirror, as if acting of its own impulse, moved slowly aside, and disclosed a dark aperture in the wall, nearly as large as an ordinary door; a figure evidently stood in this; but the light was too dim to define it accurately.

It stepped cautiously into the chamber, and with so little noise, that had I not actually seen it, I do not think I should have been aware of its presence. It was arrayed in a kind of woollen night-dress, and a white handkerchief or cloth was bound tightly about the head; I had no difficulty, spite of the strangeness of the attire in recognising the blind woman whom I so much dreaded.

She stooped down, bringing her head nearly to the ground, and in that attitude she remained motionless for some moments, no doubt in order to ascertain if any suspicious sounds were stirring.

She was apparently satisfied by her observations, for she immediately recommenced her silent progress towards a ponderous mahogany dressing-table of my husband's. When she had reached it, she paused again, and appeared to listen attentively for some minutes; she then noiselessly opened one of the drawers from which, having groped for some time, she took something which I soon perceived to be a case of razors. She opened it and tried the edge of each of the two instruments upon the skin of her hand; she quickly selected one, which she fixed firmly in her grasp. She now stooped down as before, and having listened for a time she, with the hand that was disengaged, groped her way into the dressing room where Lord Glenfallen lay fast asleep.

I was fixed as if in the tremendous spell of a nightmare. I could not stir even a finger; I could not lift my voice; I could not even breathe, and though I expected every moment to see the sleeping man murdered, I could not even close my eyes to shut out the horrible spectacle, which I had not the power to avert.

I saw the woman approach the sleeping figure, she laid the unoccupied hand lightly along his clothes, and having thus ascertained his identity she, after a brief interval, turned back and again entered my chamber; here she bent down again to listen.

I had now not a doubt but that the razor was intended for my throat; yet the terrific fascination which had locked all my powers so long, still continued to bind me fast.

I felt that my life depended upon the slightest ordinary exertion, and yet I could not stir one joint from the position in which I lay, nor even make noise enough to waken Lord Glenfallen.

The murderous woman now, with long, silent steps, approached the bed; my very heart seemed turning to ice; her left hand, that which was disengaged, was upon the pillow; she gradually slid it forward towards my head, and in an instant, with the speed of lightning, it was clutched in my hair, while, with the other hand, she dashed the razor at my throat.

A slight inaccuracy saved me from instant death; the blow fell short, the point of the razor grazing my throat. In a moment I know not how, I found myself at the other side of the bed uttering shriek after shriek; the wretch was, however, determined if possible to murder me.

Scrambling along by the curtains, she rushed round the bed towards me; I seized the handle of the door to make my escape. It was, however, fastened. At all events, I could not open it. From the mere instinct of recoiling terror, I shrunk back into a corner. She was now within a yard of me. Her hand was upon my face.

I closed my eyes fast, expecting never to open them again, when a blow, inflicted from behind by a strong arm, stretched the monster

senseless at my feet. At the same moment the door opened, and several domestics, alarmed by my cries, entered the apartment.

I do not recollect what followed, for I fainted. One swoon succeeded another so long and death-like, that my life was considered very doubtful.

At about ten o'clock, however, I sank into a deep and refreshing sleep, from which I was awakened at about two, that I might swear my deposition before a magistrate, who attended for that purpose.

I accordingly did so, as did also Lord Glenfallen; and the woman was fully committed to stand her trial at the ensuing assizes.

I shall never forget the scene which the examination of the blind woman and of the other parties afforded.

She was brought into the room in the custody of two servants. She wore a kind of flannel wrapper, which had not been changed since the night before. It was torn and soiled, and here and there smeared with blood, which had flowed in large quantities from a wound in her head. The white handkerchief had fallen off in the scuffle; and her grizzled hair fell in masses about her wild and deadly pale countenance.

She appeared perfectly composed, however, and the only regret she expressed throughout, was at not having succeeded in her attempt, the object of which she did not pretend to conceal.

On being asked her name, she called herself the Countess Glenfallen, and refused to give any other title.

'The woman's name is Flora Van-Kemp,' said Lord Glenfallen.

'It *was*, it *was*, you perjured traitor and cheat,' screamed the woman; and then there followed a volley of words in some foreign language. 'Is there a magistrate here?' she resumed; 'I am Lord Glenfallen's wife – I'll prove it – write down my words. I am willing to be hanged or burned, so *he* meets his deserts. I did try to kill that doll of his; but it was he who put it into my head to do it – two wives were too many; I was to murder her, or she was to hang me – listen to all I have to say.'

Here Lord Glenfallen interrupted.

'I think, sir,' said he, addressing the magistrate, 'that we had better proceed to business, this unhappy woman's furious recriminations but waste our time. If she refuses to answer your questions, you had better, I presume, take my depositions.'

'And are you going to swear away my life, you black perjured murderer?' shrieked the woman. 'Sir, sir, sir, you must hear me,' she continued, addressing the magistrate; 'I can convict him – he bid me murder that girl, and then when I failed, he came behind me, and struck me down, and now he wants to swear away my life – take down all I say.'

'If it is your intention,' said the magistrate, 'to confess the crime with which you stand charged, you may, upon producing sufficient evidence, criminate whom you please.'

'Evidence! – I have no evidence but myself,' said the woman. 'I will swear it all – write down my testimony – write it down, I say – we shall hang side by side, my brave Lord – all your own handiwork, my gentle husband.'

This was followed by a low, insolent and sneering laugh which, from one in her situation, was sufficiently horrible.

'I will not at present hear anything,' replied he, 'but distinct answers to the questions which I shall put to you upon this matter.'

'Then you shall hear nothing,' replied she sullenly, and no inducement or intimidation could bring her to speak again.

Lord Glenfallen's deposition and mine were then given, as also those of the servants who had entered the room at the moment of my rescue.

The magistrate then intimated that she was committed, and must proceed directly to gaol, whither she was brought in a carriage of Lord Glenfallen's, for his lordship was naturally by no means indifferent to the effect which her vehement accusations against himself might produce, if uttered before every chance hearer whom she might meet with between Cahergillagh and the place of confinement whither she was dispatched.

During the time which intervened between the committal and the trial of the prisoner, Lord Glenfallen seemed to suffer agonies of mind which baffled all description, he hardly ever slept, and when he did, his slumbers seemed but the instruments of new tortures, and his waking hours were, if possible, exceeded in intensity of terror by the dreams which disturbed his sleep.

Lord Glenfallen rested, if to lie in the mere attitude of repose were to do so, in his dressing-room, and thus I had an opportunity of witnessing, far oftener than I wished it, the fearful workings of his mind. His agony often broke out into such fearful paroxysms that delirium and total loss of reason appeared to be impending. He frequently spoke of flying from the country, and bringing with him all the witnesses of the appalling scene upon which the prosecution was founded; then again, he would fiercely lament that the blow which he had inflicted had not ended all.

The assizes arrived, however, and upon the day appointed, Lord Glenfallen and I attended in order to give our evidence.

The cause was called on, and the prisoner appeared at the bar.

Great curiosity and interest were felt respecting the trial, so that the court was crowded to excess.

The prisoner, however, without appearing to take the trouble of listening to the indictment, pleaded guilty, and no representations on the part of the court availed to induce her to retract her plea.

After much time had been wasted in a fruitless attempt to prevail upon her to reconsider her words, the court proceeded according to the usual form, to pass sentence.

This having been done, the prisoner was about to be removed, when she said in a low, distinct voice:

'A word – a word, my Lord. Is Lord Glenfallen here in the court?'

On being told that he was, she raised her voice to a tone of loud menace, and continued:

'Hardress, Earl of Glenfallen, I accuse you here in this court of justice of two crimes – first, that you married a second wife, while the first was living, and again, that you prompted me to the murder, for attempting which I am to die. secure him – chain him – bring him here!'

There was a laugh through the court at these words, which were naturally treated by the judge as a violent extemporary recrimination, and the woman was desired to be silent.

'You won't take him, then,' she said, 'you won't try him? You'll let him go free?'

It was intimated by the court that he would certainly be allowed 'to go free,' and she was ordered again to be removed.

Before, however, the mandate was executed, she threw her arms wildly into the air, and uttered one piercing shriek so full of preternatural rage and despair, that it might fitly have ushered a soul into those realms where hope can come no more.

The sound still rang in my ears, months after the voice that had uttered it was for ever silent. The wretched woman was executed in accordance with the sentence which had been pronounced.

For some time after this event, Lord Glenfallen appeared, if possible, to suffer more than he had done before, and altogether, his language, which often amounted to half confessions of the guilt imputed to him, and all the circumstances connected with the late occurrences, formed a mass of evidence so convincing that I wrote to my father, detailing the grounds of my fears, and imploring him to come to Cahergillagh without delay, in order to remove me from my husband's control, previously to taking legal steps for a final separation.

Circumstanced as I was, my existence was little short of intolerable for, besides the fearful suspicions which attached to my husband, I plainly perceived that if Lord Glenfallen were not relieved, and that speedily, insanity must supervene. I therefore expected my father's arrival, or at least a letter to announce it, with indescribable impatience.

About a week after the execution had taken place, Lord Glenfallen one morning met me with an unusually sprightly air.

'Fanny,' said he, 'I have it now for the first time, in my power to explain to your satisfaction everything which has hitherto appeared suspicious or mysterious in my conduct. After breakfast come with me to my study, and I shall, I hope, make all things clear.'

This invitation afforded me more real pleasure than I had experienced for months; something had certainly occurred to tranquillise my husband's mind, in no ordinary degree, and I thought it by no means impossible that he would, in the proposed interview, prove himself the most injured and innocent of men.

Full of this hope, I repaired to his study at the appointed hour. He was writing busily when I entered the room, and just raising his eyes, he requested me to be seated.

I took a chair as he desired, and remained silently awaiting his leisure, while he finished, folded, directed and sealed his letter. Laying it then upon the table, with the address downward, he said:

'My dearest Fanny, I know I must have appeared very strange to you and very unkind – often even cruel. Before the end of this week I will show you the necessity of my conduct – how impossible it was that I should have seemed otherwise. I am conscious that many acts of mine must have inevitably given rise to painful suspicions – suspicions which, indeed, upon one occasion, you very properly communicated to me. I have got two letters from a quarter which commands respect, containing information as to the course by which I may be enabled to prove the negative of all the crimes which even the most credulous suspicion could lay to my charge. I expected a third by this morning's post, containing documents which will set the matter for ever at rest, but owing, no doubt, to some neglect, or, perhaps, to some difficulty in collecting the papers, some inevitable delay, it has not come to hand this morning, according to my expectation. I was finishing one to the very same quarter when you came in, and if a sound rousing be worth anything, I think I shall have a special messenger before two days have passed. I have been anxiously considering with myself, as to whether I had better imperfectly clear up your doubts by submitting to your inspection the two letters which I have already received, or wait till I can triumphantly vindicate myself by the production of the documents which I have already mentioned, and I have, I think, not unnaturally decided upon the latter course. However, there is a person in the next room, whose testimony is not without its value – excuse me for one moment.'

So saying, he arose and went to the door of a closet which opened from the study, this he unlocked, and half opening the door, he said, 'It is only I,' and then slipped into the room, and carefully closed and locked the door behind him.

I immediately heard his voice in animated conversation. My curiosity upon the subject of the letter was naturally great, so, smothering any little scruples which I might have felt, I resolved to look at the address of the letter which lay as my husband had left it, with its face upon the table. I accordingly drew it over to me, and turned up the direction.

For two or three moments I could scarce believe my eyes, but there could be no mistake – in large characters were traced the words, 'To the Archangel Gabriel in Heaven.'

I had scarcely returned the letter to its original position, and in some degree recovered the shock which this unequivocal proof of insanity produced, when the closet door was unlocked, and Lord Glenfallen re-entered the study, carefully closing and locking the door again upon the outside.

'Whom have you there?' inquired I, making a strong effort to appear calm.

'Perhaps,' said he musingly, 'you might have some objection to seeing her, at least for a time.'

'Who is it?' repeated I.

'Why,' said he, 'I see no use in hiding it – the blind Dutchwoman. I have been with her the whole morning. She is very anxious to get out of that closet, but you know she is odd, she is scarcely to be trusted.'

A heavy gust of wind shook the door at this moment with a sound as if something more substantial were pushing against it.

'Ha, ha, ha! – do you hear her,' said he, with an obstreperous burst of laughter.

The wind died away in a long howl, and Lord Glenfallen, suddenly checking his merriment, shrugged his shoulders, and muttered:

'Poor devil, she has been hardly used.'

'We had better not tease her at present with questions,' said I, in as unconcerned a tone as I could assume, although I felt every moment as if I should faint.

'Humph! may be so,' said he. 'Well, come back in an hour or two, or when you please, and you will find us here.'

He again unlocked the door, and entered with the same precautions which he had adopted before, locking the door upon the inside, and as I hurried from the room, I heard his voice again exerted as if in eager parley.

I can hardly describe my emotions; my hopes had been raised to the highest, and now in an instant, all was gone; the dreadful consummation was accomplished – the fearful retribution had fallen upon the guilty man – the mind was destroyed, the power to repent was gone.

The agony of the hours which followed what I would still call my awful interview with Lord Glenfallen, I cannot describe; my solitude was, however, broken in upon by Martha, who came to inform me of the arrival of a gentleman, who expected me in the parlour.

I accordingly descended, and to my great joy, found my father seated by the fire.

This expedition, upon his part, was easily accounted for: my communications had touched the honour of the family. I speedily informed him of the dreadful malady which had fallen upon the wretched man.

My father suggested the necessity of placing some person to watch him, to prevent his injuring himself or others.

I rang the bell, and desired that one Edward Cooke, an attached servant of the family, should be sent to me.

I told him distinctly and briefly, the nature of the service required of him and, attended by him, my father and I proceeded at once to the study. The door of the inner room was still closed, and everything in the outer chamber remained in the same order in which I had left it.

We then advanced to the closet door, at which we knocked, but without receiving any answer.

We next tried to open the door, but in vain; it was locked upon the inside. We knocked more loudly, but in vain.

Seriously alarmed, I desired the servant to force the door, which was, after several violent efforts, accomplished, and we entered the closet.

Lord Glenfallen was lying on his face upon a sofa.

'Hush!' said I, 'he is asleep.' We paused for a moment.

'He is too still for that,' said my father.

We all of us felt a strong reluctance to approach the figure.

'Edward,' said I, 'try whether your master sleeps.'

The servant approached the sofa where Lord Glenfallen lay; he leant his ear towards the head of the recumbent figure, to ascertain whether the sound of breathing was audible. He turned towards us, and said:

'My lady, you had better not wait here, I am sure he is dead!'

'Let me see the face,' said I, terribly agitated, 'you *may* be mistaken.'

The man then, in obedience to my command, turned the body round, and, gracious God! what a sight met my view.

The whole breast of the shirt, with its lace frill, was drenched with his blood, as was the couch underneath the spot where he lay.

The head hung back, as it seemed, almost severed from the body by a frightful gash, which yawned across the throat. The razor which had inflicted the wound, was found under his body.

All, then, was over; I was never to learn the history in whose termination I had been so deeply and so tragically involved.

The severe discipline which my mind had undergone was not bestowed in vain. I directed my thoughts and my hopes to that place where there is no more sin, nor danger, nor sorrow.

Thus ends a brief tale, whose prominent incidents many will recognise as having marked the history of a distinguished family, and though it refers to a somewhat distant date, we shall be found not to have taken, upon that account, any liberties with the facts.

THE DEAD SEXTON
by Joseph Sheridan Le Fanu

The sunsets were red, the nights were long, and the weather pleasantly frosty; and Christmas, the glorious herald of the New Year, was at hand, when an event – still recounted by winter firesides, with a horror made delightful by the mellowing influence of years – occurred in the beautiful little town of Golden Friars, and signalised, as the scene of its catastrophe, the old inn known throughout a wide region of the Northumbrian counties as the *George and Dragon*.

Toby Crooke, the sexton, was lying dead in the old coach-house in the inn yard. The body had been discovered, only half an hour before this story begins, under strange circumstances, and in a place where it might have lain the better part of a week undisturbed; and a dreadful suspicion astounded the village of Golden Friars.

A wintry sunset was glaring through a gorge of the western mountains, turning into fire the twigs of the leafless elms, and all the tiny blades of grass on the green by which the quaint little town is surrounded. It is built of light, grey stone, with steep gables and slender chimneys rising with airy lightness from the level sward by the margin of the beautiful lake, and backed by the grand amphitheatre of the fells at the other side, whose snowy peaks show faintly against the sky, tinged with the vaporous red of the western light. As you

descend towards the margin of the lake, and see Golden Friars, its taper chimneys and slender gables, its curious old inn and gorgeous sign, and over all the graceful tower and spire of the ancient church, at this hour or by moonlight, in the solemn grandeur and stillness of the natural scenery that surrounds it, it stands before you like a fairy town.

Toby Crooke, the lank sexton, now fifty or upwards, had passed an hour or two with some village cronies, over a solemn pot of purl, in the kitchen of that cosy hostelry, the night before. He generally turned in there at about seven o'clock, and heard the news. This contented him: for he talked little, and looked always surly.

Many things are now raked up and talked over about him.

In early youth, he had been a bit of a scamp. He broke his indentures, and ran away from his master, the tanner of Bryemere; he had got into fifty bad scrapes and out again; and, just as the little world of Golden Friars had come to the conclusion that it would be well for all parties – except, perhaps, himself – and a happy riddance for his afflicted mother, if he were sunk, with a gross of quart pots about his neck, in the bottom of the lake in which the grey gables, the elms, and the towering fells of Golden Friars are mirrored, he suddenly returned, a reformed man at the ripe age of forty.

For twelve years he had disappeared, and no one knew what had become of him. Then, suddenly, as I say, he reappeared at Golden Friars – a very black and silent man, sedate and orderly. His mother was dead and buried; but the 'prodigal son' was received good-naturedly. The good vicar, Doctor Jenner, reported to his wife:

'His hard heart has been softened, dear Dolly. I saw him dry his eyes, poor fellow, at the sermon yesterday.'

'I don't wonder, Hugh darling. I know the part – 'There is joy in Heaven.' I am sure it was – wasn't it? It was quite beautiful. I almost cried myself.'

The Vicar laughed gently, and stooped over her chair and kissed her, and patted her cheek fondly.

'You think too well of your old man's sermons,' he said. 'I preach, you see, Dolly, very much to the *poor*. If *they* understand me, I am pretty sure everyone else must; and I think that my simple style goes more home to both feelings and conscience –'

'You ought to have told me of his crying before. You *are* so eloquent,' exclaimed Dolly Jenner. 'No one preaches like my man. I have never heard such sermons.'

Not many, we may be sure; for the good lady had not heard more than six from any other divine for the last twenty years.

The personages of Golden Friars talked Toby Crooke over on his return. Doctor Lincote said:

'He must have led a hard life; he had *dried in* so, and got a good deal of hard muscle; and he rather fancied he had been soldiering – he stood like a soldier; and the mark over his right eye looked like a gunshot.'

People might wonder how he could have survived a gunshot over the eye; but was not Lincote a doctor – and an army doctor to boot – when he was young; and who, in Golden Friars, could dispute with him on points of surgery? And I believe the truth is, that this mark had been really made by a pistol bullet.

Mr. Jarlcot, the attorney, would 'go bail' he had picked up some sense in his travels; and honest Turnbull, the host of the *George and Dragon*, said heartily:

'We must look out something for him to put his hand to. *Now's* the time to make a man of him.'

The end of it was that he became, among other things, the sexton of Golden Friars.

He was a punctual sexton. He meddled with no other person's business; but he was a silent man, and by no means popular. He was reserved in company; and he used to walk alone by the shore of the lake, while other fellows played at fives or skittles; and when he visited the kitchen of the *George*, he had his liquor to himself, and in the midst of the general talk was a saturnine listener. There was

something sinister in this man's face; and when things went wrong with him, he could look dangerous enough.

There were whispered stories in Golden Friars about Toby Crooke. Nobody could say how they got there. Nothing is more mysterious than the spread of rumour. It is like a vial poured on the air. It travels, like an epidemic, on the sightless currents of the atmosphere, or by the laws of a telluric influence equally intangible. These stories treated, though darkly, of the long period of his absence from his native village; but they took no well-defined shape, and no one could refer them to any authentic source.

The Vicar's charity was of the kind that thinketh no evil; and in such cases he always insisted on proof. Crooke was, of course, undisturbed in his office.

On the evening before the tragedy came to light – trifles are always remembered after the catastrophe – a boy, returning along the margin of the mere, passed him by seated on a prostrate trunk of a tree, under the 'bield' of a rock, counting silver money. His lean body and limbs were bent together, his knees were up to his chin, and his long fingers were telling the coins over hurriedly in the hollow of his other hand. He glanced at the boy, as the old English saying is, like 'the devil looking over Lincoln.' But a black and sour look from Mr. Crooke, who never had a smile for a child nor a greeting for a wayfarer, was nothing strange.

Toby Crooke lived in the grey stone house, cold and narrow, that stands near the church porch, with the window of its staircase looking out into the churchyard, where so much of his labour, for many a day, had been expended. The greater part of this house was untenanted.

The old woman who was in charge of it slept in a settle-bed, among broken stools, old sacks, rotten chests and other rattle-traps, in the small room at the rear of the house, floored with tiles.

At what time of the night she could not tell, she awoke, and saw a man, with his hat on, in her room. He had a candle in his hand,

which he shaded with his coat from her eye; his back was towards her, and he was rummaging in the drawer in which she usually kept her money.

Having got her quarter's pension of two pounds that day, however, she had placed it, folded in a rag, in the corner of her tea caddy, and locked it up in the 'eat-malison' or cupboard.

She was frightened when she saw the figure in her room, and she could not tell whether her visitor might not have made his entrance from the contiguous churchyard. So, sitting bolt upright in her bed, her grey hair almost lifting her kerchief off her head, and all over in 'a fit o' t' creepins,' as she expressed it, she demanded:

'In God's name, what want ye thar?'

'Whar's the peppermint ye used to hev by ye, woman? I'm bad wi' an inward pain.'

'It's all gane a month sin,' she answered; and offered to make him a 'het' drink if he'd get to his room.

But he said:

'Never mind, I'll try a mouthful o' gin.'

And, turning on his heel, he left her.

In the morning the sexton was gone. Not only in his lodging was there no account of him, but, when inquiry began to be extended, nowhere in the village of Golden Friars could he be found.

Still he might have gone off, on business of his own, to some distant village, before the town was stirring; and the sexton had no near kindred to trouble their heads about him. People, therefore, were willing to wait, and take his return ultimately for granted.

At three o'clock the good Vicar, standing at his hall door, looking across the lake towards the noble fells that rise, steep and furrowed, from that beautiful mere, saw two men approaching across the green, in a straight line, from a boat that was moored at the water's edge. They were carrying between them something which, though not very large, seemed ponderous.

'Ye'll ken this, sir,' said one of the boatmen as they set down,

almost at his feet, a small church bell, such as in old-fashioned chimes yields the treble notes.

'This won't be less nor five stean. I ween it's fra' the church steeple yon.'

'What! one of our church bells?' ejaculated the Vicar – for a moment lost in horrible amazement. 'Oh, no! – *no*, that can't possibly be! Where did you find it?'

He had found the boat, in the morning, moored about fifty yards from her moorings where he had left it the night before, and could not think how that came to pass; and now, as he and his partner were about to take their oars, they discovered this bell in the bottom of the boat, under a bit of canvas, also the sexton's pick and spade – 'tom-spey'ad,' they termed that peculiar, broad-bladed implement.

'Very extraordinary! We must try whether there is a bell missing from the tower,' said the Vicar, getting into a fuss. 'Has Crooke come back yet? Does anyone know where he is?'

The sexton had not yet turned up.

'That's odd – that's provoking,' said the Vicar. 'However, my key will let us in. Place the bell in the hall while I get it; and then we can see what all this means.'

To the church, accordingly, they went, the Vicar leading the way, with his own key in his hand. He turned it in the lock, and stood in the shadow of the ground porch, and shut the door.

A sack, half full, lay on the ground, with open mouth, a piece of cord lying beside it. Something clanked within it as one of the men shoved it aside with his clumsy shoe.

The Vicar opened the church door and peeped in. The dusky glow from the western sky, entering through a narrow window, illuminated the shafts and arches, the old oak carvings, and the discoloured monuments, with the melancholy glare of a dying fire.

The Vicar withdrew his head and closed the door. The gloom of the porch was deeper than ever as, stooping, he entered the narrow door that opened at the foot of the winding stair that leads to the first

loft; from which a rude ladder-stair of wood, some five and twenty feet in height, mounts through a trap to the ringers' loft.

Up the narrow stairs the Vicar climbed, followed by his attendants, to the first loft. It was very dark: a narrow bow-slit in the thick wall admitted the only light they had to guide them. The ivy leaves, seen from the deep shadow, flashed and flickered redly, and the sparrows twittered among them.

'Will one of you be so good as to go up and count the bells, and see if they are all right?' said the Vicar. 'There should be – '

'Agoy! what's that?' exclaimed one of the men, recoiling from the foot of the ladder.

'By Jen!' ejaculated the other, in equal surprise.

'Good gracious!' gasped the Vicar, who, seeing indistinctly a dark mass lying on the floor, had stooped to examine it, and placed his hand upon a cold, dead face.

The men drew the body into the streak of light that traversed the floor.

It was the corpse of Toby Crooke! There was a frightful scar across his forehead.

The alarm was given. Doctor Lincote, and Mr Jarlcot, and Turnbull, of the *George and Dragon*, were on the spot immediately; and many curious and horrified spectators of minor importance.

The first thing ascertained was that the man must have been many hours dead. The next was that his skull was fractured, across the forehead, by an awful blow. The next was that his neck was broken.

His hat was found on the floor, where he had probably laid it, with his handkerchief in it.

The mystery now began to clear a little; for a bell – one of the chime hung in the tower – was found where it had rolled to, against the wall, with blood and hair on the rim of it, which corresponded with the grizzly fracture across the front of his head.

The sack that lay in the vestibule was examined, and found to contain all the church plate; a silver salver that had disappeared,

about a month before, from Dr Lincote's store of valuables; the Vicar's gold pencil-case, which he thought he had forgot in the vestry book; silver spoons, and various other contributions, levied from time to time off a dozen different households, the mysterious disappearance of which spoils had, of late years, begun to make the honest little community uncomfortable. Two bells had been taken down from the chime; and now the shrewd part of the assemblage, putting things together, began to comprehend the nefarious plans of the sexton, who lay mangled and dead on the floor of the tower, where only two days ago he had tolled the holy bell to call the good Christians of Golden Friars to worship.

The body was carried into the yard of the *George and Dragon* and laid in the old coach-house; and the townsfolk came grouping in to have a peep at the corpse, and stood round, looking darkly, and talking as low as if they were in a church.

The Vicar, in gaiters and slightly shovel hat, stood erect, as one in a little circle of notables – the doctor, the attorney, Sir Geoffrey Mardykes, who happened to be in the town, and Turnbull, the host – in the centre of the paved yard, they having made an inspection of the body, at which troops of the village stragglers, to-ing and fro-ing, were gaping and frowning as they whispered their horrible conjectures.

'What d'ye think o' that?' said Tom Scales, the old hostler of the *George*, looking pale, with a stern, faint smile on his lips, as he and Dick Linklin sauntered out of the coach-house together.

'The deaul will hev his ain noo,' answered Dick, in his friend's ear. 'T' sexton's got a craigthraw like he gav' the lass over the clints of Scarsdale; ye mind what the ald soger telt us when he hid his face in the kitchen of the *George* here? By Jen! I'll ne'er forget that story.'

'I ween 'twas all true enough,' replied the hostler; 'and the sizzup he gav' the sleepin' man wi' t' poker across the forehead. See whar the edge o' t' bell took him, and smashed his ain, the self-same lids. By ma sang, I wonder the deaul did na carry awa' his corpse i' the night, as he did wi' Tam Lunder's at Mooltern Mill.'

'Hout, man, who ever sid t' deaul inside o' a church?'

'The corpse is ill-faur'd enew to scare Satan himsel', for that matter; though it's true what you say. Ay, ye're reet tul a trippet, thar; for Beelzebub dar'n't show his snout inside the church, not the length o' the black o' my nail.'

While this discussion was going on, the gentlefolk who were talking the matter over in the centre of the yard had dispatched a message for the coroner all the way to the town of Hextan.

The last tint of sunset was fading from the sky by this time; so, of course, there was no thought of an inquest earlier than next day.

In the meantime it was horribly clear that the sexton had intended to rob the church of its plate, and had lost his life in the attempt to carry the second bell, as we have seen, down the worn ladder of the tower. He had tumbled backwards and broken his neck upon the floor of the loft; and the heavy bell, in its fall, descended with its edge across his forehead.

Never was a man more completely killed by a double catastrophe, in a moment.

The bells and the contents of the sack, it was surmised, he meant to have conveyed across the lake that night, and with the help of his spade and pick to have buried them in Clousted Forest, and returned, after an absence of but a few hours – as he easily might – before morning, unmissed and unobserved. He would no doubt, having secured his booty, have made such arrangements as would have made it appear that the church had been broken into. He would, of course, have taken all measures to divert suspicion from himself, and have watched a suitable opportunity to repossess himself of the buried treasure and dispose of it in safety.

And now came out, into sharp relief, all the stories that had, one way or other, stolen after him into the town. Old Mrs Pullen fainted when she saw him, and told Doctor Lincote, after, that she thought he was the highwayman who fired the shot that killed the coachman the night they were robbed on Hounslow Heath. There were the

stories also told by the wayfaring old soldier with the wooden leg, and fifty others, up to this more than half disregarded, but which now seized on the popular belief with a startling grasp.

The fleeting light soon expired, and twilight was succeeded by the early night.

The inn yard gradually became quiet; and the dead sexton lay alone, in the dark, on his back, locked up in the old coach-house, the key of which was safe in the pocket of Tom Scales, the trusty old hostler of the *George*.

It was about eight o'clock, and the hostler, standing alone on the road in the front of the open door of the *George and Dragon*, had just smoked his pipe out. A bright moon hung in the frosty sky. The fells rose from the opposite edge of the lake like phantom mountains. The air was stirless. Through the boughs and sprays of the leafless elms no sigh or motion, however hushed, was audible. Not a ripple glimmered on the lake, which at one point only reflected the brilliant moon from its dark blue expanse like burnished steel. The road that runs by the inn door, along the margin of the lake, shone dazzlingly white.

White as ghosts, among the dark holly and juniper, stood the tall piers of the Vicar's gate, and their great stone balls, like heads, overlooking the same road, a few hundred yards up the lake, to the left. The early little town of Golden Friars was quiet by this time. Except for the townsfolk who were now collected in the kitchen of the inn itself, no inhabitant was now outside his own threshold.

Tom Scales was thinking of turning in. He was beginning to fell a little queer. He was thinking of the sexton, and could not get the fixed features of the dead man out of his head, when he heard the sharp though distant ring of a horse's hoof upon the frozen road. Tom's instinct apprised him of the approach of a guest to the *George and Dragon*. His experienced ear told him that the horseman was approaching by the Dardale road, which, after crossing that wide and dismal moss, passes the southern fells by Dunner Cleugh and

finally enters the town of Golden Friars by joining the Mardykes road, at the edge of the lake, close to the gate of the Vicar's house.

A clump of tall trees stood at this point; but the moon shone full upon the road and cast their shadow backward.

The hoofs were plainly coming at a gallop, with a hollow rattle. The horseman was a long time in appearing. Tom wondered how he had heard the sound – so sharply frosty as the air was – so very far away.

He was right in his guess. The visitor was coming over the mountainous road from Dardale Moss; and he now saw a horseman, who must have turned the corner of the Vicar's house at the moment when his eye was wearied; for when he saw him for the first time he was advancing, in the hazy moonlight, like the shadow of a cavalier, at a gallop, upon the level strip of road that skirts the margin of the mere, between the *George* and the Vicar's piers.

The hostler had not long to wonder why the rider pushed his beast at so furious a pace, and how he came to have heard him, as he now calculated, at least three miles away. A very few moments sufficed to bring horse and rider to the inn door.

It was a powerful black horse, something like the great Irish hunter that figured a hundred years ago, and would carry sixteen stone with ease across country. It would have made a grand charger. Not a hair turned. It snorted, it pawed, it arched its neck; then threw back its ears and down its head, and looked ready to lash, and then to rear; and seemed impatient to be off again, and incapable of standing quiet for a moment.

The rider got down

"As light as shadow falls."

But he was a tall, sinewy figure. He wore a cape or short mantle, a cocked hat, and a pair of jack-boots, such as held their ground in some primitive corners of England almost to the close of the last century.

'Take him, lad,' said he to old Scales. 'You need not walk or wisp

him – he never sweats or tires. Give him his oats, and let him take his own time to eat them. House!' cried the stranger – in the old-fashioned form of summons which still lingered, at that time, in out-of-the-way places – in a deep and piercing voice.

As Tom Scales led the horse away to the stables it turned its head towards its master with a short, shill neigh.

'About *your* business, old gentleman – we must not go too fast,' the stranger cried back again to his horse, with a laugh as harsh and piercing; and he strode into the house.

The hostler led this horse into the inn yard. In passing, it sidled up to the coach-house gate, within which lay the dead sexton – snorted, pawed and lowered its head suddenly, with ear close to the plank, as if listening for a sound from within; then uttered again the same short, piercing neigh.

The hostler was chilled at this mysterious coquetry with the dead. He liked the brute less and less every minute.

In the meantime, its master had proceeded.

'I'll go to the inn kitchen,' he said, in his startling bass, to the drawer who met him in the passage.

And on he went, as if he had known the place all his days: not seeming to hurry himself – stepping leisurely, the servant thought – but gliding on at such a rate, nevertheless, that he had passed his guide and was in the kitchen of the *George* before the drawer had got much more than half-way to it.

A roaring fire of dry wood, peat and coal lighted up this snug but spacious apartment – flashing on pots and pans, and dressers high-piled with pewter plates and dishes; and making the uncertain shadows of the long 'hanks' of onions and many a flitch and ham, depending from the ceiling, dance on its glowing surface.

The doctor and the attorney, even Sir Geoffrey Mardykes, did not disdain on this occasion to take chairs and smoke their pipes by the kitchen fire, where they were in the thick of the gossip and discussion excited by the terrible event.

The tall stranger entered uninvited.

He looked like a gaunt, athletic Spaniard of forty, burned half black in the sun, with a bony, flattened nose. A pair of fierce black eyes were just visible under the edge of his hat; and his mouth seemed divided, beneath the moustache, by the deep scar of a hare-lip.

Sir Geoffrey Mardykes and the host of the *George*, aided by the doctor and the attorney, were discussing and arranging, for the third or fourth time, their theories about the death and the probable plans of Toby Crooke, when the stranger entered.

The new-comer lifted his hat, with a sort of smile, for a moment from his black head.

'What do you call this place, gentlemen?' asked the stranger.

'The town of Golden Friars, sir,' answered the doctor politely.

'The *George and Dragon*, sir: Anthony Turnbull, at your service,' answered mine host, with a solemn bow, at the same moment – so that the two voices went together, as if the doctor and the innkeeper were singing a catch.

'The *George and the Dragon*,' repeated the horseman, expanding his long hands over the fire which he had approached. 'Saint George, King George, the Dragon, the Devil: it is a very grand idol, that outside your door, sir. You catch all sorts of worshippers – courtiers, fanatics, scamps: all's fish, eh? Everybody welcome, provided he drinks like one. Suppose you brew a bowl or two of punch. I'll stand it. How many are we? *Here* – count, and let us have enough. Gentlemen, I mean to spend the night here, and my horse is in the stable. What holiday, fun, or fair has got so many pleasant faces together? When I last called here – for, now I bethink me, I have seen the place before – you all looked sad. It was on a Sunday, that dismalest of holidays; and it would have been positively melancholy only that your sexton – that saint upon earth – Mr Crooke, was here.' He was looking round, over his shoulder, and added: 'Ha! don't I see him there?'

Frightened a good deal were some of the company. All gaped in the direction in which, with a nod, he turned his eyes.

'He's *not* thar – he *can't* be thar – we *see* he's not thar,' said Turnbull, as dogmatically as old Joe Willet might have delivered himself – for he did not care that the *George* should earn the reputation of a haunted house. 'He's met an accident, sir: he's dead – he's elsewhere – and therefore can't be here.'

Upon this the company entertained the stranger with the narrative – which they made easy by a division of labour, two or three generally speaking at a time, and no one being permitted to finish a second sentence without finding himself corrected and supplanted.

'The man's in Heaven, so sure as you're not,' said the traveller so soon as the story was ended. 'What! he was fiddling with the church bell, was he, and d——d for that – eh? Landlord, get us some drink. A sexton d——d for pulling down a church bell he has been pulling at for ten years!'

'You came, sir, by the Dardale road, I believe?' said the doctor (village folk are curious). 'A dismal moss is Dardale Moss, sir; and a bleak clim' up the fells on t' other side.'

'I say 'Yes' to all – from Dardale Moss, as black as pitch and as rotten as the grave, up that zigzag wall you call a road, that looks like chalk in the moonlight, through Dunner Cleugh, as dark as a coal-pit, and down here to the *George and the Dragon*, where you have a roaring fire, wise men, good punch – here it is – and a corpse in your coach-house. Where the carcase is, there will the eagles be gathered together. Come, landlord, ladle out the nectar. Drink, gentlemen – drink, all. Brew another bowl at the bar. How divinely it stinks of alcohol! I hope you like it, gentlemen: it smells all over of spices, like a mummy. Drink, friends. Ladle, landlord. Drink, all. Serve it out.'

The guest fumbled in his pocket, and produced three guineas, which he slipped into Turnbull's fat palm.

'Let punch flow till that's out. I'm an old friend of the house. I call here, back and forward. I know you well, Turnbull, though you don't recognise me.'

'You have the advantage of me, sir,' said Mr Turnbull, looking hard on that dark and sinister countenance – which, or the like of which, he could have sworn he had never seen before in his life. But he liked the weight and colour of his guineas, as he dropped them into his pocket. 'I hope you will find yourself comfortable while you stay.'

'You have given me a bedroom?'

'Yes, sir – the cedar chamber.'

'I know it – the very thing. No – no punch for me. By and by, perhaps.'

The talk went on, but the stranger had grown silent. He had seated himself on an oak bench by the fire, towards which he extended his feet and hands with seeming enjoyment; his cocked hat being, however, a little over his face.

Gradually the company began to thin. Sir Geoffrey Mardykes was the first to go; then some of the humbler townsfolk. The last bowl of punch was on its last legs. The stranger walked into the passage and said to the drawer:

'Fetch me a lantern. I must see my nag. Light it – hey! That will do. No – you need not come.'

The gaunt traveller took it from the man's hand and strode along the passage to the door of the stableyard, which he opened and passed out.

Tom Scales, standing on the pavement, was looking through the stable window at the horses when the stranger plucked his shirt-sleeve. With an inward shock the hostler found himself alone in presence of the very person he had been thinking of.

'I say – they tell me you have something to look at in there' – he pointed with his thumb at the old coach-house door. 'Let us have a peep.'

Tom Scales happened to be at that moment in a state of mind highly favourable to anyone in search of a submissive instrument. He was in great perplexity, and even perturbation. He suffered the stranger to lead him to the coach-house gate.

'You must come in and hold the lantern,' said he. 'I'll pay you handsomely.'

The old hostler applied his key and removed the padlock.

'What are you afraid of? Step in and throw the light on his face,' said the stranger grimly. 'Throw open the lantern: stand *there*. Stoop over him a little – he won't bite you. Steady, or you may pass the night with him!'

*   *   *   *   *

In the meantime the company at the *George* had dispersed; and, shortly after, Anthony Turnbull – who, like a good landlord, was always last in bed, and first up, in his house – was taking, alone, his last look round the kitchen before making his final visit to the stable-yard, when Tom Scales tottered into the kitchen, looking like death, his hair standing upright; and he sat down on an oak chair, all in a tremble, wiped his forehead with his hand, and, instead of speaking, heaved a great sigh or two.

It was not till after he had swallowed a dram of brandy that he found his voice, and said:

'We'ev the deaul himsel' in t' house! By Jen! ye'd best send fo t' sir' (the clergyman). 'Happen he'll tak him in hand wi' holy writ, and send him elsewhidder deftly. Lord atween us and harm! I'm a sinfu' man. I tell ye, Mr Turnbull, I dar' n't stop in t' *George* to-night under the same roof wi' him.'

'Ye mean the ra-beyoned, black-feyaced lad, wi' the brocken neb? Why, that's a gentleman wi' a pocket ful o' guineas, man, and a horse worth fifty pounds!'

'That horse is no better nor his rider. The nags that were in the stable wi' him, they all tuk the creepins, and sweated like rain down a thack. I tuk them all out o' that, away from him, into the hack-stable, and I thocht I cud never get them past him. But that's not all. When I was keekin inta t' winda at the nags, he comes behint me and claps

his claw on ma shouther, and he gars me gang wi' him, and open the aad coach-house door, and haad the cannle for him, till he pearked into the deed man't feyace; and, as God's my judge, I sid the corpse open its eyes and wark its mouth, like a man smoorin' and strivin' to talk. I cudna move or say a word, though I felt my hair rising on my heed; but at lang-last I gev a yelloch, and say I, "La! what is that?" And he himsel' looked round on me, like the devil he is; and, wi' a skirl o' a laugh, he strikes the lantern out o' my hand. When I cum to myself we were outside the coach-house door. The moon was shinin' in, ad I cud see the corpse stretched on the table whar we left it; and he kicked the door to wi' a purr o' his foot. "Lock it," says he; and so I did. And here's the key for ye – tak it yoursel', sir. He offer'd me money: he said he'd mak me a rich man if I'd sell him the corpse, and help him awa' wi' it.'

'Hout, man! What cud he want o' t' corpse? He's not doctor, to do a' that lids. He was takin' a rise out o' ye, lad,' said Turnbull.

'Na, na – he wants the corpse. There's summat you a' me can't tell he wants to do wi' 't; and he'd liefer get it wi' sin and thievin', and the damage of my soul. He's one of them freytens a boo or a dobbies off Dardale Moss, that's always astir wi' the like after nightfall; unless – Lord save us! – he be the deaul himsel'.'

'Whar is he noo?' asked the landlord, who was growing uncomfortable.

'He spang'd up the back stair to his room. I wonder you didn't hear him trampin' like a wild horse; and he clapt his door that the house shook again – but Lord knows whar he is noo. Let us gang awa' up to the Vicar's, and gan *him* come down, and talk wi' him.'

'Hoity toity, man – you're too easy scared,' said the landlord, pale enough by this time. ''Twould be a fine thing, truly, to send abroad that the house was haunted by the deaul himsel'! Why, 'twould be the ruin o' the *George*. You're sure ye locked the door on the corpse?'

'Aye, sir – sartain.'

'Come wi' me, Tom – we'll gi' a last look round the yard.'

So, side by side, with many a jealous look right and left, and over their shoulders, they went in silence. On entering the old-fashioned quadrangle, surrounded by stables and other offices – built in the antique cage-work fashion – they stopped for a while under the shadow of the inn gable, and looked round the yard, and listened. All was silent – nothing stirring.

The stable lantern was lighted; and with it in his hand Tony Turnbull, holding Tom Scales by the shoulder, advanced. He hauled Tom after him for a step or two; then stood still and shoved him before him for a step or two more; and thus cautiously – as a pair of skirmishers under fire – they approached the coach-house door.

'There, ye see – all safe,' whispered Tom, pointing to the lock, which hung – distinct in the moonlight – in its place. 'Cum back, I say!'

'Cum on, say I!' retorted the landlord valorously. 'It would never do to allow any tricks to be played with the chap in there' – he pointed to the coach-house door.

'The coroner here in the morning, and never a corpse to sit on!' He unlocked the padlock with these words, having handed the lantern to Tom. 'Here, keck in, Tom,' he continued; 'ye hev the lantern – and see if all's as ye left it.'

'Not me – na, not for the *George* and a' that's in it!' said Tom, with a shudder, sternly, as he took a step backward.

'What the – what are ye afraid on? Gi' me the lantern – it is all one: *I* will.'

And cautiously, little by little, he opened the door; and, holding the lantern over his head in the narrow slit, he peeped in – frowning and pale – with one eye, as if he expected something to fly in his face. He closed the door without speaking, and locked it again.

'As safe as a thief in a mill,' he whispered with a nod to his companion. And at that moment a harsh laugh overhead broke the silence startlingly, and set all the poultry in the yard gabbling.

'Thar he be!' said Tom, clutching the landlord's arm – 'in the winda – see!'

The window of the cedar-room, up two pair of stairs, was open; and in the shadow a darker outline was visible of a man, with his elbows on the window-stone, looking down upon them.

'Look at his eyes – like two live coals!' gasped Tom.

The landlord could not see all this so sharply, being confused, and not so long-sighted as Tom.

'Time, sir,' called Tony Turnbull, turning cold as he thought he saw a pair of eyes shining down redly at him – 'time for honest folk to be in their beds, and asleep!'

'As sound as your sexton!' said the jeering voice from above.

'Come out of this,' whispered the landlord fiercely to his hostler, plucking him hard by the sleeve.

They got into the house, and shut the door.

'I wish we were shot of him,' said the landlord, with something like a groan, as he leaned against the wall of the passage. 'I'll sit up, anyhow – and, Tom, you'll sit wi' me. Cum into the gun-room. No one shall steal the dead man out of my yard while I can draw a trigger.'

The gun-room in the *George* is about twelve feet square. It projects into the stable-yard and commands a full view of the old coach-house; and, through a narrow side window, a flanking view of the back door of the inn, through which the yard is reached.

Tony Turnbull took down the blunderbuss – which was the great ordnance of the house – and loaded it with a stiff charge of pistol bullets.

He put on a great-coat which hung there, and was his covering when he went out at night, to shoot wild ducks. Tom made himself comfortable likewise. They then sat down at the window, which was open, looking into the yard, the opposite side of which was white in the brilliant moonlight.

The landlord laid the blunderbuss across his knees, and stared into the yard. His comrade stared also. The door of the gun-room was locked; so they felt tolerably secure.

An hour passed; nothing had occurred. Another. The clock struck one. The shadows had shifted a little; but still the moon shone full on the old coach-house, and the stable where the guest's horse stood.

Turnbull thought he heard a step on the back-stair. Tom was watching the back-door through the side window, with eyes glazing with the intensity of his stare. Anthony Turnbull, holding his breath, listened at the room door. It was a false alarm.

When he came back to the window looking into the yard:

'Hish! Look thar!' said he in a vehement whisper.

From the shadow at the left they saw the figure of the gaunt horseman, in short cloak and jack-boots, emerge. He pushed open the stable door, and led out his powerful black horse. He walked it across the front of the building till he reached the old coach-house door; and there, with its bridle on its neck, he left it standing, while he stalked to the yard gate; and, dealing it a kick with his heel, it sprang back with the rebound, shaking from top to bottom, and stood open. The stranger returned to the side of his horse; and the door which secured the corpse of the dead sexton seemed to swing slowly open of itself as he entered, and returned with the corpse in his arms, and swung it across the shoulders of the horse, and instantly sprang into the saddle.

'Fire!' shouted Tom, and bang went the blunderbuss with a stunning crack. A thousand sparrows' wings winnowed through the air from the thick ivy. The watch-dog yelled a furious bark. There was a strange ring and whistle in the air. The blunderbuss had burst to shivers right down to the very breech. The recoil rolled the inn-keeper upon his back on the floor, and Tom Scales was flung against the side of the recess of the window, which had saved him from a tumble as violent. In this position they heard the searing laugh of the departing horseman, and saw him ride out of the gate with his ghastly burden.

* * * * *

Perhaps some of my readers, like myself, have heard this story told by Roger Turnbull, now host of the *George and Dragon*, the grandson of the very Tony who then swayed the spigot and keys of that inn, in the identical kitchen of which the fiend treated so many of the neighbours to punch.

*   *   *   *   *

What infernal object was subserved by the possession of the dead villain's body, I have not learned. But a very curious story, in which a vampire resuscitation of Crooke the sexton figures, may throw a light upon this part of the tale.

The result of Turnbull's shot at the disappearing fiend certainly justifies old Andrew Moreton's dictum, which is thus expressed in his curious *History of Apparitions*: 'I warn rash brands who, pretending not to fear the devil, are for using the ordinary violences with him, which affect one man from another – or with an apparition, in which they may be sure to receive some mischief. I knew one fired a gun at an apparition and the gun burst in a hundred pieces in his hand; another struck at an apparition with a sword, and broke his sword in pieces and wounded his hand grievously; and 'tis next to madness for anyone to go that way to work with any spirit, be it angel or be it devil.'

THE ITALIAN'S STORY
by Catherine Crowe
from GHOST STORIES AND FAMLY LEGENDS

'Ｈow well your friend speaks English!' I remarked one day to an acquaintance when I was abroad, alluding to a gentleman who had just quitted the room. 'What is his name?'

'Count Francesco Ferraldi.'

'I suppose he has been in England?'

'Oh, yes; he was exiled and taught Italian there. His history is very curious and would interest you, who like wonderful things.'

'Can you tell it me.'

'Not correctly, as I never heard it from himself. But I believe he has no objection to tell it – with the exception of the political transactions in which he was concerned, and which caused his being sent out of the Austrian dominions; that part of it I believe he thinks it prudent not to allude to. We'll ask him to dinner, if you'll meet him, and perhaps we may persuade him to tell the story.' Accordingly, the meeting took place; we dined *en petit comité*, – and the Count very good-naturedly yielded to our request; 'but you must excuse me,' he said, 'beginning a long way back, for my story commences three hundred years ago.

'Our family claims to be of great antiquity, but we were not very wealthy till about the latter half of the tenth century, when Count

Jacopo Ferraldi made very considerable additions to the property; not only by getting, but also by saving – he was in fact a miser. Before that period the Ferraldis had been warriors, and we could boast of many distinguished deeds of arms recorded in our annals; but Jacopo, although by the death of his brother, he ultimately inherited the title and the estates, had begun life as a younger son, and being dissatisfied with his portion, had resolved to increase it by commerce.

'Florence then was a very different city to what it is now; trade flourished, and its merchants had correspondence and large dealings with all the chief cities of Europe. My ancestor invested his little fortune so judiciously, or so fortunately, that he trebled it in his first venture; and as people grow rapidly rich who gain and don't spend, he soon had wealth to his heart's content. But I am wrong in using that term as applied to him – he was never content with his gains but still worked on to add to them, for he grew to love the money for itself, and not for what it might purchase.

'At length, his two elder brothers died, and as they left no issue he succeeded to their inheritance, and dwelt in the palace of his ancestors; but instead of circulating his riches he hoarded them; and being too miserly to entertain his friends and neighbours, he lived like an anchorite in his splendid halls, exulting in his possessions but never enjoying them. His great pleasure and chief occupation seems to have been counting his money, which he kept hidden in strange out-of-the-way places, or in strong iron chests clamped to the floors and walls. But notwithstanding these precautions, and that he guarded it like a watch-dog, to his great dismay he one day missed a sum of two thousand pounds which he had concealed in an ingeniously contrived receptacle under the floor of his dining-room, the existence of which was only known to the man who made it; at least, so he believed. Small as was this sum in proportion to what he possessed, the shock was tremendous; he rushed out of his house like a madman with the intention of dragging the criminal to justice, but when he arrived at the man's shop he found him in bed and at the point of death. His friends and the doctor swore that he had not quitted it for a fortnight; in short, according to their showing, he was taken ill on his return from working at the Count's, the very day he finished the job.

'If this were true, he could not be the thief, as the money was not deposited there till some days afterwards, and although the Count had his doubts, it was not easy to disprove what everybody swore, more especially as the man died on the following day, and was buried. Baffled and furious, he next fell foul of his two servants – he kept but two, for he only inhabited a small part of the palace. There was not the smallest reason to suspect them, nor to suppose they knew anything of the hiding place, for every precaution had been used to conceal it; moreover, he had found it locked as he himself had locked it after depositing the money, and he was quite sure the key had never been absent from his own person. Nevertheless, he discharged them and took no others. The thief, whoever he was, had evinced so much ingenuity, that he trembled to think what such skill might compass with opportunity. So he resolved to afford none; and henceforth to have his meals sent in from a neighbouring eating-house, and to have a person once a week to sweep and clean his rooms, whom he could keep an eye on while it was doing. As he had no clue to the perpetrators of the robbery, and the man whom he had most reason to suspect was dead, he took no further steps in the business, but kept it quiet lest he should draw too much attention towards his secret hoards; nevertheless, though externally calm, the loss preyed upon his mind and caused him great anguish.

'Shortly after this occurrence, he received a letter from a sister of his who had several years before married an Englishman, saying that her husband was dead, and it being advisable that her dear and only son should enter into commerce, that she was going to send him to Florence, feeling assured that her brother would advise him for the best, and enable him to employ the funds he brought with him advantageously.

'This was not pleasing intelligence; he did not want to promote anybody's interest but his own, and he felt that the young man would be a spy on his actions, an intruder in his house, and no doubt an expectant and greedy heir, counting the hours till he died; for this sister and her family were his nearest of kin, and would inherit if he left no will to the contrary. However, his arrival could not be prevented; letters travelled slowly in those days, and ere his could reach England his nephew would have quitted it, so he resolved to give him a cold reception and send him back as soon as he could.

'In the meantime, the young man had started on his journey, full of hope and confidence, and immediately on his arrival hastened to present himself to this rich uncle who was to show him the path he had himself followed to fortune. It was not for his own sake alone he coveted riches, but his mother and sister were but poorly provided for, and they had collected the whole of their little fortune and risked it upon this venture hoping, with the aid of their relative, to be amply repaid for the present sacrifice.

'A fine open-countenanced lad was Arthur Allen, just twenty years of age; such a face and figure had not beamed upon those old halls for many a day. Well brought up and well instructed too; he spoke Italian as well as English, his mother having accustomed him to it from infancy.

'Though he had heard his uncle was a miser, he had no conception of the amount to which the mania had arisen; and his joyous anticipations were somewhat damped when he found himself so coldly received, and when he looked into those hard, grey eyes and contracted features that had never expanded with a genial smile; so fearing the old man might be apprehensive that he had come as an applicant for assistance to set him up in trade, he hastened to inform him of the true state of the case, saying that they had got together two thousand pounds.

'"Of course, my mother," he said, "would not have entrusted my

inexperience with such a sum; but she desired me to place it in your hands, and to act entirely under your direction."

'To use the miser's own expression – for we have learnt all these particulars from a memoir left by himself – "When I heard these words the devil entered into me, and I bade the youth bring the money and dine with me on the following day."

'I daresay you will think the devil had entered into him long before; however, now he recognised his presence, but that did not deter him from following his counsel.

'Pleased that he had so far thawed his uncle's frigidity, Arthur arrived the next day with his money bags at the appointed hour, and was received in an inner chamber; their contents were inspected and counted, and then placed in one of the old man's iron chests. Soon afterwards the tinkle of a bell announced that the waiter from the neighbouring traiteur's had brought the dinner, and the host left the room to see that all was ready. Presently he re-entered, and led his guest to the table. The repast was not sumptuous, but there was a bottle of old Lacryma Christi which he much recommended, and which the youth tasted with great satisfaction. But strange! He had no sooner swallowed the first glass, than his eyes began to stare – there was a gurgle in his throat – a convulsion passed over his face – and his body stiffened.

"'I did not look up," says the old man in his memoir, "for I did not like to see the face of the boy that had sat down so hearty to his dinner, so I kept on eating mine – but I heard the gurgle, and I knew what had happened; and presently lest the servant should come to fetch the dinner things, I pushed the table aside and opened the receptacle from which my two thousand pounds had been stolen – curses on the thief! – and I laid the body in it, and the wine therewith. I locked it and drove in two strong nails. Then I put back the table – moved away the lad's chair and plate, unlocked the door which was fast, and sat down to finish my dinner. I could not help chuckling as I ate, to think how his had been spoilt.

"'I closed up that apartment, as I thought there might be a smell that would raise observation, and I selected one on the opposite side of the gallery for my dining-room. All went well till the following day. I counted my two thousand pounds again and again, and I kept gloating over the recovery of it – for I felt as if it was my own money, and that I had a right to seize it where I could. I wrote also to my sister, saying, that her son had not arrived; but that when he did, I would do my best to forward his views. My heart was light that day – they say that's a bad sign.

"'Yes, all was so far well; but the next day we were two of us at dinner! And yet I had invited no guest; and the next – and the next – and so on – always! As I was about to sit down, he entered and took a chair opposite me, an unbidden guest. I ceased dining at home, but it made no difference; he came, dine where I would. This preyed upon me; I tried not to mind, but I could not help it. Argument was vain. I lost my appetite, and was reduced nearly to death's door. At last, driven to desperation, I consulted Fra Giuseppe. He had been a fast fellow in his time, and it was said had been too impatient for his father's succession; howbeit, the old man died suddenly; Giuseppe spent the money and then took to religion. I thought he was a proper person to consult, so I told him my case. He recommended repentance and restitution. I tried, but I could not repent, for I had got the money; but I thought, perhaps, if I parted with it to another, I might be released; so I looked about for an advantageous purchase, and hearing that Bartolomeo Malfi was in difficulties, I offered him two thousand pounds, money down, for his land – I knew it was worth three times the sum. We signed the agreement, and then I went home and opened the door of the room where it was; but lo! he sat there upon the chest where the money was fast locked, and I could not get it. I peeped in two or three times, but he was always there; so I was obliged to expend other moneys in this purchase, which vexed me, albeit the bargain was a good one. Then I consulted friend Giuseppe again, and he said nothing would do but restitution

– but that was hard, so I waited; and I said to myself, 'I'll eat and care not whether he sit there or no.' But woe be to him! He chilled the marrow of my bones, and I could not away with him; so I said one day, 'What if I go to England with the money?' and he bowed his head."

'The old man accordingly took the money-bags from the chest and started for England. His sister and her daughter were still living in the house they had inhabited during the husband's lifetime; in short, it was their own; and being attached to the place they hoped, if the young man succeeded in his undertakings, to be able to keep it. It was a small house with a garden full of flowers, which the ladies cultivated themselves. The village church was close at hand, and the churchyard adjoined the garden. The poor ladies had become very uneasy at not hearing of Arthur's arrival; and when the old man presented himself and declared he had never seen anything of him, great was their affliction and dismay; for it was clear that either some misfortune had happened to the boy, or he had appropriated the money and gone off in some other direction. They scarcely admitted the possibility of the last contingency, although it was the one their little world universally adopted, in spite of his being a very well conducted and affectionate youth; but people said it was too great a temptation for his years, and blamed his mother for entrusting him with so much money. Whichever it was, the blow fell very heavy on them in all ways, for Arthur was their sole stay and support, and they loved him dearly.

'Since he had set out on this journey, the old man had been relieved from the company of his terrible guest, and was beginning to recover himself a little, but it occasioned him a severe pang when he remembered that this immunity was to be purchased with the sacrifice of two thousand pounds, and he set himself to think how he could jockey the ghost. But while he was deliberating on this subject, an event happened that alarmed him for the immediate safety of the money.

'He had found on the road, that the great weight of a certain chest he brought with him, had excited observation whenever his luggage had to be moved; on his arrival two labouring men had been called in to carry it into the house, and he had overheard some remarks that induced him to think they had drawn a right conclusion with regard to its contents. Subsequently, he saw these two men hovering about the house in a suspicious manner, and he was afraid to leave it or to go to sleep at night, lest he should be robbed.

'So far we learn from Jacopo Ferraldi himself; but there the memoir stops and tradition says that he was found one morning murdered in his bed and his chest rifled. All the family, that is the mother and daughter and their one servant, were accused of the murder; and notwithstanding their protestation of innocence were declared guilty and executed.

'The memoir I have quoted was found on his dressing-table, and he appears to have been writing it when he was surprised by the assassins; for the last words were – "I think I've baulked them, and nobody will understand the –" then comes a large blot and a mark, as if the pen had fallen out of his hand. It seems wonderful that this man, so suspicious and secretive, should thus have entrusted to paper what it was needful he should conceal; but the case is not singular; it has been remarked in similar instances, when some dark mystery is pressing on a human soul, that there exists an irresistible desire to communicate it, notwithstanding the peril of betrayal; and when no other confidant can be found, the miserable wretch has often had recourse to paper.

'The family of Arthur Allen being now extinct, a cousin of Jacopo's, who was a penniless soldier, succeeded to the title and estate, and the memoir, with a full account of what had happened, being forwarded to Italy, inquiries were made about the missing two thousand pounds; but it was not forthcoming; and it was at first supposed that the ladies had had some accomplice who had carried it off. Subsequently, however, one of the two men who had borne the

money-chest into the house, at the period of the old man's arrival, was detected in endeavouring to dispose of some Italian gold coin and a diamond ring, which Jacopo was in the habit of wearing. This led to investigation, and he ultimately confessed to the murder committed by himself and his companion, thus exonerating the unfortunate women. He nevertheless declared that they had not rifled the strong box, as they could not open it, and were disturbed by the barking of a dog before they could search for the keys. The box itself they were afraid to carry away, it being a remarkable one and liable to attract notice; and that therefore their only booty was some loose coin and some jewels that were found on the old man's person. But this was not believed, especially as his accomplice was not to be found, and appeared, on inquiry, to have left that part of the country immediately after the catastrophe.

'There the matter rested for nearly two centuries and a half. Nobody sorrowed for Jacopo Ferraldi, and the fate of the Allens was a matter of indifference to the public, who were glad to see the estate fall into the hands of his successor, who appears to have made a much better use of his riches. The family, in the long period that elapsed, had many vicissitudes; but at the period of my birth my father inhabited the same old palace, and we were in tolerably affluent circumstances. I was born there, and I remember as a child the curiosity I used to feel about the room with the secret receptacle under the floor where Jacopo had buried the body of his guest. It had been found there and received Christian burial; but the receptacle still remained, and the room was shut up being said to be haunted. I never *saw* anything extraordinary, but I can bear witness to the frightful groans and moans that issued from it sometimes at night, when, if I could persuade anybody to accompany me, I used to stand in the gallery and listen with wonder and awe. But I never passed the door alone, nor would any of the servants do so after dark. There had been an attempt made to exclude the sounds by walling up the door; but so far from this succeeding they became twenty times worse, and as the wall was a disfigurement as well as a failure, the unquiet spirit was placated by taking it down again.

'The old man's memoir is always preserved among the family papers, and his picture still hangs in the gallery. Many strangers who have heard something of this extraordinary story, have asked to see it. The palace is now inhabited by an Austrian nobleman. Whether the ghost continues to annoy the inmates by his lamentations, I do not know.

'I now,' said Count Francesco, 'come to my personal history. Political reasons a few years since obliged me to quit Italy with my family. I had no resources except a little ready money that I had brought with me, and I had resolved to utilise some musical talent which I had cultivated for my amusement. I had not voice enough to sing in public, but I was capable of giving lessons and was considered, when in Italy, a successful amateur. I will not weary you with the sad details of my early residence in England; you can imagine the difficulties that an unfortunate foreigner must encounter before he can establish a connexion. Suffice it to say that my small means were wholly exhausted, and that very often I, and what was worse, my wife and child were in want of bread, and indebted to one of my more prosperous countrymen for the very necessaries of life. I was almost in despair, and I do not know what rash thing I might have done if I had been a single man; but I had my family depending on me, and it was my duty not to sink under my difficulties however great they were.

'One night I had been singing at the house of a nobleman, in St James's Square, and had received some flattering compliments from a young man who appeared to be very fond of Italian music, and to understand it. My getting to this party was a stroke of good luck in the first instance, for I was quite unknown to the host, but Signor A, an acquaintance of mine, who had been engaged for the occasion, was taken ill at the last moment, and had sent me with a note of introduction to supply his place.

'I knew, of course, that I should be well paid for my services, but

I would have gladly accepted half the sum I expected if I could have had it that night, for our little treasury was wholly exhausted, and we had not sixpence to purchase a breakfast for the following day. When the great hall door shut upon me, and I found myself upon the pavement, with all that luxury and splendour on one side, and I and my desolation on the other, the contrast struck me cruelly, for I too had been rich, and dwelt in illuminated palaces, and had a train of liveried servants at my command, and sweet music had echoed through my halls. I felt desperate, and drawing my hat over my eyes, I began pacing the square, forming wild plans for the relief or escape from my misery. No doubt I looked frantic; for you know we Italians have such a habit of gesticulating, that I believe my thoughts were accompanied by movements that must have excited notice; but I was too much absorbed to observe anything, till I was roused by a voice saying, "Signor Ferraldi, still here this damp chilly night! Are you not afraid for your voice – it is worth taking care of."

"'To what purpose," I said savagely, "It will not give me bread!"

'If the interruption had not been so sudden, I should not have made such an answer, but I was surprised into it before I knew who had addressed me. When I looked up I saw it was the young man I had met at Lord L.'s, who had complimented me on my singing. I took off my hat and begged his pardon, and was about to move away, when he took my arm.

"'Excuse me," he said, "let us walk together," and then after a little pause, he added, with an apology, "I think you are an exile."

"'I am," I said.

"'And I think," he continued, "I have surprised you out of a secret that you would not voluntarily have told me. I know well the hardships that beset many of your countrymen – as good gentlemen as we are ourselves – when you are obliged to leave your country; and I beg therefore you will not think me impertinent or intrusive, if I beg you to be frank with me and tell me how you are situated!"

'This offer of sympathy was evidently so sincere, and it was so

welcome, at such a moment, that I did not hesitate to comply with my new friend's request – I told him everything – adding that in time I hoped to get known, and that then I did not fear being able to make my way; but that meanwhile we were in danger of starving.

'During this conversation we were walking round and round the square, where in fact he lived. Before we parted at his own door, he had persuaded me to accept of a gift, I call it, for he had then no reason to suppose I should ever be able to repay him, but he called it an advance of ten guineas upon some lessons I was to give him; the first instalment of which was to be paid the following day.

'I went home with a comparatively light heart, and the next morning waited upon my friendly pupil, whom I found, as I expected, a very promising scholar. He told me with a charming frankness, that he had not much influence in fashionable society, for his family, though rich, was *parvenu*, but he said he had two sisters, as fond of music as himself, who would be shortly in London, and would be delighted to take lessons, as I had just the voice they liked to sing with them.

'This was the first auspicious incident that had occurred to me, nor did the omen fail in its fulfilment. I received great kindness from the family when they came to London. I gave them lessons, sang at their parties, and they took every opportunity of recommending me to their friends.

'When the end of the season approached, however, I felt somewhat anxious about the future – there would be no parties to sing at, and my pupils would all be leaving town; but my new friends, whose name, by the way, was Greathead, had a plan for me in their heads, which they strongly recommended me to follow. They said they had a house in the country with a large neighbourhood – in fact, near a large watering-place; and that if I went there during the summer months, they did not doubt my getting plenty of teaching; adding, "We are much greater people there than we are here, you see; and our recommendation will go a great way."

'I followed my friend's advice, and soon after they left London, I joined them at Salton, which was the name of their place. As I had left my wife and children in town, with very little money, I was anxious that they should join me as soon as possible; and therefore the morning after my arrival, I proceeded to look for a lodging at S., and to take measures to make my object known to the residents and visitors there. My business done, I sent my family directions for their journey, and then returned to Salton to spend a few days, as I had promised my kind patrons.

'The house was modern, in fact it had been built by Mr Greathead's grandfather, who was the architect of their fortunes; the grounds were extensive, and the windows looked on a fine lawn, a picturesque ruin, a sparkling rivulet and a charming flower-garden; there could not be a prettier view than we enjoyed while sitting at breakfast. It was my first experience of the lovely and graceful English homes, and it fully realised all my expectations, both within doors and without. After breakfast Mr Greathead and his son asked me to accompany them round the grounds, as they were contemplating some alterations.

'"Among other things," said Mr G., "we want to turn this rivulet; but my wife has a particular fancy for that old hedge, which is exactly in the way, and she won't let me root it up."

'The hedge alluded to enclosed two sides of the flower-garden, but seemed rather out of place, I thought.

'"Why?" said I. "What is Mrs Greathead's attachment to the hedge?"

'"Why? it's very old; it formerly bordered the churchyard, for that old ruin you see there, is all that remains of the parish church; and this flower-garden, I fancy, is all the more brilliant for the rich soil of the burial-ground. But what is remarkable is, that the hedge and that side of the garden are full of Italian flowers, and always have been so as long as anybody can remember. Nobody knows how it happens, but they must spring up from some old seeds that have been long in the ground. Look at this cyclamen growing wild in the hedge."

'The subject of the alterations was renewed at dinner, and Mrs

Greathead, still objecting to the removal of the hedge, her younger son, whose name was Harry, said, "It is very well for mamma to pretend it is for the sake of the flowers, but I am quite sure that the real reason is that she is afraid of offending the ghost."

"'What nonsense, Harry," she said. "You must not believe him, Mr. Ferraldi."

"'Well, mamma," said the boy, "you know you will never be convinced that that was not a ghost you saw."

"'Never mind what it was," she said; "I won't have the hedge removed. Presently," she added, "I suppose you would laugh at the idea of anybody believing in a ghost, Mr Ferraldi."

"'Quite the contrary," I answered; "I believe in them myself, and upon very good grounds, for we have a celebrated ghost in our family."

"'Well," she said, "Mr Greathead and the boys laugh at me: but when I came to live here, upon the death of Mr Greathead's grandfather, – for his father never inhabited the place, having died by an accident before the old gentleman – I had never heard a word of the place being haunted; and, perhaps, I should not have believed it if I had. But, one evening, when the younger children were gone to bed, and Mr Greathead and George were sitting with some friends in the dining-room, I and my sister, who was staying with me, strolled into the garden. It was in the month of August, and a bright starlight night. We were talking on a very interesting matter, for my sister had that day, received an offer from the gentleman she afterwards married. I mention this, to show you that we were not thinking of anything supernatural but, on the contrary, that our minds were quite absorbed with the subject we were discussing. I was looking on the ground, as one often does, when listening intently to what another person is saying; my sister was speaking, when she suddenly stopped, and laid her hand on my arm, saying, 'Who's that?'

"'I raised my eyes and saw, not many yards from us, an old man, withered and thin, dressed in a curious antique fashion, with a high peaked hat on his head. I could not conceive who he could be, or what he could be doing there, for it was close to the flower-garden; so we stood still to observe him. I don't know whether you saw the remains of an old tombstone in a corner of the garden? It is said to be that of a former rector of the parish; the date, 1550, is still legible upon it. The old man walked from one side of the hedge to that stone, and seemed to be counting his steps. He walked like a person pacing the ground, to measure it; then he stopped, and appeared to be noting the result of his measurement with a pencil and paper he held in his hand; then he did the same thing, the other side of the hedge, pacing up to the tombstone and back.

"'There was a talk, at that time, of removing the hedge, and digging up the old tombstone; and it occurred to me, that my husband might have been speaking to somebody about it, and that this man might be concerned in the business, though, still, his dress and appearance puzzled me. It seemed odd, too, that he took no notice of us; and I might have remarked, that we heard no footsteps, though we were quite close enough to do so; but these circumstances did not strike me then. However, I was just going to advance, and ask him what he was doing, when I felt my sister's hand release the hold she had of my arm, and she sank to the ground; at the same instant I lost sight of the mysterious old man, who suddenly disappeared.

"'My sister had not fainted; but she said her knees had bent under her, and she had slipped down, collapsed by terror. I did not feel very comfortable myself, I assure you; but I lifted her up, and we hastened back to the house and told what we had seen. The gentlemen went out, and, of course, saw nothing, and laughed at us; but shortly afterwards, when Harry was born, I had a nurse from the village, and she asked me one day, if I had ever happened to see 'the old gentleman that walks!' I had ceased to think of the circumstance, and inquired what old gentleman she meant. And then she told me that, long ago, a foreign gentleman had been murdered here; that is, in the old house that Mr Greathead's grandfather pulled down when he built this; and that, ever since, the place has been haunted, and that nobody will pass by the hedge, and the old tombstone after dark; for that is the spot to which the ghost confines himself."

"'But I should think," said I, "that so far from desiring to preserve these objects, you would rather wish them removed, since the ghost would, probably, cease to visit the spot at all."

"'Quite the contrary," answered Mr G. "The people of the neighbourhood say, that the former possessor of the place entertained the same idea, and had resolved to remove them; but that then, the old man became very troublesome, and was even seen in the house; the nurse positively assured me, that her mother had told her, old Mr Greathead had also intended to remove them; but that he quite suddenly counter-ordered the directions he had given, and, though he did not confess to anything of the sort, the people all believed that he had seen the ghost. Certain, it is, that this hedge has always been maintained by the proprietors of the place."

'The young men laughed and quizzed their mother for indulging in such superstitions; but the lady was quite firm in her opposition, alledging that, independently of all considerations connected with the ghost, she liked the hedge on account of the wild Italian flowers; and she liked the old tombstone on account of its antiquity.

'Consequently, some other plan was devised for Mr Greathead's alterations, which led the course of the rivulet quite clear of the hedge and the tombstone.

'In a few days, my family arrived, and I established myself at S., for the summer. The speculation answered very well, and through the recommendations of Mr and Mrs Greathead, and their personal kindness to myself and my wife, we passed the time very pleasantly. When the period for our returning to London approached, they invited us to spend a fortnight with them before our departure and, accordingly, the day we gave up our lodgings, we removed to Salton.

'Preparations for turning the rivulet had then commenced; and soon after my arrival, I walked out with Mr Greathead to see the works. There was a boy, about fourteen, amongst the labourers;

and while we were standing close to him, he picked up something, and handed it to Mr G., saying, "Is this yours, sir?" which, on examination, proved to be a gold coin of the sixteenth century – the date on it was 1545. Presently, the boy who was digging, picked up another, and then several more.

"'This becomes interesting," said Mr Greathead, "I think we are coming upon some buried treasure;" and he whispered to me, that he had better not leave the spot.

'Accordingly, he did stay, till it was time to dress for dinner; and, feeling interested, I remained also. In the interval, many more coins were found; and when he went in, he dismissed the workmen, and sent a servant to watch the place – for he saw by their faces, that if he had not happened to be present he would, probably, never have heard of the circumstance. A few more turned up the following day, and then the store seemed exhausted. When the villagers heard of this money being discovered, they all looked upon it as the explanation of the old gentleman haunting that particular spot. No doubt he had buried the money, and it remained to be seen whether, now, that it was found, his spirit would be at rest.

'My two children were with me at Salton on this occasion. They slept in a room on the third floor, and one morning, my wife having told me that the younger of the two seemed unwell, I went upstairs to look at her. It was a cheerful room, with two little white beds in it, and several old prints and samplers, and bits of work such as you see in nurseries, framed and hung against the wall. After I had spoken to the child, and while my wife was talking to the maid, I stood with my hands in my pockets, idly looking at these things. Amongst them was one that arrested my attention, because at first I could not understand it, nor see why this discoloured parchment, with a few lines and dots on it, should have been framed and glazed. There were some words here and there which I could not decipher; so I lifted the frame off the nail and carried it to the window. Then I saw that the words were Italian, written in a crabbed, old-fashioned hand, and the whole seemed to be a plan, or sketch, rudely drawn, of what I at first thought was a camp – but, on closer examination, I saw was part of a churchyard, with tombstones, from one of which lines were drawn to various dots, and along these lines were numbers, and here and there a word as *right, left, &c.* There were also two lines forming a right angle, which intersected the whole, and after contemplating the thing for some time, it struck me that it was a rude sort of map of the old churchyard and the hedge, which had formed the subject of conversation some days before.

'At breakfast, I mentioned what I had observed to Mr and Mrs Greathead, and they said they believed it was; it had been found when the old house was pulled down, and was kept on account of its antiquity.

'"Of what period is it," I asked, "and how happens it to have been made by an Italian?"

'"The last question I can't answer," said Mr. Greathead; "but the date is on it, I believe."

'"No," said I, "I examined it particularly – there is no date."

'"Oh, there is a date and name, I think – but I never examined it myself;" and to settle the question he desired his son Harry to run up and fetch it, adding, "you know Italian architects and designers of various kinds, were not rare in this country a few centuries ago."

'Harry brought the frame, and we were confirmed in our conjectures of what it represented, but we could find no date or name.

'"And yet I think I've heard there was one," said Mr. Greathead. "Let us take it out of the frame?"

'This was easily done, and we found the date and the name; the count paused, and then added:

'I dare say you can guess it?'

'Jacopo Ferraldi?' I said.

'It was,' he answered; and it immediately occurred to me that he had buried the money supposed to have been stolen on the night he was murdered, and that this was a plan to guide him in finding

it again. So I told Mr Greathead the story I have now told you, and mentioned my reasons for supposing that if I was correct in my surmise, more gold would be found.

'With the old man's map as our guide, we immediately set to work – the whole family vigorously joining in the search; and, as I expected, we found that the tombstone in the garden was the point from which all the lines were drawn, and that the dots indicated where the money lay. It was in different heaps, and appeared to have been enclosed in bags, which had rotted away with time. We found the whole sum mentioned in the memoir, and Mr Greathead being Lord of the Manor, was generous enough to make it all over to me, as being the lawful heir, which, however, I certainly was not, for it was the spoil of a murderer and a thief, and it properly belonged to the Allens. But that family had become extinct; at least, so we believed, when the two unfortunate ladies were executed, and I accepted the gift with much gratitude and a quiet conscience. It relieved us from our pressing difficulties, and enabled me to wait for better times.

'And,' said I, 'now of the ghost? was he pleased or otherwise, by the *dénouement*?'

'I cannot say,' replied the count; 'I have not heard of his being seen since; I believe, however, that the villagers, who understand these things better than we do, say, that they should not be surprised if he allowed the hedge and tombstone to be removed now without opposition; but Mr Greathead, on the contrary, wished to retain them as mementoes of these curious circumstances.'

ROUND THE FIRE
by Catherine Crowe
from GHOST STORIES AND FAMILY LEGENDS
SEVENTH EVENING

'**M**y story will be a very short one,' said Mrs M.; 'for I must tell you that though, like everybody else, I have heard a great many ghost stories, and have met people who assured me they had seen such things, I cannot, for my own part, bring myself to believe in them; but a circumstance occurred when I was abroad, that you may perhaps consider of a ghostly nature, though I cannot.

'I was travelling through Germany, with no one but my maid – it was before the time of railways, and on my road from Leipzic to Dresden, I stopped at an inn that appeared to have been long ago part of an aristocratic residence – a castle, in short; for there was a stone wall and battlements, and a tower at one side; while the other was a prosaic-looking, square building that had evidently been added in modern times. The inn stood at one end of a small village, in which some of the houses looked so antique that they might, I thought, be coeval with the castle itself. There were a good many travellers, but the host said he could accommodate me; and when I asked to see my room, he led me up to the towers, and showed me a tolerably comfortable one. There were only two apartments on each floor; so I asked him if I could have the other for my maid,

and he said yes, if no other traveller arrived. None came, and she slept there.

'I supped at the *table d'hôte*, and retired to bed early, as I had an excursion to make on the following day; and I was sufficiently tired with my journey to fall asleep directly.

'I don't know how long I had slept – but I think some hours, when I awoke quite suddenly, almost with a start, and beheld near the foot of the bed, the most hideous, dreadful-looking old woman, in an antique dress, that imagination can conceive. She seemed to be approaching me – not as if walking, but gliding, with her left arm and hand extended towards me.

'"Merciful God, deliver me!" I exclaimed under my first impulse of amazement; and as I said the words she disappeared.'

'Then, though you don't believe in ghosts, you thought it was one when you saw it,' said I.

'I don't know what I thought – I admit I was a good deal frightened, and it was a long time before I fell asleep again.

'In the morning,' continued Mrs M., 'my maid knocked, and I told her to come in; but the door was locked, and I had to get out of bed to admit her – I thought I might have forgotten to fasten it. As soon as I was up, I examined every part of the room, but I could find nothing to account for this intrusion. There was neither trap nor moving panel, nor door that I could see, except the one I had locked. However, I made up my mind not to speak of the circumstance, for I fancied I must have been deceived in supposing myself awake, and that it was only a dream; more particularly as there was no light in my room, and I could not comprehend how I could have seen this woman.

'I went out early, and was away the greater part of the day. When I returned I found more travellers had arrived, and that they had given the room next mine to a German lady and her daughter, who were at the *table d'hôte*. I therefore had a bed made up in my room for my maid; and before I lay down, I searched thoroughly, that I might be sure nobody was concealed there.

'In the middle of the night – I suppose about the same time I had been disturbed on the preceding one – I and my maid were awakened by a piercing scream; and I heard the voice of the German girl in the adjoining room, exclaiming, "*Ach! meine mutter! meine mutter!*"

'For some time afterwards I heard them talking, and then I fell asleep – wondering, I confess, whether they had had a visit from the frightful old woman. They left me in no doubt the next morning. They came down to breakfast greatly excited – told everybody the cause – described the old woman exactly as I had seen her, and departed from the house incontinently, declaring they would not stay there another hour.'

'What did the host say to it?' we asked.

'Nothing; he said we must have dreamed it – and I suppose we did.'

'Your story,' said I, 'reminds me of a very interesting letter which I received soon after the publication of *The Nightside of Nature*. It was from a clergyman who gave his name, and said he was chaplain to a nobleman. He related that in a house he inhabited, or had inhabited, a lady had one evening gone upstairs, and seen, to her amazement, in a room, the door of which was open, a lady in an antique dress, standing before a chest of drawers, and apparently examining their contents. She stood still, wondering who this stranger could be, when the figure turned her face towards her, and, to her horror, she saw there were no eyes. Other members of the family saw the same apparition also. I believe there were further particulars; but I unfortunately lost this letter, with some others, in the confusion of changing my residence.

'The absence of eyes I take to be emblematical of moral blindness; for in the world of spirits there is no deceiving each other by false seemings; as we are, so we appear.'

'Then,' said Mrs W. C., 'the apparition – if it was an apparition – that two of my servants saw lately, must be in a very degraded state.'

'There is a road, and on one side of it a path, just beyond my garden wall. Not long ago two of my servants were in the dusk of

the evening walking up this path, when they saw a large, dark object coming towards them. At first, they thought it was an animal; and when it got close, one of them stretched out her hand to touch it; but she could feel nothing, and it passed on between her and the garden wall, although there was *no space*, the path being only wide enough for two; and on looking back, they saw it walking down the hill behind them. Three men were coming up on the path; and as the thing approached, they jumped off into the road.

"'Good heavens, what is that!" cried the women.

"'I don't know," replied the men; "I never saw such a thing as that before."

'The women came home greatly agitated; and we have since heard there is a tradition that the spot is haunted by the ghost of a man who was killed in a quarry close by.'

'I have travelled a great deal,' said our next speaker, the Chevalier de La C. G.; and, certainly, I have never been in any country where instances of these spiritual appearances were not adduced on apparently credible authority. I have heard numerous stories of the sort, but the one that most readily occurs to me at present, was told to me not long ago, in Paris, by Count P. – the nephew of the celebrated Count P. whose name occurs in the history of the remarkable incidents connected with the death of the Emperor Paul.

'Count P., my authority for the following story, was attached to the Russian embassy; and he told me, one evening, when the conversation turned on the inconveniences of travelling in the East of Europe, that, on one occasion, when in Poland, he found himself about seven o'clock in an autumn evening on a forest road, where there was no possibility of finding a house of public entertainment within many miles. There was a frightful storm; the road, not good at the best, was almost impracticable from the weather, and his horses were completely knocked up. On consulting his people what was best to be done, they said, that to go back was as impossible as to go forward; but that by turning a little out of the main road, they

should soon reach a castle where possibly shelter might be procured for the night. The count gladly consented, and it was not long before they found themselves at the gate of what appeared a building on a very splendid scale. The courier quickly alighted and rang at the bell, and while waiting for admission, he enquired who the castle belonged to, and was told that it was Count X's.

'It was some time before the bell was answered, but at length an elderly man appeared at a wicket, with a lantern, and peeped out. On perceiving the equipage, he came forward and stepped up to the carriage, holding the light aloft to discover who was inside. Count P. handed him his card, and explained his distress.

'"There is no one here, my lord," replied the man, "but myself and my family; the castle is not inhabited."

'"That's bad news," said the count; "but nevertheless, you can give me what I am most in need of, and that is – shelter for the night."

'"Willingly," said the man, "if your lordship will put up with such accommodation as we can hastily prepare."

'"So," said the count, "I alighted and walked in; and the old man unbarred the great gates to admit my carriages and people. We found ourselves in an immense *couer*, with the castle *en face*, and stables and offices on each side. As we had a *fourgon* with us, with provender for the cattle and provisions for ourselves, we wanted nothing but beds and a good fire; and as the only one lighted was in the old man's apartments, he first took us there. They consisted of a *suite* of small rooms in the left wing, that had probably been formerly occupied by the upper servants. They were comfortably furnished, and he and his large family appeared to be very well lodged. Besides the wife, there were three sons, with their wives and children, and two nieces; and in a part of the offices, where I saw a light, I was told there were labourers and women servants, for it was a valuable estate, with a fine forest, and the sons acted as *gardes chasse*.

'"Is there much game in the forest?" I asked.

'"A great deal of all sorts," they answered.

"'Then I suppose during the season the family live here?"

"'Never," they replied. "None of the family ever reside here."

"'Indeed!" I said; "how is that? It seems a very fine place."

"'Superb," answered the wife of the custodian; "but the castle is haunted."

'She said this with a simple gravity that made me laugh; upon which they all stared at me with the most edifying amazement.

"'I beg your pardon," I said; "but you know, perhaps, in great cities, such as I usually inhabit, there are no ghosts."

"'Indeed!" said they. "No ghosts!"

"'At least," I said, "I never heard of any; and we don't believe in such things."

'They looked at each other with surprise, but said nothing; not appearing to have any desire to convince me. "But do you mean to say," said I, "that that is the reason the family don't live here, and that the castle is abandoned on that account?"

"'Yes," they replied, "that is the reason nobody has resided here for many years."

"'But how can you live here then?"

"'We are never troubled in this part of the building," said she. "We hear noises, but we are used to that."

"'Well, if there is a ghost, I hope I shall see it," said I.

"'God forbid!" said the woman, crossing herself. "But we shall guard against that; your *seigneurie* will sleep not far from this, where you will be quite safe."

"'Oh! but," said I, "I am quite serious, if there is a ghost, I should particularly like to see him, and I should be much obliged to you to put me in the apartments he most frequents."

'They opposed this proposition earnestly, and begged me not to think of if; besides, they said if anything was to happen to my lord, how should they answer for it; but as I insisted, the women went to call the members of the family who were lighting fires and preparing beds in some rooms on the same floor as they occupied themselves.

When they came they were as earnest against the indulgence of my wishes as the women had been. Still I insisted.

"'Are you afraid,' I said, "to go yourselves in the haunted chambers?"

"'No,' they answered. "We are the custodians of the castle and have to keep the rooms clean and well-aired lest the furniture be spoiled – my lord talks always of removing it, but it has never been removed yet – but we would not sleep up there for all the world."

"'Then it is the upper floors that are haunted?'"

"'Yes, especially the long room, no one could pass a night there; the last that did is in a lunatic asylum now at Warsaw," said the custodian.

"'What happened to him?'"

"'I don't know,' said the man; "he was never able to tell."

"'Who was he?' I asked.

"'He was a lawyer. My lord did business with him; and one day he was speaking of this place, and saying that it was a pity he was not at liberty to pull it down and sell the materials; but he cannot, because it is family property and goes with the title; and the lawyer said he wished it was his, and that no ghost should keep him out of it. My lord said that it was easy for anyone to say that who knew nothing about it, and that he must suppose the family had not abandoned such a fine place without good reasons. But the lawyer said it was some trick, and that it was coiners, or robbers, who had got a footing in the castle, and contrived to frighten people away that they might keep it to themselves; so my lord said if he could prove that he should be very much obliged to him, and more than that, he would give him a great sum – I don't know how much. So the lawyer said, he would; and my lord wrote to me that he was coming to inspect the property, and I was to let him do anything he liked.

"'Well, he came, and with him his son, a fine young man and a soldier. They asked me all sorts of questions, and went over the castle and examined every part of it. From what they said, I could see that they thought the ghost was all nonsense, and that I and my family were in collusion with the robbers or coiners. However, I did not care for that, my lord knew that the castle had been haunted before I was born.

"'I had prepared rooms on this floor for them – the same I am preparing for your lordship, and they slept there, keeping the keys of the upper rooms to themselves, so I did not interfere with them. But one morning, very early, we were awakened by someone knocking at our bedroom door, and when we opened it, we saw Mr Thaddeus – that was the lawyer's son – standing there half-dressed and as pale as a ghost; and he said his father was very ill and he begged us to go to him; to our surprise he led us upstairs to the haunted chamber, and there we found the poor gentleman speechless, and we thought they had gone up there early and that he had had a stroke. But it was not so; Mr Thaddeus said, that after we were all in bed, they had gone up there to pass the night. I know they thought that there was no ghost but us, and that's why they would not let us know their intention. They laid down upon some sofas, wrapped up in their fur cloaks, and resolved to keep awake, and they did so for some time, but at last the young man was overcome by drowsiness, he struggled against it, but could not conquer it, and the last thing he recollects was his father shaking him and saying 'Thaddeus, Thaddeus, for God's sake keep awake!' But he could not, and he knew no more till he woke and saw that day was breaking, and found his father sitting in a corner of the room speechless, and looking like a corpse; and there he was when we went up. The young man thought he'd been taken ill or had a stroke, as we supposed at first; but when we found they had passed the night in the haunted chambers, we had no doubt what had happened – he had seen some terrible sight and so lost his senses."

"He lost his senses, I should say, from terror when his son fell asleep," said I, "and he felt himself alone. He could have been a man of no nerve. At all events, what you tell me raises my curiosity. Will you take me upstairs and show me those rooms?"

"'Willingly,' said the man, and fetching a bunch of keys and a light, and calling one of his sons to follow him with another, he led

the way up the great staircase to a suite of apartments on the first floor. The rooms were lofty and large, and the man said the furniture was very handsome, but old. Being all covered with canvas cases, I could not judge of it. "Which is the long room?" I said.

'Upon which he led me into a long narrow room that might rather have been called a gallery. There were sofas along each side, something like a dais at the upper end; and several large pictures hanging on the walls.

'I had with me a bulldog, of a very fine breed, that had been given me in England by Lord F. She had followed me upstairs – indeed, she followed me everywhere – and I watched her narrowly as she went smelling about, but there were no indications of her perceiving anything extraordinary. Beyond this gallery there was only a small octagon room, with a door that led out upon another staircase. When I had examined it all thoroughly, I returned to the long room and told the man, as that was the place especially frequented by the ghost, I should feel much obliged if he would allow me to pass the night there. I could take upon myself to say that Count X., would have no objection.

'"It is not that," replied the man; "but the danger to your lordship," and he conjured me not to insist on such a perilous experiment.

'When he found I was resolved, he gave way, but on condition that I signed a paper, stating that in spite of his representations I had determined to sleep in the long room.

'I confess, the more anxious these people seemed to prevent my sleeping there, the more curious I was; not that I believed in the ghost the least in the world. I thought that the lawyer had been right in his conjecture, but that he hadn't nerve enough to investigate whatever he saw or heard; and that they had succeeded in frightening him out of his senses. I saw what an excellent place these people had got, and how much it was their interest to maintain the idea that the castle was uninhabitable. Now, I have pretty good nerves – I have been in situations that have tried them severely – and I did not believe

that any ghost, if there was such a thing, or any jugglery by which a semblance of one might be contrived, would shake them. As for any real danger, I did not apprehend it; the people knew who I was, and any mischief happening to me would have led to consequences they well understood. So they lighted fires in both the grates of the gallery, and as they had abundance of dry wood, they soon blazed up. I was determined not to leave the room after I was once in it, lest, if my suspicions were correct, they might have time to make their arrangements; so I desired my people to bring up my supper, and I ate it there.

'My courier said he had always heard the castle was haunted, but he dare say there was no ghost but the people below, who had a very comfortable berth of it; and he offered to pass the night with me, but I declined any companion and preferred trusting to myself and my dog. My valet, on the contrary, strongly advised me against the enterprise, assuring me that he had lived with a family in France whose *château* was haunted, and had left his place in consequence.

'By the time I had finished my supper it was ten o'clock, and everything was prepared for the night. My bed, though an impromptu, was very comfortable, made of amply stuffed cushions and thick coverlets, placed in front of the fire. I was provided with light and plenty of wood; and I had my regimental cutlass, and a case of excellent pistols, which I carefully primed and loaded in presence of the custodian, saying, "You see I am determined to fire at the ghost, so if he cannot stand a bullet, he had better not pay me a visit."

'The old man shook his head calmly, but made no answer. Having desired the courier, who said he should not go to bed, to come upstairs immediately if he heard the report of firearms, I dismissed my people and locked the doors, barricading each with a heavy ottoman besides. There was no arras or hangings of any sort behind which a door could be concealed; and I went round the room, the walls of which were panelled with white and gold, knocking every

part, but neither the sound, nor Dido, the dog, gave any indications of there being anything unusual. Then I undressed and lay down with my sword and my pistols beside me; and Dido at the foot of my bed, where she always slept.

'I confess I was in a state of pleasing excitement; my curiosity and my love of adventure were roused; and whether it was ghost, or robber, or coiner, I was to have a visit from, the interview was likely to be equally interesting. It was half-past ten when I lay down; my expectations were too vivid to admit of sleep; and after an attempt at a French novel, I was obliged to give it up; I could not fix my attention to it. Besides, my chief care was not to be surprised. I could not help thinking the custodian and his family had some secret way of getting into the room, and I hoped to detect them in the act; so I lay with my eyes and ears open in a position that gave me a view of every part of it, till my travelling clock struck twelve, which being pre-eminently the ghostly hour, I thought the critical moment was arrived. But no, no sound, no interruption of any sort to the silence and solitude of the night occurred. When half-past twelve, and one struck, I pretty well made up my mind that I should be disappointed in my expectations, and that the ghost, whoever he was, knew better than to encounter Dido and a brace of well charged pistols; but just as I arrived at this conclusion, an unaccountable *frisson* came over me, and I saw Dido, who tired with her day's journey, had lain till now quietly curled up asleep, begin to move, and slowly get upon her feet. I thought she was only going to turn, but, instead of lying down, she stood still with her ears erect and her head towards the dais, uttering a low growl.

'The dais, I should mention, was but the skeleton of a dais, for the draperies were taken off. There was only remaining a canopy covered with crimson velvet, and an armchair covered with velvet too, but cased in canvas like the rest of the furniture. I had examined this part of the room thoroughly, and had moved the chair aside to ascertain that there was nothing under it.

'Well, I sat up in bed and looked steadily in the same direction as the dog, but I could see nothing at first, though it appeared that she did; but as I looked, I began to perceive something like a cloud in the chair, while at the same time a chill which seemed to pervade the very marrow in my bones crept through me, yet the fire was good; and it was not the chill of fear, for I cocked my pistols with perfect self-possession and abstained from giving Dido the signal to advance, because I wished eagerly to see the denouement of the adventure.

'Gradually, this cloud took a form, and assumed the shape of a tall white figure that reached from the ceiling to the floor of the dais, which was raised by two steps. "At him, Dido! At him!" I said, and away she dashed to the steps, but instantly turned and crept back completely cowed. As her courage was undoubted, I own this astonished me, and I should have fired, but that I was perfectly satisfied that what I saw was not a substantial human form, for I had seen it grow into its present shape and height from the undefined cloud that first appeared in the chair. I laid my hand on the dog who had crept up to my side, and I felt her shaking in her skin. I was about to rise myself and approach the figure, though I confess I was a good deal awestruck, when it stepped majestically from the dais, and seemed to be advancing. "At him!" I said, "At him, Dido!" and I gave the dog every encouragement to go forward; she made a sorry attempt, but returned when she had got halfway and crouched beside me whining with terror. The figure advanced upon me; the cold became icy; the dog crouched and trembled; and I, as it approached, honestly confess,' said Count P., 'that I hid my head under the bedclothes and did not venture to look up till morning. I know not what it was – as it passed over me I felt a sensation of undefinable horror, that no words can describe – and I can only say that nothing on earth would tempt me to pass another night in that room, and I am sure if Dido could speak, you'd find her of the same opinion.

'I had desired to be called at seven o'clock, and when the custodian, who accompanied my valet, found me safe and in my perfect senses,

I must say the poor man appeared greatly relieved; and when I descended the whole family seemed to look upon me as a hero. I thought it only just to them to admit that something had happened in the night that I felt impossible to account for, and that I should not recommend anybody who was not very sure of their nerves to repeat the experiment.'

When the Chevalier had concluded this extraordinary story, I suggested that the apparition of the castle very much resembled that mentioned by the late Professor Gregory, in his letters on mesmerism, as having appeared in the Tower of London some years ago, and from the alarm it created, having occasioned the death of a lady, the wife of an officer quartered there, and one of the sentries. Everyone who had read that very interesting publication was struck by the resemblance.

THE MYSTERIOUS STRANGER
(Translated from German)
from ODDS AND ENDS

'To die? to sleep!
Perchance to dream? Ay, there's the rub.' – *Hamlet*

BOREAS, that fearful north-west wind, which in the spring and autumn stirs up the lowest depths of the wild Adriatic, and is then so dangerous to vessels, was howling through the woods, and tossing the branches of the old knotty oaks in the Carpathian Mountains, when a party of five riders, who surrounded a litter drawn by a pair of mules, turned into a forest-path, which offered some protection from the April weather, and allowed the travellers in some degree to recover their breath. It was already evening, and bitterly cold; the snow fell every now and then in large flakes. A tall old gentleman, of aristocratic appearance, rode at the head of the troop. This was the Knight of Fahnenberg, in Austria. He had inherited from a childless brother a considerable property, situated in the Carpathian Mountains; and he had set out to take possession of it, accompanied by his daughter Franziska, and a niece about twenty years of age, who had been brought up with her. Next to the knight rode a fine young man some twenty and odd years – the Baron Franz

von Kronstein; he wore, like the former, the broad-brimmed hat with hanging feathers, the leather collar, the wide riding-boots – in short, the travelling-dress which was in fashion at the commencement of the seventeenth century. The features of the young man had much about them that was open and friendly, as well as some mind; but the expression was more that of dreamy and sensitive softness than of youthful daring, although no one could deny that he possessed much of youthful beauty. As the cavalcade turned into the oak wood the young man rode up to the litter, and chatted with the ladies who were seated therein. One of these – and to her his conversation was principally addressed – was of dazzling beauty. Her hair flowed in natural curls round the fine oval of her face, out of which beamed a pair of star-like eyes, full of genius, lively fancy and a certain degree of archness. Franziska von Fahnenberg seemed to attend but carelessly to the speeches of her admirer, who made many kind inquiries as to how she felt herself during the journey, which had been attended with many difficulties: she always answered him very shortly; almost contemptuously; and at length remarked, that if it had not been for her father's objections, she would long ago have requested the baron to take her place in their horrid cage of a litter, for, to judge by his remarks, he seemed incommoded by the weather; and she would so much rather be mounted on the spirited horse, and face wind and storm, than be mewed up there, dragged up the hills by those long-eared animals, and mope herself to death with ennui. The young lady's words and, still more, the half-contemptuous tone in which they were uttered, appeared to make the most painful impression on the young man: he made her no reply at the moment, but the absent air with which he attended to the kindly-intended remarks of the other young lady, showed how much he was disconcerted.

'It appears, dear Franziska,' said he at length in a kindly tone, 'that the hardships of the road have affected you more than you will acknowledge. Generally so kind to others, you have been very often out of humour during the journey, and particularly with regard to your humble servant and cousin, who would gladly bear a double or treble share of the discomforts, if he could thereby save you from the smallest of them.'

Franziska showed by her look that she was about to reply with some bitter jibe, when the voice of the knight was heard calling for his nephew, who galloped off at the sound.

'I should like to scold you well, Franziska,' said her companion somewhat sharply, 'for always plaguing your poor Cousin Franz in this shameful way; he who loves you so truly, and who, whatever you may say, will one day be your husband.'

'My husband!' replied the other angrily. 'I must either completely alter my ideas, or he his whole self, before that takes place. No, Bertha! I know that this is my father's darling wish, and I do not deny the good qualities Cousin Franz may have, or really has, since I see you are making a face; but to marry an effeminate man – never!'

'Effeminate! you do him great injustice,' replied her friend quickly. 'Just because instead of going off to the Turkish war, where little honour was to be gained, he attended to your father's advice, and stayed at home, to bring his neglected estate into order, which he accomplished with care and prudence; and because he does not represent this howling wind as a mild zephyr – for reasons such as these you are pleased to call him effeminate.'

'Say what you will, it is so,' cried Franziska obstinately. 'Bold, aspiring, even despotic, must be the man who is to gain my heart; these soft, patient and thoughtful natures are utterly distasteful to me. Is Franz capable of deep sympathy, either in joy or sorrow? He is always the same – always quiet, soft and tiresome.'

'He has a warm heart, and is not without genius,' said Bertha.

'A warm heart! that may be,' replied the other; 'but I would rather be tyrannised over, and kept under a little by my future husband, than be loved in such a wearisome manner. You say he has genius, too. I will not exactly contradict you, since that would be impolite, but it is not easily discovered. But even allowing you

are right in both statements, still the man who does not bring these qualities into action is a despicable creature. A man may do many foolish things, he may even be a little wicked now and then, provided it is in nothing dishonourable; and one can forgive him, if he is only acting on some fixed theory for some special object. There is, for instance, your own faithful admirer, the Castellan of Glogau, Knight of Woislaw; he loves you most truly, and is now quite in a position to enable you to marry comfortably. The brave man has lost his right hand – reason enough for remaining seated behind the stove, or near the spinning-wheel of his Bertha; but what does he do? – He goes off to the war in Turkey; he fights for a noble thought – '

'And runs the chance of getting his other hand chopped off, and another great scar across his face,' put in her friend.

'Leaves his lady-love to weep and pine a little,' pursued Franziska, 'but returns with fame, marries, and is all the more honoured and admired! This is done by a man of forty, a rough warrior, not bred at court, a soldier who has nothing but his cloak and sword. And Franz – rich, noble – but I will not go on. Not a word more on this detested point, if you love me, Bertha.'

Franziska leaned back in the corner of the litter with a dissatisfied air, and shut her eyes as though, overcome by fatigue, she wished to sleep.

'This awful wind is so powerful, you say, that we must make a detour to avoid its full force,' said the knight to an old man, dressed in a fur-cap and a cloak of rough skin, who seemed to be the guide of the party.

'Those who have never personally felt the Boreas storming over the country between Sessano and Triest, can have no conception of the reality,' replied the other. 'As soon as it commences, the snow is blown in thick long columns along the ground. That is nothing to what follows. These columns become higher and higher, as the wind rises, and continue to do so until you see nothing but

snow above, below and on every side – unless, indeed, sometimes, when sand and gravel are mixed with the snow, and at length it is impossible to open your eyes at all. Your only plan for safety is to wrap your cloak around you, and lie down flat on the ground. If your home were but a few hundred yards off, you might lose your life in the attempt to reach it.'

'Well, then, we owe you thanks, old Kumpan,' said the knight, though it was with difficulty he made his words heard above the roaring of the storm; 'we owe you thanks for taking us this round, as we shall thus be enabled to reach our destination without danger.'

'You may feel sure of that, noble sir,' said the old man. 'By midnight we shall have arrived, and that without any danger by the way, if –' Suddenly the old man stopped, he drew his horse sharply up, and remained in an attitude of attentive listening.

'It appears to me we must be in the neighbourhood of some village,' said Franz von Kronstein; 'for between the gusts of the storm I hear a dog howling.'

'It is no dog, it is no dog!' said the old man uneasily, and urging his horse to a rapid pace. 'For miles around there is no human dwelling; and except in the castle of Klatka, which indeed lies in the neighbourhood, but has been deserted for more than a century, probably no one has lived here since the creation. – But there again,' he continued; 'well, if I wasn't sure of it from the first.'

'That howling seems to fidget you, old Kumpan,' said the knight, listening to a long-drawn fierce sound, which appeared nearer than before, and seemed to be answered from a distance.

'That howling comes from no dogs,' replied the old guide uneasily. 'Those are reed-wolves; they may be on our track; and it would be as well if the gentlemen looked to their firearms.'

'Reed-wolves ? What do you mean?' inquired Franz in surprise.

'At the edge of this wood,' said Kumpan, 'there lies a lake about a mile long, whose banks are covered with reeds. In these a number of wolves have taken up their quarters, and feed on wild birds, fish

and such like. They are shy in the summer-time, and a boy of twelve might scare them; but when the birds migrate, and the fish are frozen up, they prowl about at night, and then they are dangerous. They are worst, however, when Boreas rages, for then it is just as if the fiend himself possessed them: they are so mad and fierce that man and beast become alike their victims; and a party of them have been known even to attack the ferocious bears of these mountains, and, what is more, to come off victorious.' The howl was now again repeated more distinctly, and from two opposite directions. The riders in alarm felt for their pistols, and the old man grasped the spear which hung at his saddle.

'We must keep close to the litter; the wolves are very near us,' whispered the guide. The riders turned their horses, surrounded the litter, and the knight informed the ladies, in a few quieting words, of the cause of this movement.

'Then we *shall* have an adventure – some little variety!' cried Franziska with sparkling eyes.

'How can you talk so foolishly?' said Bertha in alarm.

'Are we not under manly protection? Is not Cousin Franz on our side?' said the other mockingly.

'See, there is a light gleaming among the twigs; and there is another,' cried Bertha. 'there must be people close to us.'

'No, no,' cried the guide quickly. 'Shut up the door, ladies. Keep close together, gentlemen. It is the eyes of wolves you see sparkling there.' The gentlemen looked towards the thick underwood, in which every now and then little bright spots appeared, such as in summer would have been taken for glow-worms; it was just the same greenish-yellow light, but less unsteady, and there were always two flames together. The horses began to be restive, they kicked and dragged at the rein; but the mules behaved tolerably well.

'I will fire on the beasts, and teach them to keep their distance,' said Franz, pointing to the spot where the lights were thickest.

'Hold, hold, Sir Baron!' cried Kumpan quickly, and seizing the

young man's arm. 'You would bring such a host together by the report, that, encouraged by numbers, they would be sure to make the first assault. However, keep your arms in readiness, and if an old she-wolf springs out – for these always lead the attack – take good aim and kill her, for then there must be no further hesitation.' By this time the horses were almost unmanageable, and terror had also infected the mules. Just as Franz was turning towards the litter to say a word to his cousin, an animal, about the size of a large hound, sprang from the thicket and seized the foremost mule.

'Fire, baron! A wolf!' shouted the guide.

The young man fired, and the wolf fell to the ground. A fearful howl rang through the wood.

'Now, forward! Forward without a moment's delay!' cried Kumpan. 'We have not above five minutes' time. The beasts will tear their wounded comrade to pieces, and, if they are very hungry, partially devour her. We shall, in the meantime, gain a little start, and it is not more than an hour's ride to the end of the forest. There – do you see – these are the towers of Klatka between the trees – out there where the moon is rising, and from that point the wood becomes less dense.'

The travellers endeavoured to increase their pace to the utmost, but the litter retarded their progress. Bertha was weeping with fear, and even Franziska's courage had diminished, for she sat very still. Franz endeavoured to reassure them. They had not proceeded many moments when the howling recommenced, and approached nearer and nearer.

'There they are again and fiercer and more numerous than before,' cried the guide in alarm.

The lights were soon visible again, and certainly in greater numbers. The wood had already become less thick, and the snow storm having ceased, the moonbeams discovered many a dusky form amongst the trees, keeping together like a pack of hounds, and advancing nearer and nearer till they were within twenty paces, and on the very path of the travellers. From time to time a fierce howl arose from their centre, which was answered by the whole pack, and was at length taken up by single voices in the distance.

The party now found themselves some few hundred yards from the ruined castle of which Kumpan had spoken. It was, or seemed by moonlight to be, of some magnitude. Near the tolerably preserved principal building lay the ruins of a church, which must have once been beautiful, placed on a little hillock, dotted with single oak-trees and bramble-bushes. Both castle and church were still partially roofed in; and a path led from the castle gate to an old oak-tree, where it joined at right angles the one along which the travellers were advancing.

The old guide seemed in much perplexity.

'We are in great danger, noble sir,' said he. 'The wolves will very soon make a general attack. There will then be only one way of escape: leaving the mules to their fate, and taking the young ladies on your horses.'

'That would be all very well, if I had not thought of a better plan,' replied the knight. 'Here is the ruined castle; we can surely reach that, and then, blocking up the gates, we must just await the morning.'

'Here? In the ruins of Klatka? – Not for all the wolves in the world!' cried the old man. 'Even by daylight no one likes to approach the place, and, now, by night! – The castle, Sir Knight, has a bad name.'

'On account of robbers?' asked Franz.

'No; it is haunted,' replied the other.

'Stuff and nonsense!' said the baron. 'Forward to the ruins; there is not a moment to be lost.'

And this was indeed the case. The ferocious beasts were but a few steps behind the travellers. Every now and then they retired, and set up a ferocious howl. The party had just arrived at the old oak before mentioned, and were about to turn into the path to the ruins, when the animals, as though perceiving the risk they ran of losing their prey, came so near that a lance could easily have struck them. The knight and Franz faced sharply about, spurring their horses amidst the advancing crowds, when suddenly, from the shadow of the oak stepped forth a man, who in a few strides placed himself between the travellers and their pursuers. As far as one could see in the dusky light, the stranger was a man of a tall and well-built frame; he wore a sword by his side, and a broad-brimmed hat was on his head. If the party were astonished at his sudden appearance, they were still more so at what followed. As soon as the stranger appeared, the wolves gave over their pursuit, tumbled over each other, and set up a fearful howl. The stranger now raised his hand, appeared to wave it, and the wild animals crawled back into the thickets like a pack of beaten hounds.

Without casting a glance at the travellers, who were too much overcome by astonishment to speak, the stranger went up the path which led to the castle, and soon disappeared beneath the gateway.

'Heaven have mercy on us!' murmured old Kumpan in his beard, as he made the sign of the cross.

'Who was that strange man?' asked the knight with surprise, when he had watched the stranger as long as he was visible, and the party had resumed their way.

The old guide pretended not to understand and, riding up to the mules, busied himself with arranging the harness, which had become disordered in their haste: more than a quarter of an hour elapsed before he rejoined them.

'Did you know the man who met us near the ruins, and who freed us from our four-footed pursuers in such a miraculous way?' asked Franz of the guide.

'Do I know him? No, noble sir; I never saw him before,' replied the guide hesitatingly.

'He looked like a soldier, and was armed,' said the baron. 'Is the castle, then, inhabited?'

'Not for the last hundred years,' replied the other. 'It was dismantled because the possessor in those days had iniquitous dealings with

some Turkish-Sclavonian hordes, who had advanced as far as this; or rather' – he corrected himself hastily – 'he is *said* to have had such, for he might have been as upright and good a man as ever ate cheese fried in butter.'*

'And who is now the possessor of the ruins and of these woods?' inquired the knight.

'Who but yourself, noble sir?' replied Kumpan. 'For more than two hours we have been on your estate, and we shall soon reach the end of the wood.'

'We hear and see nothing more of the wolves,' said the baron after a pause. 'Even their howling has ceased. The adventure with the stranger still remains to me inexplicable, even if one were to suppose him a huntsman –'

'Yes, yes; that is most likely what he is,' interrupted the guide hastily, whilst he looked uneasily round him. 'The brave good man, who came so opportunely to our assistance, must have been a huntsman. Oh, there are many powerful woodsmen in this neighbourhood! Heaven be praised!' he continued, taking a deep breath, 'there is the end of the wood, and in a short hour we shall be safely housed.'

And so it happened. Before an hour had elapsed, the party passed through a well-built village, the principal spot on the estate, towards the venerable castle, the windows of which were brightly illuminated, and at the door stood the steward and other dependants, who, having received their new lord with every expression of respect, conducted the party to the splendidly furnished apartments.

Nearly four weeks passed before the travelling adventures again came on the *tapis*. The knight and Franz found such constant employment in looking over all the particulars of the large estate, and endeavouring to introduce various German improvements,

---

* A favourite dish in these parts.

that they were very little at home. At first, Franziska was charmed with everything in a neighbourhood so entirely new and unknown. It appeared to her so romantic, so very different from her German Fatherland, that she took the greatest interest in everything, and often drew comparisons between the countries, which generally ended unfavourably for Germany. Bertha was of exactly the contrary opinion: she laughed at her cousin, and said that her liking for novelty and strange sights must indeed have come to a pass, when she preferred hovels in which the smoke went out of the doors and windows instead of the chimney, walls covered with soot, and inhabitants not much cleaner, and of unmannerly habits, to the comfortable dwellings and polite people of Germany. However, Franziska persisted in her notions, and replied that everything in Austria was flat, *ennuyant*, and common; and that a wild peasant here, with his rough coat of skin, had ten times more interest for her than a quiet Austrian in his holiday suit, the mere sight of whom was enough to make one yawn.

As soon as the knight had got the first arrangements into some degree of order, the party found themselves more together again. Franz continued to show great attention to his cousin, which, however, she received with little gratitude, for she made him the butt of all her fanciful humours, that soon returned when after a longer sojourn she had become more accustomed to her new life. Many excursions into the neighbourhood were undertaken, but there was little variety in the scenery, and these soon ceased to amuse.

The party were one day assembled in the old-fashioned hall, dinner had just been removed, and they were arranging in which direction they should ride. 'I have it,' cried Franziska suddenly, 'I wonder we never thought before of going to view by day the spot where we fell in with our night-adventure with wolves and the Mysterious Stranger.'

'You mean a visit to the ruins – what were they called?' said the knight.

'Castle Klatka,' cried Franziska gaily. 'Oh, we really must ride there! It will be so charming to go over again by daylight, and in safety, the ground where we had such a dreadful fright.'

'Bring round the horses,' said the knight to a servant 'and tell the steward to come to me immediately.' The latter, an old man, soon after entered the room.

'We intend taking a ride to Klatka,' said the knight: 'we had an adventure there on our road –'

'So old Kumpan told me,' interrupted the steward.

'And what do you say about it?' asked the knight.

'I really don't know what to say,' replied the old man, shaking his head. 'I was a youth of twenty when I first came to this castle, and now my hair is grey; half a century has elapsed during that time. Hundreds of times my duty has called me into the neighbourhood of those ruins, but never have I seen the Fiend of Klatka.'

'What do you say? Whom do you call by that name?' inquired Franziska, whose love of adventure and romance was strongly awakened.

'Why, people call by that name the ghost or spirit who is supposed to haunt the ruins,' replied the steward. 'They say he only shows himself on moonlight nights –'

'That is quite natural,' interrupted Franz smiling. 'Ghosts can never bear the light of day; and if the moon did not shine, how could the ghost be seen? For it is not supposed that any one BUT a mere freak would visit the ruins by torch-light.'

'There are some credulous people who pretend to have seen this ghost,' continued the steward. 'Huntsmen and wood-cutters say they have met him by the large oak on the cross-path. That, noble sir, is supposed to be the spot he inclines most to haunt, for the tree was planted in remembrance of the man who fell there.'

'And who was he?' asked Franziska with increasing curiosity.

'The last owner of the castle, which at that time was a sort of robber's den, and the headquarters of all depredators in the neighbourhood,' answered the old man. 'They say this man was of superhuman strength,

and was feared not only on account of his passionate temper, but of his treaties with the Turkish hordes. Any young woman, too, in the neighbourhood to whom he took a fancy, was carried off to his tower and never heard of more. When the measure of his iniquity was full, the whole neighbourhood rose in a mass, besieged his stronghold, and at length he was slain on the spot where the huge oak-tree now stands.'

'I wonder they did not burn the whole castle, so as to erase the very memory of it,' said the knight.

'It was a dependency of the church, and that saved it,' replied the other. 'Your great-grandfather afterwards took possession of it, for it had fine lands attached. As the Knight of Klatka was of good family, a monument was erected to him in the church, which now lies as much in ruin as the castle itself.'

'Oh, let us set off at once! Nothing shall prevent my visiting so interesting a spot,' said Franziska eagerly. 'The imprisoned damsels who never reappeared, the storming of the tower, the death of the knight, the nightly wanderings of his spirit round the old oak, and, lastly, our own adventure, all draw me thither with an indescribable curiosity.'

When a servant announced that the horses were at the door, the young girls tripped laughingly down the steps which led to the coach-yard. Franz, the knight, and a servant well acquainted with the country, followed; and in a few minutes the party were on their road to the forest.

The sun was still high in the heavens when they saw the towers of Klatka rising above the trees. Everything in the wood was still, except the cheerful twitterings of the birds as they hopped about amongst the bursting buds and leaves, and announced that spring had arrived.

The party soon found themselves near the old oak at the bottom of the hill on which stood the towers, still imposing in their ruin. Ivy and bramble bushes had wound themselves over the walls, and forced deep roots so firmly between the stones that they in a great

measure held these together. On the top of the highest spot, a small bush in its young fresh verdure swayed lightly in the breeze.

The gentlemen assisted their companions to alight, and leaving the horses to the care of the servant, ascended the hill to the castle. After having explored this in every nook and cranny, and spent much time in a vain search for some trace of the extraordinary stranger, whom Franziska declared she was determined to discover, they proceeded to an inspection of the adjoining church. This they found to have better withstood the ravages of time and weather; the nave, indeed, was in complete dilapidation, but the chancel and altar were still under roof, as well as a sort of chapel which appeared to have been a place of honour for the families of the old knights of the castle. Few traces remained, however, of the magnificent painted glass which must once have adorned the windows, and the wind entered at pleasure through the open spaces.

The party were occupied for some time in deciphering the inscriptions on a number of tombstones, and on the walls, principally within the chancel. They were generally memorials of the ancient lords, with figures of men in armour, and women and children of all ages. A flying raven and various other devices were placed at the corners. One gravestone, which stood close to the entrance of the chancel, differed widely from the others: there was no figure sculptured on it, and the inscription, which, on all besides, was a mere mass of flattering eulogies, was here simple and unadorned; it contained only these words: 'Ezzelin von Klatka fell like a knight at the storming of the castle' – on such a day and year.

'That must be the monument of the knight whose ghost is said to haunt these ruins,' cried Franziska eagerly. 'What a pity he is not represented in the same way as the others – I should so like to have known what he was like!'

'Oh, there is the family vault, with steps leading down to it, and the sun is lighting it up through a crevice,' said Franz, stepping from the adjoining vestry.

The whole party followed him down the eight or nine steps which led to a tolerably airy chamber, where were placed a number of coffins of all sizes, some of them crumbling into dust. Here, again, one close to the door was distinguished from the others by the simplicity of its design, the freshness of its appearance, and the brief inscription: 'Ezzelinus de Klatka, Eques.'

As not the slightest effluvium was perceptible, they lingered some time in the vault; and when they reascended to the church, they had a long talk over the old possessors, of whom the knight now remembered he had heard his parents speak. The sun had disappeared, and the moon was just rising as the explorers turned to leave the ruins. Bertha had made a step into the nave, when she uttered a slight exclamation of fear and surprise. Her eyes fell on a man who wore a hat with drooping feathers, a sword at his side, and a short cloak of somewhat old-fashioned cut over his shoulders. The stranger leaned carelessly on a broken column at the entrance; he did not appear to take any notice of the party; and the moon shone full on his pale face.

The party advanced towards the stranger.

'If I am not mistaken,' commenced the knight; 'we have met before.'

Not a word from the unknown.

'You released us in an almost miraculous manner,' said Franziska, 'from the power of those dreadful wolves. Am I wrong in supposing it is to you we are indebted for that great service?'

'The beasts are afraid of me,' replied the stranger in a deep fierce tone, while he fastened his sunken eyes on the girl, without taking any notice of the others.

'Then you are probably a huntsman,' said Franz, 'and wage war against the fierce brutes.'

'Who is not either the pursuer or the pursued? All persecute or are persecuted, and Fate persecutes all,' replied the stranger without looking at him.

'Do you live in these ruins?' asked the knight hesitatingly.

'Yes; but not to the destruction of your game, as you may fear, Knight of Fahnenberg,' said the unknown contemptuously. 'Be quite assured this; of your property shall remain untouched –'

'Oh! my father did not mean that,' interrupted Franziska, who appeared to take the liveliest interest in the stranger. 'Unfortunate events and sad experiences have, no doubt, induced you to take up your abode in these ruins, of which my father would by no means dispossess you.'

'Your father is very good, if that is what he meant,' said the stranger in his former tone; and it seemed as though his dark features were drawn into a slight smile; 'but people of my sort are rather difficult to turn out.'

'You must live very uncomfortably here,' said Franziska, half vexed, for she thought her polite speech had deserved a better reply.

'My dwelling is not exactly uncomfortable, only somewhat small, still quite suitable for quiet people,' said the unknown with a kind of sneer. 'I am not, however, always quiet; I sometimes pine to quit the narrow space, and then I dash away through forest and field, over hill and dale; and the time when I must return to my little dwelling always comes too soon for me.'

'As you now and then leave your dwelling,' said the knight, 'I would invite you to visit us, if I knew – '

'That I was in a station to admit of your doing so,' interrupted the other; and the knight started slightly, for the stranger had exactly expressed the half-formed thought. 'I lament,' he continued coldly, 'that I am not able to give you particulars on this point – some difficulties stand in the way: be assured, however, that I am a knight, and of at least as ancient a family as yourself.'

'Then you must not refuse our request,' cried Franziska, highly interested in the strange manners of the unknown. 'You must come and visit us.'

'I am no boon-companion, and on that account few have invited me of late,' replied the other with his peculiar smile; 'besides, I

generally remain at home during the day; that is my time for rest. I belong, you must know, to that class of persons who turn day into night, and night into day, and who love everything uncommon and peculiar.'

'Really? So do I! And for that reason, you must visit us,' cried Franziska. 'Now,' she continued smiling, 'I suppose you have just risen, and you are taking your morning airing. Well, since the moon is your sun, pray pay a frequent visit to our castle by the light of its rays. I think we shall agree very well, and that it will be very nice for us to be acquainted.'

'You wish it? – You press the invitation?' asked the stranger earnestly and decidedly.

'To be sure, for otherwise you will not come,' replied the young lady shortly.

'Well, then, come I will!' said the other, again fixing his gaze on her. ' If my company does not please you at any time, you will have yourself to blame for an acquaintance with one who seldom forces himself, but is difficult to shake off.'

When the unknown had concluded these words, he made a slight motion with his hand, as though to take leave of them, and passing under the doorway, disappeared among the ruins. The party soon after mounted their horses, and took the road home.

It was the evening of the following day, and all were again seated in the hall of the castle. Bertha had that day received good news. The knight Woislaw had written from Hungary, that the war with the Turks would be brought to a conclusion during the year, and that although he had intended returning to Silesia, hearing of the knight of Fahnenberg having gone to take possession of his new estates, he should follow the family there, not doubting that Bertha had accompanied her friend. He hinted that he stood so high in the opinion of his duke on account of his valuable services, that in future his duties would be even more important and extensive; but before settling down to them, he should come and claim Bertha's promise to become his wife. He had been much enriched by his master, as well as by booty taken from the Turks. Having formerly lost his right hand in the duke's service, he had essayed to fight with his left; but this did not succeed very admirably, and so he had an iron one made by a very clever artist. This hand performed many of the functions of a natural one, but there had been still much wanting; now, however, his master had presented him with one of gold, an extraordinary work of art, produced by a celebrated Italian mechanic. The knight described it as something marvellous, especially as to the superhuman strength with which it enabled him to use the sword and lance. Franziska naturally rejoiced in the happiness of her friend, who had had no news of her betrothed for a long time before. She launched out every now and then, partly to plague Franz, and partly to express her own feelings, in the highest praise and admiration of the bravery and enterprise of the knight, whose adventurous qualities she lauded to the skies. Even the scar on his face, and his want of a right hand, were reckoned as virtues; and Franziska at last saucily declared that a rather ugly man was infinitely more attractive to her than a handsome one, for as a general rule handsome men were conceited and effeminate. Thus, she added, no one could term their acquaintance of the night before handsome, but attractive and interesting he certainly was. Franz and Bertha simultaneously denied this. His gloomy appearance, the deadly hue of his complexion, the tone of his voice, were each in turn depreciated by Bertha, while Franz found fault with the contempt and arrogance obvious in his speech. The knight stood between the two parties. He thought there was something in his bearing that spoke of good family, though much could not be said for his politeness; however, the man might have had trials enough in his life to make him misanthropical. Whilst they were conversing in this way, the door suddenly opened, and the subject of their remarks himself walked in.

'Pardon me, Sir Knight,' he said coldly, 'that I come, if not

uninvited, at least unannounced; there was no one in the ante-chamber to do me that service.'

The brilliantly lighted chamber gave a full view of the stranger. He was a man about forty, tall and extremely thin. His features could not be termed uninteresting – there lay in them something bold and daring; but the expression was on the whole anything but benevolent. There was contempt and sarcasm in the cold grey eyes, whose glance, however, was at times so piercing, that no one could endure it long. His complexion was even more peculiar than the features: it could neither be called pale nor yellow; it was a sort of grey, or, so to speak, dirty white, like that of an Indian who has been suffering long from fever; and was rendered still more remarkable by the intense blackness of his beard and short cropped hair. The dress of the unknown was knightly, but old-fashioned and neglected; there were great spots of rust on the collar and breastplate of his armour; and his dagger and the hilt of his finely-worked sword were marked in some places with mildew. As the party were just going to supper, it was only natural to invite the stranger to partake of it; he complied, however, only in so far that he seated himself at the table, for he ate no morsel. The knight, with surprise, inquired the reason.

'For a long time past, I have accustomed myself never to eat at night,' he replied with a strange smile.

'My digestion is quite unused to solids, and indeed would scarcely confront them. I live entirely on liquids.'

'Oh, then, we can empty a bumper of Rhine-wine together,' cried the host.

'Thanks; but I neither drink wine nor any cold beverage,' replied the other; and his tone was full of mockery. It appeared as if there was some amusing association connected with the idea.

'Then I will order you a cup of hippocras' – a warm drink composed of herbs – 'it shall be ready immediately,' said Franziska.

'Many thanks, fair lady; not at present,' replied the other. 'But if I refuse the beverage you offer me now, you may be assured that as soon as I require it – perhaps very soon – I will request that, or some other of you.'

Bertha and Franz thought the man had something inexpressibly repulsive in his whole manner, and they had no inclination to engage him in conversation; but the baron, thinking that perhaps politeness required him to say something, turned towards the guest, and commenced in a friendly tone: 'It is now many weeks since we first became acquainted with you; we then had to thank you for a signal service –'

'And I have not yet told you my name, although you would gladly know it,' interrupted the other dryly. 'I am called Azzo; and as' – this he said again with his ironical smile – 'with the permission of the Knight of Fahnenberg, I live at the castle of Klatka, you can in future call me Azzo von Klatka.'

'I only wonder you do not feel lonely and uncomfortable amongst those old walls,' began Bertha. 'I cannot understand –'

'What my business is there? Oh, about that I will willingly give you some information, since you and the young gentleman there takes such a kindly interest in my person,' replied the unknown in his tone of sarcasm.

Franz and Bertha both started, for he had revealed their thoughts as though he could read their souls. 'You see, lady,' he continued, 'there are a variety of strange whims in the world. As I have already said, I love what is peculiar and uncommon, at least what would appear so to you. It is wrong in the main to be astonished at anything, for, viewed in one light, all things are alike; even life and death, this side of the grave and the other, have more resemblance than you would imagine. You perhaps consider me rather touched a little in my mind, for taking up my abode with the bat and the owl; but if so, why not consider every hermit and recluse insane? You will tell me that those are holy men. I certainly have no pretension that way; but as they find pleasure in praying and singing psalms, so I amuse myself with hunting. Oh, you can have no idea of the intense pleasure of dashing away in the pale moonlight, on a horse that never tires, over hill and dale, through forest and woodland! I rush among the wolves, which fly at my approach, as you yourself perceived, as though they were puppies fearful of the lash.'

'But still it must be lonely, very lonely for you,' remarked Bertha.

'So it would by day; but I am then asleep,' replied the stranger dryly; 'at night I am merry enough.'

'You hunt in an extraordinary way,' remarked Franz hesitatingly.

'Yes; but, nevertheless, I have no communication with robbers, as you seem to imagine,' replied Azzo coldly.

Franz again started – that very thought had just crossed his mind. 'Oh, I beg your pardon; I do not know – ' he stammered.

'What to make of me,' interrupted the other. 'You would, therefore, do well to believe just what I tell you, or at least to avoid making conjectures of your own, which will lead to nothing.'

'I understand you: I know how to value your ideas, if no one else does,' cried Franziska eagerly. 'The humdrum, everyday life of the generality of men is repulsive to you; you have tasted the joys and pleasures of life, at least what are so called, and you have found them tame and hollow. How soon one tires of the things one sees all around! Life consists in change. Only in what is new, uncommon and peculiar, do the flowers of the spirit bloom and give forth scent. Even pain may become a pleasure if it saves one from the shallow monotony of everyday life – a thing I shall hate till the hour of my death.'

'Right, fair lady – quite right! Remain in this mind: this was always my opinion, and the one from which I have derived the highest reward,' cried Azzo; and his fierce eyes sparkled more intensely than ever. 'I am doubly pleased to have found in you a person who shares my ideas. Oh, if you were a man, you would make me a splendid companion; but even a woman may have fine experiences when once these opinions take root in her, and bring forth action!'

As Azzo spoke these words in a cold tone of politeness, he turned from the subject, and for the rest of his visit only gave the knight monosyllabic replies to his inquiries, taking leave before the table was cleared. To an invitation from the knight, backed by a still more pressing one from Franziska to repeat his visit, he replied that he would take advantage of their kindness, and come sometimes.

When the stranger had departed, many were the remarks made on his appearance and general deportment. Franz declared his most decided dislike to him. Whether it was as usual to vex her cousin, or whether Azzo had really made an impression on her, Franziska took his part vehemently. As Franz contradicted her more eagerly than usual, the young lady launched out into still stronger expressions; and there is no knowing what hard words her cousin might have received had not a servant entered the room.

The following morning Franziska lay longer than usual in bed. When her friend went to her room, fearful lest she should be ill, she found her pale and exhausted. Franziska complained she had passed a very bad night; she thought the dispute with Franz about the stranger must have excited her greatly, for she felt quite feverish and exhausted, and a strange dream, too, had worried her, which was evidently a consequence of the evening's conversation. Bertha, as usual, took the young man's part, and added, that a common dispute about a man whom no one knew, and about whom anyone might form his own opinion, could not possibly have thrown her into her present state. 'At least,' she continued, 'you can let me hear this wonderful dream.'

To her surprise; Franziska for a length of time refused to do so.

'Come, tell me,' inquired Bertha, 'what can possibly prevent you from relating a dream – a mere dream? I might almost think it credible, if the idea were not too horrid, that poor Franz is not very far wrong when he says that the thin, corpse-like, dried-up, old-fashioned stranger has made a greater impression on you than you will allow.'

'Did Franz say so?' asked Franziska. 'Then you can tell him he is not mistaken. Yes, the thin, corpse-like, dried-up, whimsical stranger is far more interesting to me than the rosy-checked, well-dressed, polite and prosy cousin.'

Strange,' cried Bertha. 'I cannot at all comprehend the almost magic influence which this man, so repulsive, exercises over you.'

'Perhaps the very reason I take his part, may be that you are all so prejudiced against him,' remarked Franziska pettishly. 'Yes, it must be so; for that his appearance should please my eyes, is what no one in his senses could imagine. But,' she continued, smiling and holding out her hand to Bertha, 'is it not laughable that I should get out of temper even with you about this stranger? – I can more easily understand it with Franz – and that this unknown should spoil my morning, as he has already spoiled my evening and my night's rest?'

'By that dream, you mean?' said Bertha, easily appeased, as she put her arm round her cousin's neck and kissed her. 'Now, do tell it to me. You know how I delight in hearing anything of the kind.'

'Well, I will, as a sort of compensation for my peevishness towards you,' said the other, clasping her friend's hands. 'Now, listen! I had walked up and down my room for a long time; I was excited – out of spirits – I do not know exactly what. It was almost midnight ere I lay down, but I could not sleep. I tossed about, and at length it was only from sheer exhaustion that I dropped off. But what a sleep it was! An inward fear ran through me perpetually. I saw a number of pictures before me, as I used to do in childish sicknesses. I do not know whether I was asleep or half awake. Then I dreamed, but as clearly as if I had been wide awake, that a sort of mist filled the room, and out of it stepped the knight Azzo. He gazed at me for a time, and then letting himself slowly down on one knee, imprinted a kiss on my throat. Long did his lips rest there; and I felt a slight pain, which always went on increasing, until I could bear it no more. With all my strength I tried to force the vision from me, but succeeded only after a long struggle. No doubt I uttered a scream, for that awoke me from my trance. when I came a little to my senses, I felt a sort of superstitious fear creeping over me – how great you may imagine when I tell you that, with my eyes open and awake, it appeared to me as if Azzo's figure were still by my bed, and then disappearing gradually into the mist, vanished at the door!'

'You must have dreamed very heavily, my poor friend,' began Bertha, but suddenly paused. She gazed with surprise at Franziska's throat. 'Why, what is that?' she cried. ' Just look: how extraordinary – a red streak on your throat!'

Franziska raised herself, and went to a little glass that stood in the window. She really saw a small red line about an inch long on her neck, which began to smart when she touched it with her finger.

'I must have hurt myself by some means in my sleep,' she said after a pause; 'and that in some measure will account for my dream.'

The friends continued chatting for some time about this singular coincidence – the dream and the stranger; and at length it was all turned into a joke by Bertha.

Several weeks passed. The knight had found the estate and affairs in greater disorder than he at first imagined; and instead of remaining three or four weeks, as was originally intended, their departure was deferred to an indefinite period. This postponement was likewise in some measure occasioned by Franziska's continued indisposition. She who had formerly bloomed like a rose in its young fresh beauty, was becoming daily thinner, more sickly and exhausted, and at the same time so pale, that in the space of a month not a tinge of red was perceptible on the once glowing cheek. The knight's anxiety about her was extreme, and the best advice was procured which the age and country afforded; but all to no purpose. Franziska complained from time to time that the horrible dream with which her illness commenced was repeated, and that always on the day following she felt an increased and indescribable weakness. Bertha naturally set this down to the effect of fever, but the ravages of that fever on the usually clear reason of her friend filled her with alarm.

The knight Azzo repeated his visits every now and then. He always came in the evening, and when the moon shone brightly. His manner was always the same. He spoke in monosyllables, and was coldly polite to the knight; to Franz and Bertha, particularly to the former, contemptuous and haughty; but to Franziska, friendliness itself. Often when, after a short visit, he again left the house, his peculiarities became the subject of conversation. Besides his old way of speaking, in which Bertha said there lay a deep hatred, a cold detestation of all mankind with the exception of Franziska, two other singularities were observable. During none of his visits, which often took place at supper-time, had he been prevailed upon to eat or drink anything, and that without giving any good reason for his abstinence. A remarkable alteration, too, had taken place in his appearance; he seemed an entirely different creature. The skin, before so shrivelled and stretched, seemed smooth and soft, while a slight tinge of red appeared in his cheeks, which began to look round and plump. Bertha, who could not at all conceal her ill-will towards him, said often, that much as she hated his face before, when it was more like a death's-head than a human being's, it was now more than ever repulsive; she always felt a shudder run through her veins whenever his sharp piercing eyes rested on her. Perhaps it was owing to Franziska's partiality, or to the knight Azzo's own contemptuous way of replying to Franz, or to his haughty way of treating him in general, that made the young man dislike him more and more. It was quite observable, that whenever Franz made a remark to his cousin in the presence of Azzo, the latter would immediately throw some ill-natured light on it, or distort it to a totally different meaning. This increased from day to day, and at last Franz declared to Bertha, that he would stand such conduct no longer, and that it was only out of consideration for Franziska that he had not already called him to account.

At this time the party at the castle was increased by the arrival of Bertha's long-expected guest. He came just as they were sitting down to supper one evening, and all jumped up to greet their old friend. The knight Woislaw was a true model of the soldier, hardened and strengthened by war with men and elements. His face would not have been termed ugly, if a Turkish sabre had not left a mark running from the right eye to the left cheek, and standing out bright red from the sunburned skin. The frame of the Castellan of Glogau might almost be termed colossal. Few would have been able to carry his armour, and still fewer move with his lightness and ease under its weight. He did not think little of this same armour, for it had been a present from the Palatine of Hungary on his leaving the camp. The blue wrought-steel was ornamented all over with patterns in gold; and he had put it on to do honour to his bride-elect, together with the wonderful gold hand, the gift of the duke.

Woislaw was questioned by the knight and Franz on all the concerns of the campaign; and he entered into the most minute particulars relating to the battles which, with regard to plunder, had been more successful than ever. He spoke much of the strength of the Turks in a hand-to-hand fight, and remarked that he owed the duke many thanks for his splendid gift, for in consequence of its strength many of the enemy regarded him as something superhuman. The sickliness and deathlike paleness of Franziska was too perceptible not to be immediately noticed by Woislaw; accustomed to see her so fresh and cheerful, he hastened to inquire into the cause of the change. Bertha related all that had happened, and Woislaw listened with the greatest interest. This increased to the utmost at the account of the often-repeated dream, and Franziska

had to give him the most minute particulars of it; it appeared as though he had met with a similar case before, or at least had heard of one. When the young lady added, that it was very remarkable that the wound on her throat which she had at first felt had never healed, and still pained her, the knight Woislaw looked at Bertha as much as to say, that this last fact had greatly strengthened his idea as to the cause of Franziska's illness.

It was only natural that the discourse should next turn to the knight Azzo, about whom every one began to talk eagerly. Woislaw inquired as minutely as he had done with regard to Franziska's illness, about what concerned this stranger, from the first evening of their acquaintance down to his last visit, without, however, giving any opinion on the subject. The party were still in earnest conversation, when the door opened, and Azzo entered. Woislaw's eyes remained fixed on him, as he, without taking any particular notice of the new arrival, walked up to the table, and seating himself, directed most of the conversation to Franziska and her father, and now and then made some sarcastic remark when Franz began to speak. The Turkish war again came on the *tapis*, and though Azzo only put in an occasional remark, Woislaw had much to say on the subject. Thus they had advanced late into the night, and Franz said smiling to Woislaw: 'I should not wonder if day had surprised us, whilst listening to your entertaining adventures.'

'I admire the young gentleman's taste,' said Azzo, with an ironical curl of the lip. 'Stories of storm and shipwreck are, indeed, best heard on *terra firma*, and those of battle and death at a hospitable table or in the chimney-corner. One had then the comfortable feeling of keeping a whole skin, and being in no danger, not even of taking cold.' With the last words, he gave a hoarse laugh, and turning his back on Franz, rose, bowed to the rest of the company, and left the room. The knight, who always accompanied Azzo to the door, now expressed himself fatigued, and bade his friends good night.

'That Azzo's impertinence is unbearable,' cried Bertha when he was gone. 'He becomes daily more rough, impolite and presuming. If only on account of Franziska's dream, though of course he cannot help that, I detest him. Now, tonight, not one civil word has he spoken to any one but Franziska, except, perhaps, some casual remark to my uncle.'

'I cannot deny that you are right, Bertha,' said her cousin. 'One may forgive much to a man whom fate had probably made somewhat misanthropical; but he should not overstep the bounds of common politeness. But where on earth is Franz?' added Franziska, as she looked uneasily round. – The young man had quietly left the room whilst Bertha was speaking.

'He cannot have followed the knight Azzo to challenge him?' cried Bertha in alarm.

'It were better he entered a lion's den to pull his mane!' said Woislaw vehemently. 'I must follow him instantly,' he added, as he rushed from the room.

He hastened over the threshold, out of the castle and through the court, before he came up to them. Here a narrow bridge with a slight balustrade passed over the moat by which the castle was surrounded. It appeared that Franz had only just addressed Azzo in a few hot words, for as Woislaw, unperceived by either, advanced under the shadow of the wall, Azzo said gloomily: 'Leave me, foolish boy – leave me; for by that sun' – and he pointed to the full moon above them – 'you will see those rays no more if you linger another moment on my path.'

'And I tell you, wretch, that you either give me satisfaction for your repeated insolence, or you die,' cried Franz, drawing his sword.

Azzo stretched forth his hand, and grasping the sword in the middle, it snapped like a broken reed. 'I warn you for the last time,' he said in a voice of thunder, as he threw the pieces into the moat. 'Now, away – away, boy, from my path, or, by those below us, you are lost!'

'You or I! you or I!' cried Franz madly, as he made a rush at the sword of his antagonist, and strove to draw it from his side. Azzo replied not; only a bitter laugh half escaped from his lips; then seizing Franz by the chest, he lifted him up like an infant, and was in the act of throwing him over the bridge, when Woislaw stepped to his side. With a grasp of his wonderful hand, into the springs of which he threw all his strength, he seized Azzo's arm, pulled it down, and obliged him to drop his victim. Azzo seemed in the highest degree astonished. Without concerning himself further about Franz, he gazed in amazement on Woislaw.

'Who are thou who darest to rob me of my prey?' he asked hesitatingly. 'Is it possible? Can you be – '

'Ask not, thou bloody one! Go, seek thy nourishment! Soon comes thy hour!' replied Woislaw in a calm but firm tone.

'Ha, now I know!' cried Azzo eagerly. 'Welcome, blood-brother! I give up to you this worm, and for your sake will not crush him. Farewell; our paths will soon meet again.'

'Soon, very soon; farewell!' cried Woislaw, drawing Franz towards him. Azzo rushed away, and disappeared.

Franz had remained for some moments in a state of stupefaction, but suddenly started as from a dream. 'I am dishonoured, dishonoured for ever!' he cried, as he pressed his clenched hands to his forehead.

'Calm yourself; you could not have conquered,' said Woislaw.

'But I will conquer, or perish!' cried Franz incensed. 'I will seek this adventurer in his den, and he or I must fall.'

'You could not hurt him,' said Woislaw. 'You would infallibly be the victim.'

'Then show me a way to bring the wretch to judgment,' cried Franz, seizing Woislaw's hands, while tears of anger sprang to his eyes. 'Disgraced as I am, I cannot live.'

'You shall be revenged, and that within twenty-four hours, I hope; but only on two conditions –'

'I agree to them! I will do anything –' began the young man eagerly.

'The first is, that you do nothing, but leave everything in my hands,' interrupted Woislaw. 'The second, that you will assist me in persuading Franziska to do what I shall represent to her as absolutely necessary. That young lady's life is in more danger from Azzo than your own!'

'How? What?' cried Franz fiercely. 'Franziska's life in danger! and from that man? Tell me, Woislaw, who is this fiend?'

'Not a word will I tell either the young lady or you, until the danger is passed,' said Woislaw firmly. 'The smallest indiscretion would ruin everything. No one can act here but Franziska herself, and if she refuses to do so she is irretrievably lost.'

'Speak, and I will help you. I will do all you wish, but I must know –'

'Nothing, absolutely nothing,' replied Woislaw. 'I must have both you and Franziska yield to me unconditionally. Come now, come to her. You are to be mute on what has passed, and use every effort to induce her to accede to my proposal.'

Woislaw spoke firmly, and it was impossible for Franz to make any further objection; in a few moments they both entered the hall, where they found the young girls still anxiously awaiting them.

'Oh, I have been so frightened,' said Franziska, even paler than usual, as she held out her hand to Franz. 'I trust all has ended peaceably.'

'Everything is arranged; a couple of words were sufficient to settle the whole affair,' said Woislaw cheerfully. 'But Master Franz was less concerned in it than yourself, fair lady.'

'I! How do you mean?' said Franziska in surprise.

'I allude to your illness,' replied the other.

'And you spoke of that to Azzo? Does he, then, know a remedy which he could not tell me himself?' she inquired, smiling painfully.

'The knight Azzo must take part in your cure; but speak to you about it he cannot, unless the remedy is to lose all its efficacy,' replied Woislaw quietly.

'So it is some secret elixir, as the learned doctors say, who have so long attended me, and through whose means I only grow worse,' said Franziska mournfully.

'It is certainly a secret, but is as certainly a cure,' replied Woislaw.

'So said all, but none has succeeded,' said the young lady peevishly.

'You might at least try it,' began Bertha.

'Because your friend proposes it,' said the other smiling. 'I have no doubt that you, with nothing ailing you, would take all manner of drugs to please your knight; but with me the inducement is wanting, and therefore also the faith.'

'I did not speak of any medicine,' said Woislaw.

'Oh! a magical remedy! I am to be cured – what was it the quack who was here the other day called it? – "by sympathy." Yes, that was it.'

'I do not object to your calling it so, if you like,' said Woislaw smiling; 'but you must know, dear lady, that the measures I shall propose must be attended to literally, and according to the strictest directions.'

'And you trust this to me?' asked Franziska.

'Certainly,' said Woislaw hesitating; 'but – '

'Well, why do you not proceed? Can you think that I shall fail in courage?' she asked.

'Courage is certainly necessary for the success of my plan,' said Woislaw gravely; 'and it is because I give you credit for a large share of that virtue, I venture to propose it at all, although for the real harmlessness of the remedy I will answer with my life, provided you follow my directions exactly.'

'Well, tell me the plan, and then I can decide,' said the young lady.

'I can only tell you that when we commence our operations,' replied Woislaw.

'Do you think I am a child to be sent here, there and everywhere, without a reason?' asked Franziska, with something of her old pettishness.

'You did me great injustice, dear lady, if you thought for a moment I would propose anything disagreeable to you, unless demanded by the sternest necessity,' said Woislaw; 'and yet I can only repeat my former words.'

'Then I will not do it,' cried Franziska. 'I have already tried so much, and all ineffectually.'

'I give you my honour as a knight, that your cure is certain, but – you must pledge yourself solemnly and unconditionally to do implicitly what I shall direct,' said Woislaw earnestly.

'Oh, I implore you to consent, Franziska. Our friend would not propose anything unnecessary,' said Bertha, taking both her cousin's hands.

'And let me join my entreaties to Bertha's,' said Franz.

'How strange you all are!' exclaimed Franziska, shaking her head; 'you make such a secret of that which I must know if I am to accomplish it, and then you declare so positively that I shall recover, when my own feelings tell me it is quite hopeless.'

'I repeat, that I will answer for the result,' said Woislaw, 'on the condition I mentioned before, and that you have courage to carry out what you commence.'

'Ha! now I understand; this, after all, is the only thing which appears doubtful to you,' cried Franziska. 'Well, to show you that our sex are neither wanting in the will nor in the power to accomplish deeds of daring, I give my consent.'

With the last words, she offered Woislaw her hand.

'Our compact is thus sealed,' she pursued smiling. 'Now say, Sir Knight, how am I to commence this mysterious cure?'

'It commenced when you gave your consent,' said Woislaw gravely. 'Now, I have only to request that you will ask no more questions, but hold yourself in readiness to take a ride with me tomorrow an hour before sunset. I also request that you will not mention to your father a word of what has passed.'

'Strange!' said Franziska.

'You have made the compact; you are not wanting in resolution; and I will answer for everything else,' said Woislaw encouragingly.

'Well, so let it be. I will follow your directions,' said the lady, although she still looked incredulous.

'On our return you shall know everything; before that, it is quite impossible,' said Woislaw in conclusion. 'Now go, dear lady, and take some rest; you will need strength for tomorrow.'

It was on the morning of the following day, the sun had not risen above an hour, and the dew still lay like a veil of pearls on the grass, or dripped from the petals of the flowers, swaying in the early breeze, when the knight Woislaw hastened over the fields towards the forest, and turned into a gloomy path, which by the direction, one could perceive, led towards the towers of Klatka. When he arrived at the old oak tree we have before had occasion to mention, he sought carefully along the road for traces of human footsteps, but only a deer had passed that way; and seemingly satisfied with his search, he proceeded on his way, though not before he had half drawn his dagger from its sheath, as though to assure himself that it was ready for service in time of need.

Slowly he ascended the path; it was evident he carried something beneath his cloak. Arrived in the court, he left the ruins of the castle to the left, and entered the old chapel. In the chancel, he looked eagerly and earnestly around. A deathlike stillness reigned in the deserted sanctuary, only broken by the whispering of the wind in an old thorn-tree which grew outside. Woislaw had looked round him ere he perceived the door leading down to the vault; he hurried towards it, and descended. The sun's position enabled its rays to penetrate the crevices, and made the subterranean chamber so light, that one could read easily the inscriptions at the head and feet of the coffins. The knight first laid on the ground the packet he had hitherto carried under his cloak, and then going from coffin to coffin, at last remained stationary before the oldest of them. He read the inscription carefully, drew his dagger thoughtfully from its case, and endeavoured to raise the lid with its point. This was no difficult matter, for the rusty iron nails kept but a slight hold of the rotten wood. On looking in, only a heap of ashes, some remnants of dress, and a skull were the contents. He quickly closed it again, and went on to the next, passing over those of a woman and two children. Here things had much the same appearance, except that the corpse held together till the lid was raised, and then fell into dust, a few linen rags and bones being alone perceptible. In the third, fourth, and nearly the next half-dozen, the bodies were in better preservation: in some, they looked a sort of yellow brown mummy; whilst in others, a skinless skull covered with hair grinned from the coverings of velvet, silk or mildewed embroideries; all, however, were touched with the loathsome marks of decay. Only one more coffin now remained to be inspected; Woislaw approached it, and read the inscription. It was the same that had before attracted the Knight of Fahnenberg: Ezzelin von Klatka, the last possessor of the tower, was described as lying therein. Woislaw found it more difficult to raise the lid here; and it was only by the exertion of much strength he at length succeeded in extracting the nails. He did all, however, as quietly as if afraid of rousing some sleeper within; he then raised the cover, and cast a glance on the corpse. An involuntary 'Ha!' burst from his lips as he stepped back a pace. If he had less expected the sight that met his eyes, he would have been far more overcome. In the coffin lay Azzo as he lived and breathed, and as Woislaw had seen him at the supper-table only the evening before. His appearance, dress and all were the same; besides, he had more the semblance of sleep than of death – no trace of decay was visible – there was even a rosy tint on his cheeks. Only the circumstance that the breast did not heave, distinguished him from one who slept. For a few moments Woislaw did not move; he could only stare into the coffin. With a hastiness in his movements not usual with him, he suddenly seized the lid, which had fallen from his hands, and laying it on the coffin, knocked the nails into their places. As soon as he had completed this work, he fetched the packet he had left at the entrance, and laying it on the top of the coffin, hastily ascended the steps, and quitted the church and the ruins.

The day passed. Before evening, Franziska requested her father to allow her to take a ride with Woislaw, under pretence of showing him the country. He, only too happy to think this a sign of amendment in his daughter, readily gave his consent; so followed by a single servant, they mounted and left the castle. Woislaw was unusually silent and serious. When Franziska began to rally him about his gravity, and the approaching sympathetic care, he replied that what was before her was no laughing matter; and that although the result would be certainly a cure, still it would leave an impression on her whole future life. In such discourse they reached the wood, and at length the oak, where they left their horses. Woislaw gave Franziska his arm, and they ascended the hill slowly and silently. They had just reached one of the half-dilapidated outworks where they could catch a glimpse of the open country, when Woislaw, speaking more to himself than to his companion, said: 'In a quarter of an hour, the sun will set, and in another hour the moon will have risen; then all must be accomplished. It will soon be time to commence the work.'

'Then, I should think it was time to entrust me with some idea of what it is,' said Franziska, looking at him.

'Well, lady,' he replied, turning towards her, and his voice was very solemn, 'I entreat you, Franziska von Fahnenberg, for your own good, and as you love the father who clings to you with his whole soul, that you will weigh well my words, and that you will not interrupt me with questions which I cannot answer until the work is completed. Your life is in the greatest danger from the illness under which you are labouring; indeed, you are irrecoverably lost if you do not fully carry out what I shall now impart to you. Now, promise me to do implicitly as I shall tell you; I pledge you my knightly word it is nothing against Heaven, or the honour of your house; and, besides, it is the sole means for saving you.' With these words, he held out his right hand to his companion, while he raised the other to heaven in confirmation of his oath.

'I promise you,' said Franziska, visibly moved by Woislaw's solemn tone, as she laid her little white and wasted hand in his.

'Then, come; it is time,' was his reply, as he led her towards the church. The last rays of the sun were just pouring through the broken windows. They entered the chancel, the best preserved part of the whole building; here there were still some old kneeling-stools, placed before the high-altar, although nothing remained of that but the stonework and a few steps; the pictures and decorations had all vanished.

'Say an *Ave*; you will have need of it,' said Woislaw, as he himself fell on his knees.

Franziska knelt beside him, and repeated a short prayer. After a few moments, both rose.

'The moment has arrived! The sun sinks, and before the moon rises, all must be over,' said Woislaw quickly.

'What am I to do?' asked Franziska cheerfully.

'You see there that open vault!' replied the knight Woislaw, pointing to the door and flight of steps: 'You must descend. You must go alone; I may not accompany you. When you have reached the vault you will find, close to the entrance, a coffin, on which is placed a small packet. Open this packet, and you will find three long iron nails and a hammer. Then pause for a moment; but when I begin to repeat the *Credo* in a loud voice, knock with all your might, first one nail, then a second, and then a third, into the lid of the coffin, right up to their heads.'

Franziska stood thunderstruck; her whole body trembled, and she could not utter a word. Woislaw perceived it.

'Take courage, dear lady!' said he. 'Think that you are in the hands of Heaven, and that without the will of your Creator, not a

hair can fall from your head. Besides, I repeat, there is no danger.'

'Well, then, I will do it,' cried Franziska, in some measure regaining courage.

'Whatever you may hear, whatever takes place inside the coffin,' continued Woislaw, 'must have no effect upon you. Drive the nails well in, without flinching: your work must be finished before my prayer comes to an end.'

Franziska shuddered, but again recovered herself. 'I will do it; Heaven will send me strength,' she murmured softly.

'There is one thing more,' said Woislaw hesitatingly; 'perhaps it is the hardest of all I have proposed, but without it your cure will not be complete. When you have done as I have told you, a sort of' – he hesitated – 'a sort of liquid will flow from the coffin; in this dip your finger, and besmear the scratch on your throat.'

'Horrible!' cried Franziska. 'This liquid is blood. A human being lies in the coffin.'

'An *unearthly one* lies therein! That blood is your own, but it flows in other veins,' said Woislaw gloomily. 'Ask no more; the sand is running out.'

Franziska summoned up all her powers of mind and body, went towards the steps which led to the vault, and Woislaw sank on his knees before the altar in quiet prayer. When the lady had descended, she found herself before the coffin on which lay the packet before mentioned. A sort of twilight reigned in the vault, and everything around was so still and peaceful, that she felt more calm, and going up to the coffin, opened the packet. She had hardly seen that a hammer and three long nails were its contents when suddenly Woislaw's voice rang through the church, and broke the stillness of the aisles. Franziska started, but recognised the appointed prayer. She seized one of the nails, and with one stroke of the hammer drove it at least an inch into the cover. All was still; nothing was heard but the echo of the stroke. Taking heart, the maiden grasped the hammer with both hands, and struck the nail twice with all her might, right up to the head into the wood. At this moment commenced a rustling noise; it seemed as though something in the interior began to move and to struggle. Franziska drew back in alarm. She was already on the point of throwing away the hammer, and flying up the steps, when Woislaw raised his voice so powerfully, and it sounded so entreatingly, that in a sort of excitement, such as would induce one to rush into a lion's den, she returned to the coffin, determined to bring things to a conclusion. Hardly knowing what she did, she placed a second nail in the centre of the lid, and after some strokes, this was likewise buried to its head. The struggle now increased fearfully, as if some living creature were striving to burst the coffin. This was so shaken by it, that it cracked and split on all sides. Half distracted, Franziska seized the third nail; she thought no more of her ailments, she only knew herself to be in terrible danger, of what kind she could not guess: in an agony that threatened to rob her of her senses, and in the midst of the turning and cracking of the coffin, in which low groans were now heard, she struck the third nail in equally tight. At this moment, she began to lose consciousness. She wished to hasten away, but staggered; and mechanically grasping at something to save herself by, she seized the corner of the coffin, and sank fainting beside it on the ground.

A quarter of an hour might have elapsed, when she again opened her eyes. She looked around her. Above was the starry sky, and the moon, which shed her cold light on the ruins and on the tops of the old oak trees. Franziska was lying outside the church walls, Woislaw on his knees beside her, holding her hand in his.

'Heaven be praised that you live!' he cried, with a sigh of relief. 'I was beginning to doubt whether the remedy had not been too severe, and yet it was the only thing to save you.'

Franziska recovered her full consciousness very gradually. The past seemed to her like a dreadful dream. Only a few moments before, that fearful scene; and now this quiet all around her. She hardly dared at first to raise her eyes, and shuddered when she found herself only a few paces removed from the spot where she had undergone such terrible agony. She listened half unconsciously, now to the pacifying words Woislaw addressed to her, now to the whistling of the servant, who stood by the horses, and who, to wile away his time, was imitating the evening-song of a belated cow herd.

'Let us go,' whispered Franziska, as she strove to raise herself 'But what is this? My shoulder is wet, my throat, my hand –'

'It is probably the evening dew on the grass,' said Woislaw gently.

'No; it is blood!' she cried, springing up with horror in her tone. 'See, my hand is full of blood!'

'Oh, you are mistaken – surely mistaken,' said Woislaw stammering. 'Or perhaps the wound on your neck may have opened! Pray, feel whether this is the case.' He seized her hand, and directed it to the spot.

'I do not perceive anything; I feel no pain,' she said at length, somewhat angrily.

'Then, perhaps, when you fainted, you may have struck a corner of the coffin, or have torn yourself with the point of one of the nails,' suggested Woislaw.

'Oh, of what do you remind me!' cried Franziska shuddering. 'Let us away – away! I entreat you, come! I will not remain a moment longer near this dreadful, dreadful place.'

They descended the path much quicker than they came. Woislaw placed his companion on her horse, and they were soon on their way home.

When they approached the castle, Franziska began to inundate her protector with questions about the preceding adventure; but he declared that her present state of excitement must make him defer all explanations till the morning, when her curiosity should be satisfied. On their arrival, he conducted her at once to her room, and told the knight his daughter was too much fatigued with her ride to appear at the supper-table. On the following morning,

Franziska rose earlier than she had done for a long time. She assured her friend it was the first time since her illness commenced that she had been really refreshed by her sleep and, what was still more remarkable, she had not been troubled by her old terrible dream. Her improved looks were not only remarked by Bertha, but by Franz and the knight; and with Woislaw's permission, she related the adventures of the previous evening. No sooner had she concluded, than Woislaw was completely stormed with questions about such a strange occurrence.

'Have you' said the latter, turning towards his host, 'ever heard of Vampires?'

'Often,' replied he; 'but I have never believed in them.'

'Nor did I,' said Woislaw; 'but I have been assured of their existence by experience.'

'Oh, tell us what occurred,' cried Bertha eagerly, as a light seemed to dawn on her.

'It was during my first campaign in Hungary,' began Woislaw, 'when I was rendered helpless for some time by this sword-cut of a janizary across my face, and another on my shoulder. I had been taken into the house of a respectable family in a small town. It consisted of the father and mother, and a daughter about twenty years of age. They obtained their living by selling the very good wine of the country, and the taproom was always full of visitors. Although the family were well to do in the world, there seemed to brood over them a continual melancholy, caused by the constant illness of the only daughter, a very pretty and excellent girl. She had always bloomed like a rose, but for some months she had been getting so thin and wasted, and that without any satisfactory reason: they tried every means to restore her, but in vain. As the army had encamped quite in the neighbourhood, of course a number of people of all countries assembled in the tavern. Amongst these there was one man who came every evening, when the moon shone, who struck everybody by the peculiarity of his manners and appearance; he looked dried up and deathlike, and hardly spoke at all; but what he did say was bitter and sarcastic. Most attention was excited towards him by the circumstance, that although he always ordered a cup of the best wine, and now and then raised it to his lips, the cup was always as full after his departure as at first.'

'This all agrees wonderfully with the appearance of Azzo,' said Bertha, deeply interested.

'The daughter of the house,' continued Woislaw, 'became daily worse, despite the aid not only of Christian doctors, but of many amongst the heathen prisoners, who were consulted in the hope that they might have some magical remedy to propose. It was singular that the girl always complained of a dream, in which the unknown guest worried and plagued her.'

'Just the same as your dream, Franziska,' cried Bertha.

'One evening,' resumed Woislaw, 'an old Sclavonian – who had made many voyages to Turkey and Greece, and had even seen the New World – and I were sitting over our wine, and sat down at the table. The bottle passed quickly between my friend and me, whilst we talked of all manner of things, of our adventures, and of passages in our lives, both horrible and amusing. We went on chatting thus for about an hour, and drank a tolerable quantity of wine. The unknown had remained perfectly silent the whole time, only smiling contemptuously every now and then. He now paid his money, and was going away. All this had quietly worried me – perhaps the wine had got a little into my head – so I said to the stranger: "Hold, you stony stranger; you have hitherto done nothing but listen, and have not even emptied your cup. Now you shall take your turn in telling us something amusing, and if you do not drink up your wine, it shall produce a quarrel between us." "Yes," said the Sclavonian, "you must remain; you shall chat and drink, too;" and he grasped – for although no longer young, he was big and very strong – the stranger by the shoulder, to pull him down to his seat again: the latter, however, although as thin as a skeleton, with one movement of his hand flung the Sclavonian to the middle of the room, and half stunned him for a moment. I now approached to hold the stranger back. I caught him by the arm; and although the springs of my iron hand were less powerful than those I have at present, I must have gripped him rather hard in my anger, for after looking grimly at me for a moment, he bent towards me and whispered in my ear: "Let me go: from the gripe of your fist, I see you are my brother, therefore do not hinder me from seeking my bloody nourishment. I am hungry!" Surprised by such words, I let him loose, and almost before I was aware he had left the room. As soon as I had in some degree recovered from my astonishment, I told the Sclavonian what I had heard. He started, evidently alarmed. I asked him to tell me the cause of his fears, and pressed him for an explanation of those extraordinary words. On our way to his lodging, he complied with my request. "The stranger," said he, "is a vampire!"

'How?' cried the knight, Franziska, and Bertha simultaneously, in a voice of horror. 'So this Azzo was –'

'Nothing less. He also was a Vampire!' replied Woislaw. 'But at all events *his* hellish thirst is quenched for ever; he will never return. – But I have not finished. As in my country vampires had never been heard of, I questioned the Sclavonian minutely. He said that in Hungary, Croatia, Dalmatia and Bosnia, these hellish guests were not uncommon. They were deceased persons, who had either once served as nourishment to vampires, or who had died in deadly sin, or under excommunication; and that whenever the moon shone, they rose from their graves, and sucked the blood of the living.'

'Horrible!' cried Franziska. 'If you had told me all this beforehand, I should never have accomplished the work.'

'So I thought; and yet it must be executed by the sufferers themselves, while some one else performs the devotions,' replied Woislaw. 'The Sclavonian,' he continued after a short pause, 'added many other facts with regard to these unearthly visitants. He said that whilst their victim wasted, they themselves improved in appearance, and that a vampire possessed enormous strength –'

'Now I can understand the change your false hand produced on Azzo,' interrupted Franz.

'Yes, that was it,' replied Woislaw. 'Azzo, as well as the other vampire, mistook its great power for that of a natural one, and concluded I was one of his own species. – You may now imagine, dear lady,' he continued, turning to Franziska, 'how alarmed I was at your appearance when I arrived: all you and Bertha told me increased my anxiety; and when I saw Azzo, I could doubt no longer that he was a vampire. As I learned from your account that a grave with the name Ezzelin von Klatka lay in the neighbourhood, I had no doubt that you might be saved if I could only induce you to assist me. It did not appear to me advisable to impart the whole facts of the case, for your bodily powers were so impaired, that an idea of the horrors before you might have quite unfitted you for the exertion; for this reason, I arranged everything in the manner in which it has taken place.'

'You did wisely,' replied Franziska shuddering. 'I can never be grateful enough to you. Had I known what was required of me, I never could have undertaken the deed.'

'That was what I feared,' said Woislaw; 'but fortune has favoured us all through.'

'And what became of the unfortunate girl in Hungary?' inquired Bertha.

'I know not,' replied Woislaw. 'That very evening there was an alarm of Turks, and we were ordered off. I never heard anything more of her.'

The conversation upon these strange occurrences continued for some time longer. The knight determined to have the vault at Klatka walled up for ever. This took place on the following day; the knight alleging as a reason that he did not wish the dead to be disturbed by irreverent hands.

Franziska recovered gradually. Her health had been so severely shaken, that it was long ere her strength was so much restored as to allow of her being considered out of danger. The young lady's character underwent a great change in the interval. Its former strength was, perhaps, in some degree diminished, but in place of that, she had acquired a benevolent softness, which brought out all her best qualities. Franz continued his attentions to his cousin; but, perhaps, owing to a hint from Bertha, he was less assiduous in his exhibition of them. His inclinations did not lead him to the battle, the camp or the attainment of honours; his great aim was to increase the good condition and happiness of his tenants, and to this he contributed the whole energy of his mind. Franziska could not withstand the unobtrusive signs of the young man's continued attachment; and it was not long ere the credit she was obliged to yield to his noble efforts for the welfare of his fellow-creatures, changed into a liking, which went on increasing, until at length it assumed the character of love. As Woislaw insisted on making Bertha his wife before he returned to Silesia, it was arranged that the marriage should take place at their present abode. How joyful was the surprise of the knight of Fahnenberg, when his daughter and Franz likewise entreated his blessing, and expressed their desire of being united on the same day! That day soon came round, and it saw the bright looks of two happy couples.

THE GHOST DETECTIVE
by Mark Lemon

'You take an interest in Christmas legends, I believe?' said my friend Carraway, passing the claret.

Yes, I think they are as good as any other,' I replied.

'And have faith in ghosts?'

'Well, I must answer that question with an equivocation. Yes – no.'

'Then if you care to listen, I can, I fancy, remove your scepticism,' said Carraway.

I professed my willingness to be converted, provided I might smoke whilst my friend talked, and the conditions being agreed to, Carraway commenced:

'When I first came into the City – now some thirty years ago – I formed an intimacy with a young man in the wine trade, and we passed most of our leisure time together. He was much liked by his employers, whose principal business was with publicans and tavern-keepers, and after a time my friend became their town traveller – a position of trust and fair emolument. This advancement enabled my friend, James Loxley, to carry out a long-cherished desire, and that was to marry a fair cousin to whom he had been attached from his boyhood. The girl was one of those pretty *blondes* that are so attractive to young fellows with a turn for the sentimental, and a

tendency to sing about violet eyes and golden hair and all that. I was never given that way myself, and I confess Loxley's cousin would not have been the woman I should have chosen for a wife had I ever thought of taking to myself an encumbrance. I had had a step-mother, and she cured me of any matrimonial inclinations which I might have had at one time. Well, Loxley thought differently from me, and his marriage with his cousin, Martha Lovett, was settled, and I was appointed best man upon the occasion.

'The bride certainly looked very pretty in her plain white dress – very pretty, though somewhat paler than usual, and that perhaps made me think more than ever that Martha was not the wife my friend James should have selected, knowing as I did that they would only have his salary to live upon, and that much would depend upon her to make his means sufficient for decent comfort. However, they were sincerely attached to each other, and that, I was told, was worth one or two hundred a year, which I did not believe. Martha was greatly agitated at the altar, and at one time I thought she would have fainted before the ceremony, as they call it, had finished. As it was, she had a slight attack of hysteria in the vestry, but the pew-opener told me that was nothing unusual with brides, especially with those who had been widows.

'The wedding-breakfast was a quiet affair – nothing like the sacrificial feasts of the present day – and we were all merry enough until the happy pair were to leave for their own home, and the poor little Martha hung about her mother's neck and sobbed – much more than I thought was complimentary to her new husband – but then I was not a fair judge of the sex, having been worried all my life by a step-mother.

'When Loxley and his wife were fairly settled in their new home I used frequently to pop in for a game at cribbage or a chat with my old friend, and a more loving couple I never saw in my life. Not being by any means rich, they had babies, of course, and in less than three years, there were two most charming creatures – when they

didn't cry or poke out their eyes with tea-spoons, or perform any other of those antics which are the delight of parents, but can only be designated as inflictions to unattached spectators.

'I have thought it only fair to mention these little matters; you will see wherefore by and by.

'Loxley had invited me to take my Christmas dinner with him, and a pleasant day we had! He was partial to keeping Christmas with all the honours, and his little dining-room – it was his drawing-room also – was sprigged about with holly, even to the picture frames. He had only two oil paintings – portraits of his father and mother, both long deceased, but the likenesses, he said, were so good, that he could always fancy his parents were present.

'Well, as I have mentioned, we passed a happy day and night; Loxley had arranged to go with me for a couple of days into the country, on a visit to a good old uncle of mine, as an atonement for keeping me away from the family dinner.

'The visit was paid; but I was rather annoyed at the effort which Loxley evidently made to appear entertained, and I thought he was homesick, or vexed that I had not invited his wife to join us, as there were lady visitors at my uncle's. Whatever was the cause of his frequent abstractions, I could only regret it, as I had given him such a good character for cheerfulness and pleasant companionship, that one of my cousins twitted me, with rural delicacy, for having brought a thorough wet blanket from London.

'During our journey back to town Loxley was silent and thoughtful, and I longed to ask if anything troubled him. But we had passed such a jovial Christmas Day together that I could not suppose he had any other anxiety than what the restoration to the arms of his Martha would remove. We parted, however, without any explanation being asked or volunteered.

'On the second day after our return, I was astounded at receiving a message from Loxley to come to him at the Mansion House. The officer who brought the note told me that Loxley was in custody,

charged, he believed, by his employer with no less an offence than embezzlement.

'Such an accusation seemed at first to me, who had known Loxley so long, so intimately, preposterous – impossible. As I walked to the Mansion House a cold sweat seized me, and for a moment I thought I should have fallen, as the strange conduct of my friend during the past two days came to my recollection. Had he found his means too small for his home requirements? Had he been tempted, and yielded as good men had done before him? No, no! – a thousand times, no! – if I knew James Loxley rightly.

'He was standing at the prisoners' bar when I reached the Mansion House, and I was not permitted to speak to him. He saw me, however, and knew his friend was with him.

'The junior principal, who had recently joined the firm of X and Co. – by the by, he had for some reason never taken kindly to Loxley – was giving his evidence. He said: "That John Rogers, a customer of the house, had caused a great deal of trouble with his overdue account, and that it was thought he would prove a defaulter. Mr X (the prosecutor) had heard accidentally that Rogers had received a large sum of money, and as Mr Loxley was away from business Mr X had called upon the debtor to demand payment of his debt. Mr X was received with much insolence by Rogers; and his conduct was accounted for subsequently by the production of Loxley's receipt for the money, dated the 24th of December. The man had paid £40 by a cheque to Loxley, and no such amount was credited in the books of X and Co. Rogers produced his banker's book, and the cheque with Loxley's signature on the back. It was found, also, that a person answering by description to Loxley had received two notes of £20 each, one of which had been paid at the Bank of England in gold early on the morning after Christmas Day."

'This evidence was confirmed by John Rogers, who had given the cheque; by the banker's cashier, who had paid it; and by the Bank of England clerk, who had given gold for the note.

'Loxley was asked – having received the usual caution – if he wished to say anything.

'He answered:

'"Yes;" and he thought he had been hardly used by his employers, that an explanation of the matter had not been required from him by them before he had been taken into custody as a thief. He had also heard of Rogers's accession to money; and having the interests of his employers in view, went at once to the man and with great difficulty succeeded in obtaining payment of the debt. He received the cheque but, fearing that Rogers might stop the payment of it at his banker's, he, Loxley, cashed it immediately, placing the notes he received, as he believed, in his pocket-book. As it was Christmas Eve, he did not return to X and Co.'s, the house being closed, but walked home with a friend he had met in the banking house when he received the money for Rogers's cheque. On the morning of the 26th he had intended calling at X and Co.'s on his way to his appointment with me; but, finding he was late, he attached no consequence to the omission, having a holiday. When he was at his journey's end and in his bedroom, he was looking in his pocket-book for some matter or the other, and for the first time missed the banknotes he had received for the cheque. He was completely perplexed, being certain that he had placed the notes in the case, and that he had never lost possession of them. He had employed the morning of his return to town in searching – vainly, he knew – all conceivable places at home for the missing notes, and of course without success. Before he could go to X and Co.'s offices he was taken into custody."

'"One of the notes was cashed at the Bank of England early on the morning of the 26th, was it not?" asked the Lord Mayor.

'The bank clerk who cashed the note said "Yes, it appeared so, but he could not remember exactly whether it was presented by a man or a woman. He thought it was not paid to the prisoner."

'"But it was paid, and in gold," said the Lord Mayor. "The

embezzlement of employers money is one of the gravest offences against the law, and must be severely punished and put a stop to. The statement of the prisoner is very plausible – very feasible, perhaps I should say – but I cannot feel it my duty to decide upon its truth or falsehood. He must be committed for trial."

'Loxley bowed his head and remained immovable, until a shriek in the passage of the court reached him, and he started as from a dream. He instantly looked to where I had been standing, and I understood his meaning. He was right. He had recognised the voice of his wife, who, having heard where they had taken her husband, had followed after. I found her as I had seen her on her wedding day – hysterical, but the attack was very violent; it was with great difficulty I conveyed her to her mother's, and thence to her own home.

'I said all I could to comfort her. I told her my own conviction of Loxley's innocence, my full belief in the explanation which he had given, and the certainty of his speedy liberation. But I spoke to a stricken woman, to a distracted wife, a half mad mother. She sat for some time with her children in her lap, rocking to and fro, and sobbing as though her heart would burst. She cried to me to succour her husband, to bring him home, if not for her sake, for that of her innocent children. She would not let her mother speak, but continued to appeal to me until – yes, I own it – until I fairly broke down and could not answer her. And all this while the green holly garnishing the room, and the faces of the father and mother looking on placidly from the walls.'

The recollection of the painful scene he had been describing made Carraway silent for a time, and I remarked that he had the satisfaction of knowing he had done his duty to his friend, whether he proved guilty or innocent.

'Yes,' continued Carraway. 'I had that satisfaction, though I did not desire to blow my own trumpet in what I have said. Well, when the elder X, who had been away from town, heard of the matter he was inclined to believe Loxley's statement, and blamed his son for

his precipitancy. The matter, however, was beyond his control now, and the law had to vindicate its supremacy.

'The trial came on, and the gentleman whose professional business it was to prove Loxley guilty necessarily did all that was possible to show the weakness of the defence. He asked why Loxley had not instantly returned to town when he had discovered the loss of the notes? Why had he not written to his employers? Why had he not mentioned his loss to me – the friend who he had called to speak of his character? No satisfactory answer could be given for such omissions. What had become of the other note? If a dishonest person had found the notes – supposing them to have been lost – would they not have changed both of them for gold? The most favourable construction which could be placed upon the case was the supposition that the prisoner had need of twenty pounds and had taken his employer's money, intending, very likely, to replace it. That was no uncommon case. The pressure of what seemed to be only a temporary difficulty had often led well-meaning men into such unpardonable breaches of trust. And now, having placed the case as fairly as he could before the jury, his duty was done, and it rested with the twelve intelligent men in the box to pronounce their verdict.

'"Embezzlement," the judge said, very properly, "was a serious crime, and must be repressed by the punishment of offenders. The jury had heard the prosecutor's statement – proved by highly respectable witnesses; and the prisoner's defence – unsupported by any corroborative evidence. The jury had to judge between them."

'Without leaving their box the jury, after a brief consultation, pronounced a verdict of "Guilty," and my friend – my dear friend James Loxley – was sentenced to transportation.

'This terrible sentence was almost fatal to Mrs Loxley. Her delicate constitution would have given way under her excess of grief had not – well, had not I set before her the duty she owed to her children, who had a right to a share in her affection. Poor thing! she struggled

bravely to overcome her great sorrow, but I doubt much if she would have succeeded but for what I am now about to relate to you. Stay – I must mention one or two matters before I tell you that portion of my story.

'The Loxleys occupied only part of the house in which they lived. They had their own furniture, but the landlady of the house provided servants, excepting a little girl who acted as nurse.

'The general servant who waited upon the Loxleys was one of those patient drudges often found in lodging-houses. Her name was Susan, but Loxley had given her the sobriquet of "Dormouse," as she was a drowsy, stupid – perhaps sullen is the better word – girl, who moved about more like a piece of machinery than a living being. She never showed any feeling, either of displeasure or gratification, excepting in her strong attachment to Loxley's children. That arose, perhaps, from her womanly instinct. But when Mrs Loxley's great trouble came, when the girl had come to understand what had befallen Mr Loxley, and that misery and ruin had overtaken them and their children, Susan's whole nature appeared to undergo a change. She seemed to watch every want, every movement of Mrs Loxley. More than once she was found sitting on the stairs near Mrs Loxley's door, when that poor lady was in her paroxysms of grief, as though desirous to lend what aid she could in subduing them. I was so struck by the devotion and sympathy of this poor, stupid creature that I could not help noticing her, and on one occasion offered her money. She refused to take it.

'"No, thank'ee, sir," she said; "that's not what I want; but I should like to be of use to poor missus, if I could, sir."

'I told her she had been of great use, great comfort, to Mrs Loxley, who had seen, as I had, how much she felt for her misfortunes.

'"Yes, sir, that's true enough. And what will they do to Mr Loxley, sir?" she asked.

'"He will have to suffer a great deal, Susan – great misery; but neither you nor I can help him."

'The girl burst into tears, and cried so bitterly that Mrs Loxley overheard her, and I have no doubt questioned her when I was gone.

'Mrs Loxley's mother was staying with her, the elder Mr X having insisted upon making a temporary provision for the unhappy wife of the man he still believed to be innocent – I say Mrs Loxley's mother was staying with her daughter. She had gone to bed in an adjoining room, as Mrs Loxley frequently begged to be allowed to sit alone, as she found it difficult to sleep. I have reason to believe that after her mother had gone to rest, Mrs Loxley had an interview with Susan; but, for reasons which will appear, I never questioned her on that point. It was past midnight, according to Mrs Loxley's statement, when, sitting with her head resting on her hands, she saw the door of her room open, and her husband enter; saw him as plainly and like himself as she had ever seen him. She rose up; but the figure motioned her to remain where she was. She complied; now conscious that it was not her husband in the flesh upon which she looked. The figure sat down in his accustomed place, and then appeared to gaze steadfastly on the portrait of his father, still ornamented with the faded holly twigs which had been placed there at Christmas-time. This continued for some minutes. The figure then rose up and, looking towards Mrs Loxley with a most loving expression on its face, walked from the room, opening and closing the door after it.

'Mrs Loxley tried to follow, but could not. She was not asleep, she had not been even dozing – she was sure of that, but had seen with her waking senses the apparition of her husband, then lying in Newgate prison.

'What followed seemed equally inexplicable to me, who had more than once witnessed her tendency to hysteria and fainting. She said she had felt no alarm at what she had seen. She was stupefied for a few moments, but not alarmed. She went to her mother; but finding her quietly sleeping Mrs Loxley lay down beside her without disturbing her. In the morning she narrated to her mother what she

had witnessed during the past night, and subsequently repeated her story – word for word, her mother said – to me, in the presence of her landlady and the maid Susan.

'The effect upon the poor, dull-witted servant was very remarkable. She fixed her eyes on the portrait which had attracted the notice of the apparition as though she were fascinated by it. She then asked Mrs Loxley, with a voice and look of terror, "Did you speak to the ghost, missus?" And when Mrs Loxley replied "No," Susan inquired, "And didn't the ghost speak to you?"

'Mrs Loxley answered that she had told all that had occurred, adding nothing, keeping back nothing; and this assurance seemed to have a consolatory effect upon the girl, who then busied herself with her work. I had made inquiries at the prison, as Mrs Loxley foreboded illness or death to her husband, and learned that my unfortunate friend was in health, and had become more resigned to the cruel future which awaited him. Mrs Loxley appeared to be satisfied with this account of her husband.

'The night which succeeded Mrs Loxley proposed to pass in the same manner; but her mother insisted upon remaining with her, and that night no apparition came.

'Mrs Loxley was disappointed, and attributed the absence of the spirit to the presence of her mother, and it was now her turn to insist. Mrs Lovett went to her room, having promised to go to bed and not seek to watch or return to her daughter. It was impossible, however, for the old lady to sleep, and she listened to every noise in the street, and to those unaccountable sounds which we have all heard in our lonely rooms.

'It was again past midnight, and Mrs Loxley had, she admitted, worked herself into a high state of expectancy, when, without the opening of the door, the figure of her husband stood in the room. Again it regarded her most tenderly for a few seconds, and then fixed its gaze on the portrait of Loxley's father. It had not seated itself, as on the former visitation, but stood, with its hands folded,

as though in supplication. It then turned its face to Mrs Loxley and opened its arms, as if inviting her to its embrace. Without a moment's hesitation she rose, and almost rushed to the bosom of the shadow. But the impalpable figure offering no resistance, she dashed herself against the panelling of the room, and the withered holly sprigs in the frame of the picture above her fell rustling to the ground. The shade was gone!

'Mrs Lovett, hearing the noise against the panel and the scratching of the falling holly, immediately went to her daughter. Mrs Loxley had not borne the second visitation so bravely as she had done the former one, and it was necessary to call for assistance, as a violent attack of hysteria succeeded the vision.

'The "Dormouse," usually most difficult to arouse, was the first to hear the calling of Mrs Lovett and to go to her assistance.

'"Has she seen it again?" asked Susan, almost directly she had entered.

'"Yes."

'"And did he speak to her this time, missus?" asked Susan. Mrs Lovett could not satisfy the girl's curiosity, but when Mrs Loxley revived sufficiently to tell what she had seen, Susan repeated her inquiries and appeared to be relieved when she heard that the ghost had been silent.

'I was sent for early in the morning and, having dispatched what pressing business matters I had, I went to Mrs Loxley. She was, as before, perfectly circumstantial in her account of what she had seen, not varying in the least from her first statement; and she and her mother believed that she had seen with her corporeal eyes the spirit of her living husband. I could not bring myself quite to this conclusion. I therefore suggested that it was possibly the association of the portrait with her husband, acting upon her over-taxed brain, that had conjured up these shadows. Mrs Loxley admitted the possibility of such a solution and readily acceded to my proposal to take down the portrait which had attracted, as it seemed, the attention of the figure, and then to abide the result of another night, if Mrs Loxley felt equal to courting the return of the vision.

'I rang the bell for the maid, and requested her to bring the steps.'

'"What for?" she asked quickly.

'"To take down one of the pictures," I replied.

'"There ain't no steps," she said firmly.

'I could have sworn I had seen a pair in the passage as I entered, but I might have been mistaken, and I did not press the request. The picture was easily removed by my standing on a chair.

'As I turned to place the picture on the floor I was perfectly thunderstruck to see the change which had come over Susan. She stood transfixed as it were, her mouth and eyes distended to the full, her hands stretched out, as though she were looking upon the ghost which had disturbed us all.

'"What is the matter with the girl?" I exclaimed, and all eyes were directed to her.

'Susan fell upon her knees and hid her face almost on the ground and screamed out, "I'm guilty, missus! I'm found out! I knowed why the ghost come! I'm guilty!"

'We were all astounded! After a few moments, as I stood on the chair with the face of the portrait towards me, Mrs Loxley uttered a shrill cry and rushed to the picture. From the inside of the frame to which the canvas was attached she took out a note for £20 – the note which Loxley had received and had lost so mysteriously!

'There was no doubt who had been the thief. Susan had already confessed herself guilty, and I did not hesitate to obtain what other confession I could from her. It seemed that Loxley had been mistaken in supposing he had placed the notes in his pocket-hook. Owing to his surprise at meeting the friend he had spoken to at the banker's he had placed the notes in his trousers-pocket, and the force of habit had induced him to think he had otherwise disposed of them. These notes, so carelessly placed, he had drawn forth with his hand whilst ascending his own stairs, and Susan had found them. The half-witted creature showed her prize to an old man employed to clean shoes and knives, and he counselled the changing of one of the notes, with what success we know. Susan received none of the money, as the old scoundrel declared himself a partner in the waif, and told Susan she might keep the other note. But what Susan saw and heard subsequently had so terrified her and filled her with remorse, that she dared not dispose of her ill-gotten money, but, strangely enough, concealed it behind the portrait of Loxley's father.

'My friend, by the exertions of X., was soon liberated, and by the honourable conduct of the same gentleman, who did all he could to repair the wrong unwittingly done to Loxley, an excellent appointment was found in Australia. There James and Martha and their progeny are now, and thriving, I am glad to say.

'I'll trouble you for the claret,' added Carraway. 'And now do you believe in ghosts?'

'I must make the answer I did before,' I replied. 'Yes – no. I think the apparition was provoked by the cause you at first suggested – namely, the association of Loxley's with his father's portrait and Mrs Loxley's over-taxed brain. You have heard, no doubt, of the well-known case of M. Nikolai, the Berlin banker, who, according to his own account, having experienced several unpleasant circumstances, saw phantasms of the living and the dead by dozens, and was yet convinced they were not ghosts. Mrs Loxley might have also been dreaming, without being aware of it, as others have done; and it is rather against the ghost, if he appeared only to discover the lost note, that he came not when Mrs Lovett was present.'

'But the note was found behind the portrait at which the ghost looked so earnestly. How can you account for that?' asked Carraway.

'Well, I am so much a doubter of spiritual manifestation that I can satisfy myself, though not you, perhaps, on that particular. Suppose this stupid Dormouse had taken it into her silly head that Mr Loxley's ghost had come for Mr Loxley's money, and under that impression had placed the note behind the picture after she had heard Mrs Loxley's account of the first visitation, in order to get rid of the money which the ghost wanted?'

'I don't believe that!' said Carraway. 'I believe it was a real, actual ghost!'

'I don't,' I replied, 'and so we end as we began. I'll thank you for the cigars.'

THE SHADOW OF A SHADE
by Tom Hood

My sister Lettie has lived with me ever since I had a home of my own. She was my little housekeeper before I married. Now she is my wife's constant companion, and the 'darling auntie' of my children, who go to her for comfort, advice and aid in all their little troubles and perplexities.

But, though she has a comfortable home, and loving hearts around her, she wears a grave, melancholy look on her face, which puzzles acquaintances and grieves friends.

A disappointment! Yes, the old story of a lost lover is the reason for Lattie's looks. She has had good offers often; but since she lost the first love of her heart she has never indulged in the happy dream of loving and being loved.

George Mason was a cousin of my wife's – a sailor by profession. He and Lettie met one another at our wedding, and fell in love at first sight. George's father had seen service before him on the great mysterious sea, and had been especially known as a good Arctic sailor, having shared in more than one expedition in search of the North Pole and the North-West Passage.

It was not a matter of surprise to me, therefore, when George volunteered to go out in the *Pioneer*, which was being fitted out for

a cruise in search of Franklin and his missing expedition. There was a fascination about such an undertaking that I felt I could not have resisted had I been in his place. Of course, Lettie did not like the idea at all, but he silenced her by telling her that men who volunteered for Arctic search were never lost sight of, and that he should not make as much advance in his profession in a dozen years as he would in the year or so of this expedition. I cannot say that Lettie, even after this, was quite satisfied with the notion of his going but, at all events, she did not argue against it any longer. But the grave look, which is now habitual with her, but was a rare thing in her young and happy days, passed over her face sometimes when she thought no one was looking.

My younger brother, Harry, was at this time an academy student. He was only a beginner then. Now he is pretty well known in the art world, and his pictures command fair prices. Like all beginners in art, he was full of fancies and theories. He would have been a pre-Raphaelite, only pre-Raphaelism had not been invented then. His peculiar craze was for what he styled the Venetian School. Now, it chanced that George had a fine Italian-looking head, and Harry persuaded him to sit for him for his portrait. It was a fair likeness, but a very moderate work of art. The background was so very dark, and George's naval costume so very deep in colour, that the face came out too white and staring. It was a three-quarter picture; but only one hand showed in it, leaning on the hilt of a sword. As George said, he looked much more like the commander of a Venetian galley than a modern mate.

However, the picture pleased Lettie, who did not care much about art provided the resemblance was good. So the picture was duly framed – in a tremendously heavy frame, of Harry's ordering – and hung up in the dining-room.

And now the time for George's departure was growing nearer. The *Pioneer* was nearly ready to sail, and her crew only waited orders. The officers grew acquainted with each other before sailing, which was an

advantage. George took up very warmly with the surgeon, Vincent Grieve, and, with my permission, brought him to dinner once or twice.

'Poor chap, he has no friends nearer than the Highlands, and it's precious lonely work.'

'Bring him by all means, George! You know that any friends of yours will be welcome here.'

So Vincent Grieve came. I am bound to say I was not favourably impressed by him, and almost wished I had not consented to his coming. He was a tall, pale, fair young man, with a hard Scotch face and a cold, grey eye. There was something in his expression, too, that was unpleasant – something cruel or crafty, or both.

I considered that it was very bad taste for him to pay such marked attention to Lettie, coming, as he did, as the friend of her fiancé. He kept by her constantly and anticipated George in all the little attentions which a lover delights to pay. I think George was a little put out about it, though he said nothing, attributing his friend's offence to lack of breeding.

Lettie did not like it at all. She knew that she was not to have George with her much longer, and she was anxious to have him to herself as much as possible. But as Grieve was her lover's friend she bore the infliction with the best possible patience.

The surgeon did not seem to perceive in the least that he was interfering where he had no business. He was quite self-possessed and happy, with one exception. The portrait of George seemed to annoy him. He had uttered a little impatient exclamation when he first saw it which drew my attention to him; and I noticed that he tried to avoid looking at it. At last, when dinner came, he was told to sit exactly facing the picture. He hesitated for an instant and then sat down, but almost immediately rose again.

'It's very childish and that sort of thing,' he stammered, 'but I cannot sit opposite that picture.'

'It is not high art,' I said, 'and may irritate a critical eye.'

'I know nothing about art,' he answered, 'but it is one of those

unpleasant pictures whose eyes follow you about the room. I have an inherited horror of such pictures. My mother married against her father's will, and when I was born she was so ill she was hardly expected to live. When she was sufficiently recovered to speak without delirious rambling she implored them to remove a picture of my grandfather that hung in the room, and which she vowed made threatening faces at her. It's superstitious, but constitutional – I have a horror of such paintings!'

I believe George thought this was a ruse of his friend's to get a seat next to Lettie; but I felt sure it was not, for I had seen the alarmed expression of his face.

At night, when George and his friend were leaving, I took an opportunity to ask the former, half in a joke, if he should bring the surgeon to see us again. George made a very hearty assertion to the contrary, adding that he was pleasant enough company among men at an inn, or on board ship, but not where ladies were concerned.

But the mischief was done. Vincent Grieve took advantage of the introduction and did not wait to be invited again. He called the next day, and nearly every day after. He was a more frequent visitor than George now, for George was obliged to attend to his duties, and they kept him on board the *Pioneer* pretty constantly, whereas the surgeon, having seen to the supply of drugs, etc., was pretty well at liberty. Lettie avoided him as much as possible, but he generally brought, or professed to bring, some little message from George to her, so that he had an excuse for asking to see her.

On the occasion of his last visit – the day before the *Pioneer* sailed – Lettie came to me in great distress. The young cub had actually the audacity to tell her he loved her. He knew, he said, about her engagement to George, but that did not prevent another man from loving her too. A man could no more help falling in love than he could help taking a fever. Lettie stood upon her dignity and rebuked him severely; but he told her he could see no harm in telling her of his passion, though he knew it was a hopeless one.

'A thousand things may happen,' he said at last, 'to bring your engagement with George Mason to an end. Then perhaps you will not forget that another loves you!'

I was very angry, and was forthwith going to give him my opinion on his conduct, when Lettie told me he was gone, that she had bade him go and had forbidden him the house. She only told me in order to protect herself, for she did not intend to say anything to George, for fear it should lead to a duel or some other violence.

That was the last we saw of Vincent Grieve before the *Pioneer* sailed.

George came the same evening, and was with us till daybreak, when he had to tear himself away and join his ship.

After shaking hands with him at the door, in the cold, grey, drizzly dawn, I turned back into the dining-room, where poor Lettie was sobbing on the sofa.

I could not help starting when I looked at George's portrait, which hung above her. The strange light of daybreak could hardly account for the extraordinary pallor of the face. I went close to it and looked hard at it. I saw that it was covered with moisture, and imagined that that possibly made it look so pale. As for the moisture, I supposed poor Lettie had been kissing the beloved's portrait, and that the moisture was caused by her tears.

It was not till a long time after, when I was jestingly telling Harry how his picture had been caressed, that I learnt the error of my conjecture. Lettie assured me most solemnly that I was mistaken in supposing she had kissed it.

'It was the varnish blooming, I expect,' said Harry. And thus the subject was dismissed, for I said no more, though I knew well enough, in spite of my not being an artist, that the bloom of varnish was quite another sort of thing.

The *Pioneer* sailed. We received – or, rather, Lettie received – two letters from George, which he had taken the opportunity of sending by homeward-bound whalers. In the second he said it was hardly likely he should have an opportunity of sending another, as they were sailing into high latitudes – into the solitary sea, to which none but expedition ships ever penetrated. They were all in high spirits, he said, for they had encountered very little ice and hoped to find clear water further north than usual. Moreover, he added, Grieve had held a sinecure so far, for there had not been a single case of illness on board.

Then came a long silence, and a year crept away very slowly for poor Lettie. Once we heard of the expedition from the papers. They were reported as pushing on and progressing favourably by a wandering tribe of Esquimaux with whom the captain of a Russian vessel fell in. They had laid the ship up for the winter, and were taking the boats on sledges, and believed they had met with traces of the lost crews that seemed to show they were on the right track.

The winter passed again, and spring came. It was a balmy, bright spring such as we get occasionally, even in this changeable and uncertain climate of ours.

One evening we were sitting in the dining-room with the window open for, although we had long given up fires, the room was so oppressively warm that we were glad of the breath of the cool evening breeze.

Lettie was working. Poor child, though she never murmured, she was evidently pining at George's long absence. Harry was leaning out of the window, studying the evening effect on the fruit blossom, which was wonderfully early and plentiful, the season was so mild. I was sitting at the table, near the lamp, reading the paper.

Suddenly there swept into the room a chill. It was not a gust of cold wind, for the curtain by the open window did not swerve in the least. But the deathly cold pervaded the room – came, and was gone in an instant. Lettie shuddered, as I did, with the intense icy feeling.

She looked up. 'How curiously cold it has got all in a minute,' she said.

'We are having a taste of poor George's polar weather,' I said with a smile.

At the same moment I instinctively glanced towards his portrait. What I saw struck me dumb, A rush of blood, at fever heat, dispelled the numbing influence of the chill breath that had seemed to freeze me.

I have said the lamp was lighted; but it was only that I might read with comfort, for the violet twilight was still so full of sunset that the room was not dark. But as I looked at the picture I saw it had undergone a strange change. I saw it as plainly as possible. It was no delusion, coined for the eye by the brain.

I saw, in the place of George's head, a grinning skull! I stared at it hard; but it was no trick of fancy. I could see the hollow orbits, the gleaming teeth, the fleshless cheekbones – it was the head of death!

Without saying a word, I rose from my chair and walked straight up to the painting. As I drew nearer a sort of mist seemed to pass before it; and as I stood close to it, I saw only the face of George. The spectral skull had vanished.

'Poor George!' I said unconsciously.

Lettie looked up. The tone of my voice had alarmed her, the expression of my face did not reassure her.

'What do you mean? Have you heard anything? Oh, Robert, in mercy tell me!'

She got up and came over to me and, laying her hands on my arm, looked up into my face imploringly.

'No, my dear; how should I hear? Only I could not help thinking of the privation and discomfort he must have gone through. I was reminded of it by the cold – '

'Cold!' said Harry, who had left the window by this time. 'Cold! what on earth are you talking about? Cold, such an evening as this! You must have had a touch of ague, I should think.'

'Both Lettie and I felt it bitterly cold a minute or two ago. Did not you feel it?'

'Not a bit; and as I was three parts out of the window I ought to have felt it if anyone did.'

It was curious, but that strange chill had been felt only in the

room. It was not the night wind, but some supernatural breath connected with the dread apparition I had seen. It was, indeed, the chill of polar winter – the icy shadow of the frozen North.

'What is the day of the month, Harry?' I asked.

'Today – the 23rd, I think,' he answered; then added, taking up the newspaper I had been reading: 'Yes, here you are. Tuesday, February the 23rd, if the *Daily News* tells truth, which I suppose it does. Newspapers can afford to tell the truth about dates, whatever they may do about art.' Harry had been rather roughly handled by the critic of a morning paper for one of his pictures a few days before, and he was a little angry with journalism generally.

Presently Lettie left the room, and I told Harry what I had felt and seen, and told him to take note of the date, for I feared that some mischance had befallen George.

"I'll put it down in my pocket-book, Bob. But you and Lettie must have had a touch of the cold shivers, and your stomach or fancy misled you – they're the same thing, you know. Besides, as regards the picture, there's nothing in that! There is a skull there, of course. As Tennyson says:

> "Any face, however full,
> Padded round with flesh and fat,
> Is but modelled on a skull."

The skull's there – just as in every good figure-subject the nude is there under the costumes. You fancy that is a mere coat of paint. Nothing of the kind! Art lives, sir! That is just as much a real head as yours is with all the muscles and bones, just the same. That's what makes the difference between art and rubbish.'

This was a favourite theory of Harry's, who had not yet developed from the dreamer into the worker. As I did not care to argue with him, I allowed the subject to drop after we had written down the date in our pocket-books. Lettie sent down word presently that she

did not feel well and had gone to bed. My wife came down presently and asked what had happened. She had been up with the children and had gone in to see what was the matter with Lettie.

'I think it was very imprudent to sit with the window open, dear. I know the evenings are warm, but the night air strikes cold at times – at any rate, Lettie seems to have caught a violent cold, for she is shivering very much. I am afraid she has got a chill from the open windows.'

I did not say anything to her then, except that both Lettie and I had felt a sudden coldness; for I did not care to enter into an explanation again, for I could see Harry was inclined to laugh at me for being so superstitious.

At night, however, in our own room, I told my wife what had occurred, and what my apprehensions were. She was so upset and alarmed that I almost repented having done so.

The next morning Lettie was better again, and as we did not either of us refer to the events of the preceding night the circumstance appeared to be forgotten by us all.

But from that day I was ever inwardly dreading the arrival of bad news. And at last it came, as I expected.

One morning, just as I was coming downstairs to breakfast, there came a knock at the door, and Harry made his appearance. It was a very early visit from him, for he generally used to spend his mornings at the studio, and drop in on his way home at night.

He was looking pale and agitated.

'Lettie's not down, is she, yet?' he asked; and then, before I could answer, added another question:

'What newspaper do you take?'

'The *Daily News*,' I answered. 'Why?'

'She's not down?'

'No.'

'Thank God! Look here!'

He took a paper from his pocket and gave it to me, pointing out a short paragraph at the bottom of one of the columns.

I knew what was coming the moment he spoke about Lettie.

The paragraph was headed, 'Fatal Accident to one of the Officers of the *Pioneer* Expedition Ship'. It stated that news had been received at the Admiralty stating that the expedition had failed to find the missing crews, but had come upon some traces of them. Want of stores and necessaries had compelled them to turn back without following those traces up; but the commander was anxious, as soon as the ship could be refitted, to go out and take up the trail where he left it. An unfortunate accident had deprived him of one of his most promising officers, Lieutenant Mason, who was precipitated from an iceberg and killed while out shooting with the surgeon. He was beloved by all, and his death had flung a gloom over the gallant little troop of explorers.

'It's not in the *News* today, thank goodness, Bob,' said Harry, who had been searching that paper while I was reading the one he brought – 'but you must keep a sharp look-out for some days and not let Lettie see it when it appears, as it is certain to do sooner or later.'

Then we both of us looked at each other with tears in our eyes. 'Poor George! – poor Lettie!' we sighed softly.

'But she must be told at some time or other?' I said despairingly.

'I suppose so,' said Harry; 'but it would kill her to come on it suddenly like this. Where's your wife?'

She was with the children, but I sent up for her and told her the ill-tidings.

She had a hard struggle to conceal her emotion, for Lettie's sake. But the tears would flow in spite of her efforts.

'How shall I ever find courage to tell her?' she asked,

'Hush!' said Harry, suddenly grasping her arm and looking towards the door.

I turned. There stood Lettie, with her face pale as death, with her lips apart, and with a blind look about her eyes. She had come in without our hearing her. We never learnt how much of the story she had overheard; but it was enough to tell her the worst. We all sprang towards her; but she only waved us away, turned round, and went

upstairs again without saying a word. My wife hastened up after her and found her on her knees by the bed, insensible.

The doctor was sent for, and restoratives were promptly administered. She came to herself again, but lay dangerously ill for some weeks from the shock.

It was about a month after she was well enough to come downstairs again that I saw in the paper an announcement of the arrival of the *Pioneer*. The news had no interest for any of us now, so I said nothing about it. The mere mention of the vessel's name would have caused the poor girl pain.

One afternoon shortly after this, as I was writing a letter, there came a loud knock at the front door. I looked up from my writing and listened; for the voice which inquired if I was in sounded strange, but yet not altogether unfamiliar. As I looked up, puzzling whose it could he, my eye rested accidentally upon poor George's portrait. Was I dreaming or awake?

I have told you that the one hand was resting on a sword. I could see now distinctly that the forefinger was raised, as if in warning. I looked at it hard, to assure myself it was no fancy, and then I perceived, standing out bright and distinct on the pale face, two large drops, as if of blood.

I walked up to it, expecting the appearance to vanish, as the skull had done. It did not vanish; but the uplifted finger resolved itself into a little white moth which had settled on the canvas. The red drops were fluid, and certainly not blood, though I was at a loss for the time to account for them.

The moth seemed to be in a torpid state, so I took it off the picture and placed it under an inverted wine-glass on the mantelpiece. All this took less time to do than to describe. As I turned from the mantelpiece the servant brought in a card, saying the gentleman was waiting in the hall to know if I would see him.

On the card was the name of 'Vincent Grieve, of the exploring vessel *Pioneer*'.

'Thank Heaven, Lettie is out,' thought I; and then added aloud to the servant, 'Show him in here; and Jane, if your mistress and Miss Lettie come in before the gentleman goes, tell them I have someone with me on business and do not wish to be disturbed.'

I went to the door to meet Grieve. As he crossed the threshold, and before he could have seen the portrait, he stopped, shuddered and turned white, even to his thin lips.

'Cover that picture before I come in,' he said hurriedly, in a low voice. 'You remember the effect it had upon me. Now, with the memory of poor Mason, it would be worse than ever.'

I could understand his feelings better now than at first; for I had come to look on the picture with some awe myself. So I took the cloth off a little round table that stood under the window and hung it over the portrait.

When I had done so Grieve came in. He was greatly altered. He was thinner and paler than ever; hollow-eyed and hollow-cheeked. He had acquired a strange stoop, too, and his eyes had lost the crafty look for a look of terror, like that of a hunted beast. I noticed that he kept glancing sideways every instant, as if unconsciously. It looked as if he heard someone behind him.

I had never liked the man; but now I felt an insurmountable repugnance to him – so great a repugnance that, when I came to think of it, I felt pleased that the incident of covering the picture at his request had led to my not shaking hands with him.

I felt that I could not speak otherwise than coldly to him; indeed, I had to speak with painful plainness.

I told him that, of course, I was glad to see him back, but that I could not ask him to continue to visit us. I should be glad to hear the particulars of poor George's death, but that I could not let him see my sister, and hinted, as delicately as I could, at the impropriety of which he had been guilty when he last visited.

He took it all very quietly, only giving a long, weary sigh when I told him I must beg him not to repeat his visit. He looked so weak

and ill that I was obliged to ask him to take a glass of wine – an offer which he seemed to accept with great pleasure.

I got out the sherry and biscuits and placed them on the table between us, and he took a glass and drank it off greedily.

It was not without some difficulty that I could get him to tell me of George's death. He related, with evident reluctance, how they had gone out to shoot a white bear which they had seen on an iceberg stranded along the shore. The top of the berg was ridged like the roof of a house, sloping down on one side to the edge of a tremendous overhanging precipice. They had scrambled along the ridge in order to get nearer the game, when George incautiously ventured on the sloping side.

'I called out to him', said Grieve, 'and begged him to come back, but too late. The surface was as smooth and slippery as glass. He tried to turn back, but slipped and fell. And then began a horrible scene. Slowly, slowly, but with ever-increasing motion, he began to slide down towards the edge. There was nothing to grasp at – no irregularity or projection on the smooth face of the ice. I tore off my coat, and hastily attaching it to the stock of my gun, pushed the latter towards him; but it did not reach far enough. Before I could lengthen it, by tying my cravat to it, he had slid yet further away, and more quickly. I shouted in agony; but there was no one within hearing. He, too, saw his fate was sealed; and he could only tell me to bring his last farewell to you, and – and to her!' – Here Grieve's voice broke – 'and it was all over! He clung to the edge of the precipice instinctively for one second, and was gone!'

Just as Grieve uttered the last word, his jaw fell; his eyeballs seemed ready to start from his head; he sprang to his feet, pointed at something behind me, and then flinging up his arms, fell, with a scream, as if he had been shot. He was seized with an epileptic fit.

I instinctively looked behind me as I hurried to raise him from the floor. The cloth had fallen from the picture, where the face of George, made paler than ever by the gouts of red, looked sternly down.

I rang the bell. Luckily, Harry had come in; and, when the servant told him what was the matter, he came in and assisted me in restoring Grieve to consciousness. Of course, I covered the painting up again.

When he was quite himself again, Grieve told me he was subject to fits occasionally.

He seemed very anxious to learn if he had said or done anything extraordinary while he was in the fit, and appeared reassured when I said he had not. He apologised for the trouble he had given, and said as soon as he was strong enough he would take his leave. He was leaning on the mantelpiece as he said this. The little white moth caught his eye.

'So you have had someone else from the *Pioneer* here before me?' he said, nervously.

I answered in the negative, asking what made him think so.

'Why, this little white moth is never found in such southern latitudes. It is one of the last signs of life northward. Where did you get it?'

'I caught it here, in this room,' I answered.

'That is very strange. I never heard of such a thing before. We shall hear of showers of blood soon, I should not wonder.'

'What do you mean?' I asked.

'Oh, these little fellows emit little drops of a red-looking fluid at certain seasons, and sometimes so plentifully that the superstitious think it is a shower of blood. I have seen the snow quite stained in places. Take care of it, it is a rarity in the south.'

I noticed, after he left, which he did almost immediately, that there was a drop of red fluid on the marble under the wine-glass. The blood-stain on the picture was accounted for; but how came the moth here?

And there was another strange thing about the man, which I had scarcely been able to assure myself of in the room, where there were cross-lights, but about which there was no possible mistake, when I saw him walking away up the street.

'Harry, here – quick!' I called to my brother, who at once came to the window. 'You're an artist, tell me, is there anything strange about that man?'

'No; nothing that I can see,' said Harry, but then suddenly, in an altered tone, added, 'Yes, there is. By Jove, *he has a double shadow!*'

That was the explanation of his sidelong glances, of the habitual stoop. There was a something always at his side, which none could see, but which cast a shadow.

He turned, presently, and saw us at the window. Instantly, he crossed the road to the shady side of the street. I told Harry all that had passed, and we agreed that it would be as well not to say a word to Lettie.

Two days later, when I returned from a visit to Harry's studio, I found the whole house in confusion.

I learnt from Lettie that while my wife was upstairs, Grieve had called, had not waited for the servant to announce him, but had walked straight into the dining-room, where Lettie was sitting. She noticed that he avoided looking at the picture, and, to make sure of not seeing it, had seated himself on the sofa just beneath it. He had then, in spite of Lettie's angry remonstrances, renewed his offer of love, strengthening it finally by assuring her that poor George with his dying breath had implored him to seek her, and watch over her, and marry her.

'I was so indignant I hardly knew how to answer him,' said Lettie. 'When, suddenly, just as he uttered the last words, there came a twang like the breaking of a guitar – and – I hardly know how to describe it – but the portrait had fallen, and the corner of the heavy frame had struck him on the head, cutting it open, and rendering him insensible.'

They had carried him upstairs, by the direction of the doctor, for whom my wife at once sent on hearing what had occurred. He was laid on the couch in my dressing-room, where I went to see him. I intended to reproach him for coming to the house, despite my prohibition, but I found him delirious. The doctor said it was a queer case; for, though the blow was a severe one, it was hardly enough to account for the symptoms of brain-fever. When he learnt that Grieve had but just returned in the *Pioneer* from the North, he said it was possible that the privation and hardship had told on his constitution and sown the seeds of the malady.

We sent for a nurse, who was to sit up with him, by the doctor's directions.

The rest of my story is soon told. In the middle of the night I was roused by a loud scream. I slipped on my clothes, and rushed out to find the nurse, with Lettie in her arms, in a faint. We carried her into her room, and then the nurse explained the mystery to us.

It appears that about midnight Grieve sat up in bed, and began to talk. And he said such terrible things that the nurse became alarmed. Nor was she much reassured when she became aware that the light of her single candle flung what seemed to be two shadows of the sick man on the wall.

Terrified beyond measure, she had crept into Lettie's room, and confided her fears to her; and Lettie, who was a courageous and kindly girl, dressed herself, and said she would sit with her. She, too, saw the double shadow – but what she heard was far more terrible.

Grieve was sitting up in bed, gazing at the unseen figure to which the shadow belonged. In a voice that trembled with emotion, he begged the haunting spirit to leave him, and prayed its forgiveness.

'You know the crime was not premeditated. It was a sudden temptation of the devil that made me strike the blow, and fling you over the precipice. It was the devil tempting me with the recollection of her exquisite face – of the tender love that might have been mine, but for you. But she will not listen to me. See, she turns away from me, as if she knew I was your murderer, George Mason!'

It was Lettie who repeated in a horrified whisper this awful confession.

I could see it all now! As I was about to tell Lettie of the many

strange things I had concealed from her, the nurse, who had gone to see her patient, came running back in alarm.

Vincent Grieve had disappeared. He had risen in his delirious terror, had opened the window, and leaped out. Two days later his body was found in the river.

A curtain hangs now before poor George's portrait, though it is no longer connected with any supernatural marvels; and never, since the night of Vincent Grieve's death, have we seen aught of that most mysterious haunting presence – the Shadow of a Shade.

THE DEAD MAN OF VARLEY GRANGE
Anonymous

'Hallo, Jack! Where are you off to? Going down to the governor's place for Christmas?'

Jack Darent, who was in my old regiment, stood drawing on his dogskin gloves upon the 23rd of December the year before last. He was equipped in a long ulster and top hat, and a hansom, already loaded with a gun-case and portmanteau, stood awaiting him. He had a tall, strong figure, a fair, fresh-looking face, and the merriest blue eyes in the world. He held a cigarette between his lips, and late as was the season of the year there was a flower in his buttonhole. When did I ever see handsome Jack Darent when he did not look well dressed and well-fed and jaunty? As I ran up the steps of the Club he turned round and laughed merrily.

'My dear fellow, do I look the sort of man to be victimised at a family Christmas meeting? Do you know the kind of business they have at home? Three maiden aunts and a bachelor uncle, my eldest brother and his insipid wife, and all my sister's six noisy children at dinner. Church twice a day, and snap-dragon between the services! No, thank you! I have a great affection for my old parents, but you

don't catch me going in for that sort of national festival!'

'You irreverent ruffian!' I replied, laughing. 'Ah, if you were a married man–'

'Ah, if I were a married man!' replied Captain Darent with something that was almost a sigh, and then lowering his voice, he said hurriedly, 'How is Miss Lester, Fred?'

'My sister is quite well, thank you,' I answered with becoming gravity; and it was not without a spice of malice that I added, 'She has been going to a great many balls and enjoying herself very much.'

Captain Darent looked profoundly miserable.

'I don't see how a poor fellow in a marching regiment, a younger son too, with nothing in the future to look to, is ever to marry nowadays,' he said almost savagely; 'when girls, too, are used to so much luxury and extravagance that they can't live without it. Matrimony is at a deadlock in this century, Fred, chiefly owing to the price of butcher's meat and bonnets. In fifty years' time it will become extinct and the country be depopulated. But I must be off, old man, or I shall miss my train.'

'You have never told me where you are going to, Jack.'

'Oh, I am going to stay with old Henderson, in Westernshire; he has taken a furnished house, with some first-rate pheasant shooting, for a year. There are seven of us going – all bachelors, and all kindred spirits. We shall shoot all day and smoke half the night. Think what you have lost, old fellow, by becoming a Benedick!'

'In Westernshire, is it?' I inquired. 'Whereabouts is this place, and what is the name of it? For I am a Westernshire man by birth myself, and I know every place in the county.'

'Oh, it's a tumbledown sort of old house, I believe,' answered Jack carelessly. 'Gables and twisted chimneys outside, and uncomfortable spindle-legged furniture inside – you know the sort of thing; but the shooting is capital, Henderson says, and we must put up with our quarters. He has taken his French cook down, and plenty of liquor, so I've no doubt we shan't starve.'

'Well, but what is the name of it?' I persisted, with a growing interest in the subject.

'Let me see,' referring to a letter he pulled out of his pocket. 'Oh, here it is – Varley Grange.'

'Varley Grange!' I repeated, aghast. 'Why, it has not been inhabited for years.'

'I believe not,' answered Jack unconcernedly. 'The shooting has been let separately; but Henderson took a fancy to the house too and thought it would do for him, furniture and all, just as it is. My dear Fred, what are you looking so solemnly at me for?'

'Jack, let me entreat of you not to go to this place,' I said, laying my hands on his arm.

'Not go! Why, Lester, you must be mad! Why on earth shouldn't I go there?'

'There are stories – uncomfortable things said of that house.' I had not the moral courage to say, 'It is haunted,' and I felt myself how weak and childish was my attempt to deter him from his intended visit; only – I knew all about Varley Grange.

I think handsome Jack Darent thought privately that I was slightly out of my senses, for I am sure I looked unaccountably upset and dismayed by the mention of the name of the house that Mr Henderson had taken.

'I dare say it's cold and draughty and infested with rats and mice,' he said laughingly; 'and I have no doubt the creature-comforts will not be equal to Queen's Gate; but I stand pledged to go now, and I must be off this very minute, so have no time, old fellow, to inquire into the meaning of your sensational warning. Goodbye, and – and remember me to the ladies.'

He ran down the steps and jumped into the hansom.

'Write to me if you have time!' I cried out after him; but I don't think he heard me in the rattle of the departing cab. He nodded and smiled at me and was swiftly whirled out of sight.

As for me, I walked slowly back to my comfortable house in

Queen's Gate. There was my wife presiding at the little five o'clock tea-table, our two fat, pink and white little children tumbling about upon the hearthrug amongst dolls and bricks, and two utterly spoilt and over-fed pugs; and my sister Bella – who, between ourselves, was the prettiest as well as dearest girl in all London – sitting on the floor in her handsome brown, velvet gown, resigning herself gracefully to be trampled upon by the dogs, and to have her hair pulled by the babies.

'Why, Fred, you look as if you had heard bad news,' said my wife, looking up anxiously as I entered.

'I don't know that I have heard of anything very bad; I have just seen Jack Darent off for Christmas,' I said, turning instinctively towards my sister. He was a poor man and a younger son, and of course a very bad match for the beautiful Miss Lester; but for all that I had an inkling that Bella was not quite indifferent to her brother's friend.

'Oh!' says that hypocrite. 'Shall I give you a cup of tea, Fred!'

It is wonderful how women can control their faces and pretend not to care a straw when they hear the name of their lover mentioned. I think Bella overdid it, she looked so supremely indifferent.

'Where on earth do you suppose he is going to stay, Bella?'

'Who? Oh, Captain Darent! How should I possibly know where he is going? Archie, pet, please don't poke the doll's head quite down Ponto's throat; I know he will bite it off if you do.'

This last observation was addressed to my son and heir.

'Well, I think you will be surprised when you hear: he is going to Westernshire, to stay at Varley Grange.'

'*What!*' No doubt about her interest in the subject now! Miss Lester turned as white as her collar and sprang to her feet impetuously, scattering dogs, babies and toys in all directions away from her skirts as she rose.

'You cannot mean it, Fred! Varley Grange, why, it has not been inhabited for ten years; and the last time – Oh, do you remember those poor people who took it? What a terrible story it has!' She shuddered.

'Well, it is taken now,' I said, 'by a man I know, called Henderson

– a bachelor; he has asked down a party of men for a week's shooting, and Jack Darent is one of them.'

'For Heaven's sake prevent him from going!' cried Bella, clasping her hands.

'My dear, he is gone!'

'Oh, then write to him – telegraph – tell him to come back!' she urged breathlessly.

'I am afraid it is no use,' I said gravely. 'He would not come back; he would not believe me; he would think I was mad.'

'Did you tell him anything?' she asked faintly.

'No, I had not time. I did say a word or two, but he began to laugh.'

'Yes, that is how it always is!' she said distractedly. 'People laugh and pooh-pooh the whole thing, and then they go there and see for themselves, and it is too late!'

She was so thoroughly upset that she left the room. My wife turned to me in astonishment; not being a Westernshire woman, she was not well up in the traditions of that venerable county.

'What on earth does it all mean, Fred?' she asked me in amazement. 'What is the matter with Bella, and why is she so distressed that Captain Darent is going to stay at that particular house?'

'It is said to be haunted, and–'

'You don't mean to say you believe in such rubbish, Fred?' interrupted my wife sternly, with a side-glance of apprehension at our first-born, who, needless to say, stood by, all eyes and ears, drinking in every word of the conversation of his elders.

'I never know what I believe or what I don't believe,' I answered gravely. 'All I can say is that there are very singular traditions about that house, and that a great many credible witnesses have seen a very strange thing there, and that a great many disasters have happened to the persons who have seen it.'

'What has been seen, Fred? Pray tell me the story! Wait, I think I will send the children away.'

My wife rang the bell for the nurse, and as soon as the little ones

had been taken from the room she turned to me again.

'I don't believe in ghosts or any such rubbish one bit, but I should like to hear your story.'

'The story is vague enough,' I answered. 'In the old days Varley Grange belonged to the ancient family of Varley, now completely extinct. There was, some hundred years ago, a daughter, famed for her beauty and her fascination. She wanted to marry a poor, penniless squire, who loved her devotedly. Her brother, Dennis Varley, the new owner of Varley Grange, refused his consent and shut his sister up in the nunnery that used to stand outside his park gates – there are a few ruins of it left still. The poor nun broke her vows and ran away in the night with her lover. But her brother pursued her and brought her back with him. The lover escaped, but the lord of Varley murdered his sister under his own roof, swearing that no scion of his race should live to disgrace and dishonour his ancient name.

'Ever since that day Dennis Varley's spirit cannot rest in its grave – he wanders about the old house at night time, and those who have seen him are numberless. Now and then the pale, shadowy form of a nun flits across the old hall, or along the gloomy passages, and when both strange shapes are seen thus together misfortune and illness, and even death, is sure to pursue the luckless man who has seen them, with remorseless cruelty.'

'I wonder you believe in such rubbish,' says my wife at the conclusion of my tale.

I shrug my shoulders and answer nothing, for who are so obstinate as those who persist in disbelieving everything that they cannot understand?

*   *   *   *   *

It was little more than a week later that, walking by myself along Pall Mall one afternoon, I suddenly came upon Jack Darent walking towards me.

'Hallo, Jack! Back again? Why, man, how odd you look!'

There was a change in the man that I was instantly aware of. His frank, careless face looked clouded and anxious, and the merry smile was missing from his handsome countenance.

'Come into the Club, Fred,' he said, taking me by the arm. 'I have something to say to you.'

He drew me into a corner of the Club smoking-room.

'You were quite right. I wish to Heaven I had never gone to that house.'

'You mean – have you seen anything?' I inquired eagerly.

'I have seen *everything*,' he answered with a shudder. 'They say one dies within a year – '

'My dear fellow, don't be so upset about it,' I interrupted; I was quite distressed to see how thoroughly the man had altered.

'Let me tell you about it, Fred.'

He drew his chair close to mine and told me his story, pretty nearly in the following words:

'You remember the day I went down you had kept me talking at the Club door; I had a race to catch the train; however, I just did it. I found the other fellows all waiting for me. There was Charlie Wells, the two Harfords, old Colonel Riddell, who is such a crack shot, two fellows in the Guards, both pretty fair, a man called Thompson, a barrister, Henderson and myself – eight of us in all. We had a remarkably lively journey down, as you may imagine, and reached Varley Grange in the highest possible spirits. We all slept like tops that night.

The next day we were out from eleven till dusk among the coverts, and a better day's shooting I never enjoyed in the whole course of my life, the birds literally swarmed. We bagged a hundred and thirty brace. We were all pretty well tired when we got home, and did full justice to a very good dinner and first-class Perrier-Jouet. After dinner we adjourned to the hall to smoke. This hall is quite the feature of the house. It is large and bright, panelled half-way up with sombre old oak, and vaulted with heavy carved oaken rafters. At the farther end runs a gallery, into which opened the door of my bedroom, and shut off from the rest of the passages by a swing door at either end.

'Well, all we fellows sat up there smoking and drinking brandy and soda, and jawing, you know – as men always do when they are together – about sport of all kinds, hunting and shooting and salmon-fishing; and I assure you not one of us had a thought in our heads beyond relating some wonderful incident of a long shot or big fence by which we could each cap the last speaker's experiences. We were just, I recollect, listening to a long story of the old Colonel's, about his experiences among bisons in Cachemire, when suddenly one of us – I can't remember who it was – gave a sort of shout and started to his feet, pointing up to the gallery behind us. We all turned round, and there – I give you my word of honour, Lester – stood a man leaning over the rail of the gallery, staring down upon us.

'We all saw him. Every one of us. Eight of us, remember. He stood there full ten seconds, looking down with horrible glittering eyes at us. He had a long tawny beard, and his hands, that were crossed together before him, were nothing but skin and bone. But it was his face that was so unspeakably dreadful. It was livid – the face of a dead man!'

'How was he dressed?'

'I could not see; he wore some kind of a black cloak over his shoulders, I think, but the lower part of his figure was hidden behind the railings. Well, we all stood perfectly speechless for, as I said, about ten seconds; and then the figure moved, backing slowly into the door of the room behind him, which stood open. It was the door of my bedroom! As soon as he had disappeared our senses seemed to return to us. There was a general rush for the staircase, and, as you may imagine, there was not a corner of the house that was left unsearched; my bedroom especially was ransacked in every part of it. But all in vain; there was not the slightest trace to be found of any

living being. You may suppose that not one of us slept that night. We lighted every candle and lamp we could lay hands upon and sat up till daylight, but nothing more was seen.

'The next morning, at breakfast, Henderson, who seemed very much annoyed by the whole thing, begged us not to speak of it any more. He said that he had been told, before he had taken the house, that it was supposed to be haunted; but, not being a believer in such childish follies, he had paid but little attention to the rumour. He did not, however, want it talked about, because of the servants, who would be so easily frightened. He was quite certain he said, that the figure we had seen last night must be somebody dressed up to practise a trick upon us, and he recommended us all to bring our guns down loaded after dinner, but meanwhile to forget the startling apparition as far as we could.

'We, of course, readily agreed to do as he wished, although I do not think that one of us imagined for a moment that any amount of dressing-up would be able to simulate the awful countenance that we had all of us seen too plainly. It would have taken a Hare or an Arthur Cecil, with all the theatrical appliances known only to those two talented actors, to have "made-up" the face, that was literally that of a corpse. Such a person could not be amongst us – actually in the house – without our knowledge.

'We had another good day's shooting, and by degrees the fresh air and exercise and the excitement of the sport obliterated the impression of what we had seen in some measure from the minds of most of us. That evening we all appeared in the hall after dinner with our loaded guns beside us; but, although we sat up till the small hours and looked frequently up at the gallery at the end of the hall, nothing at all disturbed us that night.

'Two nights thus went by and nothing further was seen of the gentleman with the tawny beard. What with the good company, the good cheer and the pheasants, we had pretty well forgotten all about him.

'We were sitting as usual upon the third night, with our pipes and our cigars; a pleasant glow from the bright wood fire in the great chimney lighted up the old hall, and shed a genial warmth about us; when suddenly it seemed to me as if there came a breath of cold, chill air behind me, such as one feels when going down into some damp, cold vault or cellar.

'A strong shiver shook me from head to foot. Before even I saw it I knew that it was there.

'It leant over the railing of the gallery and looked down at us all just as it had done before. There was no change in the attitude, no alteration in the fixed, malignant glare in those stony, lifeless eyes; no movement in the white and bloodless features. Below, amongst the eight of us gathered there, there arose a panic of terror. Eight strong, healthy, well-educated nineteenth century Englishmen, and yet I am not ashamed to say that we were paralysed with fear. Then one, more quickly recovering his senses than the rest, caught at his gun, that leant against the wide chimney-corner, and fired.

'The hall was filled with smoke, but as it cleared away every one of us could see the figure of our supernatural visitant slowly backing, as he had done on the previous occasion, into the chamber behind him, with something like a sardonic smile of scornful derision upon his horrible, death-like face.

'The next morning it is a singular and remarkable fact that four out of the eight of us received by the morning post – so they stated – letters of importance which called them up to town by the very first train! One man's mother was ill, another had to consult his lawyer, whilst pressing engagements, to which they could assign no definite name, called away the other two.

'There were left in the house that day but four of us – Wells, Bob Harford, our host, and myself. A sort of dogged determination not to be worsted by a scare of this kind kept us still there. The morning light brought a return of common sense and of natural courage to us. We could manage to laugh over last night's terrors whilst discussing

our bacon and kidneys and hot coffee over the late breakfast in the pleasant morning-room, with the sunshine streaming cheerily in through the diamond-paned windows.

"'It *must* be a delusion of our brains," said one.

"'Our host's champagne," suggested another.

"'A well-organied hoax," opined a third.

"'I will tell you what we will do," said our host. "Now that those other fellows have all gone – and I suppose we don't any of us believe much in those elaborate family reasons which have so unaccountably summoned them away – we four will sit up regularly night after night and watch for this thing, whatever it may be. I do not believe in ghosts. However, this morning I have taken the trouble to go out before breakfast to see the Rector of the parish, an old gentleman who is well up in all the traditions of the neighbourhood, and I have learnt from him the whole of the supposed story of our friend of the tawny beard, which, if you like, I will relate to you."

'Henderson then proceeded to tell us the tradition concerning the Dennis Varley who murdered his sister, the nun – a story which I will not repeat to you, Lester, as I see you know it already.

'The clergyman had furthermore told him that the figure of the murdered nun was also sometimes seen in the same gallery, but that this was a very rare occurrence. When both the murderer and his victim are seen together, terrible misfortunes are sure to assail the unfortunate living man who sees them; and if the nun's face is revealed, death within the year is the doom of the ill-fated person who has seen it.

"'Of course," concluded our host, "I consider all these stories to be absolutely childish. At the same time I cannot help thinking that some human agency – probably a gang of thieves or housebreakers – is at work, and that we shall probably be able to unearth an organised system of villainy by which the rogues, presuming on the credulity of the persons who have inhabited the place, have been able to plant themselves securely among some secret passages and hidden rooms in the house, and have carried on their depredations undiscovered and unsuspected. Now, will all of you help me to unravel this mystery?"

'We all promised readily to do so. It is astonishing how brave we felt at eleven o'clock in the morning; what an amount of pluck and courage each man professed himself to be endued with; how lightly we jested about the "old boy with the beard", and what jokes we cracked about the murdered nun!

"'She would show her face oftener if she was good-looking. No fear of her looking at Bob Harford, he was too ugly. It was Jack Darent who was the showman of the party; she'd be sure to make straight for him if she could, he was always run after by the women," and so on, till we were all laughing loudly and heartily over our own witticisms. That was eleven o'clock in the morning.

'At eleven o'clock at night we could have given a very different report of ourselves.

'At eleven o'clock at night each man took up his appointed post in solemn and somewhat depressed silence.

'The plan of our campaign had been carefully organised by our host. Each man was posted separately with about thirty yards between them, so that no optical delusion, such as an effect of firelight upon the oak panelling, nor any reflection from the circular mirror over the chimneypiece, should be able to deceive more than one of us. Our host fixed himself in the very centre of the hail, facing the gallery at the end; Wells took up his position half-way up the short, straight flight of steps; Harford was at the top of the stairs upon the gallery itself; I was opposite to him at the further end. In this manner, whenever the figure – ghost or burglar – should appear, it must necessarily be between two of us, and be seen from both the right and the left side. We were prepared to believe that one amongst us might be deceived by his senses or by his imagination, but it was clear that two persons could not see the same object from a different point of view and be simultaneously deluded by any effect of light or any optical hallucination.

'Each man was provided with a loaded revolver, a brandy and soda and a sufficient stock of pipes or cigars to last him through the night. We took up our positions at eleven o'clock exactly, and waited.

'At first we were all four very silent and, as I have said before, slightly depressed; but as the hour wore away and nothing was seen or heard we began to talk to each other. Talking, however, was rather a difficulty. To begin with, we had to shout – at least we in the gallery had to shout to Henderson, down in the hall; and though Harford and Wells could converse quite comfortably, I, not being able to see the latter at all from my end of the gallery, had to pass my remarks to him second-hand through Harford, who amused himself in misstating every intelligent remark that I entrusted him with; added to which natural impediments to the "flow of the soul", the elements thought fit to create such a hullabaloo without that conversation was rendered still further a work of difficulty.

'I never remember such a night in all my life. The rain came down in torrents; the wind howled and shrieked wildly amongst the tall chimneys and the bare elm trees without. Every now and then there was a lull, and then, again and again, a long sobbing moan came swirling round and round the house, for all the world like the cry of a human being in agony. It was a night to make one shudder, and thank Heaven for a roof over one's head.

'We all sat on at our separate posts hour after hour, listening to the wind and talking at intervals; but as the time wore on insensibly we became less and less talkative, and a sort of depression crept over us.

'At last we relapsed into a profound silence; then suddenly there came upon us all that chill blast of air, like a breath from a charnel-house, that we had experienced before, and almost simultaneously a hoarse cry broke from Henderson in the body of the hall below, and from Wells half-way up the stairs.

'Harford and I sprang to our feet, and we too saw it.

'The dead man was slowly coming up the stairs. He passed silently up with a sort of still, gliding motion, within a few inches of poor Wells, who shrank back, white with terror, against the wall. Henderson rushed wildly up the staircase in pursuit, whilst Harford and I, up on the gallery, fell instinctively back at his approach.

'He passed between us.

We saw the glitter of his sightless eyes – the shrivelled skin upon his withered face – the mouth that fell away, like the mouth of a corpse, beneath his tawny beard. We felt the cold death-like blast that came with him, and the sickening horror of his terrible presence. Ah! can I ever forget it?'

With a strong shudder Jack Darent buried his face in his hands, and seemed too much overcome for some minutes to be able to proceed.

'My dear fellow, are you *sure*?' I said in an awe-struck whisper.

He lifted his head.

'Forgive me, Lester; the whole business has shaken my nerves so thoroughly that I have not yet been able to get over it. But I have not yet told you the worst.'

'Good Heavens – is there worse?' I ejaculated.

He nodded.

'No sooner,' he continued, 'had this awful creature passed us than Harford clutched at my arm and pointed to the farther end of the gallery.

'"Look!" he cried hoarsely, "the nun!"

'There, coming towards us from the opposite direction, was the veiled figure of a nun.

'There were the long, flowing black and white garments – the gleam of the crucifix at her neck – the jangle of her rosary-beads from her waist; but her face was hidden.

'A sort of desperation seized me. With a violent effort over myself I went towards this fresh apparition.

'"It *must* be a hoax," I said to myself and there was a half-formed intention in my mind of wrenching aside the flowing draperies and of seeing for myself who and what it was. I strode towards the figure

– I stood within half a yard of it. The nun raised her head slowly – and, Lester – *I saw her face!*'

There was a moment's silence.

'What was it like, Jack?' I asked him presently.

He shook his head.

'That I can never tell to any living creature.'

'Was it so horrible?'

He nodded assent, shuddering.

'And what happened next?'

'I believe I fainted. At all events I remembered nothing further. They made me go to the vicarage the next day. I was so knocked over by it all – I was quite ill. I could not have stayed in the house. I stopped there all yesterday, and I got up to town this morning. I wish to Heaven I had taken your advice, old man, and had never gone to the horrible house.'

'I wish you had, Jack,' I answered fervently.

'Do you know that I shall die within the year?' he asked me presently.

I tried to pooh-pooh it.

'My dear fellow, don't take the thing so seriously as all that. Whatever may be the meaning of these horrible apparitions, there can be nothing but an old wives' fable in *that* saying. Why on earth should you die – you of all people, a great strong fellow with a constitution of iron? You don't look much like dying!'

'For all that I shall die. I cannot tell you why I am so certain – but I know that it will be so,' he answered in a low voice. 'And some terrible misfortune will happen to Harford – the other two never saw her – it is he and I who are doomed.'

*   *   *   *   *

A year has passed away. Last summer fashionable society rang for a week or more with the tale of poor Bob Harford's misfortune.

The girl whom he was engaged to and to whom he was devotedly attached – young, beautiful and wealthy – ran away on the eve of her wedding-day with a drinking, swindling villain who had been turned out of ever so many clubs and tabooed for ages by every respectable man in town, and who had nothing but a handsome face and a fascinating manner to recommend him, and who by dint of these had succeeded in gaining a complete ascendancy over the fickle heart of poor Bob's lovely *fiancée*. As to Harford, he sold out and went off to the backwoods of Canada, and has never been heard of since.

And what of Jack Darent? Poor, handsome Jack, with his tall figure and his bright, happy face, and the merry blue eyes that had wiled Bella Lester's heart away! Alas! far away in Southern Africa, poor Jack Darent lies in an unknown grave – slain by a Zulu *assegai* on the fatal plain of Isandula!

And Bella goes about clad in sable garments, heavy-eyed and stricken with sore grief. A widow in heart, if not in name.

THE STORY OF MEDHANS LEA
by E. and H. Heron

The following story has been put together from the account of the affair given by Nare-Jones, sometime house-surgeon at Bart's, of his strange terror and experiences both in Medhans Lea and the pallid avenue between the beeches; of the narrative of Savelsan, of what he saw and heard in the billiard room and afterwards; of the silent and indisputable witness of big, bull-necked Harland himself; and, lastly, of the conversation which subsequently took place between these three men and Mr Flaxman Low, the noted psychologist.

It was by the merest chance that Harland and his two guests spent that memorable evening of the 18th of January, 1889, in the house of Medhans Lea. The house stands on the slope of a partially wooded ridge in one of the Midland Counties. It faces south, and overlooks a wide valley bounded by the blue outlines of the Bredon hills. The place is secluded, the nearest dwelling being a small public-house at the crossroads some mile and a half from the lodge gates.

Medhans Lea is famous for its long straight avenue of beeches, and for other things. Harland, when he signed the lease, was thinking of the avenue of beeches; not of the other things, of which he knew nothing until later.

Harland had made his money by running tea plantations in

Assam, and he owned all the virtues and faults of a man who has spent most of his life abroad. The first time he visited the house he weighed seventeen stone and ended most of his sentences with 'don't yer know?' His ideas could hardly be said to travel on the higher planes of thought, and his chief aim in life was to keep himself down to the seventeen stone. He had a red neck and a blue eye, and was a muscular, inoffensive, good-natured man, with courage to spare, and an excellent voice for accompanying the banjo.

After signing the lease, he found that Medhans Lea needed an immense amount of putting in order and decorating. While this was being done, he came backwards and forwards to the nearest provincial town, where he stopped at a hotel, driving out almost daily to superintend the arrangements of his new habitation. Thus he had been away for the Christmas and New Year, but about the 15th January he returned to the *Red Lion*, accompanied by his friends Nare-Jones and Savelsan, who proposed to move with him into his new house during the course of the ensuing week.

The immediate cause of their visit to Medhans Lea on the evening of the 18th inst. was the fact that the billiard table at the *Red Lion* was not fit, as Harland remarked, to play shinty on, while there was an excellent table just put in at Medhans Lea, where the big billiard-room in the left wing had a wide window with a view down a portion of the beech avenue.

'Hang it!' said Harland, 'I wish they would hurry up with the house. The painters aren't out of it yet, and the people don't come to the Lodge till Monday.'

'It's a pity, too,' remarked Savelsan regretfully, 'when you think of that table.'

Savelsan was an enthusiast in billiards, who spent all the time he could spare from his business, which happened to be teabroking, at the game. He was the more sorry for the delay, since Harland was one of the few men he knew to whom it was not necessary to give points.

'It's a ripping table,' returned Harland. 'Tell you what,' he added,

struck by a happy idea, 'I'll send out Thoms to make things straight for us tomorrow, and we'll put a case of syphons and a bottle of whisky under the seat of the trap, and drive over for a game after dinner.'

The other two agreed to this arrangement, but in the morning Nare-Jones found himself obliged to run up to London to see about securing a berth as ship's doctor. It was settled, however, that on his return he was to follow Harland and Savelsan to Medhans Lea.

He got back by the 8.30, entirely delighted, because he had booked a steamer bound for the Persian Gulf and Karachi, and had gained the cheering intelligence that a virulent type of cholera was lying in wait for the advent of the Mecca pilgrims in at any rate two of the chief ports of call, which would give him precisely the experience he desired.

Having dined, and the night being fine, he ordered a dogcart to take him out to Medhans Lea. The moon had just risen by the time he reached the entrance to the avenue, and as he was beginning to feel cold he pulled up, intending to walk to the house. Then he dismissed the boy and cart, a carriage having been ordered to come for the whole party after midnight. Nare-Jones stopped to light a cigar before entering the avenue, then he walked past the empty lodge. He moved briskly in the best possible temper with himself and all the world. The night was still, and his collar up, his feet fell silently on the dry carriage road, while his mind was away on blue water forecasting his voyage on the S.S. *Sumatra*.

He says he was quite halfway up the avenue before he became conscious of anything unusual. Looking up at the sky, he noticed what a bright, clear night it was, and how sharply defined the outline of the beeches stood out against the vault of heaven. The moon was yet low, and threw netted shadows of bare twigs and branches on the road which ran between black lines of trees in an almost straight vista up to the dead grey face of the house now barely two hundred yards away. Altogether it struck him as forming a pallid picture, etched in like a steel engraving in black, and grey and white.

He was thinking of this when he was aware of words spoken rapidly in his ear, and he turned half expecting to see someone behind him. No one was visible. He had not caught the words, nor could he define the voice; but a vague conviction of some horrible meaning fixed itself in his consciousness.

The night was very still, ahead of him the house glimmered grey and shuttered in the moonlight. He shook himself, and walked on oppressed by a novel sensation compounded of disgust and childish fear; and still, from behind his shoulder, came the evil, voiceless murmuring.

He admits that he passed the end of the avenue at an amble, and was abreast of a semi-circle of shrubbery, when a small object was thrust out from the shadow of the bushes, and lay in the open light. Though the night was peculiarly still, it fluttered and balanced a moment, as if windblown, then came in skimming flights to his feet. He picked it up and made for the door, which yielded to his hand, and he flung it to and bolted it behind him.

Once in the warmly-lit hall his senses returned, and he waited to recover breath and composure before facing the two men whose voices and laughter came from a room on his right. But the door of the room was thrown open, and the burly figure of Harland in his shirt sleeves appeared on the threshold.

'Hullo, Jones, that you? Come along!' he said genially.

'Bless me!' exclaimed Nare-Jones irritably, 'there's not a light in any of the windows. It might be a house of the dead!'

Harland stared at him, but all he said was: 'Have a whisky-and-soda?'

Savelsan, who was leaning over the billiard table, trying side-strokes with his back to Nare-Jones, added:

'Did you expect us to illuminate the place for you? There's not a soul in the house but ourselves.'

'Say when,' said Harland, poising the bottle over a glass.

Nare-Jones laid down what he held in his hand on the corner of the billiard table, and took up his glass.

'What in creation's this?' asked Savelsan.

'I don't know; the wind blew it to my feet just outside,' replied Nare-Jones, between two long pulls at the whisky-and-soda.

'*Blown* to your feet?' repeated Savelsan, taking up the the thing and weighing it in his hand. 'It must be blowing a hurricane then.'

'It isn't blowing at all,' returned Nare-Jones blankly. 'The night is dead calm.'

For the object that had fluttered and rolled so lightly across the turf and gravel was a small, battered, metal calf, made of some heavy brass amalgam.

Savelsan looked incredulously into Nare-Jones' face, and laughed.

'What's wrong with you? You look queer.'

Nare-Jones laughed too; he was already ashamed of the last ten minutes.

Harland was meantime examining the metal calf.

'It's a Bengali idol,' he said. 'It's been knocked about a good bit, by Jove! You say it blew out of the shrubbery?'

'Like a bit of paper. I give you my word, though there was not a breath of wind going,' admitted Nare-Jones.

'Seems odd, don't yer know?' remarked Harland carelessly. 'Now you two fellows had better begin; I'll mark.'

Nare-Jones happened to be in form that night, and Savelsan became absorbed in the delightful difficulty of giving him a sound thrashing.

Suddenly Savelsan paused in his stroke.

What the sin's that?' he asked.

They stood listening. A thin, broken crying could be heard.

'Sounds like green plover.' remarked Nare-Jones, chalking his cue.

'It's a kitten they've shut up somewhere.' said Harland.

'That's a child, and in the deuce of a fright, too,' said Savelsan. 'You'd better go and tuck it up in its little bed, Harland,' he added, with a laugh.

Harland opened the door. There could no longer be any doubt

about the sounds; the stifled shrieks and thin whimpering told of a child in the extremity of pain and fear.

'It's upstairs,' said Harland. 'I'm going to see.'

Nare-Jones picked up a lamp and followed him.

'I stay here,' said Savelsan sitting down by the fire.

In the hall the two men stopped and listened again. It is hard to locate a noise, but this seemed to come from the upper landing.

'Poor little beggar!' exclaimed Harland, as he bounded up the staircase. The bedroom doors opening on the square central landing above were all locked, the keys being on the outside. But the crying led them into a side passage which ended in a single room.

'It's in here, and the door's locked,' said Nare-Jones. 'Call out and see who's there.'

But Harland was set on business. He flung his weight against the panel, and the door burst open, the lock ricocheting noisily into a corner. As they passed in, the crying ceased abruptly.

Harland stood in the centre of the room, while Nare-Jones held up the light to look round.

'The dickens!' exclaimed Harland exhaustively.

The room was entirely empty.

Not so much as a cupboard broke the smooth surface of the walls, only the two low windows and the door by which they had entered.

'This is the room above the billiard-room, isn't it?' said Nare-Jones at last.

'Yes. This is the only one I have not had furnished yet. I thought I might – '

He stopped short, for behind them burst out a peal of harsh, mocking laughter, that rang and echoed between the bare walls.

Both men swung round simultaneously, and both caught a glimpse of a tall, thin figure in black, rocking with laughter in the doorway, but when they turned it was gone. They dashed out into the passage and landing. No one was to be seen. The doors were locked as before, and the staircase and hall were vacant.

After making a prolonged search through every corner of the house, they went back to Savelsan in the billiard-room.

'What were you laughing about? What is it anyway?' began Savelsan at once.

'It's nothing. And we didn't laugh.' replied Nare-Jones definitely.

'But I heard you,' insisted Savelsan. 'And where's the child?'

'I wish you'd go up and find it,' returned Harland grimly. 'We heard the laughing and saw, or thought we saw, a man in black – '

'Something like a priest in a cassock,' put in Nare-Jones.

'Yes, like a priest,' assented Harland, 'but as we turned he disappeared.'

Savelsan sat down and gazed from one to the other of his companions.

'The house behaves as if it was haunted,' he remarked; 'only there is no such thing as an authenticated ghost outside the experiences of the Psychical Research Society. I'd ask the Society down if I were you, Harland. You never can tell what you may find in these old houses.'

'It's not an old house,' replied Harland. 'It was built somewhere about '40. I certainly saw that man; and, look to it, Savelsan. I'll find out who or what he is. That I swear! The English law makes no allowance for ghosts – nor will I.'

'You'll have your hands full, or I'm mistaken,' exclaimed Savelsan, grinning. 'A ghost that laughs and cries in a breath, and rolls battered idols about your front door, is not to be trifled with. The night is young yet – not much past eleven. I vote for a peg all round and then I'll finish off Jones.'

Harland, sunk in a fit of sullen abstraction, sat on a settee, and watched them. On a sudden he said:

'It's turned beastly cold.'

'There's a beastly smell, you mean,' corrected Savelsan crossly, as he went round the table. He had made a break of forty and did not want to be interrupted. 'The draught is from the window.'

'I've not noticed it before this evening,' said Harland, as he opened the shutters to make sure.

As he did so the night air rushed in heavy with the smell as of an old well that has not been uncovered for years, a smell of slime and unwholesome wetness. The lower part of the window was wide open and Harland banged it down.

'It's abominable!' he said, with an angry sniff. 'Enough to give us all typhoid.'

'Only dead leaves,' remarked Nare-Jones. 'There are the rotten leaves of twenty winters under the trees and outside this window. I noticed them when we came over on Tuesday.'

'I'll have them cleared away tomorrow. I wonder how Thoms came to leave this window open,' grumbled Harland, as he closed and bolted the shutter. 'What do you say – forty-five?' and he went over to mark it up.

The game went on for some time, and Nare-Jones was lying across the table with the cue poised, when he heard a slight sound behind him. Looking round he saw Harland, his face flushed and angry, passing softly – wonderfully softly for so big a man, Nare-Jones remembers thinking – along the angle of the wall towards the window.

All three men unite in declaring that they were watching the shutter, which opened inwards as if thrust by some furtive hand from the outside. At the moment Nare-Jones and Savelsan were standing directly opposite to it on the further side of the table, while Harland crouched behind the shutter intent on giving the intruder a lesson.

As the shutter unfolded to its utmost the two men opposite saw a face pressed against the glass, a furrowed evil face, with a wide laugh perched upon its sinister features.

There was a second of absolute stillness, and Nare-Jones' eyes met those other eyes with the fascinated horror of a mutual understanding, as all the foul fancies that had pursued him in the avenue poured back into his mind.

With an uncontrollable impulse of resentment, he snatched a billiard ball from the table and flung it with all his strength at the face. The ball crashed through the glass and through the face beyond it! The glass fell shattered, but the face remained for an instant peering and grinning at the aperture, then as Harland sprang forward it was gone.

'The ball went clean through it!' said Savelsan with a gasp.

They crowded to the window, and throwing up the sash, leant out. The dank smell clung about the air, a boat-shaped moon glimmered between the bare branches, and on the white drive beyond the shrubbery the billiard ball could be seen a shining spot under the moon. Nothing more.

'What was it?' asked Harlad.

'"Only a face at the window,"' quoted Savelsan with an awkward attempt at making light of his own scare. 'Devillish queer face too, eh, Jones?'

'I wish I'd got him!' returned Harland frowning. 'I'm not going to put up with any tricks about the place, don't yer know?'

'You'd bottle any tramp loafing around,' said Nare-Jones

Harland looked down at his immense arms outlined in his shirt-sleeves.

'I could that,' he answered. 'But this chap – did you hit him?'

'Clean through the face! Or, at any rate, it looked like it,' replied Savelsan, as Nare-Jones stood silent.

Harland shut the shutter and poked up the fire.

'It's a cursed creepy affair!' he said, 'I hope the servants won't get hold of this nonsense. Ghosts play the very mischief with a house. Though I don't believe them myself,' he concluded.

Then Savelsan broke out in an unexpected place.

'Nor do I – as a rule,' he said slowly. 'Still you know it is a sickening idea to think of a spirit condemned to haunt the scene of its crime waiting for the world to die.'

Harland and Nare-Jones looked at him.

'Have a whisky neat,' suggested Harland, soothingly. 'I never knew you taken that way before.'

Nare-Jones laughed out. He says he does not know why he laughed nor why he said what follows.

'It's this way,' he said. 'The moment of foul satisfaction is gone for ever, yet for all time the guilty spirit must perpetuate its sin – the sin that brought no lasting reward, only a momentary reward experienced, it may be, centuries ago, but to which still clings the punishment of eternally rehearsing in loneliness, and cold, and gloom, the sin of other days. No punishment can be conceived more horrible. Savelsan is right.'

'I think we've had enough about ghosts,' said Harland cheerfully, 'let's go on. Hurry-up, Savelsan.'

'There's the billiard ball,' said Nare-Jones. 'Who'll go fetch?'

'Not I,' replied Savelsan promptly. 'When that – was at the window, I felt sick.'

Nare-Jones nodded. 'And I wanted to bolt!' he said emphatically.

Harland faced about from the fire.

'And I, though I saw nothing but the shutter, I – hang it! – don't yer know – so did I! There was panic in the air for a minute. But I'm shot if I'm afraid now,' he concluded doggedly, 'I'll go.'

His heavy animal face was lit with courage and resolution.

'I've spent close upon five thousand pounds over this blessed house first and last, and I'm not going to be done out of it by any infernal spiritualism!' he added, as he took down his coat and pulled it on.

'It's all in view from the window except those few yards through the shrubbery,' said Savelsan. 'Take a stick and go. Though, on second thoughts, I bet you a fiver you don't.'

'I don't want a stick,' answered Harland. 'I'm not afraid – not now – and I'd meet most men with my hands.'

Nare-Jones opened the shutters again; the sash was low, and he pushed the window up and leant far out.

'It's not much of a drop,' he said, and slung his legs out over the lintel; but the night was full of the smell, and something else. He

leapt back into the room. 'Don't go, Harland!'

Harland gave him a look that set his blood burning.

'What is there, after all, to be afraid of in a ghost?' he asked heavily.

Nare-Jones, sick with the sense of his own newly-born cowardice, yet entirely unable to master it, answered feebly:

'I can't say, but don't go.'

The words seemed inevitable, though he could have kicked himself for hanging back.'

There was a forced laugh from Savelsan.

'Give it up and stop at home, little man,' he said.

Harland merely snorted in reply, and laid his great leg over the window ledge. The other two watched his big, tweed-clad figure as it crossed the grass and disappeared into the shrubbery.

'You and I are in a preposterous funk,' said Savelsan with unpleasant explicitness, as Harland, whistling loudly, passed into the shadow.

But this was a point on which Nare-Jones could not bring himself to speak at the moment. Then they sat on the sill and waited. The moon shone out clearly above the avenue, which now lay white and undimmed between its crowding trees.

'And he's whistling because he's afraid,' continued Savelsan.

'He's not often afraid,' replied Nare-Jones shortly; 'besides, he's doing what neither of us were very keen on.'

The whistling stopped suddenly. Savelsan said afterwards that he fancied he saw Harland's grey-clad shoulders, with uplifted arms, rise for a second above the bushes.

Then out of the silence came peal upon peal of that infernal laughter, and, following it, the thin pitiful crying of the child. That too ceased, and an absolute stillness seemed to fall upon the place.

They leant out and listened. The minutes passed slowly. In the middle of the avenue the billiard ball glinted on the gravel, but there was no sign of Harland emerging from the shrubbery path.

'He should be there by now,' said Nare-Jones anxiously.

They listened again; everything was quiet. The ticking of Harland's big watch on the mantelpiece was distinctly audible.

'This is too much,' said Nare-Jones. 'I'm going to see where he is.'

He swung himself out on the grass, and Savelsan called to him to wait as he was coming also. While Nare-Jones stood waiting, there was a sound as of a pig grunting and rooting among the dead leaves in the shrubbery.

They ran forward into the darkness, and found the shrubbery path. A minute later they came across something that tossed and snorted and rolled under the shrubs.

'Great Heavens!' cried Nare-Jones, 'it's Harland!'

'He's breaking somebody's neck,' added Savelsan, peering into the gloom.

Nare-Jones was himself again. The powerful instinct of his profession – the help-giving instinct, possessed him to the exclusion of every other feeling.

'He's in a fit – just a fit,' he said in matter of fact tones, as he bent over the struggling form; 'that's all.'

With the assistance of Savelsan, he managed to carry Harland out into the open drive. Harland's eyes were fearful, and froth hung about his blue puffing lips as they laid him down upon the ground. He rolled over, and lay still, while from the shadows broke another shout of laughter.

'It's apoplexy. We must get him away from here,' said Nare-Jones. 'But, first, I'm going to see what is in those bushes.'

He dashed through the shrubbery, backwards and forwards. He seemed to feel the strength of ten men as he wrenched and tore and trampled the branches, letting in the light of the moon to its darkness. At last he paused, exhausted.

'Of course, there's nothing,' said Savelsan wearily. 'What did you expect after the incident of the billiard ball?'

Together, with awful toil, they bore the big man down the narrow avenue, and at the lodge gates they met the carriage.

Some time later the subject of their common experiences at Medhans Lea was discussed amongst the three men. Indeed, for many weeks Harland had not been in a state to discuss any subject at all, but as soon as he was allowed to do so, he invited Nare-Jones and Savelsan to meet Mr Flaxman Low, the scientist, whose works on psychology and kindred matters are so well known, at the Metropole, to thresh out the matter.

Flaxman Low listened with his usual air of gentle abstraction, from time to time making notes on the back of an envelope. He looked at each narrator in turn as he took up the thread of the story. He understood perfectly that the man who stood furthest from the mystery must inevitably have been the self-centred Savelsan; next in order came Nare-Jones, with sympathetic possibilities, but a crowded brain; closest of all would be big, kindly Harland, with more than one strong animal instinct about him, and whose bulk of matter was evidently permeated by a receptive spirit.

When they had ended, Savelsan turned to Flaxman Low.

'There you have the events, Mr Low. Now, the question is how to deal with them.'

'Classify them,' replied Flaxman Low.

'The crying would seem to indicate a child,' began Savelsan, ticking off the list on his fingers; 'the black figure, the face at the window, and the laughter are naturally connected. So far I can go alone. I conclude that we saw the apparition of a man, possibly a priest, who had during his lifetime ill-treated a child, and whose punishment it is to haunt the scene of his crime.'

'Precisely – the punishment being worked out under conditions which admit of human observation,' returned Flaxman Low. 'As for the child the sound of crying was merely part of the *mise-en-scène*. The child was not there.'

'But that explanation stops short of several points. Now about the suggestive thoughts experienced by my friend, Nare-Jones; what brought on the fit in the case of Mr Harland, who assures us that he was not suffering from fright or other violent emotion; and what connection can be traced between all these things and the Bengali idol?' Savelsan ended.

'Let us take the Bengali idol first,' said Low. 'It is just one of those discrepant particulars which, at first sight, seem wholly irreconcilable with the rest of the phenomena, yet these often form a test point, by which our theories are proved or otherwise.' Flaxman Low took up the metal calf from the table as he spoke. 'I should be inclined to connect this with the child. Observe it. It has not been roughly used; it is rubbed and dinted as a plaything usually is. I should say the child may have had Anglo-Indian relations.'

At this, Nare-Jones bent forward, and in his turn examined the idol, while Savelsan smiled his thin, incredulous smile.

'These are ingenious theories,' he said; 'but we are really no nearer to facts, I am afraid.'

'The only proof would be an inquiry into the former history of Medhans Lea; if events had happened there which would go to support this theory, why, then – But I cannot supply that information since I never heard of Medhans Lea or the ghost until I entered this room.'

'I know something of Medhans Lea,' put in Nare-Jones. 'I found out a good deal about it before I left the place. And I must congratulate Mr Low on his methods, for his theory tallies in a wonderful manner with the facts of the case. The house was long known to be haunted. It seems that many years ago a lady, the widow of an Indian officer, lived there with her only child, a boy, for whom she engaged a tutor, a dark-looking man. who wore a long black coat like a cassock, and was called "the Jesuit" by the country people.

'One evening the man took the boy out into the shrubbery. Screams were heard, and when the child was brought in he was found to have lost his reason. He used to cry and shriek incessantly, but was never able to tell what had been done to him as long as he

lived. As for this idol, the mother probably brought it with her from India, and the child used it as a toy, perhaps, because he was allowed no others. Hullo!' In handling the calf, Nare-Jones had touched some hidden spring, the head opened, disclosing a small cavity, from which dropped a little ring of blue beads, such as children make. He held it up. 'This affords good proof.'

'Yes,' admitted Savelsan grudgingly. 'But how about your sensations and Harland's seizure? You must know what was done to the child, Harland – what did you see in the shrubbery?'

Harland's florid face assumed a queer pallor.

'I saw something,' replied he hesitatingly, 'but I can't recall what it was. I only remember being possessed by a blind terror, and then nothing more until I recovered consciousness at the hotel next day.'

'Can you account for this, Mr Low?' asked Nare-Jones, 'and there was also my strange notion of the whispering in the avenue.'

'I think so,' replied Flaxman Low. 'I believe that the theory of atmospheric influences, which includes the power of environment to reproduce certain scenes and also thoughts, would throw light upon your sensations as well as Mr Harland's. Such influences play a far larger part in our everyday experience than we have as yet any idea of.'

There was a silence of a few moments; then Harland spoke:

'I fancy that we have said all that there is to be said upon the matter. We are much obliged to you, Mr Low'. I don't know how it strikes you other fellows but, speaking for myself, I have seen enough of ghosts to last me for a very long time.'

'And now' ended Harland wearily, 'if you have no objection, we will pass on to pleasanter subjects.'

THE TOMB OF SARAH
by Frederick George Loring

My father was the head of a celebrated firm of church restorers and decorators about sixty years ago. He took a keen interest in his work, and made an especial study of any old legends or family histories that came under his observation. He was necessarily very well read and thoroughly well posted in all questions of folklore and mediæval legend. As he kept a careful record of every case he investigated the manuscripts he left at his death have a special interest. From amongst them I have selected the following, as being a particularly weird and extraordinary experience. In presenting it to the public I feel it is superfluous to apologise for its supernatural character.

MY FATHER'S DIARY

1841. – *June 17th*. Received a commission from my old friend Peter Grant to enlarge and restore the chancel of his church at Hagarstone, in the wilds of the West Country.

July 5th. Went down to Hagarstone with my head man, Somers. A very long and tiring journey.

July 7th. Got the work well started. The old church is one of special interest to the antiquarian, and I shall endeavour while restoring it to

alter the existing arrangements as little as possible. One large tomb, however, must be moved bodily ten feet at least to the southward. Curiously enough, there is a somewhat forbidding inscription upon it in Latin, and I am sorry that this particular tomb should have to be moved. It stands amongst the graves of the Kenyons, an old family which has been extinct in these parts for centuries. The inscription on it runs thus:

SARAH.

1630.

FOR THE SAKE OF THE DEAD AND THE WELFARE

OF THE LIVING, LET THIS SEPULCHRE REMAIN

UNTOUCHED AND ITS OCCUPANT UNDISTURBED TILL

THE COMING OF CHRIST.

IN THE NAME OF THE FATHER, THE SON, AND

THE HOLY GHOST.

July 8th. Took counsel with Grant concerning the 'Sarah Tomb'. We are both very loth to disturb it, but the ground has sunk so beneath it that the safety of the church is in danger; thus we have no choice. However, the work shall be done as reverently as possible under our own direction.

Grant says there is a legend in the neighbourhood that it is the tomb of the last of the Kenyons, the evil Countess Sarah, who was murdered in 1630. She lived quite alone in the old castle, whose ruins still stand three miles from here on the road to Bristol. Her reputation was an evil one even for those days. She was a witch or were-woman, the only companion of her solitude being a familiar in the shape of a huge Asiatic wolf. This creature was reputed to seize upon children, or failing these, sheep and other small animals, and convey them to the castle, where the Countess used to suck their blood. It was popularly supposed that she could never be killed. This, however, proved a fallacy, since she was strangled one day by a mad peasant woman who had lost two children, she declaring that they had both been seized and carried off by the Countess's familiar. This is a very interesting story, since it points to a local superstition very similar to that of the Vampire, existing in Slavonic and Hungarian Europe.

The tomb is built of black marble, surmounted by an enormous slab of the same material. On the slab is a magnificent group of figures. A young and handsome woman reclines upon a couch; round her neck is a piece of rope, the end of which she holds in her hand. At her side is a gigantic dog with bared fangs and lolling tongue. The face of the reclining figure is a cruel one: the corners of the mouth are curiously lifted, showing the sharp points of long canine or dog teeth. The whole group, though magnificently executed, leaves a most unpleasant sensation.

If we move the tomb it will have to be done in two pieces, the covering slab first and then the tomb proper. We have decided to remove the covering slab tomorrow.

July 9th. – 6 p.m. A very strange day.

By noon everything was ready for lifting off the covering stone, and after the men's dinner we started the jacks and pulleys. The slab lifted easily enough, though it fitted closely into its seat and was further secured by some sort of mortar or putty, which must have kept the interior perfectly air-tight.

None of us were prepared for the horrible rush of foul, mouldy air that escaped as the cover lifted clear of its seating. And the contents that gradually came into view were more startling still. There lay the fully dressed body of a woman, wizened and shrunk and ghastly pale as if from starvation. Round her neck was a loose cord and, judging by the scars still visible, the story of death of strangulation was true enough.

The most horrible part, however, was the extraordinary freshness of the body. Except for the appearance of starvation, life might have been only just extinct. The flesh was soft and white, the eyes were wide open and seemed to stare at us with a fearful understanding in them. The body itself lay on mould, without any pretence to coffin or shell.

For several moments we gazed with horrible curiosity, and then it became too much for my work-men, who implored us to replace the covering slab. That, of course, we would not do; but I set the carpenters to work at once to make a temporary cover while we moved the tomb to its new position. This is a long job, and will take two or three days at least.

July 9th. – 9 p.m. Just at sunset we were startled by the howling of, seemingly, every dog in the village. It lasted for ten minutes or a quarter of an hour, and then ceased as suddenly as it began. This, and a curious mist that has risen round the church, makes me feel rather anxious about the 'Sarah Tomb'. According to the best-established traditions of the Vampire-haunted countries, the disturbance of dogs or wolves at sunset is supposed to indicate the presence of one of these fiends, and local fog is always considered to be a certain sign. The Vampire has the power of producing it for the purpose of concealing its movements near its hiding-place at any time.

I dare not mention or even hint my fears to the Rector, for he is, not unnaturally perhaps, a rank disbeliever in many things that I know, from experience, are not only possible but even probable. I must work this out alone at first, and get his aid without his knowing in what direction he is helping me. I shall now watch till midnight at least.

10.15 p.m. As I feared and half expected. Just before ten there was another outburst of the hideous howling. It was commenced most distinctly by a particularly horrible and blood-curdling wail from the vicinity of the churchyard. The chorus lasted only a few minutes, however, and at the end of it I saw a large dark shape, like a huge dog, emerge from the fog and lope away at a rapid canter towards

the open country. Assuming this to be what I fear, I shall see it return soon after midnight.

12.30 p.m. I was right. Almost as midnight struck I saw the beast returning. It stopped at the spot where the fog seemed to commence, and lifting its head, gave tongue to that particularly horrible long-drawn wail that I had noticed as preceding the outburst earlier in the evening.

Tomorrow I shall tell the Rector what I have seen; and if, as I expect, we hear of some neighbouring sheepfold having been raided, I shall get him to watch with me for this nocturnal marauder. I shall also examine the 'Sarah Tomb' for something which he may notice without any previous hint from me.

July 10th. I found the workmen this morning much disturbed in mind about the howling of the dogs. 'We doan't like it, zur,' one of them said to me – 'we doan't like it; there was summat abroad last night that was unholy.' They were still more uncomfortable when the news came round that a large dog had made a raid upon a flock of sheep, scattering them far and wide, and leaving three of them dead with torn throats in the field.

When I told the Rector of what I had seen and what was being said in the village, he immediately decided that we must try and catch or at least identify the beast I had seen. 'Of course,' said he, 'it is some dog lately imported into the neighbourhood, for I know of nothing about here nearly as large as the animal you describe, though its size may be due to the deceptive moonlight.'

This afternoon I asked the Rector, as a favour, to assist me in lifting the temporary cover that was on the tomb, giving as an excuse the reason that I wished to obtain a portion of the curious mortar with which it had been sealed. After a slight demur he consented, and we raised the lid. If the sight that met our eyes gave me a shock, at least it appalled Grant.

'Great God!' he exclaimed; 'the woman is alive!'

And so it seemed for a moment. The corpse had lost much of its

starved appearance and looked hideously fresh and alive. It was still wrinkled and shrunken, but the lips were firm, and of the rich red hue of health. The eyes, if possible, were more appalling than ever, though fixed and staring. At one corner of the mouth I thought I noticed a slight dark-coloured froth, but I said nothing about it then.

'Take your piece of mortar, Harry,' gasped Grant, 'and let us shut the tomb again. God help me! Parson though I am, such dead faces frighten me!'

Nor was I sorry to hide that terrible face again; but I got my bit of mortar, and I have advanced a step towards the solution of the mystery.

This afternoon the tomb was moved several feet towards its new position, but it will be two or three days yet before we shall be ready to replace the slab.

10.15 p.m. Again the same howling at sunset, the same fog enveloping the church, and at ten o'clock the same great beast slipping silently out into the open country. I must get the Rector's help and watch for its return. But precautions we must take, for if things are as I believe, we take our lives in our hands when we venture out into the night to waylay the – Vampire. Why not admit it at once? For that the beast I have seen is the Vampire of that evil thing in the tomb I can have no reasonable doubt.

Not yet come to its full strength, thank Heaven! after the starvation of nearly two centuries, for at present it can only maraud as a wolf apparently. But, in a day or two, when full power returns, that dreadful woman in new strength and beauty will be able to leave her refuge. Then it would not be sheep merely that would satisfy her disgusting lust for blood, but victims that would yield their life-blood without a murmur to her caressing touch – victims that, dying of her foul embrace, themselves must become Vampires in their turn to prey on others.

Mercifully my knowledge gives me a safeguard; for that little piece of mortar that I rescued today from the tomb contains a portion of the Sacred Host, and who holds it, humbly and firmly believing in its virtue, may pass safely through such an ordeal as I intend to submit myself and the Rector to tonight.

12.30 p.m. Our adventure is over for the present, and we are back safe.

After writing the last entry recorded above, I went off to find Grant and tell him that the marauder was out on the prowl again. 'But, Grant,' I said, 'before we start out tonight I must insist that you will let me prosecute this affair in my own way; you must promise to put yourself completely under my orders, without asking any questions as to the why and wherefore.'

After a little demur, and some excusable chaff on his part at the serious view I was taking of what he called a 'dog hunt', he gave me his promise. I then told him that we were to watch tonight and try and track the mysterious beast, but not to interfere with it in any way. I think, in spite of his jests, that I impressed him with the fact that there might be, after all, good reason for my precautions.

It was just after eleven when we stepped out into the still night.

Our first move was to try and penetrate the dense fog round the church, but there was something so chilly about it, and a faint smell so disgustingly rank and loathsome, that neither our nerves nor our stomachs were proof against it. Instead, we stationed ourselves in the dark shadow of a yew tree that commanded a good view of the wicket entrance to the churchyard.

At midnight the howling of the dogs began again, and in a few minutes we saw a large grey shape, with green eyes shining like lamps, shamble swiftly down the path towards us.

The Rector started forward, but I laid a firm hand upon his arm and whispered a warning 'Remember!' Then we both stood very still and watched as the great beast cantered swiftly by. It was real enough, for we could hear the clicking of its nails on the stone flags. It passed within a few yards of us, and seemed to be nothing more nor less than a great grey wolf, thin and gaunt, with bristling hair and dripping jaws. It stopped where the mist commenced, and

turned round. It was truly a horrible sight, and made one's blood run cold. The eyes burnt like fires, the upper lip was snarling and raised, showing the great canine teeth, while round the mouth clung and dripped a dark-coloured froth.

It raised its head and gave tongue to its long wailing howl, which was answered from afar by the village dogs. After standing for a few moments it turned and disappeared into the thickest part of the fog.

Very shortly afterwards the atmosphere began to clear, and within ten minutes the mist was all gone, the dogs in the village were silent, and the night seemed to reassume its normal aspect. We examined the spot where the beast had been standing and found, plainly enough upon the stone flags, dark spots of froth and saliva.

'Well, Rector,' I said, 'will you admit now, in view of the things you have seen today, in consideration of the legend, the woman in the tomb, the fog, the howling dogs and, last but not least, the mysterious beast you have seen so close, that there is something not quite normal in it all? Will you put yourself unreservedly in my hands and help me, *whatever I may do*, to first make assurance doubly sure, and finally take the necessary steps for putting an end to this horror of the night?' I saw that the uncanny influence of the night was strong upon him, and wished to impress it as much as possible.

'Needs must,' he replied, 'when the Devil drives: and in the face of what I have seen I must believe that some unholy forces are at work. Yet, how can they work in the sacred precincts of a church? Shall we not call rather upon Heaven to assist us in our need.'

'Grant,' I said solemnly, 'that we must do, each in his own way. God helps those who help themselves, and by His help and the light of my knowledge we must fight this battle for Him and the poor lost soul within.'

We then returned to the rectory and to our rooms, though I have sat up to write this account while the scene is fresh in my mind.

July 11th. Found the workmen again very much disturbed in their minds, and full of a strange dog that had been seen during the night by several people, who had hunted it. Farmer Stotman, who had been watching his sheep (the same flock that had been raided the night before), had surprised it over a fresh carcass and tried to drive it off, but its size and fierceness so alarmed him that he had beaten a hasty retreat for a gun. When he returned the animal was gone, though he found that three more sheep from his flock were dead and torn.

The 'Sarah Tomb' was moved today to its new position; but it was a long, heavy business, and there was not time to replace the covering slab. For this I was glad, as in the prosaic light of day the Rector almost disbelieves the events of the night, and is prepared to think everything to have been magnified and distorted by our imagination.

As, however, I could not possibly proceed with my war of extermination against this foul thing without assistance, and as there is nobody else I can rely upon, I appealed to him for one more night – to convince him that it was no delusion, but a ghastly, horrible truth, which must be fought and conquered for our own sakes, as well as that of all those living in the neighbourhood.

'Put yourself in my hands, Rector,' I said, 'for tonight at least. Let us take those precautions which my study of the subject tells me are the right ones. Tonight you and I must watch in the church; and I feel assured that tomorrow you will be as convinced as I am, and be equally prepared to take those awful steps which I know to be proper, and I must warn you that we shall find a more startling change in the body lying there than you noticed yesterday.'

My words came true; for on raising the wooden cover once more the rank stench of a slaughterhouse arose, making us feel positively sick. There lay the Vampire, but how changed from the starved and shrunken corpse we saw two days ago for the first time! The wrinkles had almost disappeared, the flesh was firm and full, the crimson lips grinned horribly over the long pointed teeth, and a distinct smear of blood had trickled down one corner of the mouth. We set our teeth, however, and hardened our hearts. Then we replaced the cover and put what we had collected into a safe place in the vestry. Yet even now Grant could not believe that there was any real or pressing danger concealed in that awful tomb, as he raised strenuous objections to any apparent desecration of the body without further proof. This he shall have tonight. God grant that I am not taking too much on myself. If there is any truth in old legends it would be easy enough to destroy the Vampire now; but Grant will not have it.

I hope for the very best of this night's work, but the danger in waiting is very great.

6 p.m. I have prepared everything: the sharp knives, the pointed stake, fresh garlic, and the wild dog-roses. All these I have taken and concealed in the vestry, where we can get at them when our solemn vigil commences.

If either or both of us die with our fearful task undone, let those reading my record see that this is done. I lay it upon them as a solemn obligation. 'That the Vampire be pierced through the heart with the stake, then let the Burial Service be read over the poor clay at last released from its doom. Thus shall the Vampire cease to be, and a lost soul rest.'

July 12th. All is over. After the most terrible night of watching and horror one Vampire at least will trouble the world no more. But how thankful should we be to a merciful Providence that that awful tomb was not disturbed by anyone not having the knowledge necessary to deal with its dreadful occupant! I write this with no feelings of self-complacency, but simply with a great gratitude for the years of study I have been able to devote to this special subject.

And now to my tale.

Just before sunset last night the Rector and I locked ourselves into the church, and took up our position in the pulpit. It was one of those pulpits, to be found in some churches, which is entered from the vestry, the preacher appearing at a good height through an

arched opening in the wall. This gave us a sense of security (which we felt we needed), a good view of the interior, and direct access to the implements which I had concealed in the vestry.

The sun set and the twilight gradually deepened and faded. There was, so far, no sign of the usual fog, nor any howling of the dogs. At nine o'clock the moon rose, and her pale light gradually flooded the aisles, and still no sign of any kind from the 'Sarah Tomb'. The Rector had asked me several times what he might expect, but I was determined that no words or thought of mine should influence him, and that he should be convinced by his own senses alone.

By half-past ten we were both getting very tired, and I began to think that perhaps after all we should see nothing that night. However, soon after eleven we observed a light mist rising from the 'Sarah Tomb'. It seemed to scintillate and sparkle as it rose, and curled in a sort of pillar or spiral.

I said nothing, but I heard the Rector give a sort of gasp as he clutched my arm feverishly. 'Great Heaven!' he whispered, 'it is taking shape.'

And, true enough, in a very few moments we saw standing erect by the tomb the ghastly figure of the Countess Sarah!

She looked thin and haggard still, and her face was deadly white; but the crimson lips looked like a hideous gash in the pale cheeks, and her eyes glared like red coals in the gloom of the church.

It was a fearful thing to watch as she stepped unsteadily down the aisle, staggering a little as if from weakness and exhaustion. This was perhaps natural, as her body must have suffered much physically from her long incarceration, in spite of the unholy forces which kept it fresh and well.

We watched her to the door, and wondered what would happen; but it appeared to present no difficulty, for she melted through it and disappeared.

'Now, Grant,' I said, 'do you believe?'

'Yes,' he replied, 'I must. Everything is in your hands, and I will

obey your commands to the letter, if you can only instruct me how to rid my poor people of this unnameable terror.'

'By God's help I will,' said I; 'but you shall be yet more convinced first, for we have a terrible work to do, and much to answer for in the future, before we leave the church again this morning. And now to work, for in its present weak state the Vampire will not wander far, but may return at any time, and must not find us unprepared.'

We stepped down from the pulpit and, taking dog-roses and garlic from the vestry, proceeded to the tomb. I arrived first and, throwing off the wooden cover, cried, 'Look! it is empty!' There was nothing there! Nothing except the impress of the body in the loose damp mould!

I took the flowers and laid them in a circle round the tomb, for legend teaches us that Vampires will not pass over these particular blossoms if they can avoid it.

Then, eight or ten feet away, I made a circle on the stone pavement, large enough for the Rector and myself to stand in, and within the circle I placed the implements that I had brought into the church with me.

'Now,' I said, 'from this circle, which nothing unholy can step across, you shall see the Vampire face to face, and see her afraid to cross that other circle of garlic and dog-roses to regain her unholy refuge. But on no account step beyond the holy place you stand in, for the Vampire has a fearful strength not her own, and, like a snake, can draw her victim willingly to his own destruction.'

Now so far my work was done, and, calling the Rector, we stepped into the Holy Circle to await the Vampire's return.

Nor was this long delayed. Presently a damp, cold odour seemed to pervade the church, which made our hair bristle and flesh to creep. And then down the aisle with noiseless feet came That which we watched for.

I heard the Rector mutter a prayer, and I held him tightly by the arm, for he was shivering violently.

Long before we could distinguish the features we saw the glowing eyes and the crimson sensual mouth. She went straight to her tomb, but stopped short when she encountered my flowers. She walked right round the tomb seeking a place to enter, and as she walked she saw us. A spasm of diabolical hate and fury passed over her face; but it quickly vanished, and a smile of love, more devilish still, took its place. She stretched out her arms towards us. Then we saw that round her mouth gathered a bloody froth, and from under her lips long pointed teeth gleamed and champed.

She spoke: a soft soothing voice, a voice that carried a spell with it, and affected us both strangely, particularly the Rector. I wished to test as far as possible, without endangering our lives, the Vampire's power.

Her voice had a soporific effect, which I resisted easily enough, but which seemed to throw the Rector into a sort of trance. More than this: it seemed to compel him to her in spite of his efforts to resist.

'Come!' she said – 'come! I give sleep and peace – sleep and peace – sleep and peace.'

She advanced a little towards us; but not far, for I noted that the Sacred Circle seemed to keep her back like an iron hand.

My companion seemed to become demoralised and spellbound. He tried to step forward and, finding me detain him, whispered, 'Harry, let go! I must go! She is calling me! I must! I must! Oh, help me! Help me!' And he began to struggle.

It was time to finish.

'Grant!' I cried, in a loud, firm voice, 'in the name of all that you hold sacred, have done and play the man!' He shuddered violently and gasped, 'Where am I?' Then he remembered, and clung to me convulsively for a moment.

At this a look of damnable hate changed the smiling face before us, and with a sort of shriek she staggered back.

'Back!' I cried: 'back to your unholy tomb! No longer shall you molest the suffering world! Your end is near.'

It was fear that now showed itself in her beautiful face (for it was beautiful in spite of its horror) as she shrank back, back and over the circlet of flowers, shivering as she did so. At last, with a low mournful cry, she appeared to melt back again into her tomb.

As she did so the first gleams of the rising sun lit up the world, and I knew all danger was over for the day.

Taking Grant by the arm, I drew him with me out of the circle and led him to the tomb. There lay the Vampire once more, still in her living death as we had a moment before seen her in her devilish life. But in the eyes remained that awful expression of hate, and cringing, appalling fear.

Grant was pulling himself together.

'Now,' I said, 'will you dare the last terrible act and rid the world for ever of this horror?'

'By God!' he said solemnly, 'I will. Tell me what to do.'

'Help me to lift her out of her tomb. She can harm us no more,' I replied.

With averted faces we set to our terrible task, and laid her out upon the flags.

'Now,' I said, 'read the Burial Service over the poor body, and then let us give it its release from this living hell that holds it.'

Reverently the Rector read the beautiful words, and reverently I made the necessary responses. When it was over I took the stake and, without giving myself time to think, plunged it with all my strength through the heart.

As though really alive, the body for a moment writhed and kicked convulsively, and an awful heart-rending shriek woke the silent church; then all was still.

Then we lifted the poor body back; and, thank God! the consolation that legend tells is never denied to those who have to do such awful work as ours came at last. Over the face stole a great and solemn peace; the lips lost their crimson hue, the prominent sharp teeth sank back into the mouth, and for a moment we saw before us

the calm, pale face of a most beautiful woman, who smiled as she slept. A few minutes more, and she faded away to dust before our eyes as we watched. We set to work and cleaned up every trace of our work, and then departed for the rectory. Most thankful were we to step out of the church, with its horrible associations, into the rosy warmth of the summer morning.

With the above end the notes in my father's diary, though a few days later this further entry occurs:

July 15th. Since the 12th everything has been quiet and as usual. We replaced and sealed up the 'Sarah Tomb' this morning. The workmen were surprised to find the body had disappeared, but took it to be the natural result of exposing it to the air.

One odd thing came to my ears today. It appears that the child of one of the villagers strayed from home the night of the 11th inst., and was found asleep in a coppice near the church, very pale and quite exhausted. There were two small marks on her throat, which have since disappeared.

What does this mean? I have, however, kept it to myself, as, now that the Vampire is no more, no further danger either to that child or any other is to be apprehended. It is only those who die of the Vampire's embrace that become Vampires at death in their turn.

EVELINE'S VISITANT
by Mary Elizabeth Braddon

It was at a masked ball at the Palais Royal that my fatal quarrel with my first cousin André de Brissac began. The quarrel was about a woman. The women who followed the footsteps of Philip of Orleans were the causes of many such disputes; and there was scarcely one fair head in all that glittering throng which, to a man versed in social histories and mysteries, might not have seemed bedabbled with blood.

I shall not record the name of her for love of whom André de Brissac and I crossed one of the bridges, in the dim August dawn on our way to the waste ground beyond the church of Saint-Germain des Prés.

There were many beautiful vipers in those days, and she was one of them. I can feel the chill breath of that August morning blowing in my face, as I sit in my dismal chamber at my château of Puy Verdun tonight, alone in the stillness, writing the strange story of my life. I can see the white mist rising from the river, the grim outline of the Châtelet, and the square towers of Notre Dame black against the pale-grey sky. Even more vividly can I recall André's fair young face, as he stood opposite to me with his two friends – scoundrels both, and alike eager for that unnatural fray. We were a strange group to be

seen in a summer sunrise, all of us fresh from the heat and clamour of the Regent's saloons – André in a quaint hunting-dress copied from a family portrait at Puy Verdun, I costumed as one of Law's Mississippi Indians; the other men in like garish frippery, adorned with broideries and jewels that looked wan in the pale light of dawn.

Our quarrel had been a fierce one – a quarrel which could have but one result, and that the direst. I had struck him; and the welt raised by my open hand was crimson upon his fair womanish face as he stood opposite to me. The eastern sun shone on the face presently, and dyed the cruel mark with a deeper red; but the sting of my own wrongs was fresh, and I had not yet learned to despise myself for that brutal outrage.

To André de Brissac such an insult was most terrible. He was the favourite of Fortune, the favourite of women; and I was nothing, a rough soldier who had done my country good service, but in the boudoir of a Parabère a mannerless boor.

We fought, and I wounded him mortally. Life had been very sweet for him; and I think that a frenzy of despair took possession of him when he felt the life-blood ebbing away. He beckoned me to him as he lay on the ground. I went, and knelt at his side.

'Forgive me, André!' I murmured.

He took no more heed of my words than if that piteous entreaty had been the idle ripple of the river near at hand.

'Listen to me, Hector de Brissac,' he said. 'I am not one who believes that a man has done with earth because his eyes glaze and his jaw stiffens. They will bury me in the old vault at Puy Verdun; and you will be master of the château. Ah, I know how lightly they take things in these days, and how Dubois will laugh when he hears that Ca has been killed in a duel. They will bury me, and sing masses for my soul; but you and I have not finished our affair yet, my cousin. I will be with you when you least look to see me, – I, with this ugly scar upon the face that women have praised and loved. I will come to you when your life seems brightest. I will come between you and

all that you hold fairest and dearest. My ghostly hand shall drop a poison in your cup of joy. My shadowy form shall shut the sunlight from your life. Men with such iron will as mine can do what they please, Hector de Brissac. It is my will to haunt you when I am dead.'

All this in short broken sentences he whispered into my ear. I had need to bend my ear close to his dying lips; but the iron will of André de Brissac was strong enough to do battle with Death, and I believe he said all he wished to say before his head fell back upon the velvet cloak they had spread beneath him, never to be lifted again.

As he lay there, you would have fancied him a fragile stripling, too fair and frail for the struggle called life; but there are those who remember the brief manhood of André de Brissac, and who can bear witness to the terrible force of that proud nature.

I stood looking down at the young face with that foul mark upon it, and God knows I was sorry for what I had done.

Of those blasphemous threats which he had whispered in my ear I took no heed. I was a soldier, and a believer. There was nothing absolutely dreadful to me in the thought that I had killed this man. I had killed many men on the battlefield; and this one had done me cruel wrong.

My friends would have had me cross the frontier to escape the consequences of my act; but I was ready to face those consequences, and I remained in France. I kept aloof from the court, and received a hint that I had best confine myself to my own province. Many masses were chanted in the little chapel of Puy Verdun, for the soul of my dead cousin, and his coffin filled a niche in the vault of our ancestors.

His death had made me a rich man; and the thought that it was so made my newly-acquired wealth very hateful to me. I lived a lonely existence in the old château, where I rarely held converse with any but the servants of the household, all of whom had served my cousin, and none of whom liked me.

It was a hard and bitter life. It galled me, when I rode through the village, to see the peasant-children shrink away from me. I have seen old women cross themselves stealthily as I passed them by. Strange reports had gone forth about me; and there were those who whispered that I had given my soul to the Evil One as the price of my cousin's heritage. From my boyhood I had been dark of visage and stern of manner; and hence, perhaps, no woman's love had ever been mine. I remembered my mother's face in all its changes of expression; but I can remember no look of affection that ever shone on me. That other woman, beneath whose feet I laid my heart, was pleased to accept my homage, but she never loved me; and the end was treachery.

I had grown hateful to myself, and had well-nigh begun to hate my fellow-creatures, when a feverish desire seized upon me, and I pined to be back in the press and throng of the busy world once again. I went back to Paris, where I kept myself aloof from the court, and where an angel took compassion upon me.

She was the daughter of an old comrade, a man whose merits had been neglected, whose achievements had been ignored, and who sulked in his shabby lodging like a rat in a hole, while all Paris went mad with the Scotch Financier, and gentlemen and lacqueys were trampling one another to death in the Rue Quincampoix. The only child of this little cross-grained old captain of dragoons was an incarnate sunbeam, whose mortal name was Eveline Duchalet.

She loved me. The richest blessings of our lives are often those which cost us least. I wasted the best years of my youth in the worship of a wicked woman, who jilted and cheated me at last.

I gave this meek angel but a few courteous words – a little fraternal tenderness – and lo, she loved me. The life which had been so dark and desolate grew bright beneath her influence; and I went back to Puy Verdun with a fair young bride for my companion.

Ah, how sweet a change there was in my life and in my home! The village children no longer shrank appalled as the dark horseman rode by, the village crones no longer crossed themselves; for a woman rode by his side – a woman whose charities had won the

love of all those ignorant creatures, and whose companionship had transformed the gloomy lord of the chateau into a loving husband and a gentle master. The old retainers forgot the untimely fate of my cousin, and served me with cordial willingness, for love of their young mistress.

There are no words which can tell the pure and perfect happiness of that time. I felt like a traveller who had traversed the frozen seas of an arctic region, remote from human love or human companionship, to find himself on a sudden in the bosom of a verdant valley, in the sweet atmosphere of home. The change seemed too bright to be real; and I strove in vain to put away from my mind the vague suspicion that my new life was but some fantastic dream.

So brief were those halcyon hours, that, looking back on them now, it is scarcely strange if I am still half inclined to fancy the first days of my married life could have been no more than a dream.

Neither in my days of gloom nor in my days of happiness had I been troubled by the recollection of André's blasphemous oath.

The words which with his last breath he had whispered in my ear were vain and meaningless to me. He had vented his rage in those idle threats, as he might have vented it in idle execrations.

That he will haunt the footsteps of his enemy after death is the one revenge which a dying man can promise himself; and if men had power thus to avenge themselves, the earth would be peopled with phantoms.

I had lived for three years at Puy Verdun; sitting alone in the solemn midnight by the hearth where he had sat, pacing the corridors that had echoed his footfall; and in all that time my fancy had never so played me false as to shape the shadow of the dead. Is it strange, then, if I had forgotten André's horrible promise? There was no portrait of my cousin at Puy Verdun. It was the age of boudoir art, and a miniature set in the lid of a gold bonbonnière, or hidden artfully in a massive bracelet, was more fashionable than a clumsy life-size image, fit only to hang on the gloomy walls of a provincial château rarely visited by its owner. My cousin's fair face had adorned more than one bonbonnière, and had been concealed in more than one bracelet; but it was not among the faces that looked down from the panelled walls of Puy Verdun.

In the library I found a picture which awoke painful associations. It was the portrait of a de Brissac, who had flourished in the time of Francis the First; and it was from this picture that my cousin André had copied the quaint hunting-dress he wore at the Regent's ball. The library was a room in which I spent a good deal of my life; and I ordered a curtain to be hung before this picture.

We had been married three months, when Eveline one day asked, 'Who is the lord of the château nearest to this?'

I looked with her in astonishment.

'My dearest,' I answered, 'do you not know that there is no other château within forty miles of Puy Verdun?'

'Indeed!' she said; 'that is strange.'

I asked her why the fact seemed strange to her; and after much entreaty I obtained from her the reason of her surprise.

In her walks about the park and woods during the last month, she had met a man who, by his dress and bearing, was obviously of noble rank. She had imagined that he occupied some château near at hand, and that his estate adjoined ours. I was at a loss to imagine who this stranger could be; for my estate of Puy Verdun lay in the heart of a desolate region, and unless when some traveller's coach went lumbering and jingling through the village, one had little more chance of encountering a gentleman than of meeting a demigod.

'Have you seen this man often, Eveline?' I asked.

She answered, in a tone which had a touch of sadness, 'I see him every day.'

'Where, dearest?'

'Sometimes in the park, sometimes in the wood. You know the little cascade, Hector, where there is some old neglected rock-work that forms a kind of cavern. I have taken a fancy to that spot, and

have spent many mornings there reading. Of late I have seen the stranger there every morning.'

'He has never dared to address you?'

'Never. I have looked up from my book, and have seen him standing at a little distance, watching me silently. I have continued reading; and when I have raised my eyes again I have found him gone. He must approach and depart with a stealthy tread, for I never hear his footfall. Sometimes I have almost wished that he would speak to me. It is so terrible to see him standing silently there.'

'He is some insolent peasant who seeks to frighten you.'

My wife shook her head.

'He is no peasant,' she answered. 'It is not by his dress alone I judge, for that is strange to me. He has an air of nobility which it is impossible to mistake.'

'Is he young or old?'

'He is young and handsome.'

I was much disturbed by the idea of this stranger's intrusion on my wife's solitude; and I went straight to the village to inquire if any stranger had been seen there. I could hear of no one. I questioned the servants closely, but without result. Then I determined to accompany my wife in her walks, and to judge for myself of the rank of the stranger.

For a week I devoted all my mornings to rustic rambles with Eveline in the park and woods; and in all that week we saw no one but an occasional peasant in sabots, or one of our own household returning from a neighbouring farm.

I was a man of studious habits, and those summer rambles disturbed the even current of my life. My wife perceived this, and entreated me to trouble myself no further.

'I will spend my mornings in the pleasaunce, Hector,' she said; 'the stranger cannot intrude upon me there.'

'I begin to think the stranger is only a phantasm of your own romantic brain,' I replied, smiling at the earnest face lifted to mine. 'A châtelaine who is always reading romances may well meet handsome cavaliers in the woodlands. I daresay I have Mdlle. Scuderi to thank for this noble stranger, and that he is only the great Cyrus in modern costume.'

'Ah, that is the point which mystifies me, Hector,' she said. 'The stranger's costume is not modern. He looks as an old picture might look if it could descend from its frame.'

Her words pained me, for they reminded me of that hidden picture in the library, and the quaint hunting costume of orange and purple, which André de Brissac wore at the Regent's ball.

After this my wife confined her walks to the pleasaunce; and for many weeks I heard no more of the nameless stranger. I dismissed all thought of him from my mind, for a graver and heavier care had come upon me. My wife's health began to droop. The change in her was so gradual as to be almost imperceptible to those who watched her day by day. It was only when she put on a rich gala dress which she had not worn for months that I saw how wasted the form must be on which the embroidered bodice hung so loosely, and how wan and dim were the eyes which had once been brilliant as the jewels she wore in her hair.

I sent a messenger to Paris to summon one of the court physicians; but I knew that many days must needs elapse before he could arrive at Puy Verdun.

In the interval I watched my wife with unutterable fear.

It was not her health only that had declined. The change was more painful to behold than any physical alteration. The bright and sunny spirit had vanished, and in the place of my joyous young bride I beheld a woman weighed down by rooted melancholy. In vain I sought to fathom the cause of my darling's sadness. She assured me that she had no reason for sorrow or discontent, and that if she seemed sad without a motive, I must forgive her sadness, and consider it as a misfortune rather than a fault.

I told her that the court physician would speedily find some cure

for her despondency, which must needs arise from physical causes, since she had no real ground for sorrow. But although she said nothing, I could see she had no hope or belief in the healing powers of medicine.

One day, when I wished to beguile her from that pensive silence in which she was wont to sit an hour at a time, I told her, laughing, that she appeared to have forgotten her mysterious cavalier of the wood, and it seemed also as if he had forgotten her.

To my wonderment, her pale face became of a sudden crimson; and from crimson changed to pale again in a breath.

'You have never seen him since you deserted your woodland grotto?' I said.

She turned to me with a heart-rending look.

'Hector,' she cried, 'I see him every day; and it is that which is killing me.'

She burst into a passion of tears when she had said this. I took her in my arms as if she had been a frightened child, and tried to comfort her.

'My darling, this is madness,' I said. 'You know that no stranger can come to you in the pleasaunce. The moat is ten feet wide and always full of water, and the gates are kept locked day and night by old Massou. The châtelaine of a mediæval fortress need fear no intruder in her antique garden.'

My wife shook her head sadly.

'I see him every day,' she said.

On this I believed that my wife was mad. I shrank from questioning her more closely concerning her mysterious visitant. It would be ill, I thought, to give a form and substance to the shadow that tormented her by too close inquiry about its look and manner, its coming and going.

I took care to assure myself that no stranger to the household could by any possibility penetrate to the pleasaunce. Having done this, I was fain to await the coming of the physician.

He came at last. I revealed to him the conviction which was my misery. I told him that I believed my wife to be mad. He saw her – spent an hour alone with her, and then came to me. To my unspeakable relief he assured me of her sanity.

'It is just possible that she may be affected by one delusion,' he said; 'but she is so reasonable upon all other points, that I can scarcely bring myself to believe her the subject of a monomania. I am rather inclined to think that she really sees the person of whom she speaks. She described him to me with a perfect minuteness. The descriptions of scenes or individuals given by patients afflicted with monomania are always more or less disjointed; but your wife spoke to me as clearly and calmly as I am now speaking to you. Are you sure there is no one who can approach her in that garden where she walks?'

'I am quite sure.'

'Is there any kinsman of your steward, or hanger-on of your household, – a young man with a fair womanish face, very pale and rendered remarkable by a crimson scar, which looks like the mark of a blow?'

'My God!' I cried, as the light broke in upon me all at once. 'And the dress – the strange old-fashioned dress?'

'The man wears a hunting costume of purple and orange,' answered the doctor.

I knew then that André de Brissac had kept his word, and that in the hour when my life was brightest his shadow had come between me and happiness.

I showed my wife the picture in the library, for I would fain assure myself that there was some error in my fancy about my cousin. She shook like a leaf when she beheld it, and clung to me convulsively.

'This is witchcraft, Hector,' she said. 'The dress in that picture is the dress of the man I see in the pleasaunce; but the face is not his.'

Then she described to me the face of the stranger; and it was my cousin's face line for line – André de Brissac, whom she had never

seen in the flesh. Most vividly of all did she describe the cruel mark upon his face, the trace of a fierce blow from an open hand.

After this I carried my wife away from Puy Verdun. We wandered far – through the southern provinces, and into the very heart of Switzerland. I thought to distance the ghastly phantom, and I fondly hoped that change of scene would bring peace to my wife.

It was not so. Go where we would, the ghost of André de Brissac followed us. To my eyes that fatal shadow never revealed itself. That would have been too poor a vengeance. It was my wife's innocent heart which André made the instrument of his revenge. The unholy presence destroyed her life. My constant companionship could not shield her from the horrible intruder. In vain did I watch her; in vain did I strive to comfort her.

'He will not let me be at peace,' she said; 'he comes between us, Hector. He is standing between us now. I can see his face with the red mark upon it plainer that I see yours.'

One fair moonlight night, when we were together in a mountain village in the Tyrol, my wife cast herself at my feet, and told me she was the worst and vilest of women. 'I have confessed all to my director,' she said; 'from the first I have not hidden my sin from Heaven. But I feel that death is near me; and before I die I would fain reveal my sin to you.'

'What sin, my sweet one?'

'When first the stranger came to me in the forest, his presence bewildered and distressed me, and I shrank from him as from something strange and terrible. He came again and again; by and by I found myself thinking of him, and watching for his coming. His image haunted me perpetually; I strove in vain to shut his face out of my mind. Then followed an interval in which I did not see him; and, to my shame and anguish, I found that life seemed dreary and desolate without him. After that came the time in which he haunted the pleasaunce; and – O, Hector, kill me if you will, for I deserve no mercy at your hands! – I grew in those days to count the hours that must elapse before his coming, to take no pleasure save in the sight of that pale face with the red brand upon it. He plucked all old familiar joys out of my heart, and left in it but one weird unholy pleasure – the delight of his presence. For a year I have lived but to see him. And now curse me, Hector; for this is my sin. Whether it comes of the baseness of my own heart, or is the work of witchcraft, I know not; but I know that I have striven against this wickedness in vain.'

I took my wife to my breast, and forgave her. In sooth, what had I to forgive? Was the fatality that overshadowed us any work of hers? On the next night she died, with her hand in mine; and at the very last she told me, sobbing and affrighted, that he was by her side.

HUGUES, THE WER-WOLF
by Sutherland Menzies

A KENTISH LEGEND OF THE MIDDLE AGES

I
'Ye hallowed bells whose voices thro' the air
The awful summons of afflictions bare.'
Honoria, or the Day of All Souls.

ON the confines of that extensive forest-tract formerly spreading over so large a portion of the county of Kent, a remnant of which, to this day, is known as the Weald* of Kent,

---

* That woody district, at the period to which our tale belongs, was an immense forrest, desolate of inhabitants and only occupied by wild swine and deer; and though it is now filled with towns and villages and well peopled, the woods that remain sufficiently indicate its former extent. 'And being at first,' says Hasted, 'neither peopled nor cultivated, and only filled with herds of deer and droves of swine, belonged wholly to the king, for there is no mention of it but in royal grants and donations. And it may be presumed that when the weald was first made to belong to certain known owners, as well as the rest of the country, it was not then allotted into tenancies, nor manured like the rest of it; but only as men we contented to inhabit it, and by piecemeal to clear it of the wood, and convert it into tillage.' —Hasted's *Kent*, vol.I, p.134.

and where it stretched its almost impervious covert midway between Ashford and Canterbury during the prolonged reign of our second Henry, a family of Norman extraction by name Hugues (or Wulfric, as they were commonly called by the Saxon inhabitants of that district) had, under protection of the ancient forest laws, furtively erected for themselves a lone and miserable habitation. And amidst those sylvan fastnesses, ostensibly following the occupation of woodcutters, the wretched outcasts, for such, from some cause or other, they evidently were, had for many years maintained a secluded and precarious existence. Whether from the rooted antipathy still actively cherished against all of that usurping nation from which they derived their origin, or from recorded malpractice by their superstitious Anglo-Saxon neighbours, they had long been looked upon as belonging to the accursed race of wer-wolves, and as such churlishly refused work on the domains of the surrounding franklins or proprietors, so thoroughly was accredited the descent of the original lycanthropic stain transmitted from father to son through several generations. That the Hugues Wulfric reckoned not a single friend among the adjacent homesteads of serf or freedman was not to be wondered at, possessing as they did so unenviable a reputation; for to them was invariably attributed even the misfortunes which chance alone might seem to have given birth. Did midnight fire consume the grange; – did the time-decayed barn, over-stored with an abundant harvest, tumble into ruins; – were the shocks of wheat lain prostrate over the fields by a tempest; – did the smut destroy the grain; – or the cattle perish, decimated by a murrain; – a child sink under some wasting malady; – or a woman give premature birth to her offspring, it was ever the Hugues Wulfric who were openly accused, eyed askaunt with mingled fear and detestation, the finger of young and old pointing them out with bitter execrations – in fine, they were almost as nearly classed *feroe natura* as their fabled prototype, and dealt with accordingly.*

Terrible, indeed, were the tales told of them round the glowing hearth at eventide, whilst spinning the flax, or plucking the geese; equally affirmed too, in broad daylight, whilst driving the cows to pasturage, and most circumstantially discussed on Sundays between mass and vespers, by the gossip groups collected within Ashford parvyse, with most seasonable admixture of anathema and devout crossings. Witchcraft, larceny, murder and sacrilege, formed prominent features in the bloody and mysterious scenes of which the Hugues Wulfric were the alleged actors: sometimes they were ascribed to the father, at others to the mother, and even the sister escaped not her share of vilification; fair would they have attributed an atrocious disposition to the unweaned babe, so great, so universal was the horror in which they held that race of Cain! The churchyard at Ashford, and the stone cross, from whence diverged the several roads to London, Canterbury and Ashford, situated midway between the two latter places, served, so tradition avouched, as nocturnal theatres for the unhallowed deeds of the Wulfrics, who thither prowled by moonlight, it was said, to batten on the freshly-buried dead, or drain the blood of any living wight who might be rash enough to venture among those solitary spots. True it was that the wolves had, during some of the severe winters, emerged from their forest lairs and, entering the cemetery by a breach in its walls, goaded by famine, had actually disinterred the dead; true was it also, that the Wolf's Cross, as the hinds commonly designated it, had been stained with gore on one occasion through

---

* King Edgar is said to have been the first who attempted to rid England of these animals; criminals even being pardoned by producing a stated number of these creatures' tongues. Some centuries after they increased to such a degree as to become again the object of royal attention; and Edward I appointed persons to extirpate this obnoxious race. It is one of the principal bearings in armoury. Hugh, surnamed Lupus, the first Earl of Kent, bore for his crest a wolf's head.

the fall of a drunken mendicant, who chanced to fracture his skull against a pointed angle of its basement. But these accidents, as well as a multitude of others, were attributed to the guilty intervention of the Wulfrics, under their fiendish guise of wer-wolves.

These poor people, moreover, took no pains to justify themselves from a prejudice so monstrous: full well apprised of what calumny they were the victims, but alike conscious of their impotence to contradict it, they tacitly suffered its infliction, and fled all contact with those to whom they knew themselves repulsive. Shunning the highways, and never venturing to pass through the town of Ashford in open day, they pursued such labour as might occupy them within doors, or in unfrequented places. They appeared not at Canterbury market, never numbered themselves amongst the pilgrims at Becket's far-famed shrine, or assisted at any sport, merry-making, hay-cutting, or harvest home: the priest had interdicted them from all communion with the church – the ale-bibbers from the hostelry.

The primitive cabin which they inhabited was built of chalk and clay, with a thatch of straw, in which the high winds had made huge rents and closed up by a rotten door, exhibiting wide gaps, through which the gusts had free ingress. As this wretched abode was situated at considerable distance from any other if, perchance, any of the neighbouring serfs strayed within its precincts towards nightfall, their credulous fears made them shun near approach so soon as the vapours of the marsh were seen to blend their ghastly wreaths with the twilight; and as that darkling time drew on which explains the diabolical sense of the old saying, 'tween dog and wolf,' 'twixt hawk and buzzard,' at that hour the will-o'-wisps began to glimmer around the dwelling of the Wulfrics, who patriarchally supped – whenever they had a supper – and forthwith betook themselves to their rest.

Sorrow, misery and the putrid exhalations of the steeped hemp, from which they manufactured a rude and scanty attire, combined

eventually to bring sickness and death into the bosom of this wretched family who, in their utmost extremity, could neither hope for pity or succour. The father was first attacked, and his corpse was scarce cold ere the mother rendered up her breath. Thus passed that fated couple to their account, unsolaced by the consolation of the confessor, or the medicaments of the leech. Hugues Wulfric, their eldest son, himself dug their grave, laid their bodies within it swathed with hempen shreds for grave cloths, and raised a few clods of earth to mark their last resting-place. A hind, who chanced to see him fulfilling this pious duty in the dusk of evening, crossed himself, and fled as fast as his legs would carry him, fully believing that he had assisted at some hellish incantation. When the real event transpired, the neighbouring gossips congratulated one another upon the double mortality, which they looked upon as the tardy chastisement of heaven: they spoke of ringing the bells, and singing masses of thanks for such an action of grace.

It was All Souls' Eve, and the wind howled along the bleak hillside, whistling drearily through the naked branches of the forest trees, whose last leaves it had long since stripped; the sun had disappeared; a dense and chilling fog spread through the air like the mourning veil of the widowed, whose day of love hath early fled. No star shone in the still and murky sky. In that lonely hut, through which death had so lately passed, the orphan survivors held their lonely vigil by the fitful blaze emitted by the reeking logs upon their hearth. Several days had elapsed since their lips had been imprinted for the last time upon the cold hands of their parents; several dreary nights had passed since the sad hour in which their eternal farewell had left them desolate on earth.

Poor lone ones! Both, too, in the flower of their youth – how sad, yet how serene did they appear amid their grief! But what sudden and mysterious terror is it that seems to overcome them? It is not, alas! the first time since they were left alone upon earth that they have found themselves at this hour of the night by their deserted hearth, enlivened of old by the cheerful tales of their mother. Full often had they wept together over her memory, but never yet had their solitude proved so appalling; and, pallid as very spectres, they tremblingly gazed upon one another as the flickering ray from the wood-fire played over their features.

'Brother! heard you not that loud shriek which every echo of the forest repeated? It sounds to me as if the ground were ringing with the tread of some gigantic phantom, and whose breath seems to have shaken the door of our hut. The breath of the dead they say is icy cold. A mortal shivering has come over me.'

'And I, too, sister, thought I heard voices as it were at a distance, murmuring strange words. Tremble not thus – am I not beside you?'

'Oh, brother! let us pray the Holy Virgin, to the end that she may restrain the departed from haunting our dwelling.'

'But, perhaps, our mother is amongst them: she comes, unshrived and unshrouded, to visit her forlorn offspring – her well-beloved! For, knowest thou not, sister, 'tis the eve on which the dead forsake their tombs. Let us open the door, that our mother may enter and resume her wonted place by the hearthstone.'

'Oh, brother, how gloomy is all without doors, how damp and cold the gust sweeps by. Hearest thou, what groans the dead are uttering round our hut? Oh, close the door, in heaven's name!'

'Take courage, sister, I have thrown upon the fire that holy branch, plucked as it flowered on last Palm Sunday, which thou knowest will drive away all evil spirits, and now our mother can enter alone.'

'But how will she look, brother? They say the dead are horrible to gaze upon; that their hair has fallen away; their eyes become hollow; and that, in walking, their bones rattle hideously. Will our mother, then, be thus?'

'No; she will appear with the features we loved to behold; with the affectionate smile that welcomes us home from our perilous labours; with the voice which, in early youth, sought us when, belated, the closing night surprised its far from our dwelling.'

The poor girl busied herself awhile in arranging a few platters of scanty fare upon the tottering board which served them for a table; and this last pious offering of filial love, as she deemed it, appeared accomplished only by the greatest and last effort, so enfeebled had her frame become.

'Let our dearly-beloved mother enter then,' she exclaimed, sinking exhausted upon the settle. 'I have prepared her evening meal, that she may not be angry with me, and all is arranged as she was wont to have it. But what ails thee, my brother, for now thou tremblest as I did awhile agone?'

'See'st thou not, sister, those pale lights which are rising at a distance across the marsh? They are the dead coming to seat themselves before the repast prepared for then. Hark! list to the funeral tones of the Allhallowtide* bells, as they come upon the gale, blended with their hollow voices. – Listen, listen!'

'Brother, this horror grows insupportable. This, I feel, of a verity, will be my last night upon earth! And is there no word of hope to cheer me, mingling with those fearful sounds? Oh, mother! mother!'

'Hush, sister, hush! see'st thou now the ghastly lights which herald the dead, gleaming athwart the horizon? Hearest thou the prolonged tolling of the bell? They come! they come!'

'Eternal repose to their ashes!' exclaimed the bereaved ones, sinking upon their knees, and bowing down their heads in the extremity of terror and lamentation; and as they uttered the words, the door was at the same moment closed with violence, as though it had been slammed to by a vigorous hand. Hugues started to his feet, for the cracking of the timber which supported the roof seemed to announce the fall of the frail tenement; the fire was suddenly extinguished, and a plaintive groan mingled itself with the blast

---

* On this eve formally the Catholic Church performed a most solemn office for the repose of the dead.

that whistled through the crevices of the door. On raising his sister, Hugues found that she too was no longer to be numbered among the living.

II

HUGUES, on becoming the head of his family, composed of two sisters younger than himself, saw them likewise descend into the grave in the short space of a fortnight; and when he had laid the last within her parent earth, he hesitated whether he should not extend himself beside them, and share their peaceful slumber. It was not by tears and sobs that grief so profound as his manifested itself, but in a mute and sullen contemplation over the supulture of his kindred and his own future happiness. During three consecutive nights he wandered, pale and haggard, from his solitary hut, to prostrate himself and kneel by turns upon the funereal turf. For three days food had not passed his lips.

Winter had interrupted the labours of the woods and fields, and Hugues had presented himself in vain among the neighbouring domains to obtain a few days' employment to thresh grain, cut wood or drive the plough; no one would employ him from fear of drawing upon himself the fallity attached to all bearing the name of Wulfric. He met with brutal denials at all hands, and not only were these accompanied by taunts and menace, but dogs were let loose upon him to rend his limbs; they deprived him even of the alms accorded to beggars by profession; in short, he found himself overwhelmed with injuries and scorn.

Was he, then, to expire of inanition or deliver himself from the tortures of hunger by suicide? He would have embraced that means, as a last and only consolation, had he not been retained earthward to struggle with his dark fate by a feeling of love. Yes, that abject being, forced in very desperation, against his better self, to abhor the human species in the abstract, and to feel a savage joy in waging war against it; that pariah who scarce longer felt confidence in that heaven which seemed an apathetic witness of his woes; that man so isolated from those social relations which alone compensate us for the toils and troubles of life, without other stay than that afforded by his conscience, with no other fortune in prospect than the bitter existence and miserable death of his departed kin: worn to the bone by privation and sorrow, swelling with rage and resentment, he yet consented to live – to cling to life; for, strange – he loved! But for that heaven-sent ray gleaming across his thorny path, a pilgrimage so lone and wearisome would he have gladly exchanged for the peaceful slumber of the grave.

Hugues Wulfric would have been the finest youth in all that part of Kent, were it not that the outrages with which he had so unceasingly to contend, and the privations he was forced to undergo, had effaced the colour from his cheeks, and sunk his eyes deep in their orbits: his brows were habitually contracted, and his glance oblique and fierce. Yet, despite that recklessness and anguish which clouded his features, one, incredulous of his atrocities, could not have failed to admire the savage beauty of his head, cast in nature's noblest mould, crowned with a profusion of waving hair, and set upon shoulders whose robust and harmonious proportions were discoverable through the tattered attire investing them. His carriage was firm and majestic; his motions were not without a species of rustic grace, and the tone of his naturally soft voice accorded admirably with the purity in which he spoke his ancestral language – the Norman-French: in short, he differed so widely from people of his imputed condition that one is constrained to believe that jealousy or prejudice must originally have been no stranger to the malicious persecution of which he was the object. The women alone ventured first to pity his forlorn condition, and endeavoured to think of him in a more favourable light.

Branda, niece of Willieblud, the flesher of Ashford, had, among other of the town maidens, noticed Hugues with a not unfavouring eye, as she chanced to pass one day on horseback, through a coppice near the outskirts of the town, into which the latter had been led by the eager chase of a wild hog, and which animal, from the nature of the country was, single-handed, exceedingly difficult of capture. The malignant falsehoods of the ancient crones, continually buzzed in her ears, in nowise diminished the advantageous opinion she had conceived of this ill-treated and good-looking wer-wolf. She sometimes, indeed, went so far as to turn considerably out of her way, in order to meet and exchange his cordial greeting: for Hugues, recognising the attention of which he had now become the object, had, in his turn, at last summoned up courage to survey more leisurely the pretty Branda; and the result was that he found her as buxom and pretty a lass as, in his hitherto restricted rambles out of the forest, his timorous gaze had ever encountered. His gratitude increased proportionally; and at the moment when his domestic losses came one after another to overwhelm him, he was actually on the eve of making Branda, on the first opportunity presenting itself, an avowal of the love he bore her.

It was chill winter – Christmas-tide – the distant roll of the curfew had long ceased, and all the inhabitants of Ashford were safe housed in their tenements for the night. Hugues, solitary, motionless, silent, his forehead grasped between his hands, his gaze dully faced upon the decaying brands that feebly glimmered upon his hearth: he heeded not the cutting north wind, whose sweeping gusts shook the crazy roof, and whistled through the chinks of the door; he started not at the harsh cries of the herons fighting for prey in the marsh, nor at the dismal croaking of the ravens perched over his smoke-vent. He thought of his departed kindred, and imagined that his hour to join them would soon be at hand; for the intense cold congealed the marrow of his bones, and fell hunger gnawed and twisted his entrails. Yet, at intervals, would a recollection of nascent love, of Branda, suddenly appease his else intolerable anguish, and cause a faint smile to gleam across his wan features.

'Oh, blessed Virgin! grant that my sufferings may speedily cease!' murmured he, despairingly. 'Oh, would I might be a wer-wolf, as they call me! I could then requite them for all the foul wrong done me. True, I could not nourish myself with their flesh; I would not shed their blood; but I would be able to terrify and torment those who have wrought my parents' and sisters' death – who have persecuted our family even to extermination! Why have I not the power to change my nature into that of a wolf, if, of a verity, my ancestors possessed it, as they avouch? I should at least find carrion to devour,* and not die thus horribly. Branda is the sole being in this world who cares for me; and that conviction alone reconciles me to life!'

Hugues gave free current to these gloomy reflections. The smouldering embers now emitted but a feeble and vacillating light, faintly struggling with the surrounding gloom, and Hugues felt the horror of darkness coming strong upon him; frozen with the ague-fit one instant, and troubled the next by the hurried pulsation of his veins, he arose, at last, to seek some fuel, and threw upon the fire a heap of faggot-chips, heath and straw, which soon raised a clear and crackling flame. His stock of wood had become exhausted, and, seeking wherewith to replenish his dying hearth-light, whilst foraging under the rude oven amongst a pile of rubbish placed there by his mother wherewith to bake bread – handles of tools, fractured joint-stools, and cracked platters, he discovered a chest rudely covered with a dressed hide, and which he had never seen before; and seizing upon it as though he had discovered a treasure, broke open the lid, strongly secured by a string.

This chest, which had evidently remained long unopened, contained the complete disguise of a wer-wolf: – a dyed sheepskin,

---

* Horseflesh was an article of food among our saxon forefathers in England.

with gloves in the form of paws, a tail, a mask with an elongated muzzle, and furnished with formidable rows of yellow horse-teeth.

Hugues started backwards, terrified at his discovery – so opportune, that it seemed to him the work of sorcery; then, on recovering from his surprise, he drew forth one by one the several pieces of this strange envelope, which had evidently seen some service, and from long neglect had become somewhat damaged. Then rushed confusedly upon his mind the marvellous recitals made him by his grandfather, as he nursed him upon his knees during earliest childhood; tales, during the narration of which his mother wept silently, as he laughed heartily. In his mind there was a mingled strife of feelings and purposes alike undefinable. He continued his silent examination of this criminal heritage, and by degrees his imagination grew bewildered with vague and extravagant projects.

Hunger and despair conjointly hurried him away: he saw objects no longer save through a bloody prism: he felt his very teeth on edge with an avidity for biting; he experienced an inconceivable desire to run: he set himself to howl as though he had practised wer-wolfery all his life, and began thoroughly to invest himself with the guise and attributes of his novel vocation. A more startling change could scarcely have been wrought in him, had that so horribly grotesque metamorphosis really been the effect of enchantment; aided, too, as it was, by the fever which generated a temporary insanity in his frenzied brain.

Scarcely did he thus find himself travestied into a wer-wolf through the influence of his vestment, ere he darted forth from the hut, through the forest and into the open country, white with hoar frost, and across which the bitter north wind swept, howling in a frightful manner and traversing the meadows, fallows, plains and marshes, like a shadow. But, at that hour, and during such a season, not a single belated wayfarer was there to encounter Hugues, whom the sharpness of the air, and the excitation of his course, had worked up to the highest pitch of extravagance and audacity: he howled the louder proportionally as his hunger increased.

Suddenly the heavy rumbling of an approaching vehicle arrested his attention; at first with indecision, then with a stupid fixity, he struggled with two suggestions, counselling him at one and the same time to fly and to advance. The carriage, or whatever it might be, continued, rolling towards him; the night was not so obscure but that he was enabled to distinguish the tower of Ashford church at a short distance off, and hard by which stood a pile of unhewn stone, destined either for the execution of some repair, or addition to the saintly edifice, in the shade of which he ran to crouch himself down, and so await the arrival of his prey.

It proved to be the covered cart of Willieblud, the Ashford flesher, who was wont twice a week to carry meat to Canterbury, and travelled by night in order that he might be among the first at market-opening. Of this Hugues was fully aware, and the departure of the flesher naturally suggested to him the inference that his niece must be keeping house by herself, for our lusty flesher had been long a widower. For an instant he hesitated whether he should introduce himself there, so favourable an opportunity thus presenting itself, or whether he should attack the uncle and seize upon his viands. Hunger got the better of love this once, and the monotonous whistle with which the driver was accustomed to urge forward his sorry jade warning him to be in readiness, he howled in a plaintive tone, and, rushing forward, seized the horse by the bit.

'Willieblud, flesher,' said he, disguising his voice, and speaking to him in the *lingua Franca* of that period, 'I hunger; throw me two pounds of meat if thou would'st have me live.'

'St Willifred have mercy on me!' cried the terrified flesher, 'is it thou, Hugues Wulfric, of Wealdmarsh, the born wer-wolf?'

'Thou say'st sooth – it is I,' replied Hugues, who had sufficient address to avail himself of the credulous superstition of Willieblud; 'I would rather have raw meat than eat of thy flesh, plump as thou art. Throw me, therefore, what I crave, and forget not to be ready with the like portion each time thou settest out for Canterbury market; or, failing thereof, I tear thee limb from limb.'

Hugues, to display his attributes of a wer-wolf before the gaze of the confounded flesher, had mounted himself upon the spokes of the wheel, and placed his forepaw upon the edge of the cart, which he made semblance of snuffing at with his snout. Willieblud, who believed in wer-wolves as devoutly as he did in his patron saint, had no sooner perceived this monstrous paw, than, uttering a fervent invocation to the latter, he seized upon his daintiest joint of meat, let it fall to the ground, and whilst Hugues sprung eagerly down to pick it up, the butcher at the same instant having bestowed a sudden and violent blow upon the flank of his beast, the latter set off at a round gallop without waiting for any reiterated invitation from the lash.

Hugues was so satisfied with a repast which had cost him far less trouble to procure than any he had long remembered, readily promised himself the renewal of an expedient, the execution of which was at once easy and diverting; for though smitten with the charms of the fair-haired Branda, he not the less found a malicious pleasure in augmenting the terror of her uncle Willieblud. The latter, for a long while, revealed not to a living being the tale of his terrible encounter and strange compact, which had varied according to circumstances, and he submitted unmurmuringly to the imposts levied each time the wer-wolf presented himself before him, without being very nice about either the weight or quality of the meat; he no longer even waited to be asked for it, anything to avoid the sight of that fiend-like form clinging to the side of his cart, or being brought into such immediate contact with that hideous mis-shapen paw stretched forth, as it were to strangle him, that paw too, which had once been a human hand. He had become dull and thoughtful of late; he set out to market unwillingly, and seemed to dread the hour of departure as it approached, and no longer beguiled the tedium of his nocturnal journey by whistling to his horse, or trolling snatches of ballads, as was his wont formerly; he now invariably returned in a melancholy and restless mood.

Branda, at loss to conceive what had given birth to this new and permanent depression which had taken possession of her uncle's mind, after in vain exhausting conjecture, proceeded to interrogate, importune and supplicate him by turns, until the unhappy flesher, no longer proof against such continued appeals, at last disburthened himself of the load which he had at heart, by recounting the history of his adventure with the wer-wolf.

Branda listened to the whole of the recital without offering interruption or comment; but, at its close –

'Hugues is no more a wer-wolf than thou or I,' exclaimed she, offended that such unjust suspicion should be cherished against one for whom she had long felt more than an interest; ''tis an idle tale, or some juggling device; I fear me thou must needs dream these sorceries, uncle Willieblud, for Hugues of the Wealmarsh, or Wulfric, as the silly fools call him, is worth far more, I trow, than his reputation.'

'Girl, it boots not saying me nay, in this matter,' replied Willieblud, pertinaciously urging the truth of his story; 'the family of Hugues, as everybody knows, were wer-wolves born and, since they are all of late, by the blessing of heaven, defunct, save one, Hugues now inherits the wolf's paw.'

'I tell thee, and will avouch it openly, uncle, that Hugues is of too gentle and seemly a nature to serve Satan, and turn himself into a wild beast, and that will I never believe until I have seen the like.'

'Mass, and that thou shalt right speedily, if thou wilt but along with me. In very troth 'tis he, besides, he made confession of his name, and did I not recognise his voice, and am I not ever bethinking me of his knavish paw, which he places me on the shaft while he stays the horse. Girl, he is in league with the foul fiend.'

Branda had, to a certain degree, imbibed the superstition

in the abstract, equally with her uncle and, excepting so far as it touched the hitherto, as she believed, traduced being on whom her affections, as if in feminine perversity, had so strangely lighted. Her woman's curiosity, in this instance, less determined her resolution to accompany the flesher on his next journey, than the desire to exculpate her lover, fully believing the strange tale of her kinsman's encounter with, and spoliation by the latter, to be the effect of some illusion, and of which to find him guilty, was the sole fear she experienced on mounting the rude vehicle laden with its ensanguined viands.

It was just midnight when they started from Ashford, the hour alike dear to wer-wolves as to spectres of every denomination. Hugues was punctual at the appointed spot; his howlings, as they drew nigh, though horrible enough, had still something human in them, and disconcerted not a little the doubts of Branda. Willieblud, however, trembled even more than she did, and sought for the wolf's portion; the latter raised himself upon his hind legs, and extended one of his forepaws to receive his pittance as soon as the cart stopped at the heap of stones.

'Uncle, I shall swoon with affright,' exclaimed Branda, clinging closely to the flesher, and tremblingly pulling the coverchief over her eyes: 'loose rein and smite thy beast, or evil will surely betide us.'

'Thou are not alone, gossip,' cried Hugues, fearful of a snare; 'if thou essay'st to play me false, thou art at once undone.'

'Harm us not friend Hugues, thou know'st I weigh not my pounds of meat with thee; I shall take care to keep my troth. It is Branda, my niece, who goes with me tonight to buy wares at Canterbury.'

'Branda with thee? By the mass 'tis she indeed, more buxom and rosy too, than ever; come pretty one, descend and tarry awhile, that I may have speech with thee.'

'I conjure thee, good Hugues, terrify not so cruelly my poor wench, who is wellnigh dead already with fear; suffer us to hold our way, for we have far to go, and the morrow is early, market-day.'

'Go thy ways then alone, uncle Willieblud, 'tis thy niece I would have speech with, in all courtesy and honour; the which, if thou permittest not readily, and of a good grace, I will rend thee both to death.'

All in vain was it that Willieblud exhausted himself in prayers and lamentations in hopes of softening the blood-thirsty wer-wolf, as he believed him to be, refusing as the latter did, every sort of compromise in avoidance of his demand, and at last replying only by horrible threats, which froze the hearts of both. Branda, although especially interested in the debate, neither stirred foot, or opened her mouth, so greatly had terror and surprise overwhelmed her; she kept her eyes fixed upon the wolf, who peered at her likewise through his mask, and felt incapable of offering resistance when she found herself forcibly dragged out of the vehicle, and deposited by an invisible power, as it seemed to her, beside the piles of stones; she swooned without uttering a single scream.

The flesher was no less dumbfounded at the turn which the adventure had taken, and he, too, fell back among his meat as though stricken by a blinding blow; he fancied that the wolf had swept his bushy tail violently across his eyes, and on recovering the use of his senses found himself alone in the cart, which rolled joltingly at a swift pace towards Canterbury. At first he listened, but in vain, for the wind bringing him either the shrieks of his niece, or the howlings of the wolf; but stop his beast he could not, which, panic-stricken, kept trotting as though bewitched, or felt the spur of some fiend pricking her flanks.

Willieblud, however, reached his journey's end in safety, sold his meat, and returned to Ashford, reckoning full sure upon having to say a *De Profundis* for his niece, whose fate he had not ceased to bemoan during the whole night. But how great was his astonishment to find her safe at home, a little pale, from recent fright and want of sleep, but without a scratch; still more was he astonished to hear that the wolf had done her no injury whatsoever, contenting himself, after she had recovered from her swoon, with conducting her back to their dwelling, and acting in every respect like a loyal suitor, rather than a sanguinary wer-wolf. Willieblud knew not what to think of it.

This nocturnal gallantry towards his niece had additionally irritated the burly Saxon against the wer-wolf, and although the fear of reprisals kept him from making a direct and public attack upon Hugues, he ruminated not the less upon taking some sure and secret revenge; but previous to putting his design into execution, it struck him that he could not do better than relate his misadventures to the ancient sacristan and parish grave-digger of St Michael's, a worthy of profound sagacity in those sort of matters, endowed with a clerk-like erudition, and consulted as an oracle by all the old crones and lovelorn maidens throughout the township of Ashford and its vicinity.

'Slay a wer-wolf thou canst not,' was the repeated rejoinder of the wiseacre to the earnest queries of the tormented flesher; 'for his hide is proof against spear or arrow, though vulnerable to the edge of a cutting weapon of steel. I counsel thee to deal him a slight flesh wound, or cut him over the paw, in order to know of a surety whether it really be Hugues or no; thou'lt run no danger, save thou strikest him a blow from which blood flows not therefrom, for, so soon as his skin is severed he taketh flight.'

Resolving implicitly to follow the advice of the sacristan, Willieblud that same evening determined to know with what wer-wolf it was with whom he had to do, and with that view hid his cleaver, newly sharpened for the occasion, under the load in his cart, and resolutely prepared to make use of it as a preparatory step towards proving the identity of Hugues with the audacious spoiler of his meat, and eke his peace. The wolf presented himself as usual, and anxiously inquired after Branda, which stimulated the flesher the more firmly to follow out his design.

'Here, Wolf,' said Willieblud, stooping down as if to choose a piece of meat; 'I give thee double portion tonight; up with thy paw, take toll, and be mindful of my frank alms.'

'Sooth, I will remember me, gossip,' rejoined our wer-wolf; 'but when shall the marriage be solemnised for certain, betwixt the fair Branda and myself?'

Hugues believing he had nothing to fear from the flesher, whose meats he so readily appropriated to himself, and of whose fair niece he hoped shortly no less to make lawful possession; both that he really loved, and viewed his union with her as the surest means of placing him within the pale of that sociality from which he had been so unjustly exiled, could he but succeed in making intercession with the holy fathers of the church to remove their interdict. Hugues placed his extended paw upon the edge of the cart; but instead of handing him his joint of beef, or mutton, Willieblud raised his cleaver, and at a single blow lopped off the paw laid there as fittingly for the purpose as though upon a block. The flesher flung down his weapon, and belaboured his beast, the wer-wolf roared aloud with agony, and disappeared amid the dark shades of the forest, in which, aided by the wind, his howling was soon lost.

The next day, on his return, the flesher, chuckling and laughing, deposited a gory cloth upon the table, among the trenchers with which his niece was busied in preparing his noonday meal, and which, on being opened, displayed to her horrified gaze a freshly severed human hand enveloped in wolf-skin. Branda, comprehending what had occurred, shrieked aloud, shed a flood of tears, and then hurriedly throwing her mantle round her, whilst her uncle amused himself by turning and twitching the hand about with a ferocious delight, exclaiming, whilst he staunched the blood which still flowed:

'The sacristan said sooth; the wer-wolf has his need I trow, at last, and now I wot of his nature, I fear no more his witchcraft.'

Although the day was far advanced, Hugues lay writhing in torture upon his couch, his coverings drenched with blood, as

well also the floor of his habitation; his countenance of a ghastly pallor, expressed as much moral, as physical pain; tears gushed from beneath his reddened eyelids, and he listened to every noise without, with an increased inquietude, painfully visible upon his distorted features. Footsteps were heard rapidly approaching, the door was hurriedly flung open, and a female threw herself beside his couch, and with mingled sobs and imprecations sought tenderly for his mutilated arm, which, rudely bound round with hempen wrappings, no longer dissembled the absence of its wrist, and from which a crimson stream still trickled. At this piteous spectacle she grew loud in her denunciations against the sanguinary flesher, and sympathetically mingled her lamentations with those of his victim.

These effusions of love and dolour, however, were doomed to sudden interruption; someone knocked at the door. Branda ran to the window that she might recognise who the visitor was that had dared to penetrate the lair of a wer-wolf, and on perceiving who it was, she raised her eyes and hands on high, in token of her extremity of despair, whilst the knocking momentarily grew louder.

"Tis my uncle', faltered she. 'Ah! woe's me, how shall I escape hence without his seeing me? Whither hide? Oh, here, here, nigh to thee, Hugues, and we will die together', and she crouched herself into an obscure recess behind his couch. 'If Willieblud should raise his cleaver to slay thee, he shall first strike through his kinswoman's body.'

Branda hastily concealed herself amidst a pile of hemp, whispering Hugues to summon all his courage, who, however, scarce found strength sufficient to raise himself to a sitting posture, whilst his eyes vainly sought around for some weapon of defence.

'A good morrow to thee, Wulfric!' exclaimed Willieblud, as he entered, holding in his hand a napkin tied in a knot, which he proceeded to place upon the coffer beside the sufferer. 'I come to offer thee some work, to bind and stack me a faggot-pile, knowing that thou art no laggard at bill-hook and wattle. Wilt do it?'

'I am sick,' replied Hugues, repressing the wrath which, despite of pain, sparkled in his wild glance; 'I am not in fitting state to work.'

'Sick, gossip, sick, art thou indeed? Or is it but a sloth fit? Come, what ails thee? Where lieth the evil? Your hand, that I may feel thy pulse.'

Hugues reddened, and for an instant hesitated whether he should resist a solicitation, the bent of which he too readily comprehended; but in order to avoid exposing Branda to discovery, he thrust forth his left hand from beneath the coverlid, all imbrued in dried gore.

'Not that hand, Hugues, but the other, the right one. Alack, and well-a-day, hast thou lost thy hand, and I must find it for thee?'

Hugues, whose purpling flush of rage changed quickly to a death-like hue, replied not to this taunt, nor testified by the slightest gesture or movement that he was preparing to satisfy a request as cruel in its preconception as the object of it was slenderly cloaked. Willieblud laughed, and ground his teeth in savage glee, maliciously revelling in the tortures he had inflicted upon the sufferer. He seemed already disposed to use violence, rather than allow himself to be baffled in the attainment of the decisive proof he aimed at. Already had he commenced untying the napkin, giving vent all the while to his implacable taunts; one hand alone displaying itself upon the coverlid, and which Hugues, wellnigh senseless with anguish, thought not of withdrawing.

'Why tender me that hand?' continued his unrelenting persecutor, as he imagined himself on the eve of arriving at the conviction he so ardently desired – 'That I should lop it off? quick, quick, Master Wulfric, and do my bidding; I demanded to see your right hand.'

'Behold it then!' ejaculated a suppressed voice, which belonged to no supernatural being, however it might seem appertaining to such; and Willieblud to his utter confusion and dismay saw a second hand, sound and unmutilated, extend itself towards him as though in silent accusation. He started back; he stammered out a cry for mercy, bent his knees for an instant, and raising himself, palsied with terror, fled from the hut, which he firmly believed under the

possession of the foul fiend. He carried not with him the severed hand, which henceforward became a perpetual vision ever present before his eyes, and which all the potent exorcisms of the sacristan, at whose hands he continually sought council and consolation, signally failed to dispel.

'Oh, that hand! To whom then, belongs that accursed hand?' groaned he, continually. 'Is it really the fiend's, or that of some werwolf? Certain 'tis, that Hugues is innocent, for have I not seen both his hands? But wherefore was one bloody? There's sorcery at bottom of it.'

The next morning, early, the first object that struck his sight on entering his stall, was the severed hand that he had left the preceding night upon the coffer in the forest hut; it was stripped of its wolf's-skin covering, and lay among the viands. He dared no longer touch that hand, which now, he verily believed to be enchanted; but in hopes of getting rid of it for ever, he had it flung down a well, and it was with no small increase of despair that he found it shortly afterwards again lying upon his block. He buried it in his garden, but still without being able to rid himself of it; it returned livid and loathsome to infect his shop, and augment the remorse which was unceasingly revived by the reproaches of his niece.

At last, flattering himself to escape all further persecution from that fatal hand, it struck him that he would have it carried to the cemetery at Canterbury, and try whether exorcism, and supulture in holy ground would effectually bar its return to the light of day. This was also done; but lo! on the following morning he perceived it nailed to his shutter. Disheartened by these dumb, yet awful reproaches, which wholly robbed him of his peace, and impatient to annihilate all trace of an action with which heaven itself seemed to upbraid him, he quitted Ashford one morning without bidding adieu to his niece, and some days after was found drowned in the River Stour. They drew out his swollen and discoloured body, which was discovered floating on the surface among the sedge, and it was

only by piecemeal that they succeeded in tearing away from his death-contracted clutch, the phantom hand, which, in his suicidal convulsions he had retained firmly grasped.

A year after this event, Hugues, although minus a hand, and consequently a confirmed wer-wolf, married Branda, sole heiress to the stock and chattels of the late unhappy flesher of Ashford.

THE BODY SNATCHER
by Robert Louis Stevenson

Every night in the year, four of us sat in the small parlour of
the *George* at Debenham – the undertaker, and the landlord,
and Fettes, and myself. Sometimes there would be more; but blow
high, blow low, come rain or snow or frost, we four would be each
planted in his own particular arm-chair. Fettes was an old drunken
Scotsman, a man of education obviously, and a man of some
property, since he lived in idleness. He had come to Debenham
years ago, while still young, and by a mere continuance of living
had grown to be an adopted townsman. His blue camlet cloak was a
local antiquity, like the church-spire. His place in the parlour at the
George, his absence from church, his old, crapulous, disreputable
vices, were all things of course in Debenham. He had some vague
Radical opinions and some fleeting infidelities, which he would
now and again set forth and emphasise with tottering slaps upon
the table. He drank rum – five glasses regularly every evening;
and for the greater portion of his nightly visit to the *George* sat,
with his glass in his right hand, in a state of melancholy alcoholic
saturation. We called him the Doctor, for he was supposed to
have some special knowledge of medicine, and had been known,
upon a pinch, to set a fracture or reduce a dislocation; but beyond

these slight particulars, we had no knowledge of his character and antecedents.

One dark winter night – it had struck nine some time before the landlord joined us – there was a sick man in the *George*, a great neighbouring proprietor suddenly struck down with apoplexy on his way to Parliament; and the great man's still greater London doctor had been telegraphed to his bedside. It was the first time that such a thing had happened in Debenham, for the railway was but newly open, and we were all proportionately moved by the occurrence.

'He's come,' said the landlord, after he had filled and lighted his pipe.

'He?' said I. 'Who? – not the doctor?'

'Himself,' replied our host.

'What is his name?'

'Doctor Macfarlane,' said the landlord.

Fettes was far through his third tumbler, stupidly fuddled, now nodding over, now staring mazily around him; but at the last word he seemed to awaken, and repeated the name 'Macfarlane' twice, quietly enough the first time, but with sudden emotion at the second.

'Yes,' said the landlord, 'that's his name, Doctor Wolfe Macfarlane.'

Fettes became instantly sober; his eyes awoke, his voice became clear, loud and steady, his language forcible and earnest. We were all startled by the transformation, as if a man had risen from the dead.

'I beg your pardon,' he said, 'I am afraid I have not been paying much attention to your talk. Who is this Wolfe Macfarlane?' And then, when he had heard the landlord out, 'It cannot be, it cannot be,' he added; 'and yet I would like well to see him face to face.'

'Do you know him, Doctor?' asked the undertaker, with a gasp.

'God forbid!' was the reply. 'And yet the name is a strange one; it were too much to fancy two. Tell me, landlord, is he old?'

'Well,' said the host, 'he's not a young man, to be sure, and his hair is white; but he looks younger than you.'

'He is older, though; years older. But,' with a slap upon the table, 'it's the rum you see in my face – rum and sin. This man, perhaps, may have an easy conscience and a good digestion. Conscience! Hear me speak. You would think I was some good, old, decent Christian, would you not? But no, not I; I never canted. Voltaire might have canted if he'd stood in my shoes; but the brains' – with a rattling fillip on his bald head – 'the brains were clear and active, and I saw and made no deductions.'

'If you know this doctor,' I ventured to remark, after a somewhat awful pause, 'I should gather that you do not share the landlord's good opinion.'

Fettes paid no regard to me.

'Yes,' he said, with sudden decision, 'I must see him face to face.'

There was another pause, and then a door was closed rather sharply on the first floor, and a step was heard upon the stair.

'That's the doctor,' cried the landlord. 'Look sharp, and you can catch him.'

It was but two steps from the small parlour to the door of the old *George* inn; the wide oak staircase landed almost in the street; there was room for a Turkey rug and nothing more between the threshold and the last round of the descent; but this little space was every evening brilliantly lit up, not only by the light upon the stair and the great signal-lamp below the sign, but by the warm radiance of the bar-room window. The *George* thus brightly advertised itself to passers-by in the cold street. Fettes walked steadily to the spot, and we, who were hanging behind, beheld the two men meet, as one of them had phrased it, face to face. Dr Macfarlane was alert and vigorous. His white hair set off his pale and placid, although energetic, countenance. He was richly dressed in the finest of broadcloth and the whitest of linen, with a great gold watchchain, and studs and spectacles of the same precious material. He wore a broad-folded tie, white and speckled with lilac, and he carried on his arm a comfortable driving-coat of fur. There was no doubt but he became his years, breathing, as he did, of wealth and consideration; and it was a surprising contrast to see our parlour sot – bald, dirty, pimpled and robed in his old camlet cloak – confront him at the bottom of the stairs.

'Macfarlane!' he said somewhat loudly, more like a herald than a friend.

The great doctor pulled up short on the fourth step, as though the familiarity of the address surprised and somewhat shocked his dignity.

'Toddy Macfarlane!' repeated Fettes.

The London man almost staggered. He stared for the swiftest of seconds at the man before him, glanced behind him with a sort of scare, and then in a startled whisper, 'Fettes!' he said, 'You!'

'Ay,' said the other, 'me! Did you think I was dead too? We are not so easy shut of our acquaintance.'

'Hush, hush!' exclaimed the doctor. 'Hush, hush! this meeting is so unexpected – I can see you are unmanned. I hardly knew you, I confess, at first; but I am overjoyed – overjoyed to have this opportunity. For the present it must be how-d'ye-do and good-bye in one, for my fly is waiting, and I must not fail the train; but you shall – let me see – yes – you shall give me your address, and you can count on early news of me. We must do something for you, Fettes. I fear you are out at elbows; but we must see to that for auld lang syne, as once we sang at suppers.'

'Money!' cried Fettes; 'money from you! The money that I had from you is lying where I cast it in the rain.'

Dr Macfarlane had talked himself into some measure of superiority and confidence, but the uncommon energy of this refusal cast him back into his first confusion.

A horrible, ugly look came and went across his almost venerable countenance. 'My dear fellow,' he said, 'be it as you please; my last thought is to offend you. I would intrude on none. I will leave you my address, however – '

'I do not wish it – I do not wish to know the roof that shelters you,' interrupted the other. 'I heard your name; I feared it might be

you; I wished to know if, after all, there were a God; I know now that there is none. Begone!'

He still stood in the middle of the rug, between the stair and the doorway; and the great London physician, in order to escape, would be forced to step to one side. It was plain that he hesitated before the thought of this humiliation. White as he was, there was a dangerous glitter in his spectacles; but while he still paused uncertain, he became aware that the driver of his fly was peering in from the street at this unusual scene and caught a glimpse at the same time of our little body from the parlour, huddled by the corner of the bar. The presence of so many witnesses decided him at once to flee. He crouched together, brushing on the wainscot, and made a dart like a serpent, striking for the door. But his tribulation was not yet entirely at an end, for even as he was passing Fettes clutched him by the arm and these words came in a whisper, and yet painfully distinct, 'Have you seen it again?'

The great rich London doctor cried out aloud with a sharp, throttling cry; he dashed his questioner across the open space, and, with his hands over his head, fled out of the door like a detected thief. Before it had occurred to one of us to make a movement the fly was already rattling toward the station. The scene was over like a dream, but the dream had left proofs and traces of its passage. Next day the servant found the fine gold spectacles broken on the threshold, and that very night we were all standing breathless by the bar-room window, and Fettes at our side, sober, pale, and resolute in look.

'God protect us, Mr Fettes!' said the landlord, coming first into possession of his customary senses. 'What in the universe is all this? These are strange things you have been saying.'

Fettes turned towards us; he looked at us each in succession in the face. 'See if you can hold your tongues,' said he. 'That man Macfarlane is not safe to cross; those that have done so already have repented it too late.'

And then, without so much as finishing his third glass, far less waiting for the other two, he bade us goodbye and went forth, under the lamp of the hotel, into the black night.

We three turned to our places in the parlour, with the big red fire and four clear candles; and as we recapitulated what had passed, the first chill of our surprise soon changed into a glow of curiosity. We sat late; it was the latest session I have known in the old *George*. Each man, before we parted, had his theory that he was bound to prove; and none of us had any nearer business in this world than to track out the past of our condemned companion, and surprise the secret that he shared with the great London doctor. It is no great boast, but I believe I was a better hand at worming out a story than either of my fellows at the *George*; and perhaps there is now no other man alive who could narrate to you the following foul and unnatural events.

In his young days, Fettes studied medicine in the schools of Edinburgh. He had talent of a kind, the talent that picks up swiftly what it hears and readily retails it for its own. He worked little at home; but he was civil, attentive and intelligent in the presence of his masters. They soon picked him out as a lad who listened closely and remembered well; nay, strange as it seemed to me when I first heard it, he was in those days well favoured, and pleased by his exterior. There was, at that period, a certain extramural teacher of anatomy, whom I shall here designate by the letter K. His name was subsequently too well known. The man who bore it skulked through the streets of Edinburgh in disguise, while the mob that applauded at the execution of Burke called loudly for the blood of his employer. But Mr K—— was then at the top of his vogue; he enjoyed a popularity due partly to his own talent and address, partly to the incapacity of his rival, the university professor. The students, at least, swore by his name, and Fettes believed himself, and was believed by others, to have laid the foundations of success when he had acquired the favour of this meteorically famous man.

Mr K—— was a *bon vivant* as well as an accomplished teacher; he liked a sly allusion no less than a careful preparation. In both capacities Fettes enjoyed and deserved his notice, and by the second year of his attendance he held the half-regular position of second demonstrator or sub-assistant in his class.

In this capacity the charge of the theatre and lecture-room devolved in particular upon his shoulders. He had to answer for the cleanliness of the premises and the conduct of the other students, and it was a part of his duty to supply, receive, and divide the various subjects. It was with a view to this last – at that time very delicate – affair that he was lodged by Mr K—— in the same wynd, and at last in the same building, with the dissecting-rooms. Here, after a night of turbulent pleasures, his hand still tottering, his sight still misty and confused, he would be called out of bed in the black hours before the winter dawn by the unclean and desperate interlopers who supplied the table. He would open the door to these men, since infamous throughout the land. He would help them with their tragic burden, pay them their sordid price, and remain alone, when they were gone, with the unfriendly relics of humanity. From such a scene he would return to snatch another hour or two of slumber, to repair the abuses of the night, and refresh himself for the labours of the day.

Few lads could have been more insensible to the impressions of a life thus passed among the ensigns of mortality. His mind was closed against all general considerations. He was incapable of interest in the fate and fortunes of another, the slave of his own desires and low ambitions. Cold, light and selfish in the last resort, he had that modicum of prudence, miscalled morality, which keeps a man from inconvenient drunkenness or punishable theft. He coveted, besides, a measure of consideration from his masters and his fellow-pupils, and he had no desire to fail conspicuously in the external parts of life. Thus he made it his pleasure to gain some distinction in his studies, and day after day rendered unimpeachable eye-service to his employer, Mr K——. For his day of work he indemnified himself by nights of roaring, blackguardly enjoyment; and when that balance had been struck, the organ that he called his conscience declared itself content.

The supply of subjects was a continual trouble to him as well as to his master. In that large and busy class, the raw material of the anatomists kept perpetually running out; and the business thus rendered necessary was not only unpleasant in itself, but threatened dangerous consequences to all who were concerned. It was the policy of Mr K—— to ask no questions in his dealings with the trade. 'They bring the body, and we pay the price,' he used to say, dwelling on the alliteration – '*quid pro quo.*' And, again, and somewhat profanely, 'Ask no questions,' he would tell his assistants, 'for conscience' sake.' There was no understanding that the subjects were provided by the crime of murder. Had that idea been broached to him in words, he would have recoiled in horror; but the lightness of his speech upon so grave a matter was, in itself, an offence against good manners, and a temptation to the men with whom he dealt. Fettes, for instance, had often remarked to himself upon the singular freshness of the bodies. He had been struck again and again by the hang-dog, abominable looks of the ruffians who came to him before the dawn; and putting things together clearly in his private thoughts, he perhaps attributed a meaning too immoral and too categorical to the unguarded counsels of his master. He understood his duty, in short, to have three branches: to take what was brought, to pay the price and to avert the eye from any evidence of crime.

One November morning this policy of silence was put sharply to the test. He had been awake all night with a racking toothache – pacing his room like a caged beast or throwing himself in fury on his bed – and had fallen at last into that profound, uneasy slumber that so often follows on a night of pain, when he was awakened by the third or fourth angry repetition of the concerted signal. There was a thin, bright moonshine; it was bitter cold, windy and frosty; the town had not yet awakened, but an indefinable stir already preluded the noise and business of the day. The ghouls had come later than usual, and they seemed more than usually eager to be gone. Fettes, sick with sleep, lighted them upstairs. He heard their grumbling Irish voices through a dream; and as they stripped the sack from their sad merchandise he leaned dozing, with his shoulder propped against the wall; he had to shake himself to find the men their money. As he did so his eyes lighted on the dead face. He started; he took two steps nearer, with the candle raised.

'God Almighty!' he cried. 'That is Jane Galbraith!'

The men answered nothing, but they shuffled nearer the door.

'I know her, I tell you,' he continued. 'She was alive and hearty yesterday. It's impossible she can be dead; it's impossible you should have got this body fairly.'

'Sure, sir, you're mistaken entirely,' said one of the men.

But the other looked Fettes darkly in the eyes, and demanded the money on the spot.

It was impossible to misconceive the threat or to exaggerate the danger. The lad's heart failed him. He stammered some excuses, counted out the sum, and saw his hateful visitors depart. No sooner were they gone than he hastened to confirm his doubts. By a dozen unquestionable marks he identified the girl he had jested with the day before. He saw, with horror, marks upon her body that might well betoken violence. A panic seized him, and he took refuge in his room. There he reflected at length over the discovery that he had made; considered soberly the bearing of Mr K——'s instructions and the danger to himself of interference in so serious a business, and at last, in sore perplexity, determined to wait for the advice of his immediate superior, the class assistant.

This was a young doctor, Wolfe Macfarlane, a high favourite among all the reckless students, clever, dissipated and unscrupulous to the last degree. He had travelled and studied abroad. His manners were agreeable and a little forward. He was an authority on the stage, skilful on the ice or the links with skate or golf-club; he dressed with nice audacity, and, to put the finishing touch upon his glory, he kept a gig and a strong trotting-horse. With Fettes he was on terms of intimacy; indeed, their relative positions called for some community of life; and when subjects were scarce the pair would drive far into the country in Macfarlane's gig, visit and desecrate some lonely graveyard, and return before dawn with their booty to the door of the dissecting-room.

On that particular morning Macfarlane arrived somewhat earlier than his wont. Fettes heard him, and met him on the stairs, told him his story, and showed him the cause of his alarm. Macfarlane examined the marks on her body.

'Yes,' he said with a nod, 'it looks fishy.'

'Well, what should I do?' asked Fettes.

'Do?' repeated the other. 'Do you want to do anything? Least said soonest mended, I should say.'

'Someone else might recognise her,' objected Fettes. 'She was as well known as the Castle Rock.'

'We'll hope not,' said Macfarlane, 'and if anybody does – well, you didn't, don't you see, and there's an end. The fact is, this has been going on too long. Stir up the mud, and you'll get K—— into the most unholy trouble; you'll be in a shocking box yourself. So will I, if you come to that. I should like to know how any one of us would look, or what the devil we should have to say for ourselves, in any Christian witness-box. For me, you know there's one thing certain – that, practically speaking, all our subjects have been murdered.'

'Macfarlane!' cried Fettes.

'Come now!' sneered the other. 'As if you hadn't suspected it yourself!'

'Suspecting is one thing – '

'And proof another. Yes, I know; and I'm as sorry as you are this should have come here,' tapping the body with his cane. 'The next best thing for me is not to recognise it; and,' he added coolly, 'I

don't. You may, if you please. I don't dictate, but I think a man of the world would do as I do; and I may add, I fancy that is what K—— would look for at our hands. The question is, Why did he choose us two for his assistants? And I answer, because he didn't want old wives.'

This was the tone of all others to affect the mind of a lad like Fettes. He agreed to imitate Macfarlane. The body of the unfortunate girl was duly dissected, and no one remarked or appeared to recognise her.

One afternoon, when his day's work was over, Fettes dropped into a popular tavern and found Macfarlane sitting with a stranger. This was a small man, very pale and dark, with coal-black eyes. The cut of his features gave a promise of intellect and refinement which was but feebly realised in his manners, for he proved, upon a nearer acquaintance, coarse, vulgar and stupid. He exercised, however, a very remarkable control over Macfarlane; issued orders like the Great Bashaw; became inflamed at the least discussion or delay, and commented rudely on the servility with which he was obeyed. This most offensive person took a fancy to Fettes on the spot, plied him with drinks, and honoured him with unusual confidences on his past career. If a tenth part of what he confessed were true, he was a very loathsome rogue; and the lad's vanity was tickled by the attention of so experienced a man.

'I'm a pretty bad fellow myself,' the stranger remarked, 'but Macfarlane is the boy – Toddy Macfarlane I call him. Toddy, order your friend another glass.' Or it might be, 'Toddy, you jump up and shut the door.' 'Toddy hates me,' he said again. 'Oh yes, Toddy, you do!'

'Don't you call me that confounded name,' growled Macfarlane.

'Hear him! Did you ever see the lads play knife? He would like to do that all over my body,' remarked the stranger.

'We medicals have a better way than that,' said Fettes. 'When we dislike a dead friend of ours, we dissect him.'

Macfarlane looked up sharply, as though this jest were scarcely to his mind.

The afternoon passed. Gray, for that was the stranger's name, invited Fettes to join them at dinner, ordered a feast so sumptuous that the tavern was thrown into commotion, and when all was done commanded Macfarlane to settle the bill. It was late before they separated; the man Gray was incapably drunk. Macfarlane, sobered by his fury, chewed the cud of the money he had been forced to squander and the slights he had been obliged to swallow. Fettes, with various liquors singing in his head, returned home with devious footsteps and a mind entirely in abeyance. Next day Macfarlane was absent from the class, and Fettes smiled to himself as he imagined him still squiring the intolerable Gray from tavern to tavern. As soon as the hour of liberty had struck he posted from place to place in quest of his last night's companions. He could find them, however, nowhere; so returned early to his rooms, went early to bed, and slept the sleep of the just.

At four in the morning he was awakened by the well-known signal. Descending to the door, he was filled with astonishment to find Macfarlane with his gig, and in the gig one of those long and ghastly packages with which he was so well acquainted.

'What?' he cried. 'Have you been out alone? How did you manage?'

But Macfarlane silenced him roughly, bidding him turn to business. When they had got the body upstairs and laid it on the table, Macfarlane made at first as if he were going away. Then he paused and seemed to hesitate; and then, 'You had better look at the face,' said he, in tones of some constraint. 'You had better,' he repeated, as Fettes only stared at him in wonder.

'But where, and how, and when did you come by it?' cried the other.

'Look at the face,' was the only answer.

Fettes was staggered; strange doubts assailed him. He looked from the young doctor to the body, and then back again. At last, with a start, he did as he was bidden. He had almost expected the sight that met his eyes, and yet the shock was cruel. To see, fixed in the rigidity of death and naked on that coarse layer of sack-cloth, the

man whom he had left well-clad and full of meat and sin upon the
threshold of a tavern, awoke, even in the thoughtless Fettes, some of
the terrors of the conscience. It was a *cras tibi* which re-echoed in
his soul, that two whom he had known should have come to lie upon
these icy tables. Yet these were only secondary thoughts. His first
concern regarded Wolfe. Unprepared for a challenge so momentous,
he knew not how to look his comrade in the face. He durst not meet
his eye, and he had neither words nor voice at his command.

It was Macfarlane himself who made the first advance. He
came up quietly behind and laid his hand gently but firmly on the
other's shoulder.

'Richardson,' said he, 'may have the head.'

Now Richardson was a student who had long been anxious for
that portion of the human subject to dissect. There was no answer,
and the murderer resumed: 'Talking of business, you must pay me;
your accounts, you see, must tally.'

Fettes found a voice, the ghost of his own: 'Pay you!' he cried.
'Pay you for that?'

'Why, yes, of course you must. By all means and on every
possible account, you must,' returned the other. 'I dare not give it
for nothing, you dare not take it for nothing; it would compromise
us both. This is another case like Jane Galbraith's. The more things
are wrong the more we must act as if all were right. Where does
old K—— keep his money?'

'There,' answered Fettes hoarsely, pointing to a cupboard in the
corner.

'Give me the key, then,' said the other, calmly, holding out his hand.

There was an instant's hesitation, and the die was cast. Macfarlane
could not suppress a nervous twitch, the infinitesimal mark of an
immense relief, as he felt the key between his fingers. He opened the
cupboard, brought out pen and ink and a paper-book that stood in
one compartment, and separated from the funds in a drawer a sum
suitable to the occasion.

'Now, look here,' he said, 'there is the payment made – first proof of your good faith: first step to your security. You have now to clinch it by a second. Enter the payment in your book, and then you for your part may defy the devil.'

The next few seconds were for Fettes an agony of thought; but in balancing his terrors it was the most immediate that triumphed. Any future difficulty seemed almost welcome if he could avoid a present quarrel with Macfarlane. He set down the candle which he had been carrying all this time, and with a steady hand entered the date, the nature and the amount of the transaction.

'And now,' said Macfarlane, 'it's only fair that you should pocket the lucre. I've had my share already. By-the-bye, when a man of the world falls into a bit of luck, has a few shillings extra in his pocket – I'm ashamed to speak of it, but there's a rule of conduct in the case. No treating, no purchase of expensive class-books, no squaring of old debts; borrow, don't lend.'

'Macfarlane,' began Fettes, still somewhat hoarsely, 'I have put my neck in a halter to oblige you.'

'To oblige me?' cried Wolfe. 'Oh, come! You did, as near as I can see the matter, what you downright had to do in self-defence. Suppose I got into trouble, where would you be? This second little matter flows clearly from the first. Mr Gray is the continuation of Miss Galbraith. You can't begin and then stop. If you begin, you must keep on beginning; that's the truth. No rest for the wicked.'

A horrible sense of blackness and the treachery of fate seized hold upon the soul of the unhappy student.

'My God!' he cried, 'but what have I done? and when did I begin? To be made a class assistant – in the name of reason, where's the harm in that? Service wanted the position; Service might have got it. Would *he* have been where *I* am now?'

'My dear fellow,' said Macfarlane, 'what a boy you are! What harm *has* come to you? What harm *can* come to you if you hold your tongue? Why, man, do you know what this life is? There are

two squads of us – the lions and the lambs. If you're a lamb, you'll come to lie upon these tables like Gray or Jane Galbraith; if you're a lion, you'll live and drive a horse like me, like K——, like all the world with any wit or courage. You're staggered at the first. But look at K——! My dear fellow, you're clever, you have pluck. I like you, and K—— likes you. You were born to lead the hunt; and I tell you, on my honour and my experience of life, three days from now you'll laugh at all these scarecrows like a high school boy at a farce.'

And with that Macfarlane took his departure and drove off up the wynd in his gig to get under cover before daylight. Fettes was thus left alone with his regrets. He saw the miserable peril in which he stood involved. He saw, with inexpressible dismay, that there was no limit to his weakness, and that, from concession to concession, he had fallen from the arbiter of Macfarlane's destiny to his paid and helpless accomplice. He would have given the world to have been a little braver at the time, but it did not occur to him that he might still be brave. The secret of Jane Galbraith and the cursed entry in the day-book closed his mouth.

Hours passed; the class began to arrive; the members of the unhappy Gray were dealt out to one and to another, and received without remark. Richardson was made happy with the head; and before the hour of freedom rang Fettes trembled with exultation to perceive how far they had already gone towards safety.

For two days he continued to watch, with increasing joy, the dreadful process of disguise.

On the third day Macfarlane made his appearance. He had been ill, he said; but he made up for lost time by the energy with which he directed the students. To Richardson in particular he extended the most valuable assistance and advice, and that student, encouraged by the praise of the demonstrator, burned high with ambitious hopes, and saw the medal already in his grasp.

Before the week was out Macfarlane's prophecy had been

fulfilled. Fettes had outlived his terrors and had forgotten his baseness. He began to plume himself upon his courage, and had so arranged the story in his mind that he could look back on these events with an unhealthy pride. Of his accomplice he saw but little. They met, of course, in the business of the class; they received their orders together from Mr K——. At times they had a word or two in private, and Macfarlane was from first to last particularly kind and jovial. But it was plain that he avoided any reference to their common secret; and even when Fettes whispered to him that he had cast in his lot with the lions and foresworn the lambs, he only signed to him smilingly to hold his peace.

At length an occasion arose which threw the pair once more into a closer union. Mr K—— was again short of subjects; pupils were eager, and it was a part of this teacher's pretensions to be always well supplied. At the same time there came the news of a burial in the rustic graveyard of Glencorse. Time has little changed the place in question. It stood then, as now, upon a crossroad, out of call of human habitations, and buried fathom deep in the foliage of six cedar trees. The cries of the sheep upon the neighbouring hills, the streamlets upon either hand, one loudly singing among pebbles, the other dripping furtively from pond to pond, the stir of the wind in mountainous old flowering chestnuts, and once in seven days the voice of the bell and the old tunes of the preceptor, were the only sounds that disturbed the silence around the rural church. The Resurrection Man – to use a by name of the period – was not to be deterred by any of the sanctities of customary piety. It was part of his trade to despise and desecrate the scrolls and trumpets of old tombs, the paths worn by the feet of worshippers and mourners, and the offerings and the inscriptions of bereaved affection. To rustic neighbourhoods, where love is more than commonly tenacious, and where some bonds of blood or fellowship unite the entire society of a parish, the body-snatcher, far from being repelled by natural respect, was attracted by the ease and

safety of the task. To bodies that had been laid in earth, in joyful expectation of a far different awakening, there came that hasty, lamp-lit, terror-haunted resurrection of the spade and mattock. The coffin was forced, the cerements torn and the melancholy relics, clad in sackcloth, after being rattled for hours on moonless by-ways, were at length exposed to uttermost indignities before a class of gaping boys.

Somewhat as two vultures may swoop upon a dying lamb, Fettes and Macfarlane were to be let loose upon a grave in that green and quiet resting-place. The wife of a farmer, a woman who had lived for sixty years, and been known for nothing but good butter and a godly conversation, was to be rooted from her grave at midnight and carried, dead and naked, to that far-away city that she had always honoured with her Sunday's best; the place beside her family was to be empty till the crack of doom; her innocent and almost venerable members to be exposed to that last curiosity of the anatomist.

Late one afternoon the pair set forth, well wrapped in cloaks and furnished with a formidable bottle. It rained without remission – a cold, dense, lashing rain. Now and again there blew a puff of wind, but these sheets of falling water kept it down. Bottle and all, it was a sad and silent drive as far as Penicuik, where they were to spend the evening. They stopped once, to hide their implements in a thick bush not far from the churchyard, and once again at the *Fisher's Tryst*, to have a toast before the kitchen fire and vary their nips of whisky with a glass of ale. When they reached their journey's end the gig was housed, the horse was fed and comforted, and the two young doctors in a private room sat down to the best dinner and the best wine the house afforded. The lights, the fire, the beating rain upon the window, the cold, incongruous work that lay before them, added zest to their enjoyment of the meal. With every glass their cordiality increased. Soon Macfarlane handed a little pile of gold to his companion.

'A compliment,' he said. 'Between friends these little d-d accommodations ought to fly like pipe-lights.'

Fettes pocketed the money, and applauded the sentiment to the echo. 'You are a philosopher,' he cried. 'I was an ass till I knew you. You and K—— between you, by the Lord Harry! but you'll make a man of me.'

'Of course we shall,' applauded Macfarlane. 'A man? I tell you, it required a man to back me up the other morning. There are some big, brawling, forty-year-old cowards who would have turned sick at the look of the d-d thing; but not you – you kept your head. I watched you.'

'Well, and why not?' Fettes thus vaunted himself. 'It was no affair of mine. There was nothing to gain on the one side but disturbance, and on the other I could count on your gratitude, don't you see?' And he slapped his pocket till the gold pieces rang.

Macfarlane somehow felt a certain touch of alarm at these unpleasant words. He may have regretted that he had taught his young companion so successfully, but he had no time to interfere, for the other noisily continued in this boastful strain:

'The great thing is not to be afraid. Now, between you and me, I don't want to hang – that's practical; but for all cant, Macfarlane, I was born with a contempt. Hell, God, Devil, right, wrong, sin, crime, and all the old gallery of curiosities – they may frighten boys, but men of the world, like you and me, despise them. Here's to the memory of Gray!'

It was by this time growing somewhat late. The gig, according to order, was brought round to the door with both lamps brightly shining, and the young men had to pay their bill and take the road. They announced that they were bound for Peebles, and drove in that direction till they were clear of the last house of the town; then, extinguishing the lamps, returned upon their course, and followed a by-road towards Glencorse. There was no sound but that of their own passage, and the incessant, strident pouring of the rain. It was pitch dark; here and there a white gate or a white stone in the wall guided them for a short space across the night; but for the most part it was at a foot pace, and almost groping, that they picked their way through that resonant blackness to their solemn and isolated destination. In the sunken woods that traverse the neighbourhood of the burying-ground the last glimmer failed them, and it became necessary to kindle a match and re-illumine one of the lanterns of the gig. Thus, under the dripping trees, and environed by huge and moving shadows, they reached the scene of their unhallowed labours.

They were both experienced in such affairs, and powerful with the spade; and they had scarce been twenty minutes at their task before they were rewarded by a dull rattle on the coffin lid. At the same moment Macfarlane, having hurt his hand upon a stone, flung it carelessly above his head. The grave, in which they now stood almost to the shoulders, was close to the edge of the plateau of the graveyard; and the gig lamp had been propped, the better to illuminate their labours, against a tree, and on the immediate verge of the steep bank descending to the stream. Chance had taken a sure aim with the stone. Then came a clang of broken glass; night fell upon them; sounds alternately dull and ringing announced the bounding of the lantern down the bank, and its occasional collision with the trees. A stone or two, which it had dislodged in its descent, rattled behind it into the profundities of the glen; and then silence, like night, resumed its sway; and they might bend their hearing to its utmost pitch, but naught was to be heard except the rain, now marching to the wind, now steadily falling over miles of open country.

They were so nearly at an end of their abhorred task that they judged it wisest to complete it in the dark. The coffin was exhumed and broken open; the body inserted in the dripping sack and carried between them to the gig; one mounted to keep it in its place, and the other, taking the horse by the mouth, groped along by wall and

bush until they reached the wider road by the *Fisher's Tryst*. Here was a faint, diffused radiancy, which they hailed like daylight; by that they pushed the horse to a good pace and began to rattle along merrily in the direction of the town.

They had both been wetted to the skin during their operations, and now, as the gig jumped among the deep ruts, the thing that stood propped between them fell now upon one and now upon the other. At every repetition of the horrid contact each instinctively repelled it with the greater haste; and the process, natural although it was, began to tell upon the nerves of the companions. Macfarlane made some ill-favoured jest about the farmer's wife, but it came hollowly from his lips, and was allowed to drop in silence. Still their unnatural burden bumped from side to side; and now the head would be laid, as if in confidence, upon their shoulders, and now the drenching sackcloth would flap icily about their faces. A creeping chill began to possess the soul of Fettes. He peered at the bundle, and it seemed somehow larger than at first. All over the countryside, and from every degree of distance, the farm dogs accompanied their passage with tragic ululations; and it grew and grew upon his mind that some unnatural miracle had been accomplished, that some nameless change had befallen the dead body, and that it was in fear of their unholy burden that the dogs were howling.

'For God's sake,' said he, making a great effort to arrive at speech, 'for God's sake, let's have a light!'

Seemingly Macfarlane was affected in the same direction; for, though he made no reply, he stopped the horse, passed the reins to his companion, got down, and proceeded to kindle the remaining lamp. They had by that time got no farther than the crossroad down to Auchendinny. The rain still poured as though the deluge were returning, and it was no easy matter to make a light in such a world of wet and darkness. When at last the flickering blue flame had been transferred to the wick and began to expand and clarify, and shed a wide circle of misty brightness round the gig, it became possible for

the two young men to see each other and the thing they had along with them. The rain had moulded the rough sacking to the outlines of the body underneath; the head was distinct from the trunk, the shoulders plainly modelled; something at once spectral and human riveted their eyes upon the ghastly comrade of their drive.

For some time Macfarlane stood motionless, holding up the lamp. A nameless dread was swathed, like a wet sheet, about the body, and tightened the white skin upon the face of Fettes; a fear that was meaningless, a horror of what could not be, kept mounting to his brain. Another beat of the watch, and he had spoken. But his comrade forestalled him.

'That is not a woman,' said Macfarlane, in a hushed voice.

'It was a woman when we put her in,' whispered Fettes.

'Hold that lamp,' said the other. 'I must see her face.'

And as Fettes took the lamp his companion untied the fastenings of the sack and drew down the cover from the head. The light fell very clear upon the dark, well-moulded features and smooth-shaven cheeks of a too familiar countenance, often beheld in dreams of both of these young men. A wild yell rang up into the night; each leaped from his own side into the roadway: the lamp fell, broke and was extinguished; and the horse, terrified by this unusual commotion, bounded and went off toward Edinburgh at a gallop, bearing along with it, sole occupant of the gig, the body of the dead and long-dissected Gray.